I'LL HATE MYSELF IN THE MORNING

IN THE MORNING

MURDER ON THE LEFT BANK

ELLIOT PAUL

I'LL HATE MYSELF IN THE MORNING

MURDER ON THE LEFT BANK

Elliot Paul

COACHWHIP PUBLICATIONS

Greenville, Ohio

I'll Hate Myself in the Morning, by Elliot Paul
Murder on the Left Bank, by Elliot Paul
© 2015 Coachwhip Publications

I'll Hate Myself in the Morning published 1945.
Murder on the Left Bank published 1951.
Elliot Paul (1891-1958)
No claims made on public domain material.

Front cover: Background © Flypaper Textures;
    Locomotive © Kristisha07

CoachwhipBooks.com

ISBN 1-61646-312-0
ISBN-13 978-1-61646-312-0

CONTENTS

I'LL HATE MYSELF IN THE MORNING

MURDER ON THE LEFT BANK

I'LL HATE MYSELF IN THE MORNING

Part One
The Death of Isaac Momblo

Introducing a Worried Young Man

HOMER EVANS, RELAXED AND CONTENT, was sitting in a comfortable chair looking out over the receding Utah landscape as the Union Pacific streamliner slid along the rails on its eastward voyage. The wind was right, so there was neither dust nor grime. The section of the track they were traversing, in spite of wartime manpower shortage, was still in fair condition. There stretched before Homer—a man who above all loved leisure and tranquility—at least twenty-four hours in which neither official duties or social obligations could intrude. In an hour the train would stop at Salt Lake City. The following noon or thereabouts it would reach Chicago. In three days, God willing, Homer would get back to New York, months or years later to Paris.

Wherever he should find himself he would be amused and companionable, and, if worse came to worst, useful. He disliked intensely to think of himself as useful, or to interpret historical, economic or social trends in material or conventional terms, but frequently in late years Evans had been drafted, as it were, by circumstances, to apply his extraordinary powers of observation and deduction in the interest of friends or mankind. One recalls the case of *The Mysterious Mickey Finn* in which the American millionaire, Hugo Weiss, was rescued; the salvaged love life of Beatrice from Boston in *Mayhem in B-flat*; many other feats of detectiveship the world knew about. There were others, perhaps the most remarkable, un-catalogued and unsung. Homer sighed with relief when he thought of them, which was seldom. He liked to assure himself that such exploits were over and done with, and that once peace had been declared, he could return to a life of ease and contemplation.

Of course, at the very moment of which we speak, Homer was a member of the secret army unit known, to the very few who even suspected its existence, as G-19. But it was a theory of Homer's that, if the public or casual observers were to be unaware that he was a secret officer and investigator, he must practically forget his role himself. He had grayed his hair slightly in order not to appear conspicuous out of uniform. Most of the time, in fact, he wore the uniform to which he was entitled, with slight changes in the insignia and decorations. As distinguished as he was, both physically and mentally, Evans could, when he desired, blend inconspicuously in almost any crowd.

For Homer to act under orders, and frequently orders that he knew were erroneous, was difficult. But he had resigned himself to it, as a part of the general disruption of the reasonable. For example: Homer and another G-19 operator had been assigned to follow and watch a certain Vichy agent who was undermining De Gaulle in Hollywood. The chief of G-19 had been informed that the traitorous French agent, one Armande de Plaitre, was leaving the screen city for Chicago on one of two railroads, the Santa Fe or the Union Pacific. Orders had been issued for Evans to cover the U.P. train, and Homer's colleague the Santa Fe "Superchief." De Plaitre had turned up on the Santa Fe train, leaving Evans and his bodyguard and assistant, Miriam Leonard, free of responsibility until Chicago, where further instructions might await them.

It is only fair to record that for several days before entraining Homer had known that the French spy would ride on the Santa Fe. But he could not disclose this knowledge to his superiors in rank, or even to his colleague, also a major, without at the same time letting it be known how he had come by the desired information. That would have had unfortunate results all around. In the first place, everyone concerned would have had his attention called to Homer's intuitive cleverness. He would be a marked man when the best interests of his country demanded that he remain obscure.

Secondly, his colleague would have suffered humiliation and official distrust because said colleague had muffed the clue. Thirdly,
De Plaitre, the prey, would not, at the moment of which we are
writing, be fatuously thinking, while under the eyes of the colleague, that he had given Homer and the department the slip.

From whatever cause or combination of circumstances Homer's
twenty-four-hour respite had stemmed, he welcomed it and was
relishing it.

Miriam, who was clearing the breakfast supplies from the table
and putting them back into the special breakfast trunk she took
with them when accompanying Homer on a tour of duty, glanced
at him unobtrusively and sighed, but with inner satisfaction. The
buzzer sounded, wasplike she started slightly. Homer paid no
attention. He had decided to be unaware of distractions, so that
although he was, when consciously attentive, the most observant
man then in Utah and probably in America, Homer did not at first
notice the porter, Moses Lemmings, who entered softly and cleared
away the cloth, dishes and implements which were company property. It was only when Moses paused to glance into the towel compartment and moved his lips almost imperceptibly, as untutored
adults do when counting, that Homer turned his head.

"What time is the inspection, Moses?" Homer asked.

The porter jumped, and frowned. He was a tall, ministerial
Negro with bald head fringed with gray hair and a resonant speaking voice that yearned for culture as a gypsy covets calico. "Sah?"
he said, to gain time.

"I noticed that in my compartment, next door, you carefully
counted the towels. Here you have just done it again. What does
that mean? That you suspect Miss Leonard of petty larceny?"

Moses' facial denials were so eloquent that Evans instantly reassured him.

"No, Moses. You are a better judge of human nature than that.
For some reason, unknown to me, you and the other veteran porters on this de-luxe train are particularly jittery about towels,
sheets, napkins and the like. That could only mean that the word
had been passed around that an inspector of company property

was either aboard or about to board the train. I have seen the passenger list, and no spotter is with us. Will he get on at Salt Lake, Moses?" Homer asked.

"I'm glad, Mr. Evans, that you-all ain't inspector," Moses Lemmings said fervently.

Evans smiled, with all his charm. "You may drop the Southern accent, Moses. You were born in East-Side Chicago."

"Some gentlemen expect it," Moses said, resignedly.

"But the inspector. Will he get on at Salt Lake?" asked Evans for the second time. From force of habit he was checking up on all the passengers on the train.

"At Omaha," Moses said. "I'm rehearsin' being frugal and accurate, one day in advance."

"Cautious man," said Homer, and again he smiled.

Moses, by that time, thought it useless to hold anything back. "And if you want to know, sir, what makes inspectors inspect more frequently and assiduously throughout the duration, it's because laundry of any kind whatsoever, either public or private, is hard to get accomplished. In the dear dead days nobody cared if the passengers took away a towel or two. Now we have to cut leakage to the minimum, because if we don't, what's lost, strayed or stolen is charged to us."

"Thanks, Moses," said Evans, but the porter had not finished.

"I'm an observant man myself, Mr. Evans," Moses said. "I observe and hereby specify that Miss Leonard must look after your laundry, or you'd have known all these things you just asked me. It's patriotic nowadays to count towels and everything else that has to be washed."

"You don't have to wash them, do you?" Evans asked.

"Not yet," said Moses, resignedly. "But all the generals and senators insist in the papers that greater sacrifices are yet to be extorted before we get that future post-war peace to come."

With that resounding phrase Moses made his exit from the drawing room, and in response to a slight nod from Miriam left the door open, so that Homer, if he wished, could see the Great Salt Lake through the corridor windows.

As Moses shuffled and swayed back to his end of the car, piquantly named Masomenus, in honor of an easygoing Ute chief who once had roamed those plains, the tall and venerable porter was thinking of Homer with immense respect. Most rich passengers were pains-in-the-neck, demanding loudly this or that, ordering impossible sandwiches and drinks at times inconvenient both for themselves and Moses. On the other hand, the few intellectual travelers were too much wrapped up in themselves and demanded no service at all, which caused Moses to worry whether his tips would be up to average. Also, most voyagers (male) either rich or poor, intellectual or dumb, were ridden and heckled by their wives, secretaries, concubines, mothers, or daughters, while Mr. Evans seemed to be able to get from lovely Miss Leonard an epic devotion, undemanding and instinctive, that upheld the fraying dignity of the sex to which Moses emphatically belonged. A man who read books in foreign languages, mused Moses, whose beautiful young companion carried along Syrian tobacco honey and a kind of strawberry jam from France which, she had told Moses, had had the seeds removed by patient old women with long needles, was the right kind of passenger for the Streamliner "City of Nuestra Senora la Reina de Los Angeles," Car 613, Masomenus, Porter: Moses Lemmings

Unconsciously Moses flattened himself against the car side as another passenger, also a gentleman of Mr. Evans' class but lacking Mr. Evans' poise and *vie intérieure*, brushed past. This gentleman, a Mr. Lancaster Primway of Bedroom A, had spent most of the morning, since an untouched breakfast at 6:30 A.M., pacing uneasily, first in his baggage-cluttered bedroom, which was lamentably lacking in pacing *platz*, then in the corridor.

Lancaster Primway was a man who looked like a movie star. To be exact, like Robert Taylor. That was fortunate for both Primway and Taylor, since the former was stand-in for the latter. Moses had portered Primway several times before, both eastbound and westbound, and had assumed, erroneously, from Mr. Primway's tips and his baggage, not to mention his Harvard accent, clothes and cuff links, that Mr. Primway was well fixed financially. Why any young man, good-looking and apparently rich, accepted socially by the best passengers, should worry, was beyond Moses' comprehension. Still, Mr. Primway was most certainly worrying.

Just as Homer Evans, sitting indolently in Compartment F, availed himself of the open door in order to glance at the Great Salt Lake, Lancaster Primway passed across his line of vision, without looking in. Homer knew and remembered young Primway, whom he had met at some Harvard function several years previously. Primway also remembered Homer Evans and had nodded politely in the dining car the evening before. But Evans had quickly sensed that Primway had something on his mind and did not wish to be engaged in conversation. Homer had merely bowed and smiled, then turned his attention back to Miriam, who was dissecting a grouse at the time.

Miriam realized that Homer and Primway were acquainted and that neither one was disposed, just then, to do anything further about it. Still, Miriam, observing Primway's distraught manner and comparing it with Homer's marvelous acceptance of things as they were, could not help reflecting how rare in men was the ability not to fidget, scratch themselves, shift their gaze fitfully, breathe stertorously, make futile and unnecessary motions, and fret when there was nothing else to do.

When Homer was at his best, either working brilliantly and intently, or lounging idly, there was an amazing affinity of spirit between him and Miriam. Her receptive mind was like a delicately adjusted instrument intercepting waves and the subtlest emanations from Homer's active brain.

Perceiving that Miriam was wondering about Primway, Homer reached over and closed the door.

"Don't let that young man make you nervous," Homer said.

"His kind of impatience is contagious, to women," Miriam said.

"Never disguise your curiosity," said Homer. "It's one of your foremost attractions."

"I know you want to rest and relax," she said, solicitously. "You don't have to analyze Mr. Primway for my benefit—unless you want to."

"To tell the truth," Evans said, "he baffles me. Either I must disregard him completely or delve more deeply into his probabilities."

"Pray do," said Miriam, seating herself gracefully to listen.

2

An Unscheduled Stop in Desperate Scenery

TWENTY-FIVE MINUTES LATER, both Homer and Miriam were sitting in the same respective positions, he musing and she still waiting. Meanwhile the train had entered the dingy Salt Lake station. A crew of rather frightening Mormon women in soiled denims, with wispy straw-colored hair, had busied themselves around the wheels and brake boxes with cotton waste and oil cans. Several military officers and men had quit the train; a larger number had got on to occupy their places. All around, factories, mills, warehouses and foundries were belching and fuming for Democracy.

As soon as the Streamliner, Car Masomenus, got into open country again, Miriam took a deep breath and seemed about to speak.

"May as well wait until we get out of Ogden," Homer said, gently. She nodded, acquiescent.

An hour later Homer turned slightly from the window and began:

"It was Lancaster Primway," he said, "who taught me to fly a plane. I met him at a smoker, at Commencement time in Cambridge, three years ago. He remarked that he had 'hopped down' from Machiasport, Maine, that afternoon. We talked about aeronautics, and the upshot was that next day he took me up in his Blansing Skyster. I brought the plane down."

"As quickly as that," said Miriam.

"I'd dipped into the theory before," Homer said. "It wasn't difficult to apply it. Primway was impressed and urged me to call on his fiancée that evening and convince her, if I could, how easy aviation was. He wanted her to be a pilot because she had a fear of planes. Being a Bostonian, with one of those rigid consciences, Primway believed that if one feared something, one should face and overcome that fear, in order to bolster up one's morale. Miss Cushing—*the* Ferdinanda Cushing whose mother was a Ledge—was essentially timid, it seemed. She had enormous social poise, never having questioned the propriety of anything a Ledge or Cushing might do, but, unlike most of the best Boston society, she was very rich—eight or ten million of her own and more to come when Uncle Leander died. Somehow, Ferdinanda's wealth had set her apart from her classmates at Miss Vincent's finishing school. She had begun to brood about whether or not she was physically attractive."

"Isn't Mr. Primway rich, too? He looks as if he might have been," said Miriam

"That's the rub," said Homer. "Primway, when I first met him, *was* rich. But his father and a couple of old-school partners made a hash of things, when the New Deal began cracking down on brokers. Lancaster, as I heard from other sources, called off his engagement to Ferdinanda the morning after he learned he was broke, and went to Hollywood to act, having been told that the big money was all there."

"The cad! To leave her just for money's sake," Miriam said, scornfully.

"He'd been taught that it was the appropriate gesture," Evans said. "His kind do not question the verities."

"Was she pretty?"

"So beautiful that she was disarming. The classic style, I mean."

"Brains?"

"An astonishing I.Q."

"Did she love him?"

"Almost pathologically," said Homer. "You know that pure New England strain that loves only once in six or seven generations."

"Oh," said Miriam, her sympathetic face showing deep concern. She was thinking of the girl, now, and taking sides against the tall and restless young man of scruples, whose love was bound by rules and precedents.

They rode along in silence fifteen minutes more.

"That can't be all," Miriam said, finally, on the verge of exasperation.

"A prize fathead among the ancients, that is to say, Aristotle," Homer continued, "laid down the principle that all stories must have a beginning, a middle and an end."

"Then what about the middle and end of this one?" asked Miriam.

Homer smiled and touched her hand. "I can supply the middle, but not the end. I'm an amateur detective, when I can't escape it, but no clairvoyant."

"You mean the end is not yet?"

"I think not. At least, I haven't heard it," Homer said. "Perhaps you'd rather not know the middle until . . ."

"Homer Evans! Don't be mean," she said, tapping with her foot. "Tell me the middle, right now or I shall denounce that young prig to his face."

Homer sighed and started again:

"Bostonians do not lend themselves readily to stage or screen acting. I'm referring to the Beacon Street, Groton, Harvard, State Street kind. They are of a type so essentially stuffy and comical inside that their restrained manners cannot adequately convey it. They have, without realizing it, studied how to be funny—that is, how to conform to a moral and social pattern that elsewhere is mirth-provoking—and at the same time they have schooled themselves to conceal their deepest feelings. In the hands of Henry James or even Marquand, they make excellent reading. The rapid medium of the screen makes them jerk like marionettes.

"I am saying all this," Homer explained, "to make it clear why our friend Primway gave up the dream of remaking his fortune as a movie star. He got a screen test because so many men of influence had had accounts with his father, and because he undoubtedly is handsome. But Harvard, while it dulls creative minds in many instances, develops to the nth degree a young man's critical side. Primway took one look at himself on the screen and said, 'I simply won't do.'"

"How absurd!" Miriam said. "Why should he have cared about earning money when Ferdinanda had practically all there was in Boston?"

"The ironic part of it is," said Homer, "it was Ferdinanda's father's firm who rooked the Primways, although, because of a middleman who was only one generation Boston, neither family understood this very well. One had got richer, the other, poorer. Very likely, if they had checked the amounts, both ways, they would have corresponded.

"Anyway," Homer continued, "whenever a Primway is confronted by a crisis, he arrives at some righteous decision that otherwise makes little sense. When he went broke in the first instance, he told Ferdinanda that she must wait."

"I know the song," said Miriam. "It may be for years and it may be forever."

"When in Hollywood it became almost immediately apparent that Lancaster Primway would never get beyond the category known as 'extra talent,' he took a graver, moralistic stand. He wrote Ferdinanda that he was a failure and that, although he always would love and respect her, she must put him out of her mind."

"An unequal contest," said Miriam, disgustedly.

"Very," agreed Homer. "For Lancaster, in spite of his other sound qualities, to put his love from his mind was like pushing a hop-toad off a floating shingle. In Ferdinanda's case the mind was excellent and her love was like a red, red coal."

"Which, when misplaced, starts fires," said Miriam.

Homer smiled. He enjoyed having Miriam a step or two ahead of him in his story. Having had a share in Miriam's creation, as it were, he was proud of it, pardonably, but frankly.

"Ferdinanda came to Hollywood, and made scenes in the Bank of America, behind a wicker window of which Lancaster eked out a puny existence, handling scrupulously each twenty minutes enough currency to have supported Ferdinanda in the style to which she had been accustomed," Homer said.

"Apple pie for breakfast," interjected Miriam.

"The symphony on Friday afternoons, and baked beans, sometimes with fish balls, on Saturday night," Homer added.

"And yards and yards of tweed," said Miriam.

"With a card to the Athenaeum," said Homer.

"And the dog races," Miriam said.

"The *Transcript* at four."

"First editions of *Lady Chatterley's Lover* and Frank Harris' *My Life and Loves.*"

"Those old English prints at Goodspeed's."

"And Bunker Hill."

By this time, the Streamliner was streaking through what the early Mormons so aptly described as "desperate scenery." Homer glanced at it for five or ten miles, in vain hopes of seeing a coyote or a jack rabbit. Then he resumed:

"Ferdinanda's touching imprecations drove Primway to more furious moral gymnastics. He decided that she must not see him, since it seemed to inflame her. So, through the aid of an executive of the bank he got a job on the M-G-M lot, as stand-in for Robert Taylor. There Ferdinanda could not follow him, since in war time the lot was doubly policed, and Houdini himself would have been hard put to gain admission without being finger-printed, photo-graphed, birth-certificated and furnished with a regulation pass. Ferdinanda, who had kept her temper fairly well up to that point, began to fume and sizzle."

"Enter the other man," said Miriam, resentfully but resignedly.

"François de la Cirage Dantan," said Homer, nodding.

"A refugee," said Miriam, sighing.

"An exile. Worse still, an actor."

"I saw him in *Homes Asunder*," Miriam said. "It should have been a wagon track."

"Naturally, Francois de la Cirage Dantan, or Frank Dante, as he is known to film fans, being the product of an older civilization than ours—in fact, a combination of three or four older civiliza-tions—had no prejudice against girls with lots of money, especially if they had that cool, clear-cut type of beauty so stimulating to jaded men of vast experience."

"What about Ferdinanda's I.Q.?" asked Miriam. "Why didn't it operate?"

"Ferdinanda's I.Q. always operates. I think she must be working according to plan," said Homer.

"Frank Dante has done in an appalling number of women, including quite a few nice ones, and some that were previously smart," Miriam said, doubtfully.

Homer sighed. "The contest, in this instance, is a fair one," he said. "I'm betting on Ferdinanda . . . but not heavily."

"Most women are foolish and impulsive, when on the rebound," said Miriam. "Is there nothing *you* can do?"

"Not unless someone is killed," he said and smiled.

Feeling that tug of the brakes which gives the illusion that the engineer had hooked a giant marlin or sailfish, both Homer and Miriam left off their consideration of the triangle Primway-Cushing-de la Cirage Dantan and looked out over the flats toward the lava-strewn foothills. Beyond the broad windows, the telegraph poles, clumps of sage, and straying cattle were receding more slowly, with longer intervals between them.

"We seem to be stopping," said Miriam

"That's strange," Homer said.

Again he reached over to open the door of the drawing room, just in time to see Lancaster Primway, this time almost frantic, halt his nervous pacing and peer out at the landscape on the north side of the tracks. It was a toss-up whether this view was more desolate, or less so than the one on the south side. He looked fearfully down the corridor, then faced about and asked of Homer: "What's wrong?"

Homer smiled reassuringly. "Maybe a troop train's ahead. That happens often this side of Green River."

"But our connection in Chicago," said Primway, agitated. "I've only two hours at best to make the Commodore."

Miriam, whose interest in Primway went way beyond anything he suspected, could not hold back an anxious inquiry.

"Then you're going back to Boston?" she murmured.

At this Primway simultaneously shuddered and froze.

"That is my intention," he said, almost curtly.

"Won't you come in?" said Homer, with a gesture indicating the roomy compartment. "We won't be stranded here long."

Primway looked questioningly at Miriam, with that Bostonian wariness which is always on the scent of possible impropriety.

"May I present Miss Leonard, my assistant?" Homer said. "Miss Leonard—Mr. Primway."

"How do you do, Miss Leonard?" said Primway, and, stepping in, sat down in the extra chair.

The train was not moving at all, and nothing stirred on the landscape except a couple of undernourished gophers near the track.

"Where are we?" Primway asked, desperately.

"A few miles over the Wyoming line," Homer replied.

"I love Wyoming," said Miriam. "It's so spacious and high. Wouldn't it be fun" (she addressed this to Homer) "if we could rope a couple of those bronchos. . . ."

"What bronchos?" asked Primway, eagerly, as if he already were contemplating a continuance of his journey on horseback, so strong was his compulsion to be moving eastward. Miriam, aware of this, began to feel her heart beating warmly. Was this misguided Bostonian repentant, in time? Was he going to Ferdinanda and beg her forgiveness, waive his Quixotic notions about bank accounts, and send Dantan or Dante back to Beverly Hills to stalk another heiress? Surely, to a man like Frank Dante, the identity of the girl who furnished the money would be inconsequential, while to Lancaster Primway it would matter vitally.

In her preoccupation with the nervous Primway, who was clasping and unclasping his hands, arranging and rearranging his necktie, clearing his throat, drumming with his shoes on the carpet, and showing all the signs of masculine disintegration in the face of unexpected obstacles, Miriam had missed what Homer was watching from the corner of his eye.

On the track, near the forward platform of Car Masomenus stood the porter, Moses Lemmings, and the conductor of the train. Lemmings was shaking like an aspen and had faded in color from ebony to slate-gray. He extended long eloquent hands to the conductor, then toward the car, then spread his arms full length and swept them across the scenery, which had remained unchanged since the last glacier had inched northward and had shaved off much of its individuality. Homer knew well the meaning of such gestures and facial contortions. Something dreadful had happened of which the porter was protesting innocence.

A few passengers descended from the platform, asked a question or two, and began to stroll up and down the right of way. Whatever the conductor told them seemed to get them nowhere. That was plain.

By the time Miriam had shifted her eyes from the faintly perspiring Primway to Homer, alert and preternaturally calm, she also was dimly aware of the pantomime and trickling procession alongside the window. She and Homer saw, coincidentally, a tremor of relief ripple upward on the long form of Moses Lemmings and a reaction from the bristling conductor. Then Moses pointed urgently, almost prayerfully, straight to the window at which Homer was sitting. The conductor responded, although reluctantly, and allowed himself to be eased back to the car platform.

A few seconds later Miriam's buzzer sounded, raggedly and tremulously. In response to Homer's invitation the door was opened. Moses stood back, his large eyes gleaming with terror. The conductor squared his jaw, tried to swell up to the appropriate stature of a commanding officer, as indisputably he was aboard the train, and both of them stood there, conveying without words, but unmistakably, their dismay at finding Homer not alone.

Whatever else may be said of Bostonians, they are never obtuse about social nuances. Primway rose stiffly.

"Perhaps I'd better go to my room. May I join you later?" he said to Homer, then bowed correctly to Miriam.

"What's your accommodation?" the conductor asked, suspiciously.

"Bedroom A," said Primway.

"I'll have to ask you not to enter any of the compartments just now," the conductor said. "Why don't you walk along the track for a while?"

At this Primway's nervous impatience broke the bonds of his New England reserve.

'What's the reason for this outrageous delay? I demand that the train proceed," he said.

"There's a box in the Nugget Car for written complaints," the conductor said. "But don't try to leave the vicinity of this car."

"Why not a little exercise?" Homer suggested, gently, to Primway. "I'll join you in a jiffy."

Primway, with a withering glare at the conductor, then at Lemmings, stalked out of the compartment and aft along the corridor.

"Watch that man," the conductor said to Moses. "He's been acting suspiciously since he got aboard. As for yourself, you know what'll happen if you try to scram."

"Yes, sir," said Moses, miserably, and shuffled along, after turning a few shades lighter gray.

The conductor now eyed Miriam in a fishy sort of way.

"Mr. Evans, could I see you alone?" he asked of Homer.

Homer smiled his hitherto irresistible smile. "Miss Leonard is my colleague," he said. "I've no secrets from her."

The conductor looked at Miriam again. She looked at Homer. Homer said to the conductor, courteously but with finality: "Please sit down."

3
The Coroner's Gone A-Hunting

IT WAS AN ODDLY ASSORTED TRIO who sat in Compartment F of Car Masomenus. The conductor, a colorless, meticulous man of medium height, looked and acted as an old sea captain might who after years of skillful navigation suddenly had lost his ship on a reef in his native harbor. Even anyone much less perspicacious than Homer could see that he was appalled, not by whatever had happened but by the consequences to himself and his long, unblemished record. Miriam was pleased, almost triumphant, because Homer had been so gallant and firm when the question of her presence arose. Homer was torn between reluctance to forsake his delicious indolence and the temptation to turn upon the riddle before him the full intensity of his unusual mind.

"That porter," said the conductor, tersely. "You know him?"

"I've enjoyed his faultless service several times," Homer said. "A very good man."

"He says he knows *you*," the conductor persisted, accusingly.

"To a certain extent, I suppose," Homer said.

"He claims you're a kind of detective, and know all about the law," the conductor went on.

"Knowledge of the law is relative," said Homer. "Do you mean the Federal law; the law of Buckskin County in which we are now sitting; the statutes, if any, of the township of West Evanston, which extends around us about six miles in four directions; the laws of the Commonwealth of Wyoming, which apply, I think, on stationary trains; the regulations of the Interstate Commerce

Commission which sometimes have the effect of the law; the war-time rulings of the O.P.A., the C.W.B., the N.D.E., the F.B.I., the orders of the Commanding Officer of the military district with headquarters at Green River . . ."

"Don't," begged the conductor, covering his ears with his hands.

Homer had accomplished what he wished and what seemed best for all concerned. He had won the initiative from the harassed conductor, gained in a measure his respect and confidence, and reduced him to a pliable state.

"I take it that the porter is in trouble, that you are badgering him about something quite serious, and that he, protesting his innocence, on which I will bet the price of my tickets, has appealed to me," Homer said. "Am I right?"

"I don't know what's right. All I know is, I had to stop the train," the conductor said.

"Now that I think of it, I understand why," Homer said. "Someone has died. I remember, although hazily, that when a passenger dies on an interstate train, the conductor is obliged to cause the said train to be stopped wherever it may be and call in the local coroner."

For answer, which was also confirmation, the conductor deepened his expression of woe and, almost as Moses had before, extended both hands toward the flats and the foothills, on which the noontide sun was glimmering.

"Call the local coroner," repeated the conductor and again cradled his head in his hands and rocked to and fro.

Miriam sighed sympathetically. "Quite an order," she said. "Couldn't you, perhaps, telephone?"

"I have telephoned. The county seat is eighty-two miles away, in Blanc Mange, and the coroner, Heber T. Allbrown, is hunting jack rabbits, on horseback. There is a branch rail connection to some cement factory reopened since the war, but their only hand-car is out of order. And the local gasoline rationing board has to hold a special meeting to decide whether, in case the coroner gets back from hunting, he would be issued enough gas to drive here to the U.P. tracks. The nearest highway, I am informed, crosses the tracks five miles east."

"Poor Primway will be distressed," Homer said. "He seems to be in a terrific hurry. I suppose there's no chance whatever of our making the connection for New York in Chicago."

What the conductor said, forgetting Miriam's presence, about New York, Chicago and any possible connection between them, must be omitted from this narrative in order that the publisher may send it through the mails. But Miriam, although trying to be patient, could not contain herself any longer. To be obliged to sit through several minutes, hearing a couple of males discuss law and territorial rights, routes, conveyances, petty officials, their where-abouts, etc., without touching upon the *corpus delicti*, overstrained her natural reluctance to assert herself.

"Who is dead?" she demanded. "How and why?"

"The result will be the same, no matter who is dead," said Homer. "Our friend Primway will lose his train out of Chicago, and probably what there is of his mind."

The conductor then had a few unprintable things to say about Primway, who could be seen pacing the cinders, tugging at his collar, scuffing his feet, glaring at the trembling Moses Lemmings, and showing other evidences that his blood pressure was approaching the danger line.

"Homer, he *does* love her," Miriam said.

The conductor on love really touched the heights.

"Who *is* dead?" interrupted Homer, as much to satisfy Miriam's curiosity as to add to his own store of facts.

"Bedroom B," said the conductor, pulling forth a frayed passenger list. "A party named Momblo, Isaac."

"Isaac Momblo," murmured Homer. "A most unusual name. Did he die from natural causes?"

"The most natural in the world," the conductor said. "That cloth-headed porter let down the upper berth, went out and forgot it, and this guy Momblo, bumped his bald head . . ."

"Bald head?" repeated Homer, suddenly sitting up straight, with real regret in his voice. "Not that rare little man with whom I spent an hour in the Nugget last evening?"

"That was probably his last happy hour," said the conductor. "If I'm any judge, this party has been dead and stiff as a mackerel quite a while."

"Then you should have stopped, according to law, in Las Vegas, Nevada," Homer said. "The act reads 'as soon as possible after the demise.' Strictly speaking, it would have been possible for you to stop, even though you were not aware that a passenger was dead. In fact, you have stopped several times. It is conceivable that a court would rule that you should take the train back to Las Vegas and look for the coroner there.'

"What about Mr. Momblo, the late Mr. Momblo?" Miriam interrupted. "And what has poor Moses to do with him, and Homer with Moses?"

"Lemmings is guilty of contributory negligence, maybe manslaughter. I'm going to put him under arrest, and have done with it," the conductor said.

"U. S. Statute 3577, 1889, as revised in 1912, would make that rather dangerous, from your point of view. Just in case—on the off-chance that Moses is not guilty of negligence, he would have a wonderful case against you and the U.P. for false arrest, defamation of character, nervous shock, and heavens knows what else," said Homer.

Miriam fairly exploded. "Will you two barristers stop arguing and take me to the scene of the crime?"

"The crime?" said Evans. Then his expression changed. "By Jove, of course. You're always right, Miriam. The crime," he added, and, turning to the conductor, he asked, "Did it occur to you that this incident may involve a charge somewhat graver than manslaughter?"

The conductor blinked, and felt for his badge, staring out of the window to make sure that Moses was still there. "You mean the shine killed him on purpose?" he asked, pale eyes bulging.

"I beg you to remember that the porter, legally, because of your own intercession and my acceptance, is my client. Whatever I might say could be used against him, and I advise you strongly to be more careful what *you* insinuate," said Homer, and this time his smile sent a chill down the conductor's spine and, for another reason, down Miriam's as well.

"Shall we go to Bedroom B?" the conductor asked, cowed.

"No hurry," Homer said, sitting down and drawing forth his leather cigar case. "The coroner, the worthy Heber T. Allbrown, won't be here for hours. If Momblo has been dead since Las Vegas, he will stay dead quite a while. Let me tell you first what I learned from the deceased, himself, in my chat with him in the Nugget Car."

With that he beckoned Moses through the window. When the porter, more dead than alive with apprehension, pressed the buzzer and opened the door, Homer smiled at him reassuringly and ordered three double sherries, remarking that in any event one must prepare for lunch, whether trains move or wait.

4
Decidedly, the Corpse Was Not Banal

ALONG THE RIGHT OF WAY, the full length of the tan-and-silver Stream-liner which stretched east to west on a reverse curve, like some serpentine creation of modern Mound Builders, the passengers were strolling, scrambling, stumbling and scurrying in a meaning-less way. There was no alarm, as yet no indignation except that of Lancaster Primway. As with other Bostonian emotions, Primway's wrath was nine-tenths submerged, like an iceberg. The remaining tenth was directed at the trembling Moses Lemmings. That is to say, until Primway peered into the window of Compartment F and saw the conductor sitting opposite Homer Evans and Miriam, sip-ping dry sherry from a water glass, and listening to a story. With that the Bostonian began a rigadoon along the car-side among the more phlegmatic passengers like a gadget shimmering along the wrong belt-line and matching none of the others.

The conductor, who, had Primway known it, was only slightly less impatient, let his attention stray from Homer's narrative just long enough to spot Primway again.

"More suspicious than ever," was his comment. "He must be wanted for something back in California. We get quite a few of those."

Homer looked at Miriam and smiled. She did not quite know why, but already she had sensed that the death of Isaac Momblo was being taken more seriously by Homer than by the conductor. The other employees on the Streamliner crew were ducking in and out of closets, under car trucks, and around mail sacks and telegraph poles in order to escape the questions fired at them by the passengers, both civil and military.

"Why had the train stopped? . . . When would it proceed? . . . Where were they, if such a God-forsaken place could have a name?"

The civilians looked at their watches, made gestures of exasperation and protest, and badgered the train crew much more assiduously than the soldiers, sailors or marines. The service men, those who had been in a week or more, had grown accustomed to unexplained stops, starts, alarums, excursions and hiatuses. They simply concluded that "someone had blundered" and let it go at that, so that at least sixty of them, in various uniforms, were stretched out under neighboring sage-brush clumps, asleep. Others were playing gambling games. Of all the weirdly assembled company, only Moses, the conductor, Homer and Miriam knew that a passenger named Isaac Momblo, occupying Bedroom B, Car 613, called "Masomenus," had been dead x hours and that a coroner living in Blanc Mange named Heber T. Allbrown was presumably on his way.

At any rate, the conductor had locked Bedroom B containing the corpse after a cursory glance following the porter's disclosure and, at Evans' suggestion, had agreed to keep it locked until the law arrived. It seemed to Miriam that the conductor might have been persuaded to unlock the bedroom and give Homer, representing Moses, the first chance to case it, but Miriam knew Homer's superb confidence in himself and his unending delight in watching professional officers and detectives commit all sorts of idiocies when first confronted with a difficult problem. On the few occasions when the professionals had been brilliant, Homer had enjoyed himself even more. He was free from vanity or envy and an ardent admirer and appreciator of what he termed "style." As fans liked to watch Sam Hirschfield's or Jim Geller's graceful sweep when driving a golf ball off the tee, Babe Ruth's powerful unerring swing with a baseball bat, or Belmonte's perfect timing with a cape in the bull ring, Homer was thrilled when observing a good mind in action. Somehow, the chances that the elusive Heber T. Allbrown's brain would prove to be remarkable seemed to Miriam infinitesimally slim. She expected that it would take Homer about five minutes to remove the cloud from the porter's reputation and career, in spite of the conductor's firm conviction that Moses Lemmings had been lax and should be arraigned.

Be that as it may, Homer, completely at his ease, was telling Miriam and the conductor, whom sherry seemed to agitate rather than soothe, about his encounter, if such a gentle incident could be thus described, with the late Isaac Momblo in the Nugget Car the evening before. Homer had been sitting not far from the bar, watching closely how the skillful Johnny Ruh was mixing a gin fizz (using a pinch of some new and obscure sulfa drug to counteract the vile taste of Cuban gin) when a little man, about five feet three, with an egg-shaped bald head which came down to a point like a kite, with a neat Vandyke beard, approached him, cleared his throat as if embarking on a studied oration, and said, in a subdued but pleasing voice, vibrant with timidity: "Good evening."

Homer had replied in kind, without the tremor. Decidedly Isaac Momblo was not banal.

The little man had owl-like green-gray eyes with a humorous glint and wore gold-rimmed spectacles. His suit was not new, and had been inexpertly pressed, Homer saw, by Momblo himself. That he was not an experienced traveler had become evident before he had said ten words.

"I suppose passengers come in here" (Isaac had indicated the red-and-gilt decorations of the Nugget and the numerous photos and tintypes of famous entertainers on the walls) "to drink, talk or play cards."

Evans, smiling, had nodded. "I have seldom seen a man more lonely, or engaging," Homer said to Miriam.

"But why did the damn fool have to die on *my* train?" the conductor interjected. "And be discovered in a stretch of country like this?"

"Good questions," Evans said. "I hope, in time, to be able to answer them."

Miriam, to her amazement, saw that Homer meant just that. To encourage Homer, she repeated Isaac's naive words: "to drink, talk or play cards."

"I can't drink. My stomach won't stand it," Momblo had said. "I can't afford to play cards and lose, and it makes me feel bad to win and take some one else's money . . ."

Isaac had hesitated, blinking and smiling hopefully.

"So," he had continued, "I thought perhaps you might be a good talker and that I could listen, and say a little something now and then."

Homer, touched, had assured his new acquaintance that nothing would give him greater pleasure.

"I don't know much to talk about—except myself, and that's not very interesting," Momblo had continued. Again reassured by Homer he had made brief and terse comments on his mode of life. It was limited, it seemed, by his very low vitality. Isaac, according to himself, had just enough strength, if he was very careful of it, to get through a daily routine. He had the vaguest and least important job in the largest electrical concern in the world, situated at Schenectady.

"He told me," Homer said, "that he didn't know exactly what he did. When a machine, huge or tiny, broke down, Momblo was assigned to it after all the experts and engineers had failed to get it going again. He would tap it, stroke it, tickle it with a feather, anoint it, unhurriedly, and almost always it responded. 'Pure instinct. I know nothing, theoretically, about machinery or electricity,' Momblo said."

Homer sighed, and went on. "According to his story, Momblo was too timid to make friends."

At this Miriam, sympathetic, reached over and touched Homer's hand. "Of course he would choose you, and trust you," she said.

Homer almost blushed. "I'm glad he did," he said. "We would have been good friends."

"Did he mention any relatives?" asked the practical conductor. "The road will have to ship his remains to somebody or other, the nearest of kin."

"He had no kin at all," Evans said. "That I remember distinctly."

"Then who shall we notify? Where shall we ship the body? How'll I get rid of him?" the conductor asked, plaintively.

"Patience," Homer said. "I was about to tell you what he said about dying."

"Dying?" The conductor sat up straight. "Did the bloody little runt have the nerve to talk about dying, in advance?"

"After all," Homer said, "death is a frequent subject of conversation."

"Gaaaaaaaad," grunted the conductor.

"Mumblo said, after telling me that he could digest almost nothing but the white meat of chicken, that he thought he would have died long before if he had felt well enough," said Homer.

"What's that? Well enough to die?" the conductor said.

"Dying, according to Momblo, was a radical change to make in one's condition. To accomplish it, well, one should be fairly fit. That was Isaac's idea," Homer said.

"*I* must be nuts," groaned the conductor.

5
It's Murder, More or Less

THE SUN WAS SETTING behind the western rim of hills behind the Streamliner when Heber T. Allbrown, accompanied by Jennie Y. Allbrown, his wife, rode into view from the south on two pintos. Just after lunch, Homer had suggested to the conductor that in order to still the passengers' questions and doubts, members of the train crew should pretend to be repairing the locomotive. Three trainmen, smeared with grease, unscrewed the cylinder head and toyed with it inside the cab. The porters all up and down the line, themselves deceived, gave out the story to the passengers. The train might move that night, or wait until the next morning, the voyagers were informed. Most of them beefed. Lancaster Primway sat grimly on the steps of Car Masomenus and yammered inwardly.

Facing south, Primway was one of the first to see approaching on horseback, if that pair of pintos could fairly be classified as horseflesh, the two Mormons, man and wife. He called Moses' attention to them and was mildly surprised when the porter practically collapsed.

"The law," whispered Lemmings hoarsely.

"The law?" repeated Primway, fretfully. "You've been seeing too many movies."

He had no way of knowing that his chance remark set Moses to wondering whether or not there would be movies in the penitentiary.

The conductor, informed of Allbrown's approach, walked a few hundred yards southward to meet the coroner, who proved to be a bony, lantern-jawed man with short eyelashes, mud- colored hair and face muscles overdeveloped from continual chewing of nothing at all. Actually, he looked a little like both of the pintos. His wife looked the way Clare Luce would, if she didn't have money.

"Coroner Allbrown, I presume," said the conductor.

"Mutually agreed," said Allbrown, chewing placidly. "Meet the wife."

"Glad to meet you, Mrs. Allbrown," the conductor said.

"Take her and welcome," said Allbrown, and looked straight ahead.

"I'm the conductor," the conductor said.

"Good job . . . Keeps a man away from home," was Allbrown's comment.

Miriam and Homer, looking from the window of Compartment F, were watching eagerly. Yes, Homer was eager, and this puzzled Miriam more than anything else that had happened that day. She had watched Homer Evans in action, and always he maintained his Olympian detachment, under circumstances beside which the current ones seemed trivial. What was his intense interest in Lemmings and the deceased gentle Momblo? Why could not a bump against an upper berth cause death to a man who, admittedly, was fragile?

"She didn't believe him," Evans, eyeing the Allbrowns, said and smiled.

"Who didn't believe whom?" asked Miriam.

"Mrs. Allbrown evidently figured her husband had trumped up this phone call in order to get away from home," Homer said.

"Mr. Allbrown was already away from home, hunting jackrabbits," Miriam said.

"That was different. That would be in the daytime," Homer said.

Out on the flat, the conductor was explaining what he could to Heber T. Allbrown, who had twice threatened to manhandle Mrs. Allbrown if she did not button up her trap, as Heber expressed it so succinctly. Mrs. Allbrown, in truth, had a marked tendency to interrupt.

"The law says . . ." the conductor began.

"What law?" asked Heber.

"The rules of the I.C.C.," the conductor said.

"Never heard of them," said Heber, and started to wheel his horse around, as if to start back to Blanc Mange.

The conductor grabbed his stirrup and held on.

"You've got to act," he said. "When a passenger dies on a train, said train must be stopped wherever it is and the nearest coroner summoned. You get mileage and a fee."

"No checks. Cash," Heber said.

"Take what you can get, you old skinflint," said Mrs. Allbrown.

"I ought to smack you in the puss," was Heber's reply.

"Not here, where there are witnesses," cautioned the conductor. Heber nodded.

"I've kept the death secret," the conductor said. "The passengers all think we had to stop to fix the engine."

"Foul play?" asked Heber.

"Just routine," the conductor said. "A porter forgot to rehoist an upper berth. A passenger bumped his head. That's all."

"'Twouldn't even a'dented that dome o' Heber's," said Mrs. Allbrown.

"I ought to whale the liver out o' you," Heber said. "I will, soon's I get my fee an' mileage and a bottle of red-eye."

"Not on railroad property," cautioned the conductor. "Now will you keep it dark, who you are, and why you're here, so the passengers won't stampede?"

"That'll cost you more," Heber said. "An extra four bits, at least."

The conductor handed him four bits and made an entry in his notebook, as they rode and he walked to the train. After Mrs. Allbrown had hitched the pintos to a pole, the trio entered Car Masomenus. Primway rose to make way for them, and Moses Lemmings, peering from his little cabinet inside, began to pray. Once the conductor and the Allbrowns were inside the car, the doors were locked, the shades drawn, and passengers, now suspecting something unusual and ominous, began to gather around, outside, until the roar and murmur of their voices swelled into a fretful chorus. First Moses was summoned from his cabinet.

"This is the culprit," the conductor said.

The firm voice of Evans brought all concerned up short. "I have warned you about false accusations," Homer said. "One more and I shall enter suit, in behalf of my client, Mr. Lemmings."

"Who's this feller?" Heber asked.

Homer handed the coroner his card, which read:

HOMER TRUESDALE EVANS

The coroner glanced at it, sighed, and handed it back. It meant nothing whatever to him.

"Who is this guy?" he asked again.

This time Moses Lemmings volunteered the information most gratefully. "That's Mr. Evans, the great detective, Mr. Sheriff, sah," the porter said. "He's on my side."

"Let's see the stiff," the coroner said.

"Right this way," said the conductor, and leading the party toward Bedroom B, fumbled with his keys, then unlocked the door. As he did so Homer stepped forward.

"Mr. Coroner, since Lemmings, the porter, has been unjustly accused of negligence, and I am representing him, would you mind if, before any of us enters the bedroom in question, I take a few pictures for the record?" Homer asked.

"Any objections?" the coroner asked the conductor.

"It ought to cost two bits," said Mrs. Allbrown.

"Shut up, Jennie," the coroner said, but he held out his hand and nodded when Homer gave him a dollar.

Homer rapidly took six exposures of the body and the interior of Bedroom B. As he did so he sighed regretfully.

The body of Isaac Momblo was lying on its side, facing the door and away from the window. On the shining bald head was a contusion and a dent. The skin had been broken and the blood had congealed.

The upper berth was horizontal, above where Momblo had fallen. Its lower convex surface showed a stain of blood in what seemed to be the appropriate spot. Momblo's head had not dented it at all.

While Homer busied himself inside the small compartment, Heber Allbrown merely squinted and grunted and chewed. Then suddenly, he asked: "Were you ever a porter, Mr. Conductor?"

Homer, Miriam, and especially the disconsolate Moses brightened.

"Not likely," the conductor said. "The porters are all colored."

"Good job," said Heber. "Takes 'em away from home. By the way. Ever play with Easter eggs?"

With that he subsided and started chewing again, but Evans was encouraged. "I did," Homer said, "as a boy. . . . This is murder."

"Murder?" gasped Miriam.

Heber turned to Mrs. Allbrown triumphantly, nodding toward Homer.

"Murder!" repeated the conductor, scornfully.

"Murder," insisted Homer, and sighed. Then he fixed the conductor with his clear, compelling eye. "Do you wish in behalf of the company, or on your own account, to charge Mr. Lemmings with murder?"

The conductor, who was beginning to be fed up with Homer's soft assurance, lost his temper and judgment. "Who else could have done it?" he said. Then he turned to Moses and was about to arrest him, when the porter suddenly wilted, and slid unconscious to the floor.

"There goes half the evidence," said Heber, tersely.

For Moses, in falling, had disarranged the position of the corpse.

"Who was the party that got killed?" asked the coroner. "He must have been a fragile feller."

Homer looked at the Mormon closely, then asked Miriam to take over while he took Mr. Allbrown to her drawing room for a private consultation. At this suggestion the conductor blew up.

"You seem to forget who's running this train," he said, hot under the collar. "Now listen to me for a while."

Unimpressed but compliant Heber prepared to listen by chewing a few degrees slower, and Homer also paused, on his lips a faint, tolerant smile

"First off," said the conductor, "I arrest Moses Lemmings . . ."

"Better wait until he revives," Homer said. "The common law, I believe . . ."

"O.K., Blackstone," said the conductor. Miriam frowned, as she always did when anyone showed Homer the slightest disrespect.

"The minute he comes to," the conductor said, splashing water from the nickel-plated carafe on the limp Lemmings, "he goes under arrest. Furthermore, if you or anybody else confers with the coroner, I sit in."

"Just a minute," Homer said, "since you seem to have suddenly got tough. I demand, in behalf of my client . . ."

The mention of Moses as a client seemed to revive him slightly. He sat up, blinking, his back to the corpse.

"That's the way," Evans said to Moses encouragingly. "Keep a stiff upper lip. I was just saying to the conductor . . . By the way, for the sake of the record, what is your name?"

"My name's Thomas Q. Rider, if it's any of your affair," the conductor said.

Again Miriam winced, and almost instinctively her hand moved toward her handbag. At this, Homer, remembering that in the handbag lay the redoubtable automatic that had sounded the "A" on a standing tuning fork without tipping it over, touched her shoulder gently.

"Don't shoot," he said. "Mr. Rider is within his rights. He's had a hard day."

The hammering and thumping on the locked car door indicated that Lancaster Primway also had had more than he could bear. No one except the hundred-odd assembled passengers paid the slightest attention to Primway, however.

Lemmings got to his feet, his whole body trembling. "I swear, Mr. Evans. I'm not guilty," he said.

"I know that, Moses," said Homer.

"You know too much for your breeches," the conductor said.

"Shut your trap," said Heber Allbrown to his wife, whose jaw was sagging as if she were about to say something.

"Since our conference must be public," Homer said to the coroner, "let's adjourn to Miss Leonard's room."

"You all through here?" asked the conductor, indicating Bedroom B.

"I'm in charge of this investigation, and what Mr. Evans says goes," the coroner said.

Miriam beamed on Heber Allbrown her most bewitching smile. The unprepossessing Mormon was a good judge of man, was her unspoken comment as the moaning porter was locked into the conductor's own compartment, and a brakeman deputized and armed to watch him and prevent his escape.

"I should like," Homer said, "to have you check the towels, used and unused, in each compartment of this car."

All were in order and the count was perfect until they reached Bedroom A. From the cabinet of this room, occupied when possible by Lancaster Primway, one towel was missing.

"Just as I thought," said Homer.

"What's that mean?" asked the coroner. "Anyone can pinch a towel."

"Not a Primway from Boston," Homer said. "There, Mr. Allbrown, you're quite wrong."

"Bah," said the conductor.

A minute search of Primway's effects, however, made at Evans' insistence and under the conductor's protest, revealed that the missing towel was not in Primway's room.

6

Concerning the Goat and the Motive

"It don't add up no way, but what can we do?" asked Heber T. Allbrown, when Heber, Homer and Miriam were seated with double whiskies in Compartment F. Outside this compartment, Mrs. Allbrown and the conductor were pacing back and forth, biting their lips, flexing their fingers, tugging at their clothes and jostling each other. Both had been excluded from the powwow by Heber, because he thought Homer would like it that way, and also from a long-suppressed desire, built up over years, to exclude Jennie Y. from anything possible.

"I'm a plain man," Heber continued, "and I see things straight. Why should the spade" (Heber's concise way of describing the dignified and apprehensive Moses Lemmings) "want to bump off the harmless little guy with the spinach?" The "spinach" was Momblo's neat Vandyke.

"Why, indeed?" agreed Homer. He wanted to draw out the rangy Mormon and get his full co-operation. For already Evans was feeling a challenge to his resourcefulness. The conductor had a certain amount of authority, the exact extent of which it would take the courts a decade at least to define. The coroner also had quite a bit of law behind him, plain man that he was. No one knew how much or how, why or where the bulk of it applied.

"Let's call back the conductor a moment," Homer suggested. "I want to ask him a question or two."

Heber thought a moment, then nodded and grinned.

"Suits me. Grill him silly. When you're through I can bounce him out again."

As the conductor was admitted, Mrs. Allbrown hopped and sashayed, uttering squealing sounds of rage.

"We all have the same objective," Homer began, pacifically. "We want to find the murderer of Isaac Momblo. He must be, or must have been on this train. Now I am anxious to know, Mr. Rider, why you suspect the porter, Moses Lemmings?"

"There has to be a goat," the conductor said, doggedly. "When a thing like this happens, someone has to take the rap. If anybody tried to pin the crime on that dude from Boston, he'd dig up a lot of influence and there'd be hell to pay."

"I see," said Homer, with disarming softness. "You mean that Moses, being colored and friendless, wouldn't be able to put up much of a defense. Is that the idea?"

"He'd get off with manslaughter. They're nice boys, the colored porters. Everybody likes 'em. But they do forget, now and then. It all works out neatly. Before we got to Las Vegas, right after dinner, perhaps, the little shrimp with the glasses . . ."

"Mr. Momblo was not a little shrimp," interrupted Miriam, eyes blazing. "He would have been a friend of Homer's."

Heber T. Allbrown was about to say, "Shut your trap," but he caught himself just in time. Homer, to quiet Miriam, used the smoother tactics. He patted her hand.

"Continue, Mr. Rider," Homer said.

"I was saying that probably the deceased called in the prisoner about ten o'clock or so and asked him to make up his berth. He hadn't traveled much . . ."

"Very interesting," interrupted Homer. "Did Momblo tell you that?"

"When I took up his ticket, just out of L.A., I buzzed and went into his bedroom and he was looking all around, like a cat in a strange closet, smiling and blinking at the conveniences. He seemed to want to talk, so I sat down a minute. 'Been out to the coast?' I says. Then he told me that the Universal Electric had sent him all the way from Schenectady to get one of the big turbines going in some war plant or other near L.A."

"Did he succeed in his mission?" Homer asked.

"So he said. And I think he was telling the truth. He didn't know just how he did it, he said, but the thing started rolling, or whatever turbines do. So he started back East again. You can't tell me a funny little gink . . ."

This time Miriam, in spite of her good resolutions, and so quickly that not even the sharp eye of Heber T. Allbrown could follow the motion of her shapely hand, did draw her automatic. The conductor turned green and started back against the cushions so violently that his false teeth were jarred loose.

"Mr. Momblo was not a *funny little gink*," said Miriam evenly. This time Homer did not interfere.

The conductor, who by this time had got both hands up, rolled his fishy eye toward Homer, and gurgled. The coroner stared at Miriam admiringly.

"The quickest draw I ever seen," he said, "barring none."

At last Homer smiled and Miriam put away the gun.

"Mr. Rider," he said, "was unfortunate in his choice of language. He meant no harm. By 'funny' he meant 'odd' and by 'gink,' 'an unaggressive man without renown.' Am I right, Mr. Rider?"

"Yeeeeees," stammered the conductor, lowering his hands to readjust his teeth. With that he started to rise, already leaning toward the door.

"Go on with your story," Homer said. "Miss Leonard will control herself."

"What I was getting at was that I didn't believe the deceased passenger would be murdered in cold blood by a porter who had nothing much to gain. It was just negligence. If Lemmings had been intending to rob somebody and beat it at Las Vegas, he would have stuck up that Boston palooka . . ."

"Who is flat broke, by the way," Homer said.

"He has six suits of clothes," said the conductor.

"Holy Cripes, I saw them," Heber said. "What can a man do with all them suits, if he hasn't any growing children?"

"He's an actor," said the conductor.

"He might be pleased to hear you say so," Homer said. "The casting directors of all the studios, including Monogram, thought differently—but frequently they are wrong."

"Why are you so anxious for a 'goat'?" Homer asked the conductor.

"If you were in my place, you'd understand. Unless there's some explanation, the case drags on and on, and I get summonses, subpoenas, lawyer's letters and phone calls, when I'm trying to sleep in Chicago, for months on end. I lost eighteen pounds after some snaky-looking Duchess lost her emeralds, in 1927. Honest, Mr. Evans, if you knew the red tape, and the bawlings out I get from the superintendent, you'd sympathize."

"Not to the extent of railroading an innocent party into the pen for five or six years," Evans said.

"I hadn't looked at it that way," said the conductor.

"Pray do," said Miriam.

The conductor ducked and started to get up again. This time they let him go.

"There's something fishy here," said Heber T. Allbrown. He looked shrewdly at Homer. Homer nodded.

"The county of Buckskin did well in electing you coroner," Homer said. "I can't tell you how pleasant it is to work with a smart man."

"Is it straight that you're a detective?" Heber asked Homer.

"Unluckily, yes," Homer said. "And it would be most inconvenient if that fact were advertised just now. The conductor knows it, so does Moses Lemmings."

"And so does my wife. If she wasn't locked in this car, the news would a got to Blanc Mange" (pronounced by Heber *blank mainge*) "by now," Heber said.

"Persuade her not to mention the fact, if you can," Homer said. "If you tried kindness . . ."

"Won't work," Heber said. "But I'll do my best."

"I'll see that you get all the credit in this case, and the fee," said Homer.

"That's Jake with me," said Heber. "Only you mustn't think I'm smarter than I am. I can see a thing when it's stuck right under my snout."

"That's more than I can do," said Miriam, ruefully.

"Women ain't supposed to notice things, unless they concern themselves, or other women, or the poor saps who marry 'em. You two sure have the right idea. If you ask me, there's always middle ground," Heber said approvingly.

Miriam blushed, but she agreed.

Heber turned again to Homer. "Here's what I mean. I'm still a'ridin' this old case, but it's got me puffin' leather. Where in heck do we go from here?"

"We must check up on the passengers," Homer said.

"And—what the hell is it the papers call the reason?"

"The motive," Homer said.

7

Two Passengers and Two Pintos Are Missing

"YOU DO THE TALKING," Heber Allbrown said to Homer after the conductor had made his brisk exit. "What you say seems to amount to
about the same as I would say, only you make it sound better and
don't get tangled up in them pronouns and things."

"Your style is less artificial and sometimes more piquant,"
Evans said, generously. "However, let me summarize."

Heber tactfully got up to go, being unfamiliar with the word,
but Homer motioned him back to his seat and poured him another
double whiskey.

"I meant," Homer explained, "let me see where we're at."

"Oh," said Heber. "That's Jake. Go ahead. Only maybe I ought
to get this idee off my chest before I plumb lose it. It struck me
that if the pint-sized bozo—gol' darn, miss, excuse me again—if
the dead gent was patching up machines for the war effort, maybe
one of them Nazzys slugged him, then tried to pin it on the Eight
Ball."

"I had thought of that," Homer said. "In that case, most probably, the enemy would have intercepted Mr. Momblo on the westward journey. Before he left Los Angeles his war work was done."

"There's that," said Heber. "Well, it's your turn now."

"Frankly, I'm stuck," said Evans. "Here is an inoffensive little
man, very shy, with few friends and no relatives. The only woman
in his life, according to what he told me, was a waitress in a health
restaurant he frequented in Schenectady. He used to take her
skating every other Sunday afternoon. His landlady, who kept a

49

middle-class boarding house, liked him because he was quiet, neat and orderly and never failed to pay his rent on Fridays. He liked her because she liked him. That was absolutely all.

"His work was not outstandingly important to the war effort. I think it had not touched it directly except for this fatal emergency trip to Los Angeles.

"He was not rich, nor destitute. His salary, I believe he said, was forty-five sixty a week."

"Them bookkeepers," Heber said. "Why couldn't they make it four bits or six bits. But anyway, the poor little scissorbill—oh, gol' darn it—"

"Don't mind me," said Miriam.

"The machine fixer," corrected Heber. "He didn't have his money with him, only one of them bank books."

"His nest egg or backlog, whatever you wish to call it, amounted to $410.19," Homer said. "We both saw his bank book."

"Them bloody pencil stiffs," grunted Heber. "They snitch the extra pennies, most likely."

"Men are sometimes killed for five dollars or for a couple of thousand. But no sum in between," Homer said. "No man is murdered for $410.19, which he hasn't got on him and which later must be extracted under false pretenses from a savings bank," he said. "As far as the motive goes, money is ruled out. So is love or jealousy."

"Say," said Heber, pounding his knee with his fist, "why not suicide? He didn't have much to live for."

"Not a chance," said Miriam, positively. "Mr. Momblo, a lonely man, had just found a friend. He would have lived out the trip, just to talk with Homer. Who wouldn't?"

Heber passed his hand across his weatherbeaten brow. "My head aches already," he said. "First time in my life I got a headache when Jennie wasn't in sight."

There was an hysterical burst of kicking and pounding on the compartment door.

"You dried-up old fathead," screamed Mrs. Allbrown through the panel. "Someone's gone and swiped them pintos."

Heber sprang to his feet, almost spilling the remains of his fourth double whiskey. He peered out the window, after raising the shade. Sure enough, the horses were nowhere in sight. It was dark outside, but the pole Jennie had used as a hitching post was visible. Horses had been there, without question, but they were elsewhere now.

"Now see what we've gone and done," said Heber. "Them cayuses set me back four bucks apiece, from a Ute Indian. If they wander back to their range, whoever really owns 'em 'll get 'em back again."

Evans, to calm his colleague slipped him a ten-dollar bill. "Don't complain," Homer said. "It may be that our man or men have played into our hands. We must question the passengers."

The conductor, having dined, was more tractable when Homer and Heber sought him out. The diner was crowded to its capacity of fifty-six. Another thirty were in the Nugget Car, drinking and grousing. That left, of the 130 passengers permitted to enter the club car and the diner, thirty-four still at large. Night having fallen, there were no more wanderers along the tracks. Conductor Rider submitted his passenger list to Homer, whose first attention was directed toward the occupants of Car Masomenus. It contained four bedrooms, two drawing rooms, and four compartments.

The rooms were occupied, in order, as follows: Bedroom "A," Lancaster Huntington Primway; Bedroom "B," Isaac Momblo; Compartment "C," Captain William Sanderson and wife; Drawing Room "D," Wen Shan; Drawing Room "E," Miss Miriam Leonard; Compartment "F," Homer Evans; Compartment "G," the Rev. Aloysius M. Quinlan, S. J.; Compartment "H," Jerry Santosuosso and Mike (Muggsy) Roth; Bedroom "I," J. Epstein; Bedroom "J," P. Epstein. That made twelve passengers, with four of whom (one dead) the reader is already acquainted.

"Never heard of any of 'em," was Heber's laconic comment.

"Perhaps we shall," Homer said.

The Rev. Quinlan, S. J., proved to be just what he appeared to be, a Jesuit priest on a missionary assignment to Bethlehem, Pa. He was distressed that poor Mr. Momblo, although not a Catholic, had died without benefit of clergy. Homer sighed and crossed him off the list.

A thorough search of the train seemed to confirm Miriam's conjecture. Mr. Lancaster Primway was nowhere to be found.

"I'm a-goin' to hold the five extra suits," said Heber Allbrown. "Them fancy ties and initialed B.V.D.'s can stay where they are."

Captain Sanderson and his bride were interviewed discreetly through the panel of the door of Compartment "C." As soon as the passengers had been readmitted to the car, Captain and Mrs. Sanderson, having been married only twenty-eight hours, and evidently having found the ceremony fatiguing, had not bothered with a porter but had made up the bed themselves and rolled into it. The captain had only three days' leave and convinced our investigators in a few well-chosen words that he had had no time in which to kill anybody. Furthermore, he was fed up with slaughter, having single-handedly wiped out a whole squad in the South Pacific, a feat he threatened to repeat informally if he were interrupted again. Homer assured him that he would not be, and wished the captain a minimum of difficulties in his married life.

There were certain indications from within that probably the Sandersons had not even heard Homer's felicitation.

"In the midst of death we are in life," beneficently murmured Father Quinlan, who had toddled along.

The spacious Drawing Room "D" was deserted, devoid of baggage, and its absent tenant, listed as Wen Shan, was missing. He was not in any of the other cars. In fact, not a single employee or voyager could remember having seen an Oriental on the train, excepting a couple of Filipinos in one of the chair cars, and they were traveling under the names of Mr. and Mrs. Stephen J. Mahoney, in order to avoid difficulties in making advance reservations.

"Wen Shan," repeated Homer, bewildered. "Now who could he be?"

"You never can tell what one of them Chinese is thinking about," Heber said.

"I do not visualize poor Momblo as being involved in a Tong war," said Homer.

The check-up continued throughout the car. The Epstein twins were at work on a script of which they were writing alternate lines simultaneously. They agreed, modestly, in unison, that it was colossal. Jerry Santusuosso and Muggsy Roth were so thoroughly sloshed, having spent the entire day at the Nugget's cozy bar, that questioning was impractical. Johnny Ruh, however, the barman known and loved by half of traveling America, had heard that same day, straight from the pair in question, about everything there was to know about them, and assured Homer that neither of the boys had killed a man recently. Muggsy, one of the niftiest lightweights in America today, had nearly knocked the head off one Kid Ory just two nights before, but he had done it according to the rules of the ring and with his manager had walked off with a purse of five thousand dollars, three thousand of which had already gone to the Government and two hundred and fifty over Johnny's bar.

"Are we goin' to grill the whole train?" asked Heber Allbrown. "What are we going to do, anyway?"

"We've got to get moving, sometime," the conductor said.

The corpse, it seemed, had to be unloaded in Buckskin County and left in the coroner's charge. Just what Heber was going to do with it, miles from a highway and much farther from home, with no means of transportation, was *his* problem. The train was to proceed and Homer was to check on as many of the passengers as possible en route to Chicago, a run of twenty-four hours, more or less.

"I won't get off and try to hitchhike on no lone prairie with this souse" (indicating Heber) "and a stiff," said Jennie Y. Allbrown. In that, she was mistaken.

Part Two
Primway's Predicament

8
Not Who, But Why

As Homer, guiding Miriam by the arm, stepped out of the Grand Central Station and saw New York once more—the upward surge, the planes, the parallelopipedons, the symphony of vertical acres, mathematically upended, cubically concentrated, astronomically assembled, windows for eyes by the hundreds of thousands, traffic streaming endlessly, Gargantuan chiaroscuro, Mephistophelian masses—he paused in awe a moment.

"Oh," gasped Miriam.

She was feeling what Homer was feeling, without words to define it, and after the days that had passed, it was a great relief to her to feel anything at all. There is somewhere or other in those recesses of literature which are most of what remains of the past, a party whose name does not readily come to mind who said something I cannot quote exactly about an idol with feet of clay. That is not precisely, but almost, what Miriam had been experiencing. She esteemed Homer too much to lose an iota of her regard on account of a failure. What tugged at her heart and kept her in a state of apprehension was Homer's own attitude. That he was filled with chagrin was unmistakable. He had showed the same symptoms in the past, when a knotty case would not yield at once to his fierce ratiocination. In this instance, however, he pretended not to care. At least, it seemed so to Miriam.

"To think that on the same great continent could co-exist Blanc Mange, Wyoming, and New York, that on the one hand vast plains with rims of hills could be thus neglected while here one of Nature's most unpromising islands, considered in the light of its physical aspects, has become man's miracle of overstatement," Homer said.

"Yes, sir. Where to?" asked Moses Lemmings, who had come up behind Evans, with a Red Cap and a truckful of baggage. The tall, dignified Negro showed effects of a recent ordeal, but more indications of a still more recent redemption. While still on a train, he had felt that the hand of the law or the U.P., or the ill luck that had brought death to his Car Masomenus and ruin to his rail career, might overtake him. Once footloose in New York, with Homer Evans as employer, needing service, Moses was himself again. He surpassed himself. The scattered impersonal service he had given thousands of travelers who were aboard today and gone tomorrow was being concentrated now on one gentleman and his lady. That was an ideal simplification, for all parties concerned. The U.P.'s loss had been Homer's gain.

"Where to?" repeated Moses, softly.

"Oh, excuse me," Homer said. "Take the things to 21 Washington Square North. Here's the key. Miss Leonard and I will walk."

Lemmings helped the Red Cap load the baggage into a taxi and started away. Homer led Miriam across the street and together they walked downtown on Park Avenue.

For a while no word was spoken between them. Miriam was fearful; Homer was frankly depressed. Thus far in his amateur career, he had never failed to solve a case. Sometimes this had occurred after three or four more innocent citizens had been added to the original death toll of one. But eventually Homer had found the reason why, the *modus operandi*, and the perpetrator's identity, dead or alive. Not so, to date, apropos the case of Isaac Momblo. As obscure and neglected as the mild little man had been in life, in death his fate seemed more disdainful. He was on ice in Blanc Mange, Wyoming, and bade fair to remain there indefinitely. For Homer would not say the word by wire which would authorize Heber T. Allbrown, the coroner, to bury Isaac, and without that instruction, as long as anyone was willing to pay storage and ice charges, Heber would not inter Momblo on his own initiative. He had a share in both the local ice plant and storage warehouse.

In truth, the body of Isaac Momblo had become, to Blanc Mange, almost what Lenin, embalmed, means to Moscow, since, for a nominal fee, Heber had permitted townsfolk and itinerants to glance at the remains and remark their excellent state of preservation. As humble as he had been in the flesh, Isaac had a Lenin-like serenity—the same intellectual forehead, the understanding eyes (lids closed), the beard, which still was growing, and a most impressive calm.

Nothing had progressed or occurred to clear up the mystery. No one knew, exactly, where authority lay or responsibility began. In all the busy war-torn world, only Miriam, Homer and Moses Lemmings had any real concern about the problem. Miriam wanted Homer's genius vindicated; he wanted just retribution to overtake the cowardly murderer of a charming little man who might have been his friend; Moses wanted to know who had tried to place the blame on him.

First it must be explained briefly how Moses got out of ambulatory stir, aboard the Streamliner, and into Homer Evans' employ. That was simple. Within the limits of Buckskin County, Wyoming, Coroner Allbrown's word was final, and, out of respect for Homer's judgment, the coroner would not receive Moses as a prisoner from the conductor's custody. Once the train had moved out of Buckskin County, Homer had wired ahead to Omaha, Nebraska, for a writ of *habeas corpus*. This had unnerved the conductor, who had begun to think he had got himself too deeply involved in the whole affair. He had released Moses and permitted him to resume his duties. When he made his report to the superintendent in Chicago, however, the superintendent told Moses he was fired. Homer, feeling even more responsible to his honest client when the latter was unemployed and without either birth certificate or availability card, had taken Moses on as valet.

The other raveled threads of the case were less satisfactorily mended. No trace had been found, thus far, of either Lancaster Primway, the mysterious Wen Shan, or the pintos. And no official, civil or military, outside of Buckskin County, seemed to give a tinker's dam whether man or beasts turned up again, in this world or the next.

In Chicago, Homer's behavior had baffled Miriam. He had been listless, absent-minded, almost inattentive. The unlucky Streamliner on which they had ridden had been delayed nine hours by the tragedy in Wyoming. They had missed their connection by seven hours and it had required Homer two days to get another reservation. Therefore they were entering New York on a Wednesday morning, whereas if they had had better luck they would have already been there since the preceding Sunday morning.

Homer had received no orders from G-19 but "his not to reason why." If the reader is curious as to why so valuable a man as Evans was left idle so many days, in the midst of the most terrible war to date for Democracy, the author, hoping not to be considered unpatriotic, will disclose that a pretty young WAC, beset in Washington by the problem of having to choose between three lieutenants and a couple of majors, had inadvertently slipped Homer's instructions into an envelope addressed to Nome, Alaska, and conversely had mailed to Chicago a general order regarding the conservation of bone buttons, the only communication Homer had received.

Near the corner of Fourth Avenue and Twenty-second Street Homer spoke, at last.

"The whole thing doesn't make a grain of sense," he said. "Momblo did not die accidentally, or at his own hand. On that I will stake not only my reputation, for which I care little, but my obscurity, which I value highly."

"Then who killed him?" asked Miriam.

"Who killed him is not the question in my mind," Homer continued. "I could probably guess who killed him in less than five minutes if only I could find out why."

"You will," said Miriam. "I know you will, Homer, if you try."

He looked at her in astonishment. "Did you think I wasn't trying?" he asked.

Miriam, much as she adored him, had always to be honest.

"In Chicago," she admitted, "you just fooled around the library, looking at pictures of Mongolian tribes, and Tartars, Polynesians, Koreans, Eskimaux, Malays, Annamites, Kalmuks . . ."

"Darling," interrupted Homer, indulgently, "have you forgotten Wen Shan?"

Miriam blushed with shame. "I'm so sorry," she said. "I never saw him."

Homer again looked troubled. "I'm not sure you ever will," he said. "As you know, I have familiarized myself with most of the principal Oriental languages, and quite a few of the minor ones and dialects. In none of them does a single name appear that resembles, to the philologist's eye, Wen Shan."

"You'll find one," Miriam said, and happily taking his arm, almost skipped like a child.

At Union Square they switched over to University Place and continued downtown to Ninth Street, where they had a late breakfast at the Lafayette. There, sitting in their old familiar corner by the window nearest the front entrance, they began to realize they were again in New York, perhaps to stay a while. Although leave for Homer was long overdue, he had hesitated to apply for it. However, since it had come to him without asking, he didn't hesitate to make use of it.

"Primway," he said, "very likely is in Boston, and let's hope he is making his peace—as they say—with the beautiful and wise Ferdinanda . . ."

"Whose mother was a Ledge," murmured Miriam. "I wonder just how that would be."

"I cannot account for his disappearance from the train and from Buckskin County, except that he was dreadfully in a hurry. Do you think any harm might have come to him?" Homer asked.

"He might have got lost," she suggested.

"Not likely. As well as I can remember the terrain, he could not have roamed far, or even circled, without striking either a road or the railroad tracks again. He certainly could read sign posts, most probably the surveyor's marks along the right of way. Eventually he must have caught another train."

"He never would have known, then, that poor Isaac had been killed," said Miriam. "After all, no one is after him."

"The towel was missing from his room," Homer said.

Miriam sat up straight in surprise. "Does that mean he was guilty? In that case he would have known . . ."

"Did he strike you as insane?" Homer asked.

"Jittery," Miriam said. "Muddled, stuffy, moralistic, inhibited, misguided, if you like, but not insane."

"He's capable of fanaticism," suggested Homer.

"He'd be a washout as a husband," said Miriam. "Poor Ferdinanda. Are you *sure* she loves him? Even that revolting François de la Cirage Dantan, or Frank Dante, would be better . . ." Miriam hesitated, or rather refrained. With Homer it was never necessary to dot the i.

"Highly-sexed women," Homer said, "often seem to waste themselves on moderate men—as the cold type of woman is fatally attractive to Don Juans. In either case, the cold potato becomes an obsession. That's why Ferdinanda, impelled no doubt by mere instinct, followed Primway to Hollywood, made scenes in the bank and outside the movie lots, then took up with the man she knew would be most repellent to him."

"Hoping Primway would resent it and fight," suggested Miriam.

"She miscalculated," Homer said. "She ought to know her Bostonians, but there she erred. Primway could easily have been wrought up to the point of attacking François. Probably it would have been easier to provoke him to it than to restrain him. There, however, the matter would end. Duty would still dictate, and convention ordain that, having mauled and humiliated her unsavory suitor, Primway again withdraw. He never could marry Ferdinanda unless they could live on his pay, and he couldn't earn enough to keep her in Symphony subscriptions."

"Then he didn't murder Momblo," said Miriam.

"I can't say who didn't until I've decided who did," Homer said. Suddenly a most disturbing thought took possession of him, causing Miriam to quail.

"Supposing, Miriam, I never did find out," he said.

"Nonsense," Miriam said.

"What if orders came from Washington right now. This minute. And I were sent to Albania or Kolombangara or Velikie Luki, left stranded in some out-of-the-way hole until every clue had disappeared," Homer said.

"It wouldn't be your fault," Miriam said, defensively.

Homer paled. "What a ghastly thing to live with . . . a failure like that . . . a wistful, gentle man struck down and unavenged . . . a nagging problem making feeble futile gestures in the depths of my mind, day after day, like the ragged claws of a blind crustacean wavering eternally on the floor of silent seas. God, Miriam! If I don't solve this, I'm lost."

"Homer!" said Miriam in alarm. "Are you feeling quite well?"

"I never was fitter or faced such inexorable clarity of mind," he said. "Not who, but why. Why?"

"You're overwrought." It was Miriam who was the paler now. She scarcely could breathe, or dared to think. Here was a threat to the man she worshiped, more deadly than any bullet, drug or blade had ever been. To this he was more vulnerable. She realized, and so did he, that a riddle like the one before him might well throw out of adjustment the delicate balance of his matchless mind.

Then she saw Homer snap into action. His eyes grew determined and clear, his shoulders were held more erect. He paid, rose, nodded, helped Miriam with her coat. She followed him to the desk.

"*Bon jour, Monsieur Michel,*" he said.

"Ah, Monsieur Evans . . . *et mademoiselle,*" replied the jovial clerk. "*D'ou arrivez-vous cette fois-ci, mon ami?*"

"From Buckskin County, Wyoming. My heart is still there," Homer said. "A telegraph blank, if you please."

Michel handed over a blank and Homer wrote: "Heber Allbrown, Blanc Mange, Wyo.—Find Wen Shan at any cost. Sending funds."

As usual, but more pronouncedly than usual on this occasion, when Homer got going, things began to happen. He beckoned to the ready Albert, who was standing near the bust of Lafayette by the elevator. Albert responded with alacrity.

"Run over to my place in Washington Square," Homer said, "and tell my new valet to repack my things and Miss Leonard's.

Get him the first and best reservation possible and ask him to take rooms in my name and wait for me at the Bellevue in Boston."

"The Bellevue?" asked Albert, bewildered. He knew there were more expensive hotels in Boston, and supposed men like Homer always stayed in them. In fact, it had always puzzled Albert why Evans patronized the Lafayette instead of the Ritz in New York.

"Tom Bowles is at the bar there," Homer explained. "And Albert, get me a taxi. John Connolly, if you can."

While Albert was calling the taxi, Homer turned to the plump and smiling Miss Codou, the telephone girl. Having relayed Homer's telegram by phone, she already had surmised that he wanted to get in touch with his bank, in order to wire the funds. So she already had vice-president Blaw on the phone. This errand, therefore, was quickly accomplished.

"*Mais, monsieur,*" Michel explained, raising his expressive eyebrows. "*Vous allez vite, vous. Mais pourquoi Boston, nom de dieu? Il n'y a presque rien de tout la bas.*"

"That remains to be seen," Homer said.

9
Boston, of All Places

IN THE SNUG MILITARY PLANE on which Homer had secured a lift to Boston for himself and Miriam, Evans sat motionlessly, hardly aware whether they were passing over the tortuous coast with ledges, beaches, tidal swamps and blue water alternating with smoky cities and drab towns, or whether the Gimlet, as the Ph-13 was aptly named, was burrowing through serrated and billowing clouds. Knowing from past experience that Homer would be absorbed, and that the pilot, she hoped, would be able to keep his eyes from her often enough to steer, Miriam picked up at random a copy of *Thyme Magazine*.

When the landscape below was obliterated by a cloudbank, Miriam took up *Thyme* and opened it to the social section. This is what she read:

"In the historic Park Street Church at Boston (Two if by Sea) next week, Socialite, Beacon Street Brahmin, and State Street tycoon, Dulcivear Cushing, will, if he is able to keep the bluest blood in New England from boiling over on his morning attire, give in marriage his only daughter, Ferdinanda (whose mother was a Ledge, and whose income is between six and seven figures) to François de la Cirage Dantan, young French nobleman formerly of Vitry-le-sec, Seine, France, but lately of Hollywood, where he is known as Frank Dante. It is the Hollywood connection that is burning up the prospective father-in-law. Nothing like it has ever before invaded Louisburg Square.

"Exclusive circles in the region of the bean and the cod are still whispering about the shattered romance between Miss Ferdinanda, who, by the way, is good to look upon as well as among the highest ten (speaking in terms of ready cash) of America's young heiresses, and the well-known Harvard ex-halfback (All-American), Lancaster Huntington Primway. It was Primway the fond father of Ferdinanda had chosen as son-in-law to be, but the unfortunate loss of the Primway millions in the Commonwealth Camphor coup on State Street sent young Primway, broke and proud, also to Hollywood, where he did conspicuously less handsomely than his successor, as it were, the sleek François, or Frank.

"The moot question on the historic hill today is: will Lancaster Primway, in order to make the last word in sportsmanlike gestures, attend the nuptials of his ex-fiancée and see her start clipping coupons with the screen wolf whose photo is to the current generation of debutantes and young matrons what Rudolph Valentino's was to our mothers?"

Miriam flipped back the page to confirm the date of the magazine and said, sincerely: "Hell!"

"Must you be garrulous?" asked Homer, almost pettishly. He was still trying, unsuccessfully, or rather unproductively, to think

"I wouldn't chatter so," Miriam said, with a faint touch of asperity, "if I hadn't come across a news item that might help you."

"Forgive me," Homer said, graciously.

"I am handing you *Thyme*, dated ten days ago. If a certain item can be credited, the wedding of Ferdinanda Cushing and François Dante, or Frank of the Shoe-blacking of Yesteryear, whatever you want to call him, took place on the Sunday morning Lancaster Primway would have arrived in Boston had not our Streamliner been delayed," Miriam said.

Homer, usually sparing with his facial expressions if they reflected his mental processes rather than his social defense, did a double-take worthy of Edward Everett Horton. Then he reached, a shade too eagerly, for the weekly magazine, so oddly out of date, and read the article. And as he read, instead of showing concern for the unlucky Lancaster Primway, Homer's smile began to shimmer, then glow.

"Now I feel easier," he said, quoting unconsciously the fair Catherine, of *La Reine Pedauque*, as, when in company with the Abbé Coignard, she squirmed out of her chemise.

"Sometimes I think you are a brute," said Miriam. "Now I understand why poor Mr. Primway paced the corridor, then the track, and lit out on a broncho. He was missing his last chance to see Ferdinanda . . ." Miriam fumbled a bit for the *mot juste*.

"Intact," Homer said.

"Serves him right," said Miriam. "The stuffy selfish prude."

"Selfish?" Homer asked.

"Selfish and cruel. Worse than that, mistaken," she insisted. "Whatever the silly story books say, people admire and envy young men who have sense enough to marry rich girls—if they love them. Especially if the men do not feel obliged, as a sop to malicious meddlers, to take some foolish job," she said. "Rich girls have been guarded and bored all the way from cradle to altar. After they escape from home and family they want some man to entertain them, and that should be a full-time job."

"Also it leaves them an out," said Homer. "The couple, I mean. When romance begins to flag and the satiated girl, now a young matron, needs more privacy, the husband can tactfully trot out the old gag about having to be useful to society, or the country, or whatever you like. Otherwise they would separate, and, in extreme cases, kill each other."

"Or drag their names through the divorce courts and try the same thing over and over again," Miriam said.

The air trip from New York to Boston is quickly over. The Gimlet swung neatly over Boston's superb harbor, once teeming with ships, now cut off from trade through the machinations of railroad financiers who wrecked first the Boston and Maine, then the New Haven. Even the relics of lost trade look dignified and outmoded in Boston.

Homer and Miriam paused on their way from East Boston Field to the Primway residence on Beacon Street to tell the clerk at the Bellevue that Moses Lemmings and their baggage would soon be arriving. Then they proceeded on foot, past the State House. Again

Evans halted and indicated the famous Bulfinch front with a sweep of his hand.

"What a pity that crimes against aesthetics and architecture are not punishable as capital offenses!" Homer said. "The law tries to stay the hand of any man who would kill another, however unpromising or even detrimental to society the victim may be. What are men? The process by which they are created is, at best, somewhat ludicrous. As dear old Dean Hathaway of Harvard said: 'The pleasure is but momentary, the risk of infection considerable . . . but, worse than that, young gentlemen, the posture is ridiculous.'"

"Not necessarily," Miriam objected.

"I was saying," continued Homer. "What is man, that ye should be mindful of him? Passing over lightly his questionable beginnings . . . What was it Housman wrote? Ah, yes. 'The night my father got me, his mind was not on me.'"

"What *does* a man think about?" began Miriam.

"We'll go into that later," Homer said, and squeezed her arm lightly. "Just now let us go on with our survey of man's preposterous development. Shakespeare's 'seven ages' should be modernized. I like James Joyce's summing up much better. For Joyce dealt not with man as if he, himself, were running the show. He saw him as a little sailor, and Fate as the Admiralty. He wound up, not in death, nearly always an accident, but with his hero being meagerly paid. He placed the blame where it squarely belongs, on 'they'."

"How true in Boston!" Miriam said.

The three plain-clothes men who guard the Bulfinch front and whoever is governor behind it inched a little nearer. They always got nervous when anyone looked at the State House. One of them was hiding, so he thought, behind the Hooker Statue; another pretended to be throwing an old newspaper into a near-by trash can; the third was taking advantage of the granite steps in order to tie his shoelaces. This is what they heard as Homer quoted:

"'They believe in rod, the scourger almighty, creator of hell upon earth and in Jacky Tar,' (the public," interjected Evans), "'the son of a gun who was conceived of unholy boast, born of the fighting Navy, suffered under rump and dozen, was scarified, flayed and curried, yelled like bloody hell. The third day he arose again from his bed, steered into haven, sitting on his beam-end till further orders whence he shall come to drudge for a living and be paid.'"

Terence Donovan, the nearest plain-clothes man (he who was pretending to tie his shoe lace) straightened up and sauntered over, fixing Homer with a baleful eye and admonitory thumb.

"What kind of talk is that? Is it code, now?" Terence demanded.

"Those are the words of the greatest Irishman of our time," Homer said, pleasantly. He again gestured toward the State House. "Beholding this elegant building, which is always filled with Irishmen, James Joyce's phrases come to mind."

"Joyce, ye say?" asked Donovan in a rollicking brogue. "I was givin' me daughter blazes just the other day. She was readin' some school books, and every last one of 'em was written by a bloody Englishman. 'What's the matter with the good Irish writers?' I says. 'Who are they?' says she. And there she had me. Now I can tell her about this—who was it?"

"Joyce. James Joyce," Homer said. "How old is your daughter, by the way?"

"Fourteen," Terence said, proudly. "She was born over here."

"Just the age for Joyce," said Homer. "I hope you'll remember, the book is *Ulysses*."

Donovan proffered his notebook, well-thumbed, and the stub of a pencil. "Will ye write it down? I can remember faces but names get all scrambled up in me skull."

Homer wrote: "James Joyce, *Ulysses*. Modern Library, one dollar and forty-five cents."

"Your good deed for the day," murmured Miriam as, after having been bade Godspeed by the dick, they continued on their way.

"I was about to point out," Homer said, "that the original Bulfinch State House was built of good honest red brick. Now it is the center of a nest of monstrosities. It was matchless and inspiring when surrounded by space and air. First the blunderers built a yellow brick office building attached to the back, then two white marble wings sticking out like flap-ears to the east and west. To match these cold excrescences the Bulfinch gem was painted white, thereby messing up the early nineteenth-century brick work. I was saying that while man, unimportant as he is, has all the law's protection against maiming, art has none whatever."

"I love to hear you talk this way," said Miriam. She knew Homer was himself again, not yet in possession of the key to the case, but in fine form to find it.

10

The Beacon Street Blues

THE PRIMWAY BROWNSTONE HOUSE on Beacon Street faced the Common, noncommittally, as it had since Augustus Peabody Primway (whose wife was a tart) had caused it to be erected in 1843, the two hundredth anniversary of the founding of the brokerage house of Primway and Leeks.

Sitting disconsolately in the parlor, splashed with sickly violet light which trickled thinly through the antique window panes, was a man whose thoughts, such as they were, were dark indeed. Lancaster Primway, for it was he, had arrived in Boston four days late. He had emerged from the smoky South Station, where the family hack, a familiar sight on State Street and outside King's Chapel and the old burying grounds, had been driven to meet him by Douse, the family coachman.

Within two hours, a cordon of police had been drawn around the Primway mansion in order to exclude reporters. The telephone had been disconnected; Douse, and the butler, McOrk, had been armed with old-fashioned revolvers; and Henry Ward Primway, Lancaster's father, had gone early to the summer place at Annisquam to escape notoriety, closing the offices of Primway and Leeks for the first time since the British evacuation. This resulted in an important family economy. The firm had been losing at least five thousand dollars a year, since 1932. Once business was suspended, this drain upon the Primway purse was stopped, and both Douse and McOrk had received part of their back wages.

It had required only twenty-four hours to convince the press that nothing was to be had from Lancaster Primway, except a couple of right crosses he handed out to a Hearst reporter who had asked him if François de la Cirage Dantan actually padded his bathing trunks. Primway was suffering. Even the callous news-hawks could see that. He exercised faithfully with Indian clubs, boxed with McOrk in the rumpus room shaded by the historic Boston elms, read James Russell Lowell from cover to cover in bed without falling asleep, and otherwise went through the motions expected of a disappointed Bostonian of the higher class. Eventually he would drop in at the Union Club, where the younger members, if any, would pretend that nothing had happened.

Reader, try to put yourself in Primway's place. Try to visualize the disturbing images which must, in spite of cold showers, New England verse, codfish balls, Indian pudding, and the like, be parading through his mind. That the mind was not a very keen one should not deprive Primway of human sympathy. That his scruples may seem distorted and his restraint unmanly should likewise be passed over tolerantly. A Primway, believe it or not, has eyes, hands, organs (however sparingly played), dimensions of a Harvard halfback, senses (however dull), and in place of affections and passions, morals, by Jove. He is fed the same food, making allowances for baked beans, Boston scrod and other delicacies which never taste the same elsewhere. He is hurt by the same weapons, subject to the same psychoses, neuroses, phobias and inhibitions. Mostly in this story, we have been dealing with the differences between a Primway and the rest of non-Bostonian mankind. So it is just as well for the reader to ponder, as Homer and Miriam descend the mild slope of Beacon Hill, on the resemblances. (*Merchant of Venice*, Act III, Scene I, Lines 63 to 70.)

If you prick a Primway, or tickle him, as Shakespeare waggishly suggests, he will first cut you dead, then sock you in a precise gymnastic way. Primways do not relish being pawed.

So! Lancaster, seated gloomily at the violet-paned window, staring at the crotch of a noble elm (*Elmus americanus*), did not recognize Homer and Miriam when they turned right into the brick walk, ascended the brownstone stairs and pulled the bellcord that had felt the touch of all the best Back Bay society, one time or another, including the rather clammy hand of the Rev. Henry Ward Beecher, Ralph Waldo Emerson, Paul Revere Frothingham, A. Z. Conrad and other divines too numerous to mention. The worn strands had likewise undergone the tug of statesmen, including John Hancock, Henry Cabot Lodge, Daniel Webster (who nearly yanked it down on one occasion, mistaking it for the night bell of the Parker House near by), Edward Everett, Edward Everett Hale—the list is too long and distinguished to continue. Of educators, Charles W. Eliot had been there to solicit funds for public inspection of the Houses of the Good Shepherd; A. Bushnell Hart had intertwined his long whiskers in that same bell cord once and had all but jerked a handful of them off; so many Cabots had had a whirl at it that an enumeration of them would be ostentatious. Henry James, William Dean Howells and Harriet Beecher Stowe had been among the literati. . . . In short, the reader, by now, has got the idea. In Hollywood there is "chi-chi," in New York, "swank." For the real authentic "class," there remains, even today, only Boston.

Of course, the Truesdales, on Homer's mother's side, belonged to one of the old Salem families who consider the residents of Boston as upstarts, but that is neither here nor there. Nevertheless, readers, especially those of the fair sex born west of Sudbury, will have a faint and sympathetic understanding of what reverence and uneasiness Miriam was feeling as McOrk responded to the bell and opened the door the correct eleven inches.

"Neither of the Messrs. Primway is at home," the butler said.

"I see Lancaster right inside the window," Miriam said, without thinking.

"I was speaking in the social, not the physical, sense," McOrk retorted and was about to close the door. Miriam's neat little foot, enchantingly shod, ran the risk of being marked if not crushed. Gallantly Homer inserted his stylish No. 11.

"It was in the physical sense that we wished to speak with Mr. Primway," Evans said. "Of course, if that is impractical, there is always the official." And Homer displayed to the formal McOrk a

small emblem concealed within his coat lapel. The butler's manner changed, became at once respectful.

"I will announce you," he said. Homer held out his card and
Miriam fumbled, vexed, in her handbag. She knew she had none,
and had never had one, but she had to stall, just the same. Homer
graciously extricated her from the predicament.

"Announce Miss Miriam Leonard first," Homer said.

The butler opened the parlor door and, stiffening to attention,
intoned: "Miss Miriam Leonard and Mr. Homer Truesdale Evans, sir."

"Eh? What's that?" said the sorrowing Primway. "Dash it, I
thought I told you . . ." Seeing Miriam enter, he rose, from force of
habit, then responded gamely as Homer advanced and extended
his hand.

"Oh, it's you, old man," Lancaster Primway said. "And Miss
Leonard. Won't you sit down? I've been so annoyed by the press
chaps that I told McOrk to let no one in."

"I quite understand," said Homer.

They all sat down, and there was an embarrassed silence during which Primway spotted the old familiar crotch of the elm on
the Common and stared at it again.

"I wanted to explain," Homer began, "why our train was delayed."

"I wrote a rather sharp letter to the *Transcript* about it. It had
slipped my mind that the *Transcript* had ceased publication three
years ago. Time flies."

"Quite," said Homer, and waited a decent interval before he
began again.

Miriam, accustomed to the breezier, conversational tempo of
Montana and Montparnasse, held herself in restraint by counting
pigeons on the Common across the way. When she got to thirty-
three, the earthly age of Our Saviour, whose debt to doves is gen-
erally conceded, Homer began speaking again.

"I hope the train delay didn't cause you any inconvenience,"
Homer said.

"I'd rather not discuss that," said Primway, and closed up like
an Ipswich clam.

"Excuse me. I know it's painful," Homer said. "I only thought you ought to know that one of the towels from your compartment was missing."

Primway's brow knitted reproachfully. He had known that Homer was frightfully long on intellect and had the reputation of being almost indecently clever. But that Homer had journeyed from New York to Boston simply to inform him that someone had pinched a towel, worth at most twenty cents, from his bedroom on a train was hard to believe.

"Toss them over a little lower, would you mind, old' man?" Primway asked. "I'm not feeling up to much today."

Either this phenomenon is the best actor in the world, all casting directors in Hollywood to the contrary, or he did not murder Momblo, was Miriam's hasty conclusion.

"You didn't chance to read about . . . the trip . . . the stranded Streamliner . . . all the facts?" Homer inquired.

"I never read the papers, since the *Transcript* passed on," Primway said. "I simply protested and waited around, then lit out on my own. Ah, well. If I'd been on time, it might have been in vain."

"Oh, surely not," said the soft-hearted Miriam.

Much as Primway's correct manner and traditional surroundings chilled her, she felt sorry for him.

"The man in the bedroom next to yours was murdered, and you ran away," Homer said. "Have you anything to say?"

"Now look here. You don't suggest that I'd kill an inoffensive little duffer . . ."

"Mr. Momblo was not a duffer," Miriam interrupted severely.

"No offense," Primway said. "I didn't realize he was a friend of yours."

"He wasn't, but he would have been," Miriam said. "That's why his loss makes me sad."

This time Primway both shook and scratched his head.

"I'm dreadfully sorry," he said, deeper in the fog than ever. "I seem to hear what you two say, and the words are all right, only, to me, they don't seem to make sense. My own fault, I daresay. It was

like that at Groton, and all the way through Harvard. I could remember signals, before that complicated chap named Haughton
took charge of the varsity squad. But talk has a way of getting away
from me. Most likely because my mother, bless her, when she was
alive, talked a blue streak from morning till night. I got so, in the
nursery, I could black right out and think about nothing at all, not
even grasp a word. Mother didn't seem to mind."

Primway turned from Miriam back to Evans, and tried his best
to concentrate. "The quiet little chap was killed, you say?"

"Murdered," Homer said.

"No," Primway said. "But I still can't hook it up with me, and
that silly towel. What about that? Give me a lift, like a good chap.
Perhaps a little drink would clear away the cobwebs?"

As neither Homer nor Miriam objected, Primway said, without
raising his voice: "McOrk."

Not only did the butler materialize, but he brought with him,
from whatever astral plane he had been occupying, a tray with a
bottle and three glasses.

"Rather decent port. DeLesseps '89," Primway murmured.
"Now what was it about the timid little party? He died, I believe
you said."

"He was murdered," Homer corrected, and watched closely the
effect. If there was any, it was most restrained. Primway by that
time had his glass in his hand and raised it, informally.

"After all, it must make little difference to a duffer how he goes.
I hope it was painless."

"Instantaneous," said Homer.

"Let's drink to the same good fortune for all of us," Primway
said, and took a generous mouthful, cocking his head with par-
donable appreciation.

"Do Boston hearts just crinkle up and fold, like patent wind-
shields?" Miriam asked herself.

Primway, warmed by the port, showed more sparkle. Of his own
accord, he took up the thread of the talk.

"Don't say he was strangled with my towel," he said. "If he was,
I've no idea about it."

He looked at Homer, slowly astonished, and a change crept over him. "You don't mean . . . I've heard you go in for criminology and all that eye-wash. You're not suggesting, old man, that I killed the chap and then ran away?"

"Why did you run away?" Homer asked.

"As plain as day," Primway said. "I had to get back to Boston. I can't tell you why, but you'll understand. I took a spotted horse, leaving a generous payment tied to the saddlestrings, jogged over to the Santa Fe, and caught another train. The conductor took my I.O.U. He'd seen me play football. Beats all, doesn't it, what sort of fellows go to games."

"You were aware, of course, that the horse you took was the property of Coroner Heber T. Allbrown, of Blanc Mange, Buckskin County, Wyoming?" Homer asked.

"Was that cowboy a coroner?" asked Primway in surprise. "I fancied he just rode around the country looking for dogies and harmonicas. After all, I didn't leave him in too much of a hole. The other horse was there."

Homer said, "Then the other horse was still there when you fled?"

"I didn't fly, or flee, whatever the verb is. I simply streaked it for another train," Primway said.

"When you *borrowed* the horse—of course, technically you stole it, which is an extraditable offense—did you see an Oriental lurking around?" asked Homer.

Primway reached for the port and gulped it, blinking reproachfully. "My fault, perhaps. I'm way behind you again."

"Was there an Oriental in sight when you pinched the pinto?" repeated Homer patiently.

"Absolutely not," Primway said.

"Ever hear of Wen Shan?" asked Homer briskly.

Again Primway frowned. "Not that Chinese game, with bamboo and pond lilies and all that unspeakable nonsense?"

"No. That's Mah Jong," Homer said, and sighed.

He was getting nowhere, again, and had to face the fact.

11

The Number-One Suspect Faces the Music

THE FIRST BOTTLE OF PORT was dwindling rapidly. Lancaster Primway, the more he drank, the more he showed, without intending to, that he was a desperate young man. With Bostonians in love, the question of timing frequently arises. The males, ultraconservative as they are, are likely to take for granted what they have, and begin to suffer keenly only when they have lost it.

As long as Ferdinanda was still single, and gunning for him, Primway had had temptation to resist. Each day for him had included a sort of moral workout. As athletes keep themselves fit by roadwork, chest-weights, skipping rope and shadow-boxing, certain types of Anglo-Saxons train their consciences by daily exercise. In the studio, standing under cameras and being shoved from chalk mark to chalk mark by directors (and even carpenters working on the set), Primway had been able to say to himself: "There, outside the iron grill, Ferdinanda is waiting for me! I must re-renounce her this very minute!" It was not an uncommon feat for him to achieve five, or as high as six, re-renouncements in a single day.

On the other hand, François was the kind of man who danced tangos in public, indulged in permanent waves, and let women pay taxi fares. He was dark and sleek, with glowing eyes and long lashes, wasp waist and zoot shoulders. His hands were long and slim, and continually seemed to be making, of their own accord, insinuating invitations and caresses. It was already whispered around Boston that, glimpsing through a window of the Cushings' reception room a passably pretty girl who was coming to the house to deliver Ferdinanda's wedding bouquet, Frank, or François, had dismissed the Cushing butler, answered the service door himself, and tried to date up the delivery maiden on the day of the ceremony.

In the minds of many readers, a popular movie star, who draws down three thousand dollars a week can hardly be rebuked with marrying for money. But the fact remains that François de la Cirage Dantan, in order to collect his pay, was expected to do a certain amount of work before the camera, and in extreme cases to report at seven in the morning. There wasn't much labor or exertion involved, but François' ideal, expressed in a moment of candor (after two double Cointreaux) to a *Variety* reporter at the Mocambo one night, was to do *no work at all*.

It must not be assumed by Southern or Western readers that the foregoing information came to Homer from Primway's lips, however drunk he might have been. Primway drank like a gentleman. The point is, that in spite of the Groton-Harvard glaze, he was taking a terrific beating, deep inside. This Miriam slowly grasped. At first he had seemed to her a type most frigid, ingrown and obsolete. Before they had started on the second of the four remaining bottles in all the world of DeLesseps '89, her heart had begun to bleed for him.

"If only he would tell us what is really on his mind. If he would break down and cry, or destroy some of this Tudor furniture, or smash a violet glass window, or chew down a historic elm," she said to herself. Instead he shrunk farther and farther into his shell.

As a matter of fact, Miriam suspected that Homer was experiencing feelings akin to hers. She knew that time was pressing, that any moment G-19 might call him to a broader duty and thus, with the ugly brand of failure and uncertainty, sear his tranquility for life. Still he stayed on and on, drawing Lancaster out as best he could. He could not bear to see a man so utterly lonely. Instead of blaming Primway for the debacle which had ended his romance, Miriam began to detest Ferdinanda. "Why could she not have compromised the man, by hook or crook, and thus wangled all the

morality and convention over to her side of the fence?" asked
Miriam of herself, indignantly. "I don't believe her old I.Q. is so
terrific, after all."

Lunch had been served and the world relieved of its entire supply of the memorable DeLesseps '89 when Homer got around to
his really astonishing maneuver. He had elicited from Primway that
the latter had left the train at Las Vegas for five minutes in order
to dispatch a telegram. This tied in with the conductor's theory in
a most important detail.

"You'll pardon my asking, old man," Homer said. "But why
didn't you let the porter send your telegram?"

Primway's blush was his answer. "After all," thought Miriam,
"a man who, at his age, can blush must have a great deal in him."

"I understand," Homer said, without pressing the question.
"The contents were . . . personal. Not the sort of thing one would
wish to have a porter read."

"Not if one had to be seeing the chap all the way to Chicago,"
Primway said.

"Did you have any difficulty finding the telegraph office in the
station?" Homer asked.

"The porter directed me. Accommodating chap. He walked part
way, to show me where it was," Primway said.

"The porter, Moses Lemmings?" persisted Homer.

"The tall, dark one who took care of our car," said Primway.

"You're sure it was Las Vegas?" Evans asked.

"That's what it said on the sign," Primway said.

They rose from the luncheon table, after as soothing a meal of
pollock's cheeks and tongues as Homer had eaten since the morning the *Titanic* went down. To Miriam's astonishment, she caught
on that she was expected to go into the drawing room and sip her
coffee and brandy by herself, while the men were to enjoy a pair of
Havana cigars right where they were. To say that she was on pins
and needles is putting it mildly. She was so distraught, in fact, that
she shocked a cough out of the otherwise imperturbable McOrk by
absent-mindedly dumping the priceless old brandy (Carlos III) into
the coffee, as she had done with Martinique rum in France.

The butler recovered in time to remove the coffee, thus extravagantly *arrosé*, and bring Miriam a fresh cup.

Coincidentally, in the dining room was taking place the conversation Miriam would have given Ferdinanda's eye teeth to hear.

"This is rather delicate, old man, no end of a nuisance, I'm afraid," Homer began. He had considerately adopted this hesitant and over-simplified mode of speech in order to be perfectly intelligible to his slower-minded companion. The technique had many advantages, since it always provided a sort of stuttering approach, a mental "ready, on your mark, get set . . ." as it were, before the pith of the communication was released.

At the word "delicate," Primway froze again. And, reader, any man, from Boston or otherwise, who can do a polite and workmanlike job of freezing after two full bottles of DeLesseps '89 and three jiggers of Spanish cognac is worthy of respect, even though he has let a lizard run away with his girl, and moralizes about it to boot.

"What I'm getting at, if you know what I mean . . ." Homer went on. He was still in his wind-up.

"Exactly. Shall we join the lady?" Primway asked.

"I wanted to . . . break the news, one might say . . . while we are alone," Homer said.

"What news?" Primway asked.

"You see . . ." Homer said. "Dash it all, it's hard to begin."

"Exactly," Primway said. "Shall we join . . ."

"The fact is," Homer said, this time letting go of the ball. "In Wyoming, where you borrowed that pinto, they're very strict. Horse stealing, you know, in a state that even today has miles and miles of free range, is a serious affair. My friend Heber T. Allbrown, the coroner, whose brother, Moroni, is sheriff of Buckskin County, can't quite get the thing hushed up. Local politics, you know. If they let a horse thief go unscathed . . ."

"A horse thief!" repeated Primway, drawing himself up at least four inches. "Did they have the impudence to call me a horse thief?"

"The pintos never turned up, that is, not yet," Homer said.

"I only took one," said Primway. "Who got the other?"

"Wen Shan," Homer said.

"Poor chap," Primway said, gravely. "Let's hope they don't lynch him."

"You ought to go back, you know, and face charges," Homer said. "That you are guilty, everyone in the county knows by now. If, by chance, you were returning to Hollywood . . ."

"I suppose I am. Nowhere else, especially, to go," Primway said. "You understand . . . of course . . . that is . . ."

Homer helped him out. "Certainly," he said.

"I don't," said Miriam, her eyes blazing. The Carlos III had strengthened her determination to assert herself as a modern young woman and not to remain in another room, with brandy, cigarettes and chocolate while the men told indecent stories or discussed the case.

Homer, a little surprised, but tolerant, turned to her and smiled.

"Mr. Primway meant to convey that Hollywood is the one place where Monsieur or Madame de la Cirage Dantan, or Mr. and Mrs. Frank Dante, most likely are not to be," he said. "Frank will shun work like the plague."

"Exactly," Primway said. "Shall we join . . . Oh, she's joined us, old man. Extraordinary!" Primway smiled. "The free and easy Western manner. Refreshing and all that. Well, shall we all start for Wyoming? I'll not wait to be extradited. Horse thief, indeed!"

Again McOrk appeared, like a dingy black-coated genie from an Aladdin's lamp.

"I have taken the liberty of packing your things, sir," he said.

"Thanks," Lancaster said. Then he turned to Homer, and with the best of bland intentions, asked the question on which Homer's future hinged: "What puzzles me, old man, is why anyone should want to murder such a harmless bloke. Could you tip me off, like a good fellow?"

Miriam saw Homer do another double-take, the second in twenty-four hours and as many years, but with magnificent aplomb he replied: "I've wondered about that," he said.

12

Of Bars and a Bartender

THE BELLEVUE BAR IN BOSTON in recent years had been honored by the presence, in official capacity as bartender, of Tom Bowles. Before that he helped make Fennel's and the old Parker House famous. And during prohibition times, although he loved his native land, the frantic importunities of good drinkers in trouble drew him to Paris, where he graced Harry's, at No. 4 rue Daunou.

Whatever outsiders think of Boston's medieval censorship, political chicanery, race and religious intolerance, stuffy scholarship and flagging trade, no one worthy of respect has cast a slur on the Boston bars. In the old days Bixby's, in the Faneuil Hall market (*The Governor of Massachusetts*, Liveright, 1929): Fennel's, Johnston's (behind the post office), Frank Locke's (now Locke Ober's), Jake Wirth's (still Jake Wirth's), the Bell-in-Hand in Pie Alley, Young's, and other drinking paradises were flourishing, and today, in memory, linger—their fragrance, dimness and comradeship, their refuge and strength, their snug hospitality, their chosen patrons and patient employees. When they were closed, temporarily, in 1919, sixteen raincoats belonging to your author were found in their back rooms, on pegs and hooks. There, in the sacred realms of the past, let us salute them.

During fifty-five years, man and boy, Tom Bowles had served his choice clientele, excepting two days in 1903, and one week in 1934. Several of his best customers knew that the earlier absence from duty had been caused by a Beacon Hill doctor, who since has died, we regret to say, from or in delirium tremens. This Dr.

Frothingham—wild horses shall not drag it from us that he was a distant relative of the famous Boston Clergyman of that name— had convinced Tom that he owed himself a vacation in Maine. Bowles had got as far as Bangor when a telegram overtook him informing him that four of his steady patrons already had succumbed to nervous breakdowns. Naturally, warm-hearted man that he was, he gave up his holiday and returned at once.

The week in '34 was the one thing on which Bowles had remained taciturn and silent. Any slight reference to it brought a blush of shame to his ruddy round and genial countenance. Only to Homer Evans, in a moment of soul-stirring confidence, had Tom disclosed the reason, and we, on the pledge of the reader's secrecy, will divulge it here. Troubled because his younger son in Boston College had received a B in Gaelic, instead of the customary A, Tom's hand had slipped in making a gin fizz. Consequently, a denizen of the Bellevue, one Joseph Lincoln, had observed on the surface of his drink a small cluster of bubbles. The shock of this had caused Tom to attend a *novena* which kept him away from his post seven days.

This is preliminary to establishing that at five o'clock in the afternoon following the lunch at Primway's residence, Homer and Miriam, facing Tom Bowles, had the Bellevue bar to themselves. Tom had such tact that he knew when and when not to listen, so they were able to speak as freely as if they had been alone.

"Is it possible that this terrible war changes everything—that nowhere or on no one does it fail to leave its mark?" Miriam had asked, looking solemn, indeed.

Homer started. He had been lost in thought, still revolving in his mind the question, asked so thoughtlessly by Primway to whom it mattered so little, pondered so intensely by Homer, to whom it was beginning to assume colossal proportions as a challenge to his gifts and a threat to his future peace of mind. Why? Why was Momblo murdered?

"Be patient, my dear," Homer said. "I shall clear this up in time."

"I find it harder and harder to understand you," said Miriam with unconcealed reproach. "Naturally I grasp what this means to you, the absolute necessity for you to find the solution. But why" (her eyes flashed) "in the midst of such a vital investigation, knowing you may be called away at any moment, do you take time off to play pranks on unfortunate Mr. Primway?"

"Oh, him," said Homer, and sighed with relief.

Miriam tapped her foot on the floor.

"Don't you say, 'Oh, him,' to me, Homer Evans. You know very well that you, alone, can prefer charges in Wyoming against Mr. Primway. You told him all that fiction about the coroners and sheriffs and lynching Orientals and extradition, knowing all the time that *you* own the missing horse or horses, if anyone does."

Homer smiled. "You still don't quite grasp the nuances of the New England mentality," he said.

"I don't want to," she almost snapped. "I want to recapture yours, if I can."

He touched her arm gently. "If I had not offered a pretext to Lancaster Primway, he would never have consented to accompany us back to Wyoming . . ."

"Us? We're going back there?" she interrupted, unable to believe her own ears.

"I arranged it all with the chief of the G-19 while you were changing," he said. "Now please let me defend myself. As I said, if Primway did not think he was 'wanted' in Wyoming and had to give himself up, to vindicate the family honor and name, he would consider it his duty to remain in Boston near Francois and Ferdinanda, suffering the torments of the damned. He's lonely, poor fellow. He's lost . . . at loose ends. Why not divert his mind, when he so sorely needs diversion?"

The flush of contrition that flooded Miriam's lovely face, and, if the truth could have been known, extended downward, brought reassurance from Homer. "We're all a little jittery today," he said.

That Tom heard. So he nodded, smiled and reached for the gin and a lime.

"As to the ownership of that pinto or pintos, the question is not so clear," Homer said. "That a Ute Indian would offer for sale two bronchos at four dollars each, if he owned them, is improbable, to say the least. Had the Ute come by them honestly, he would have charged an even five."

"Isn't he not guilty until proved un-innocent?" Miriam faltered.

"Let's hope that the pintos have wandered back home, and that their home range is not in Buckskin County," Evans said.

"Maybe Wen Shan, whoever and wherever he is, has had to cook them and eat them, to survive," said Miriam.

"My problem, just now, does not center on Wen Shan," Homer said. "I feel sure he will turn up, either dead or alive. To make certain, I don't mind telling you, I have asked our old friend, Chief Rain-No-More, (*Fracas in the Foothills*, 1940) to amble over from your native Montana into Buckskin County, Wyoming, and offer his services as deputy to Moroni S. Allbrown, the sheriff. As you know, your childhood playmate could find, on any given area of foothills and flats in Christendom, not merely an Oriental and two horses, but any given gopher with two fleas."

Miriam's expressive face now glowed with pleasure.

"It will be nice to see Elk Calf again," she said. It must be explained that in childhood on her father's ranch, adjacent to the Blackfeet reservation, Rain-No-More had nicknamed Miriam Bird Cherry and she, in return, had called him Elk Calf. The innocent and happy hours they had spent together were jewels in a carefree childhood, and one of the results had been that Miriam, at the age of ten, could shoot a June bug by starlight in mid-air, ten times out of ten. Her Indian playmate had taught her that, and she, in turn, in later years, knowing how much grief and injustice had come to the red men because of their inability to hold alcohol, had given him such sound training that at the University of California Rain-No-More had been able to drink the entire English department under the table and still recite Gray's *Elegy* without missing a word, and another chap's *Ode to a Skylark* thrown in.

"When do we start west?" asked Miriam.

"That depends," Homer said.

Miriam didn't exactly, tap her foot, but she got it in the alert position.

"Don't punish me," she said.

"Better not," Tom Bowles admonished.

So Homer came through.

"That depends on the fair Ferdinanda," he said.

"You mean . . ." Miriam was breathless with relief and joy. "You mean . . . she'll go, too?"

"Possibly. I daresay," said Homer, mimicking unmaliciously the voice and manner of Lancaster Primway. "Since I've got into this thing, I may as well go the distance. Strange, isn't it, how Primway gets under one's skin?"

For answer, Miriam, with Tom looking on and beaming, threw her arms around Homer's neck and kissed him, in a way that would have put all the Primways on crutches for generations back.

13
Hell Hath No Fury

MOSES LEMMINGS ARRIVED at the main entrance of the Bellevue in Boston with a taxi-load of suitcases and the indispensable break-fast trunk, the contents of which he had secretly sampled with awe en route. There he was told by the veteran doorman that Mr. Evans had left word that he should keep the same taxi, return to the South Station, and take himself and the baggage back to New York, there to await further orders. The tolerant ex-porter did not rant and apostrophize. He quite pontifically smiled.

"What a man!" he sighed, and the doorman, who knew Homer of old, nodded in concurrence.

"His mother broke the mold," he said, then realizing in a dim way that the metaphor was heedlessly chosen, added: "You know what I mean."

That didn't help matters, either, but he let it pass.

"Your ticket," he said, and reaching into the pocket of his uni-form overcoat, drew forth and handed Moses an envelope.

"Much obliged," Moses said. "I'm used to traveling. Back *and* forth."

Neither of them knew that, in order to supply Homer with the necessary accommodations, the President of the New Haven had cancelled space for the chairman of the Watch and Ward Society who was heading a Boston delegation to New York in order to pur-chase a full collection of books the Society had caused to be banned in Boston.

To inform the reader of the whereabouts and status of some of our characters, the following resume is inserted:

Isaac Momblo, deceased, is reposing on ice in the Allbrown Storage Warehouse in Blanc Mange, Wyoming.

Miriam is in her room at the Bellevue, Boston, wondering when, if ever, and where, if anywhere, she will get a chance to send out some laundry.

The conductor, Thomas Q. Rider, about to depart from Chicago on his annual vacation with pay.

Heber T. Allbrown is hunting jack rabbits and Wen Shan. Jennie Y. is hunting Heber.

Lancaster Primway is trying to explain by phone to his father, who is in Annisquam with an old chum he met in a cloak room years before, that he (Lancaster) has been called west to answer charges of horse stealing.

François, or Frank, de la Cirage Dantan is having a manicure—if that is the verb.

Ferdinanda, whom the reader is soon to meet, in order that he may judge for himself, is reading Lowell (Amy) and repeating after the poet: "Christ! What are patterns for!"

Not even the author can tell you, yet, the whereabouts of the elusive Wen Shan.

Let us go then, to the sacrosanct Louisburg Square, where Homer and Dulcivear Cushing, Ferdinanda's father, are in conference. The noted financier had had a hard morning. His brow was creased and furrowed, not by care but on account of a lifelong urge and inner necessity to find something to worry about. To the outsider, it would seem that Dulcivear was sitting on top of the world. He had the highest social standing in the Blue Book and the highest credit rating in Dun and Bradstreet. His health was excellent. And just within the week, his daughter Ferdinanda, who had always, because of her modern views, been a thorn in his side, even to the extent of wearing a Roosevelt button to the Junior League Prom, had got what seemed to Dulcivear a slice of her just deserts. That is, she had married de la Cirage Dantan.

"Between you and me, old man," he said to Homer, "the press Johnnies were jolly well mistaken about my resenting that French bounder. They got everything backwards. Always did. Of course I couldn't say so, but as a matter of fact I was tickled pink with that blackguard of a son-in-law. He'll skin Ferdinanda alive. I won't say I didn't favor, before I saw the actor chap, young Primway. I'd believed that Ferdinanda would have a rum enough time with him; he's such a bloody boor. But the Dago, or whatever he is, will give her what for. They do that sort of thing better on the Continent."

Homer began to glow appreciatively as the silver-haired old Brahmin warmed up to his subject.

"I only hope he badgers my daughter as she and her mother, blast 'em, have bullyragged me. Any man who can stand up to 'em and get the best of 'em—by Jove, I'll take off my hat to him. Only don't, for God's sake, tell anyone I said so."

Homer promised.

"Women," Dulcivear continued, "are the curse of this country, the respectable kind, I mean. Time and time again I've been on the point of hopping off with some chorus girl or waitress, just to spite my unspeakable family." Dulcivear sighed and extended his pink, plump hands in a gesture of futility. "Lots of chaps do," he said. "Only I couldn't stick it. Tried it once or twice, and the silly little trollops talked such rubbish that I gave it up. I wouldn't have minded 'em so much, if they'd only kept their mouths shut, but they didn't. They can't. All in all, they're as bad as the crowbait we have to live with at home. If women have money of their own, there's no way to make 'em toe the mark. If they haven't any money, they think of nothing but getting it out of a man. Six one way, half-a-dozen the other."

"Have you seen young Primway, since he came here from the west?" Homer inquired.

"He called once or twice, and bored me to distraction," Dulcivear said. "Thought it looked sporting, I fancy!"

"He didn't mention why he came . . . to Boston, just now, I mean?" Homer persisted.

"I haven't the foggiest," said the financier. "The press chaps said he was coming for the wedding. He was too late for that. Of course he would be. He's foozled everything since he stopped playing rugby, or whatever it was he was good at in school. You know what frightful asses go in for the crew and the team."

"What puzzles me is the fact that, on the train, he was in such a hurry to get here. Then, when he got here, he seemed to have nothing on his mind," Homer said.

"That's the way the young men are these days," said Dulcivear. "No stability. Does it ever strike you that this world is going to pot?"

"I won't say that I haven't considered that possibility," Homer said, and rose to go. He would have enjoyed hearing Dulcivear Cushing all day on his favorite subjects, but as far as the Momblo case was concerned, his venture was a blank.

"Come in again some time," Dulcivear said, as Homer shook his hand and departed. "Your views are very interesting—probably."

As Homer walked through the narrow alley back to Beacon Street and then down to Charles, even the squirrels that frisked around the elms and begged for bread on the paths of the Common could see that there went a man with a load on his mind.

The reader (of *Mysterious Mickey Finn*, *Hugger-Mugger in the Louvre*, etc.) already is aware that while Homer quite often heckles Miriam about what she calls "intuition," he more often resorts to it, or follows his hunches, himself. A stupendous deal of twaddle fills the library shelves with reference to the subconscious. Nevertheless it is unmistakable that fish from the depths of the human mind rise frequently to gulp a little air, while ducks drifting on the surface dip down for weeds near the bottom. To the questions already besetting Homer had now been added another, decidedly introspective. Why had he felt such an impulse to come to Boston in connection with the death of Isaac Momblo? As far as Homer knew, the deceased had never been there. Surely a man as transparent as Lancaster Primway would have betrayed the fact, had he ever heard the dead man's name, before Homer had, without warning, uttered it in his presence.

Evans had got nothing from Primway, less from his charming old father-in-law-not-to-be. From Tom Bowles he had got a few excellent gin fizzes. That was all. There remained only one more possibility—Ferdinanda Cushing de la Cirage Dantan, or Mrs. Dante. She was stopping, so her father had said, at the Glendennon, principally because she owned the place, but also to annoy her father who had hoped she would risk a honeymoon voyage on her yacht, and be *spurlos versenkt.*

"Madame Dantan is seeing no one," the old clerk with mutton-chop whiskers informed Homer at the desk.

Again Homer resorted to the handy little badge beneath his neatly rolled lapel.

"In a manner of speaking," corrected the clerk, who blinked and struck with the palm of his hand an old-fashioned bell such as the teachers of our forefathers, those that had them, used in school. A bell hop who had served with Sherman, in the incendiary squad, tottered over.

"Will you inform Mrs. Dantan that Mr. Evans is in the lobby—Mr. Homer Evans," the clerk said.

"We had a telephone," he explained to Homer, "but Mrs. Dantan ripped it out from the wall, wires and all."

"I can go up unannounced," said Homer, not having the heart to send the old soldier up three flights of stairs.

"Whom shall we notify, in case anything happens?" asked the clerk.

Homer nodded reassuringly. "I'll be tactful," he said.

The corner suite used once by the Prince of Wales, later Edward the VIIth (for what purpose again we must refrain from revealing on account of those revolting censors), overlooked both the Common and the Public Gardens. Ferdinanda, instead of greeting her visitor with firearms or Flit, as she had done in case of previous callers, seemed glad to see Homer, so glad that it took him aback. He had met her a few years before, as the reader will remember, and had enjoyed the evening well enough, but he had not expected she would remember him so well or show such an unusual interest in his call. Her receptive attitude prompted him to plunge at once into the subject nearest his heart, and, had he known it, to hers as well.

"I'm working on a murder case," he said.

"Do tell me about it," she urged. "I've been thinking of murder quite constantly in the past few days. A strange coincidence.'

"The murder to which I refer has already been committed," Homer said, and smiled. *He* was thinking that the girl before him, a product of such quaint ancestry and upbringing, was, perhaps, the justification of both. She was handsomer now, more mature, more perfect, in her way, than when he had seen her as a debutante. Her hair was dark and straight, severely coifed and of exactly the shade to accentuate the transparent ivory of her complexion. The lashes were long, almost straight, the brows finely penciled. It was a toss-up as to whether a painter or a sculptor could come nearer to doing her justice.

"You like my looks," she said, approvingly, as she crossed her silken knees and rested her long slender hands, at once capable and delicate, on twin areas of smooth clean limbs implied beneath a simple but expensive skirt.

"I hadn't thought it possible, but you surely have improved with age," Homer said. "Or is that too crude a word?"

"To say 'years' is just as bad," she said. "As you know, I'm twenty-eight."

"You haven't reached your zenith yet," he said.

She sighed. "Perhaps I never will."

Ferdinanda looked thoughtfully across the familiar stretch of treetops. "I never get exactly what I want, even when I know what it is."

"I wish you would," said Homer, sincerely. "I see no point in Nature's fashioning a superb creature like you for frustration."

"You're good for me," she said. "But I cannot deny that I envy you. Let's not be evasive. You have all the natural advantages, too. You're good-looking, in the right sort of way. You've got money. Not as much as I have, but enough. To balance that, I've got a passable intellect, but not as good as yours. There the comparison stops. You may not know it, Mr. Evans, but I've followed your career . . ."

"Career?" repeated Homer, reproachfully.

"Excuse me. Your life," she corrected.

"That's better," he said.

"The point is, you have a life. You relish it. You dip your hands and bury your arms in it, as if it were a fragrant bin of grain. The people you like, like you. The things you want agree with you. And I, for all my charms and millions, stand outside all the windows or pace in all the cells. What I have most of is least required. What attracts me moves on, maintaining its distance. When I laugh, I hear flat echoes. I need to weep, and can't."

Homer made an almost imperceptible movement expressive of his sympathy. She checked herself, and him.

"No pity, please. I'm not sorry for myself. I don't understand, that's all," she said, her determination growing. She rose, extended her hands, palms forward, fingers eloquently appealing, then swept them over her figure, from shoulders to knees.

"You've been everywhere, seen everything, known everyone. Can you tell me how a man can resist me? Oh, don't misunderstand. I don't want flattery, I don't want sympathy. I want . . . How can I express it? You must know that not more than once in a span of years do I meet a man with whom I can be candid. If you didn't love another woman, really and devotedly, and I were not cursed with this obsession for a man, you know whom I mean, but you cannot fathom why, we should not have sat here talking one-tenth as long as this. That's understood."

"Nothing is surer," Homer said. "I should reach for you now and you would respond, if both of us were not stopped short by banality."

"Thank you, my friend," she said, and impulsively extended her hand. "And now, will you help me?"

"I will if I can," Homer said. "You have just favored me with a most . . . not flattering but gratifying description. Let me confess *my* true state of mind and being."

She sat down again, her fragrance stirring with the graceful motion, just as a cool jack rose is diffused by the lightest caress of the breeze.

Homer began.

"The murder I mentioned took place on a train. A modest likable man, neither rich nor famous, sick nor well, was killed, for a reason I cannot determine. You are wondering already how this concerns you. Perhaps it doesn't, but I have to try everything.

"My method, in investigating difficult cases in an amateur way . . ."

"The best way, for anything," she said. "So I'm told."

"Each event takes place in a cluster of other events, some related, some not. That means that the death of Mr. Momblo, the man who was so unreasonably killed, may have unforeseen connections with anything that happened on that train, particularly in and around the Car Masomenus in which he was riding. Also in that car was Lancaster Primway."

"He wouldn't kill a man," she said, almost bitterly, "unless it were the proper thing to do, or not the thing not to do."

"He didn't mention to me that he was coming to attend your wedding," Homer said.

"Was he?" asked Ferdinanda eagerly. "Are you sure?"

"I can't be positive," Homer said. "Why else would he be coming? Could he have prevented it?"

Ferdinanda's clear eyes showed signs of storm.

"The chump could have prevented it by raising a finger," she said.

"Did François know that?"

"Of course," said Ferdinanda. "Lancaster could have saved me from all this nuisance and humiliation by relaxing his stupid principles and scruples and inhibitions. How can I love such a man, if one can call him a man? How could anyone? Why should I stoop . . . make public exhibitions of myself . . . pursue him, plead with him."

"He spoke of sending you a telegram," Homer said.

The storm of indignation this provoked took Evans aback, and nearly resulted in the destruction of a rather good bust of Oliver Wendell Holmes. Ferdinanda fumbled in her near-by handbag like a she-bear stripping bark from a birch and drew forth a tear-stained Western Union form. The text, which Homer read with some surprise, ran like this:

"MAY YOUR VOYAGE BE PACKED WITH THRILLS."

"The brute. The crass, unfeeling monster," Ferdinanda exclaimed, as she tore the message into shreds. One of the larger shreds, examined by Homer, was, indeed, marked "Las Vegas."

"Would you mind telling me," he said, "why, if you were so mad about him, you finally gave him up in the end?"

Ferdinanda looked at Homer almost with horror, surely with regret and disappointment. "You are upset today," she said. "Is it this perfume that addles you? I can change."

"No, no," Homer restrained her. "I spoke too hastily."

"I shall never give him up," Ferdinanda said, her eyes flashing. "I'll get some kind of resonance from his shallow tin pan of a soul if I have to beat my knuckles till the skin is worn away. You didn't think I married that detestable fatuous nincompoop and *poseur*, that subhuman scum of the studios and residue of an inept aristocracy . . ."

"Calm, friend," admonished Homer, immensely relieved but still groping. "Why did you marry Frank or François?"

"An actor's wife can get into the studio," Ferdinanda said. "I tried to buy them all, but the owners wouldn't sell. If that bleating and petrified Puritan thought he was going to stop me from entering his place of employment, he misjudged me—as he's constantly been doing since we made mud pies together in Louisburg Square, using sterilized sand and imported Vichy water. If murdering *him* wouldn't defeat my own purpose, I would have throttled him long ago. I would have strangled his silly, stilted protests in his throat. Did you ever hear of anything more ridiculous? Me, with enough money to establish and endow a dozen better systems of morality than the claptrap he learned on this hill. I can't be taken as a bride, or any other way, unless he can support me. He must work—take the bread from the mouths of those who really need jobs; get in the way of better men equipped to hold them; give *my* best years to his infantile denial of all sense and sex."

"I agree," Homer said. "Only let me explain. Granted that he felt obliged to attend your wedding, to show the world there were no hard feelings, and all that. The prospect would have been distasteful to him, *n'est-ce pas?*"

"That's why he did it, undoubtedly, or tried to. Why couldn't the worm at least have been on time?"

"He didn't tell you that?" Evans asked.

"I haven't seen him," she said. "I can't give this gigolo whose name or names I bear any pretext until I get enough on him to hang him. That may take a week or so."

"You have nothing yet?" asked Homer.

"He'll stub his toe, in time," she said. "I'm not delving into his past. That would hardly be sporting. He doesn't draw a breath, or peep into a powder room, without being watched by my agents."

"He must loathe you," Homer said.

Again her eyes darkened with anger. "That's another of my characteristic breaks of luck. He's beginning to go off the deep end. But really," she said.

"Great God," Evans said, and chuckled. "Then you can pay him off."

"I shall torture him within an inch of his life, then throw him away like a rag," she said. "As far as I can discover, there's never been a woman, of whatever race or age or previous condition of servitude, he hasn't been able to subjugate. Well, he can't subdue me. Upon my word, there's not another man I've danced with, rubbed against in subways, sat close to in church, even passed on the street or in the lobby of Symphony Hall that I haven't had some feeling for, a little tingle, a possibility, a fleeting tug of sensuosity. I'm made for men. I know it. I feel it inside. I could even stir that muttonhead of a moralist once I got him where the hair is short. But my husband!" (she emphasized the word derisively) "He could prance and smirk and paw and hiss and wriggle and stew till Kingdom Come with no more results than a gnat trying to sting a scream from the statue of Edward Everett Hale down there in the Gardens. He's frightened already. I assure you, he'll go mad. He's rushing from woman to woman, after only four days, trying to prove he's still the man he thought he was. It doesn't work. He's longing to kill me, but that would wreck his ego unless he conquered me first. Ha!" (She laughed wildly.) "What a chance! He can't believe it. He can't eat or sleep or stand up or sit down."

"What was it Nietzsche said about being discriminating even in our hates?" Homer asked, again to calm his lovely but harassed companion.

"I don't hate him," Ferdinanda said. "Perhaps I shall. But I've won the first skirmish. He thought he wasn't going back to Hollywood and act, that he'd live on my dividends in ease and lavish luxury. I'm taking him back on tomorrow's evening train."

"To catch the Superchief from Chicago?" Evans asked.

She nodded.

"Could you wait for the U. P.? We could have no end of good talk on the way," Homer suggested, persuasively. "First let me ask the question that brought me here. Knowing Primway as you do, why do you think he would have been in such a hurry to reach your side before the wedding? He bolted the Streamliner when we got stuck, stole or borrowed a horse, rode furiously all the way to the Santa Fe station at Voodoo, and, without even a ticket and no funds, and boarded the Chief only to reach Chicago too late for his reserved connection. He was held up there until after you were legally joined."

"Only legally," said Ferdinanda, grimly.

"I'm truly glad of that," Homer said. "But why the hysterical behavior in a man whose restraint has all but wrecked your life and his own, a man who never lost his temper at either Groton or Harvard, on or off the gridiron, or showed ungentlemanly haste?"

"Perhaps the fathead has a drop or two of blood in his veins, after all," Ferdinanda said, and for the first time a gleam of hope glowed in the depths of her famished and expressive eyes.

Part Three
Where Men Love Horses, and No Wonder

14
A Casualty in the Badlands

THE RUSSET LIGHT of a bulbous moon crept over Buckskin County, Wyoming, flowing over flats, humping low hills and feeling out each clump of sage-brush, lending night-colored radiance and beauty to a stretch of country otherwise as unpromising as could be found on any of the continents. The town of Blanc Mange slept, its dingy roofs and sign boards quiescent, its inhabitants twisting, turning, snoring and, if dreaming, half-awakened now and then by the melodious and lonesome whine of a coyote who bayed for want of better occupation.

Camped a half mile west of the main settlement, in a grove of cottonwoods nourished by a crusted alkaline stream, Homer, Miriam and Ferdinanda were smoking and talking over a slowly dying fire perfumed with loco weed. This kept off a small percentage of the mosquitoes and soothed the raw nerves of our Bostonienne who, on the journey from Beacon Hill to Wyoming, had been severely tried. Her legal husband, François de la Cirage Dantan, had behaved sulkily, since the prospect of a job loomed ahead, but principally because he had not been able, to use a diamond metaphor, to get to first base, with his alluring bride. At each station he had been beset by autograph collectors who little suspected what was gnawing at the vitals of their idol. From force of habit, François had pinched and prodded slyly a few of the most promising enthusiasts and had been shocked to discover that he had lost his touch. Not even the schoolgirls had responded. Most of them did not so much as resent his maneuvers, so cruelly had

François' frantic infatuation for Ferdinanda crippled his established style. For the first time since he was a boy of twelve, he slept, alone and continent, in Drawing Room D while adjacent, in C Compartment, his bride from Boston burned and yearned for Lancaster Primway, who had, for propriety's sake, insisted on being placed at the extreme end of the Car Masomenus, in Bedroom J.

It was not until François, the conductor and Homer had begun to play Gin Rummy that poor François had any diversion or company at all.

Homer had plenty, but none of a soothing kind. He had occupied the fatal Bedroom B, and on his knees had cased the carpet, let the upper berth down and latched it up again, measured distances, calculated speeds and momentums, and betweentimes had stared out at the landscape, still straining for the answer—not who, but *why*. The groan of the whistle, the click of the rails, and the indifferent swishing of the cattle's tails in fields and badlands were his only replies. The photographs he had taken when Momblo was lying dead on the floor had been printed and enlarged, and these Homer studied and passed around. Neither he nor Miriam nor Ferdinanda could derive from them a single clue they did not already possess. Neither straightforwardness nor guile, moreover, could elicit a helpful word from Lancaster Primway. Whatever had impelled him to rush eastward at the time of Ferdinanda's wedding, then shut up like the Sphinx on arriving too late, was locked in the camphor-scented coffers of his consciousness. He was polite to Ferdinanda, quite correct and distant. He acted as if François were non-existent, passing him in the narrowest of the corridors without even brushing him, let alone deigning him a glance or a nod. This performance, sustained for nights and days, won Miriam's admiration.

"It would be worth four years at Harvard," she had said to Homer, "to be able to high-hat a man like that. I wonder, myself, sometimes, if the unlucky François is not an evil spirit, after all."

"Without substance," Homer had added, and nodded his approval.

"You don't help him much—Mr. Primway, I mean," said Miriam, piqued. "Since when did you take up a silly game like Gin Rummy, and associate with gigolos, or is it gigoli?"

"Don't include the conductor," Homer said. Then he relaxed and sighed. "They both were cheating, and I think they both knew the other wasn't playing on the level. In fact, they seemed to expect it, or take it for granted. I upset the whole system by playing according to rules."

"You won, of course," said Miriam, impatiently.

"A little," admitted Homer. "Whatever they had on them."

Homer lapsed into thoughtfulness again.

"You're really worried, aren't you?" Miriam said.

"There is a most distressing possibility," said Homer. "I've tried to dismiss it, but I no longer can. If Isaac Momblo were murdered accidentally, because, let us say, he looked like some other man, we're sunk. It might take years to find out whom. Our gentle friend was of a rather common type of build and physiognomy—Lenin, Brahms, Verlaine, Garfield, Cezanne, either one of the Smith Brothers. He looked a bit like all of them, and hundreds more. I've done the best I can. Levi, of the F.B.I., is posting pictures of Momblo in all the post offices, without any name, and offering a substantial reward for anyone who supplies it. We may get results, but it's a long chance, and, while scientific enough, is the clumsiest device to which I've ever been forced to resort."

Within a few days letters and names began pouring into Blanc Mange, from all parts of the country, and in order to take care of the clerical work involved Homer hired two nieces of Heber T. Allbrown, named Reeda and Smoota. To describe one of these plump blond examples of Wyoming girlhood is to describe the other, since they were identical twins. They had placid blue eyes with arched brows, unplucked; well-rounded limbs with small wrists and ankles; shapely hands and feet. Their voices were languorous, in spite of a hearty western accent, and their speech was provocative, notwithstanding their rather meagre vocabulary. Their skin was alabaster tanned only in the areas exposed to the sun and wind, and in the strong light of their native prairies showed a soft golden down which beautified rather than marred it.

Unlike their countrywomen farther West, they did not try for the "fountain pen" figure affected by some of the mildly female movie stars. In fact, concerning those attributes which distinguish young girls from young boys, it may be said that Reeda and Smoota had duplicate sets that were esthetically delicious and socially disconcerting.

Although they did their work for Homer faithfully, the comely Mormon twins, ignoring completely the prowling François de la Cirage Dantan, made such a play for Lancaster Primway that even the animal and insect life in the neighborhood was visibly stirred. Their father, Nephi X. Allbrown, who ran the hotel, paddled the girls soundly with a lath, with an effect lamentably opposite to the one he desired, and made them both put back on the long red flannel underwear they had years before discarded in favor of flimsy modern defenses.

The spanking incident, mildly painful to the Mormon maidens, and of which Primway was completely unaware, had prompted Ferdinanda to offer secretly to the husky country girls, ten thousand dollars apiece and a four-year course at Vassar if they could get a rise out of Lancaster by any means at all.

"May as well let them do some of the spade work," Ferdinanda said to Miriam and Homer.

It was while the trio was camped on the flat east of Blanc Mange that all were startled and Ferdinanda, mistakenly thinking one or both of the girls had succeeded, was thrilled to see Reeda and Smoota streaking toward them across the prairie on the run. But as soon as the girls were within earshot, it was clear that they were calling for help. Within a few seconds they had come up, breathless, and begun their tale of woe. When one got out of wind, the other took up the story, which, as soon as Homer had grasped it, caused him and his fair companions to start for a near-by coulee on the run.

It seemed that just after supper, as soon as their strict father had gone to bed, Reeda and her sister had crept silently to

Primway's door, tried it, found it open, and got into his bed, believing that if the reserved Bostonian came home tired from his day-long search for the missing pintos he might break down and let them remain. In that way they hoped to win the coveted ten thousand and the scholarship at Vassar, which they had agreed to split between them should one succeed and the other one fail. They were wholesome, comely girls, brought up in a country school, good-looking, frank and healthy, and understandably anxious to learn, from a presentable and cultured young man, the facts of life which radio, pulp magazines and the movies, as against parental reticence and the Book of Mormon, had left rather vague in their minds.

It was a strange coincidence that the frantic François, having been warned by Ferdinanda that if he came snooping around her camp she would pot him like a gopher, and beginning to be obsessed with the fear that his spell over women had come to an inglorious end, had crept to the girls' attic room and into their double cot with designs which Dante's innumerable devotees will too well understand.

When ten o'clock struck and Primway had not returned, the girls began to get worried and decided to go out looking for him. By the light of the moon they had found Lancaster lying flat on his face, very still, shot clear through the head. There was a small wound where the bullet had entered on the right side and a larger one where it had departed from the left side. The horse he had been riding was grazing peacefully near by.

"Is he dead?" asked Reeda and Smoota in tears. Ferdinanda and Homer were both kneeling by Primway's prostrate form, listening, examining

"He's breathing. He has a pulse, but a very light one," Homer said.

Just at that moment there appeared by moonlight on the smooth horizon three horsemen at the sight of whom Miriam, the first to see them, exclaimed with joy and lit a signal fire. The horsemen saw it. The taller, Rain-No-More, responded with a whoop and a wave of his hand. They urged their horses on.

"What luck," Homer said, when his keen eye made out the identity of Rain-No-More's companions. He turned to the fainting Ferdinanda and put his arm around her shoulders reassuringly. "If anyone can save Primway, these men can. Buck up," he said.

Trout-tail III, chief medicine man of all the Blackfeet.

And the renowned ex-medical examiner of pre-war Paris, Dr. Hyacinthe Toudoux.

Since the fall of his beloved country, Dr. Toudoux had been serving De Gaulle, not at any of the fronts that make the headlines, but with his respected friend and colleague, Trout-tail, on the lava-strewn wastes of the Blackfeet reservation, capturing by the hundreds of thousands healthy specimens of the prairie rattlesnake (*crotalis confluentus*) to be distributed among the Boche by the French Underground in occupied areas. Already one of the snakes, secreted in the dress overcoat pocket of General Hedwig von und zu Bachhaus am Oder-pfui, had stung mortally the brutal officer who had sent so many innocent hostages before a firing squad, and had been rescued to rest and recuperate in preparation for another feat of fangs. The snakes, although nearly blind and quite deaf, had shown a marked affection for, and antipathy, to German soldiers, most likely because of their smell. It was a form of warfare long in use among the Blackfeet. The French and other patriots were now using it with telling effect.

Not pausing for introductions, the two doctors dismounted, knelt, glanced at the wound, felt the pulse, listened for Primway's breathing, then looked gravely at each other.

"Please, Doctor," gasped Ferdinanda to Toudoux.

The gallant Frenchman deferred to his Indian colleague. "What do you think?" he asked.

"Ytrap sih fo dia eht ot emoc ot nem doog lla rof emit eht si won," said the Medicine Man.

"My colleague does not speak English or French," he explained. "He has said, and I agree in every essential detail, that a .32 calibre bullet has passed through the prefrontal area of the brain of the young white brave, at the level of the Sylvian Fissure."

"Will he live?" asked Ferdinanda.

"Between my surgery and my Blackfeet colleague's herbs, he has a chance," Toudoux said.

"You'll forgive my agitation. I love the damn fool," Ferdinanda said.

Toudoux bowed. "In that case, the patient has everything to live for," he said.

15
Miracle of Modern Surgery

Each year since Prohibition went into effect, Thomas Q. Rider, the conductor, had spent his vacations at a place called Desert Dude Ranch, five miles out of Blanc Mange, and operated by another brother of Heber, Moroni and Nephi Allbrown, christened Orson but known locally as Highpockets. So it happened that Highpockets and Rider, having run out of hootch before midnight, had left the ranch by moonlight and driven over to Blanc Mange proper to get some from the drug store run by an elder named Pratt.

They, therefore, were astonished to see, in Pratt's back room redolent of drugs and spirits, two doctors. One was an Indian; the other had lifted the top of the skull from the head of the pale and motionless Lancaster Primway. To use the apt but rather vulgar words of Druggist Pratt: "as if it was the lid of a pisspot." They were tweaking and poking around in the rather unsightly and hitherto weak, but well-ordered, brain that had retained in its heydey enough football signals to stock a national number game. Pale, her classic face set grimly, assisting the medicos, was Ferdinanda de la Cirage Dantan. Her liberal education had included a course in emergency nursing. So she had insisted upon remaining at Primway's side, leaving Miriam, Homer and Rain-No-More to track down the assassin. That they would do so, she felt confident, more confident than she felt, in spite of the address of both doctors, that the headpiece of the man she loved, unimportant though it was in the general scheme of things, would ever, having been taken so thoroughly apart, be put back together again.

At the moment the two newcomers were gazing at the operation through the open doorway into the main drug store, Toudoux had pointed out the bullet crease to Trout-tail, and the Indian had nodded.

"Ob dick tooh weh Friedman Philadelphia," said Trout-tail, apparently well pleased.

"He says," Dr. Toudoux explained to the anxious Ferdinanda, "that Dr. Friedman of Philadelphia could scarcely have done a neater job. The crease is like the kind Friedman slices on the cerebellum of certain of his patients in the manic-depressive category."

"You mean . . ." she asked in horror. "You mean he'll be . . ." She tapped her classic forehead.

"Not necessarily," the doctor said.

"Can you pull him through?" asked the conductor, astonished. "With his dome cut up like that?"

"We shall see," sighed Toudoux, and took up his tweezers again.

"Seen enough?" the Frenchman asked Trout-tail.

"Eeeeeeeee," said the Indian, and both of them started fitting Primway's sconce back on again.

"Don't that beat all?" asked Highpockets. The conductor nodded. So did Druggist Pratt and all of the Allbrowns excepting Nephi, who was just then over at his hotel whaling the backsides off his two fair daughters because he had found Frank Dante in their room. That they had not been there with the wolf in question did not seem to matter to Nephi, who asserted, between strokes of the lath, that they were just like their dratted mother and would have been on hand for the Hollywood slicker if they hadn't been up to something worse outside.

On the summit of a flat-topped butte six miles westward, Homer and Miriam, both mounted, were leaning close together, surveying the moonlit landscape, which was hardly worth while, so dreary was the vast expanse. Their horses edged still closer, and touched noses.

"We're saved," said Homer, exultantly. "At last our adversary, clever as he is, has linked our problems."

"I don't see, for the life of me," said Miriam, "what shooting poor Primway through the head has to do with bopping or bumping the head of poor Mr. Momblo. Will you enlighten me?"

"In time," said Homer, as he gently aroused the horses from their affectionate gestures and started off toward town again. He got there just as Drs. Toudoux and Trout-tail III were finishing their work and scrubbing their hands in preparation for a well-earned rest.

"I'm sorry you couldn't stick around," said Dr. Toudoux. "That bullet cut the neatest Friedman crease I ever had the luck to see."

To the astonishment of all assembled, and much to Ferdinanda's indignation, Homer began to laugh heartily, almost uncontrollably. "A Friedman crease," he repeated, as soon as he was able, holding his aching sides. "Ho, ho. Can you beat that?"

"There's nothing to laugh at . . . or is there?" demanded Ferdinanda.

"You'll understand later," Homer said, and laughed again.

"He's being mysterious," said Miriam to the Boston belle. "Of all the men I know, he can, when he wants to, be the most exasperating. But, dear, it's an excellent sign. If he weren't sure Mr. Primway would get well . . ."

"Don't," begged Homer, doubled up with laughter again, which this time was so contagious that both doctors joined in. Toudoux, however, took time out to reassure Ferdinanda

"I'll stake my reputation. He'll recover, though he may not be the same up here." With that Dr. Toudoux touched his forehead significantly and resumed laughing again.

Druggist Pratt came in at that point with a bottle of government Bourbon which Ferdinanda, on the verge of what promised to be a violent demonstration, took from his hand, uncorked and, throwing back her aristocratic head, encompassed a slug that would have choked both pintos, if either had been found.

"As you gentlemen all know, I love him," she said, the warmth of the Bourbon glowing gently in her shapely stomach as outside the baying of the coyote, who now had a couple of pals, conveyed the idea that on the barren prairie the chill of night was crispening.

"But," continued Ferdinanda, "it is hard to see, just now, how any change in his personality could fail to be an improvement."

"One does not love on account of personalities," said Hyacinthe Toudoux, taking his turn at the Bourbon.

He coughed. "This admirable whiskey," he added, "bears the name of an illustrious, though degenerate, ruling house of France. One can only hope, and expect, that with the centuries, your American whiskey will exchange its primitive ruggedness for the suave, though effete, delicacy of our Armagnac."

"In all the years I've been running this drug store," said Tarley G. Pratt, the proprietor, "I've never heard so much talk that went over my head." He took the remains of the whiskey, notwithstanding, and disposed of them with supple Adam's apple.

The company, with the exception of Primway and Ferdinanda, who was determined to watch at his side through the night, went to their respective homes, dude ranches, hotels and shacks. Soon Blanc Mange was slumbering again, all except François or Frank Dante who, humiliated and writhing in agony, was staring at the starlight and thinking feverishly of Ferdinanda. After having failed to undo the two young girls, Reeda and Smoota, Frank had, in desperation, made a pass at Mrs. Nephi Allbrown, moustache and all (hers, we mean to say), and couldn't click even there, although Mrs. Nephi, *née* Orsonia Pratt, was none too particular. For the seventh consecutive night, an all-time record, the sleek and predatory Frank was alone and scorned.

In some ways Frank was no fool, and it would be unfair to him not to relate, here and now, that he was worried not only about what is loosely termed pleasure, but business, too. He sensed that he would, in future, unless he could vanquish Ferdinanda, be a washout on the screen. He would lose his three grand a week and have to ask his chaste bride for fives and tens. He was beginning to suspect, rather strongly, that somehow he had outsmarted himself in what was to be the crowning episode of a long and successful career.

Homer and Miriam were sitting around the embers of their camp fire. If the reader from the East is curious as to why so sensible a man and desirable a woman should elect to sleep in the open when half the rooms (four, that is to say) in the Millennium Hotel were vacant, the author can assure them that there were literally thousands of reasons, shaped just alike. How so many bedbugs, none of whom could fly, got as far from civilization as Blanc Mange, Wyoming, is a question that only a Peattie could hope to answer.

In this, reader, may be detected by the pious and discerning the mysterious Hand and Wisdom of the Ruler of Our Days. For the inconveniences He has concocted, and which demonstrate the awful scope of Divine Imagination, are not all to be found in any single region but are distributed, balanced, counter-balanced, sorted, sifted and weighed. In Boston, the censors and Puritans. In Blanc Mange, the *cimex lecturarius*.

Homer had previously explained to Rain-No-More the problem of Wen Shan and the pintos, apologizing for having called the young chief all the way from Montana for such a simple task.

"As you know," Homer said, "my race is inept at following trails and signs, except in thickly populated areas."

Now that there was a would-be murderer of Primway to find, Homer, in more ways than one, felt more justified. But as the night wore on, and the following day, and no word had been heard, not a signal or a sign, from the Blackfeet warrior, Homer's brow began to darken again. Nothing was proving as easy as he had expected.

After dinner that night, of grouse and ember-baked potatoes, preceded by an omelette of curlew eggs with wild rosemary, topped off with the fruit from a Wyoming berry known as *grossularia Zamboni*, Homer was about to saddle the horses, known respectively, because of their transparency, as Urim and Thummim, and set out to find his friend. Just in time, however, Rain-No-More appeared, dusty, weary and bedraggled.

"Bad medicine," was the way he tersely summed up the situation.

He had, as instructed, hiked over to the U.P. tracks, found the telegraph pole where the pintos had been hitched, and started from there. The trail, as Evans had warned him, led in two directions, one southeast by east toward Voodoo, on the Santa Fe, the other across cactus flats and over dreary hills to a ledge of lava rock so tough and bleak that not even a Blackfoot could have followed the track of a Panzer all the way to its edge. As far as the edge, the second (or non-Primway) pinto, bearing a rider who would have weighed approximately 170 pounds, who was tall, accustomed to the saddle, and evidently blissfully drunk, had proceeded. There the pinto tracks had vanished.

"But the rider?" asked Miriam, breathlessly. "Where could he have gone? He must have been Wen Shan."

"Unhappily, no," said Rain-No-More, helping himself to his third plump grouse and fifth baked potato.

"You didn't find him?"

"No. Instead of a Chinese, there was lying at the foot of the crumbled lava ledge the body of a man six feet tall, with carrot-colored hair and covered with freckles. He was built like the late Bob Fitzsimmons, with no waist at all, gangling long legs with bony knees, ape-like arms with knobby elbows, and powerful, broad shoulders. I think he was a Scotsman," Rain-No-More said.

Homer rose and sighed. "I'll have to have a look myself," he said. Miriam tried the cinches and stroked the waiting horses.

"The pinto?" asked Homer, still bewildered.

"It may be that the pinto, if ridden over the ledge by the drunken freckled party, whose legs must practically have hung down to the ground, lies buried in the avalanche of lava cobbles that bore Freck-les, or Wen Shan, as you call him, on its surfaces to his death. The Shan brave's head must have collided with some jutting point of rock. It was bashed in, and brains, somewhat liquefied by alcohol, which still could be detected faintly by its odor, were splashed around," the Blackfeet leader said.

"This is becoming maddening and monotonous," said Homer, disgustedly. "Brains, brains, brains. Momblo's brain was put out of commission, permanently, by an upper berth."

At this point Trout-tail III and Dr. Hyacinthe Toudoux stepped softly into the area of the dying firelight and listened silently. Evans, nodding to them, began again.

"Momblo, as I said, was killed by contact between his head and a berth on the Streamliner."

Evans turned to Toudoux. "You already, having seen Momblo's skull and the contusion, are aware, Doctor, that the conductor's theory, namely that Moses . . ."

"Review the conductor's theory, if you please," asked Toudoux.

"The conductor contends," said Homer, "that just before the train reached Las Vegas, about 11:30 at night, Momblo, who had been conversing with me in the Nugget—that I can confirm myself—went to Bedroom B, rang for the porter, and that Lemmings had just time enough to unlock and let down the berth before the train stopped in the station. Leaving the upper in a horizontal position, and intending to make up the lower as soon as he was able to leave his post at the steps when the train got in motion again—that would be ten minutes later—the porter, addled by questions from Passenger Primway about the whereabouts of the telegraph office, forgot all about Momblo and, since Momblo was dead and therefore silent and not likely to press the buzzer, Moses did not discover until the following noon that Isaac was dead."

"What killed him?" asked Miriam.

"The conductor says that Momblo spread his suitcase on the lower berth in order to find some toilet articles. This has a semblance of verity because the suitcase was spread and open in exactly the right position. Forgetting that the upper had been let down, when the train jerked to a start, Momblo, according to the conductor, must have straightened suddenly, with added force, because of the lurch of the car. He bumped his head, and, being weak and fragile, died."

"And Monsieur Primway *de* Boston," Toudoux said, "supported a bullet through both sides and the core of his head and is doing splendidly. Ho ho."

"Is Mr. Primway conscious yet?" Miriam asked.

Trout-tail III, who had followed the trend of the conversation, pointed to the moon, then held up two fingers.

"He said it may be two months before we hear a peep out of him," said Dr. Toudoux.

"I was ranting about brains," Evans said. "Momblo's brains, snuffed by a mere bump . . ."

"Surely, Monsieur Evans, you have not swallowed that preposterous theory," said Doctor Toudoux.

"Of course not," said Homer and smiled. "You noticed, of course, that the dent in Momblo's head, with triangular fracture of the skull, was much deeper than it could possibly have been had the head been moving upward and the upper berth stationary."

To illustrate, Homer took up two of the curlew's eggs, uncooked. He asked Miriam to hold one in her hand, small end upward. The other he held small end downward, and brought it down at moderate speed, held loosely, not tightly, and with very little force on the egg Miriam was holding. Result: the moving egg bore no mark whatsoever, while the static one was dented.

The demonstration took place just in time to be seen by Heber T. Allbrown, who had sauntered into the circle.

"That's what struck me, first thing," he said. "The bunk fell—or was brought down purposely—on the poor little poop—no offense, miss—and he passed on, as they say, although seeing him laid out in my warehouse each day makes me feel as if the guy is still around and may thaw out when the sun gets hotter, like a fish in a well. If you two" (he indicated the doctors) "can patch up a city sap who's been plugged clean through the bean, and stir up his brains like oatmeal, you might be able to melt a stiff who's frozen, with just a little dent in his head."

For a second, Miriam looked hopeful, but Toudoux shook his head. "Momblo died from shock. He was a sensitive man with a responsive brain and nerves keyed high. He cannot be reclaimed. Monsieur Primway, on the other hand, felt no shock at all. He was not expecting to be shot, and made no plans for it."

"You mean that the little gink was expecting to be gonked?" asked Allbrown.

"Most likely," said Toudoux.

"That means," explained Homer, not at all surprised, "that someone must have been holding him in place for the slaughter. To a man never in contact with violence, except electrical or mechanical, the shock of being grabbed and threatened with extinction would be severe indeed. He would not know how to struggle or retaliate. The whole thing would be new to him, without background of any kind whatsoever."

"Hence the finger-marks on the corpse's upper arm," said Toudoux. "Of course, we couldn't trace them. That's difficult enough if finger-marks are smeared all over a silver bowl or thermos bottle. The detective stories that tell of finger-marks on automatics are written by men of limited experience. The handle is corrugated, the barrel too small to register a print. One might remove a fingerprint intact from a cannon or a locomotive boiler, but not the barrel of a .32."

"Who held poor Mr. Momblo? And shocked him? And killed him?" again demanded Miriam.

Again Homer replied doggedly. "Not who, but why?"

"The dratted . . . what is it you call it?" asked Allbrown.

"Motive," supplied Homer, and all set out for the U.P. tracks. At Homer's suggestion, the Indians fanned out in advance of the main party to guard against attack.

"If some prowler can shoot Primway almost before our eyes," Homer said, "the same man or men can take potshots at us. And for a similar reason—perhaps."

"A reason?" gasped Miriam. "That's what you've been looking for."

Homer sighed, this time with relief. "The faintest glimmer," he said, "is beginning to dawn on the horizon of my mind—at last."

"You wouldn't let a presentable woman, however devoted, in on it, by any chance?" asked Miriam, half-reproachfully. She herself knew the time was not yet ripe.

"Just keep that automatic where you can reach it," Homer said. "And if anything moves you're not sure about . . ."

"Goody," said Miriam. "Anything at all?"

"Within reason," Homer said.

16
That Mann Act

MOST OF THE WAY TO THE RAILROAD, Homer rode side by side with Heber T. Allbrown, with Miriam deploying right and left, between them and the Indians who were farther in advance. When their trail crossed the rusty branch line from the Latter Day Cement Works, Homer, as a matter of precaution, dismounted and, kneeling, bent his ear to a rail. He raised his head, in doubt, then harkened again.

"There's some slight vibration," he said. "Let's wait. It sounds like a hand-car."

Miriam and Heber quickly dismounted. She concealed the horses in a clump of manzanita, and, following Homer's lead, hid herself, automatic in hand, in some sage brush near by, from which she could see along the track. The clicking was now audible, and coming nearer.

"Don't shoot," cautioned Homer. "First let's see who is abroad on this fine moonlit night—and why."

"We could be surer if we shot them—of their identity, I mean," she said.

"But that would seal their lips and hamper their actions," Homer said.

"And we'd still be up a tree for the dratted . . . you know."

"Motive," Homer said.

"I'm as much in the dark about Primway as poor Mr. Momblo," said Miriam.

"The motive will be one and the same for both," Homer said, positively.

"You don't say?" asked Heber in astonishment. "Now that's one on me. I thought the two crimes were as separate as night and day."

"The only person I can think of who might have just reason for killing Primway is Ferdinanda," Miriam said.

"What's he done t'her?" asked Heber, chewing placidly.

"It's what he hasn't done," explained Miriam.

"Gosh. Does a man have to, willy-nilly, back East?" Heber asked, and chewed more rapidly. His companions side-stepped that question.

"Ferdinanda was with us—with Miss Leonard and me—when Primway was shot at and drilled through the brain," Homer said. "If the shot had gone a thousandth of an inch higher or lower, or had been fired from a different angle, it would have been fatal," he continued. "What has resulted is sometimes performed by very skillful surgeons."

"You mean back East they shoot parties through the head to cure 'em of somethin' or other? I'm glad I stayed out here where I belong, in spite of Jennie," Heber said.

"Not exactly," Homer said. "The surgeons, following the great Friedman's example, slice tracks on the prefrontal area, at the level of the back of the eye. This disconnects the front and the back sections of the brain."

"What the hell for? What God hitched together . . . confound Him!"

Their talk was interrupted by the appearance, around the sharp curve of the rusty branch tracks, of the Latter Day handcar with four passengers, two men (if Frank Dante could now be described as such) and two women, if the two Mormon girls, Reeda and Smoota, were sufficiently mature to rate that category. In some ways they were, and in others, maybe not. The fourth man was the conductor.

"Let them go," said Homer. "By taking shortcuts we can keep them in sight practically all the way from here to the U.P. main line."

Miriam frowned. "I don't believe that those girls shot Primway, then came running and screaming for us," said Miriam.

"They're probably tryin' to run away from home," said Heber, laconically. "Can't say that I blame 'em. I've thought, time and time again, to be honest with you, that if I'd had the luck to have been built a little different, I'd a tried a life of ease myself. In a way, I'm glad the town'll be rid of 'em. Jennie's started raising Ned already . . . every time I look at one of 'em."

"She's jealous of your own nieces?" asked Miriam, astonished.

"Look, you're such a nice easy-goin' woman yourself that you don't know what a real she-terror can be like. Jennie got so, last winter, that she was jealous of a brindle heifer that followed me around."

"There they go," Homer said, as the hand-car slid and clicked around the bend. The liquor supply of the Millennium Cut Rate Drug Store, manned by Elder Pratt, had petered out that afternoon and the conductor had announced his intention of going to Evanston for more. This Homer himself had heard him say.

Frank Dante, Homer concluded, had been so badly frightened by his failure with country females that he was streaking out for Hollywood, where several hundred women, tried if not true, might, he hoped, offer him reassurance.

At eight o'clock in the morning, when the blistering sun already was high and heat waves shimmered sardonically over the sage, mesquite, and lizards which monopolized, and welcomed, that part of Wyoming, a physically weary but spiritually undaunted group stood looking speculatively at the remains of the deceased freckled man. That he could be, or ever had been, Wen Shan, was doubted by them all at a glance. He probably was Scotch, or maybe Australian, or a New Zealander, or in a pinch, Canadian. There was nothing on him to indicate that he had ever been on the Streamliner. Where else he might have come from, and found Pinto No. 2 tied to a pole by the car tracks, no one could conjecture. Drunks do wander around, and that Freckles had been stewed to the gills was unquestionable.

"If this man had been on the train . . ."

"How could he have been there?" asked the conductor, who, when questioned about his reasons for night flight in a hand-car, had said merely that he was thirsty and a little fed up with dude ranching. "Most years," he said, "there's a bunch of Eastern school-teachers who can do what they please so far away from home. They're safe, appreciative of attention, and there's nothing to pay. This damned war's cut down on everything," he concluded. "I'll sure be glad when the duration's over and done with."

"Amen," said Heber, fervently. "What'd you do with them nieces of mine?"

"I couldn't take a chance on them," said the conductor.

"Did that actor go an' ruin 'em both?" Heber asked.

"They didn't seem to cotton to him," said the conductor.

Miriam curled the corner of her mouth sarcastically. "You men all make me sick," she said. "You moralize when you're sober, and sentimentalize when you're drunk. No wonder women exploit you." She tapped her foot. "Where are those girls! They can't be left—like that—with no one to look after them!"

"They're going to try Salt Lake, I reckon," the conductor said.

"Try Salt Lake! Just what does that mean!" persisted Miriam, eyes blazing.

"They hope to compromise a couple of members of the armed forces, gentle-like, you know, then get their government allowance. They're not so dumb. They worked it out themselves," said the conductor.

"Plenty o' women do that," Heber said, chewing contentedly again. "Only as a gen'ral rule they put up some cock-an'-bull story about countries and flags and don't talk frank about it. Well, good luck to the danged young trollops. Lots o' soldiers could do worse—for a while."

Homer had taken little part in this conversation. He had been staring at the freckled corpse, his mind darting here and there, trying to get into a pattern the very scattered bits of information concerning Wen Shan. Beside him, getting thirstier and thirstier as the sun beat down with more insistence, stood the conductor, and facing them, across what was left of Corpse No. 2, stood Drs. Hyacinthe Toudoux and Trout-tail III, the latter in full tribal regalia.

Miriam, incensed because Reeda and Smoota had been turned loose so casually in a wicked world, ripe for worse than death in practically any style at all, was pacing the lava-strewn butte from which Wen Shan had pitched, slid or leaped to his death. That the pinto had pushed him was improbable but conceivable. In that case the animal, except by the merest chance, would not have preceded, accompanied, or followed the mysterious rider into Kingdom Come, if that description is not too ornate for the gopher- and snake-infested heap of lava stones on which Wen's brains were strewn. Rain-No-More, whose childhood memories reminded him that Miriam, when worked up about something, was likely to erupt into action, walked beside her, back and forth, with a calming word now and then.

"After all," he said, "it may be better for the young white squaws to be hustling than working in a bank or in one of those great big stores. The hours, conditions, and so forth."

They were passing just near enough to hear Homer saying: "There is the slim chance that this man, Wen Shan, who got on the train without baggage of any kind whatever, was never seen by an official or a passenger, killed Isaac Momblo in a drunken or paranoid rage, then borrowed a horse and rode, alone and without provisions, into the bleakest stretch of country known to man," Homer began.

"Then you wouldn't need a motive," Heber Allbrown said, hopefully. "The motive would be that the scissorbill was plastered and just naturally mean."

"It doesn't hold water," Homer said.

"I doubt if this type has held any water to speak of in the course of the last thirty or forty years," said Dr. Hyacinthe Toudoux, touching with his foot the stain on the lava of a small pool of brains.

Gravely the medicine man nodded in complete agreement.

"The theory doesn't hold water, I mean," Evans said. "If Wen Shan—the devil take that name—had killed Mr. Momblo, in a drunken rage, he would not have ridden on the train all night and half the next day, waiting until his victim's body was discovered, before making his getaway. Neither would he have unscrewed the chains set to retard the downward motion of the upper berth and replaced the screws again. That is a task, not for a mechanic exactly, but surely for a reasonably sober man.'

"Drat this freckled party, anyhow," Heber said. "Now I've got to pack another corpse up to my warehouse. And furthermore, if the conking of Momblo and the shooting of Primway are linked, as you said, Wen Shan, here, couldn't 'a shot at Primway a couple of weeks, at the least, after he was dead himself."

"The cases are linked?" the conductor asked, frowning. "Now who had that idea?"

"Perhaps I was mistaken," Homer said, with a shrug.

This caused Miriam to stop in her tracks. Homer, mistaken! Was he giving up in discouragement?

The answer to her unspoken question came from Homer himself, who suddenly was galvanized into action.

"The hand-car," he asked the conductor. "Where is that?"

"Back at the tracks, I suppose," the conductor said. "Dante and the girls were headed west, for Salt Lake, where he was going to hop a train to Hollywood and they're goin' to seek their fortunes."

"They are *not*," said Miriam, stamping her foot. "At least, until they have a few things explained to them."

Homer smiled to quiet her. "Perhaps they'll land in Vassar, after all," he said. "There things are all scientifically explained."

"And you?" asked Homer of the conductor.

"I was goin' to pump the hand-car down to Evanston for some hootch," the conductor said.

"A suitcase full?" asked Evans. "I noticed you brought yours with you from the dude ranch."

"I thought I might stay a few days in Evanston," the conductor explained. "There aren't any of them Eastern school marms there, but a lot of floozies who got run out of Ogden, on account of the armed forces tempting 'em, are working in a ball-bearing factory—excuse me, miss—and I thought I might date up a couple, so my vacation wouldn't go for nothing at all."

"Well. Let's amble over to the tracks," Homer said. "If the girls haven't thumbed a ride and got away, Miss Leonard can give them their pep talk, and I'd like a word with Frank or François before he leaves the state."

"That actor couldn't have killed Momblo," said Heber. "He was in Boston at the time, poor sap."

"Just a sociable chat," said Homer, and led the party northward to the railroad right of way. When near enough to see the tracks clearly, Homer waited for the conductor to come alongside and looked at the latter quizzically.

"I don't see the hand-car," began Homer.

"Never mind the hand-car. Those innocent girls!" said Miriam. "He's abducted them."

"Not yet, maybe," Rain-No-More said, but unconvincingly.

"The lousy Frog," the conductor said. "Now I got to thumb a ride myself to Evanston."

But Evans scarcely heard what the conductor said. He was smiling broadly now, and went so far as playfully to slap the back of Rain-No-More.

"Know this country?" Homer asked the Blackfeet chief with a sweep of his hand.

"My ancestors were here, in pursuit of the Shoshones and the Utes," said Rain-No-More. "I've seen many maps, on bark and hides—Shoshone hides, in fact. We could never catch enough Utes to bother skinning them, so my dear old grandfather said."

"Eeeeeeeeee," confirmed Trout-tail III.

Homer, as he talked, was unslinging his camera and adjusting it for rapid candid shots.

"Tell me how the tracks run from here to Ogden," Homer said, both to the conductor and Rain-No-More. Between them they scratched on the cinders a crude but fairly accurate sketch of how the railroad wound its way. Until the tracks began to climb in order to get over the Wasatch Mountains—which promised some of the most strenuous pumping ever attempted by a man and two young girls—the road ran fairly straight and direct. Then it started to bend, to veer, to flex, inflex, deflex, concamerate, deviate, and sinuate, at the same time mounting and contorting so that, as the railroad men expressed it, half the time the engineer could shake hands with a brakeman in the caboose.

Homer began to calculate, and Miriam's face began to glow.

"I think you're splendid, darling," she said. "I know what this case means to you, and for you to take time out to save those girls, as a favor to me, I shall never forget."

"Don't mention it, darling," he said. "I only hope we shall arrive in time."

"That's right," said Heber. "Them trollops'll get fagged out, and you know what women are when they're tired. They don't give a damn, as you might say, one way or t'other. I'd bet even money that actor's got the best of 'em by now."

"That worm would get tired before they did," Miriam said, eyes flashing again. "Come on."

The party that streaked across the flat, headed into the Wasatch foothills, was picturesque, indeed. Leading the way was Rain-No-More, Miriam and Homer, with Dr. Toudoux, Trout-tail III, Heber T. Allbrown and the conductor, in the order named. When they entered the rim of hills and saw snow on the mountains beyond, with the track like a ribbon far below in the valleys and canyons, the scenery would have impressed them had they been in less of a hurry. These same majestic mountains and valleys had caused Brigham Young, from his palette, to extend his hand over Zion and say, "This is the place." Miriam, however, was setting the pace, spurred on by visions of what might be happening to Reeda and Smoota in the lonely upland gorges and stream-watered vales. She was planning a rather drastic retaliation in the event that Frank or François Dante got in his awful work.

What was gnawing away at Heber Allbrown's mind, which was plain but surely had its points, was the question as to why, if Homer was so anxious to save Reeda and Smoota, he did not ride to the nearest settlement and phone ahead. He could have Dante and the girls headed off and apprehended for the theft of the hand-car from the Latter Day Cement Company. Not only Heber, but his brothers Moroni, Nephi, Brigham and Highpockets (christened Orson) were directors of the company and could prefer charges. Also, the three fugitives could be hauled in for using, without authorization, the U.P. tracks.

To the suggestion of possible interception by railroad officials, however, Homer had been adamant. And not until after the posse had cut across country and placed themselves well ahead of the hand-car trio did it become clear to his companions what Homer had in mind. Not even then did Dr. Toudoux, the Free Frenchman, quite grasp the situation, for in a civilized land like France a law such as the Mann Act would be unthinkable, not to say, unworkable.

Anyway, the state line running between Wyoming and Utah, at the point where the U.P. intersects, parallels a mountain stream in which the rainbow trout cavort and whose rippling lends music to the rustling of alder leaves and intensifies the soothing redolence of pine. There, standing plainly by the tracks, is the tell-tale sign inscribed on the east side, "Wyoming," and on the west side, "Utah." That is the hurdle, reader, believe it or not, between a simple misdemeanor and a Federal offense. That invisible but inexorable boundary separates, not only two of our great states, but the traveler's prospects, if he is healthy and unwary, of spending, on the one hand, from five minutes to an hour in court with a fine of ten dollars, or languishing from twenty to thirty-five years within the walls and dungeons of a Federal prison, in the company of trigger-men and bankers, and what is worse, the wardens and the guards, who are there, in a manner of speaking, from choice and, therefore, are more depraved.

According to Homer's calculations, the hand-car if pumped assiduously, would not reach the point which held such dire legal significance for two hours, and most likely three. So a good meal of trout, with a suckling bear cub and some wild pears, neatly roasted in husks of wild maize, was enjoyed by all, before, individually and separately, they concealed themselves in the underbrush to wait.

The first sign of the approach of the hand-car was a knowing glance between Trout-tail III and Rain-No-More, whose sense of hearing was phenomenal. Homer laid his ear to the rail, confirmed their findings with a nod, and unslung his camera, making careful adjustments on account of the clear mountain light.

Homer disposed his forces and witnesses as follows:

On the north side of the tracks, from which the view was excellent and the greensward restful, Miriam lay prone, and, close by her side, Dr. Hyacinthe Toudoux. They were speaking of France, of Paris the unforgettable, of the days when song and laughter, when liberty, equality and fraternity, not to mention wine, cuisine, companionship, art, science and abundance were offered, on equal terms, to those who hungered for them and knew the matchless hospitality of France. Then their thoughts strayed back to America.

"What, exactly, is this Mann Act?" asked Hyacinthe Toudoux, once they had reached the point in their reminiscences which caused both, in a surge of emotion, to turn away to hide their tears. "I have listened. My English is much better than it was. Still, I fail to understand. If I have heard correctly, a man and woman, having in mind a most salutary, and necessarily cooperative act, without which man would have to live by bread alone, are liable to years of penal servitude . . ."

"The man, not the woman," said Miriam. "She only gets six months or so. The law does not take into account the possibility that a woman might lure a man across a state line for immoral purposes."

Dr. Hyacinthe Toudoux looked around at the snow-clad mountains, the woods and stream, the dome of sky, and sighed with admiration. "I had not realized," he said, "that Americans were capable of such chivalry. The Mann Act. That is truly gallant and splendid."

And he drew from his pocket the notebook in which were jotted memoranda that one day he hoped to assemble and edit into a definitive work on American life, for the benefit of his untraveled countrymen.

17
Trouble Rides a Hand-Car

ON THE SOUTH SIDE OF THE TRACKS, by the burbling stream, was stretched Homer with his camera. Two hundred yards over the Utah line, perfectly camouflaged by the natural surroundings, Trout-tail III and Rain-No-More lurked in ambush. The conductor, who seemed increasingly nervous, was sitting cross-legged in a sheltered spot, thumbing the regulations in order to ascertain his authority in connection with unauthorized use of inter-state tracks.

"You will be able to arrest Dante in Utah, on charge of misuse of railroad property, after the Indians waylay him," Homer said. "Then you can bring him back into Wyoming, where Heber, a deputy of his brother Moroni, can apprehend him for larceny—that is, theft of the hand-car belonging to the Latter Day Cement Company. There, Heber can hold Frank, or François, long enough for me to obtain official authority, from Washington to act for the F.B.I. and make formal charges against Dante for violating the Mann White Slave Act."

"I shall shoot him, under the unwritten law of the West, if he has ruined those young girls," said Miriam.

"Shucks, miss. I keep a'tellin' you they don't amount to much. This whole business is getting screwier and screwier, if you ask me. First, a mousy little palooka bumps his head, or has it bumped for him. No one seems to know or care how or why, except maybe Mr. Evans. Then a dude from Boston gets shot through the head, and it ain't no use. He just naturally won't die. So we're told the cases are linked, and start out. Then what do we do? Start shaggin' a foreign poontang hound and a couple of young hussies all over the prairies and mountains, figuring out a dozen ways to pinch the poor guy and keep him locked up till he dies. What bothers me is poor Miss Ferdinanda. She can't get a divorce, if that scarlet man o' hers goes to the Federal pen. So how can she marry the cloth-headed clunk she dotes on?"

"I hadn't thought of that," said Miriam, "I ought to plug him, to be sure. If she's a widow . . ."

"Please," Homer said. "In just a little while, the whole pattern will be clear as day, and everyone on the side of the angels will be quite satisfied."

"I think," signaled Rain-No-More, who on account of his phenomenal hearing had been able to follow the discussion, "that the two young white squaws from the old Ute hunting grounds should be given a chance to inspect both Bryn Mawr and Goucher before making their decision to attend Vassar. Also Wellesley, if I remember correctly, offers unparalleled opportunities for Western young women on account of Babson's Institute near by in Wellesley Hills."

Having completed his signaling, Rain-No-More dropped quickly to the ground, and, taking their cue from the Chief, the others of the scattered party concealed themselves also. The hand-car was approaching, over the divide.

The two Indians, to whom ambushing was second nature, although this was the first time they had applied that ancient technique to hand-cars, had taken their position on a stiff upgrade, where the vehicle would of necessity be moving slowly.

When Miriam caught sight of the oncoming hand-car, her grip on her automatic tightened and there was a dangerous glint in her eye. But she controlled herself and waited, prompted by a glance from Homer, who already had trained his camera on the tracks and started his series of shots which, including as they would, the state boundary marker, would leave no doubt in the minds of good jurors and true that Frank or François had gone offside.

It was impressive to Miriam and to Dr. Hyacinthe Toudoux to observe that the conductor was showing signs of extreme perplexity and agitation. He seemed to be suffering pangs of apprehension, and the charitable Frenchman at once concluded that the apparent injustice of what Evans was planning had so depressed the railroad man that he could no longer conceal his chagrin. If the truth be known, in spite of his long acquaintance with Homer Evans and his confidence in his judgment, Dr. Toudoux was having doubts on his own account. His French logic made it hard for him to accept that a little bout of *amour* in Wyoming was so much graver than a similar one in Utah, all other things being equal. Also that if three persons, two female, most unmistakably, and one male, however questionably, were straining all their muscles propelling a hand-car, the lone male should be adjudged guilty of *transporting* his companions and should languish a lifetime in jail.

The hand-car was so close now that its nearest occupants could be seen distinctly, in more detail than the girls suspected. Along with home and family they had left behind the red flannel underwear prescribed by the sagacious Brigham to protect Mormon girls from certain accidents, which, because of the scantier fashions of today, threaten to become chronically epidemic.

For the first time that morning, Dr. Hyacinthe Toudoux began to enjoy himself thoroughly, and tried to think of ways and means whereby such comely girls might be induced to serve the Fighting French.

Each member of the party, and particularly the harassed conductor Rider gave a gasp as the hand-car slid over the deadly invisible line. As it started up the steep grade, barely making headway, Frank or François de la Cirage Dantan actually pushed on the bar, which formerly he had been merely holding, unaccustomed as he was to doing his share. It was impossible, even for Homer, to guess whether or not Miriam's worst fears had been realized

When out on the track stepped two Blackfeet braves, one in full paint and feathers, the other in a Rogers Peet creation which he had used while riding to the hounds, Frank Dante, in astonishment, began to bellow and reach for the sky.

"So help me, boys, I'm clean," he said.

The girls, both of whom were reaching far down, and all-unwittingly demonstrating to the redmen how prudent Brigham had been in prescribing long undies, straightened up and turned around. Miriam embraced them hastily; then turned her attention to Frank. In less time than it takes to tell, her automatic was pointing straight at what he could least afford to lose.

"What gives, Miss Leonard? Have you all one crazy?" Dante asked, his olive complexion showing a tinge of gray or green.

"Are you safe?" asked Miriam of the astonished Reeda and Smoota, who had, not exactly visions, but their tactile equivalents, of being paddled by their father back in Blanc Mange.

"Let us go," they wailed.

"What's the big idea?" demanded Frank Dante, as Homer, Dr. Toudoux and the conductor advanced along the track from the Wyoming side.

"You pinched the hand-car, and left me flat," said the conductor.

"Hell. I'll pay for it, double. Besides, that was in another state. Send the bill to my wife."

"I've got to arrest you, Frank, for misusing railroad property," Rider said, his face a picture of woe.

"Who says so?" demanded François, shifting uneasily and glancing at the inexorable barrel of Miriam's gun. There was no escape. Wherever he shifted, the barrel shifted, too.

"Mr. Evans says so," the conductor said, apologetically. "So help me, Frank, it wasn't my idea."

Frank glared at Homer, who remained calm and impassive.

"I'll get you for this, you smart aleck," Dante said. Then he turned on the conductor: "And you, too. Don't forget that!"

The gentle prodding of Frank by Trout-tail III with a sharpened rat-tail file soon eased the enraged actor back over the Wyoming line, where Heber stepped up, and showed his badge.

"I hereby arrest you, in the name of the State of Wyoming, Buckskin County, on charges of larceny of one four-passenger hand-car in operating condition from the premises of the Latter Day Cement Company situated in the township of Blanc Mange," was the substance of Heber's stern greeting.

"My wife will bail me out, and pay all the expenses," Frank said. "She wouldn't want this scandal to get out in Boston, now would she, Mr. Evans?"

"In Boston," Homer said unruffled, "a Cushing, Ledge or even a Cabot can do no wrong. As for you, I suspect very strongly that you will never see Boston again."

Meanwhile, at a discreet distance, Miriam was questioning the two husky girls. Her quick relief and the girls' rueful countenances seemed to indicate that Reeda and Smoota were still undefiled.

18
Census Totals Remain Unchanged

IT IS ALWAYS REFRESHING when a long-standing partnership or association between two men holds up in times of stress. In this case, once the two culprits had got over their initial suspicion that one had squealed, they shook hands, cursing Homer, but admiring his prowess just the same.

Of the last breakfast of the condemned men in Blanc Mange there is little to say. The local hens were not laying and, as all Westerners know, prime beef is always shipped east. However, the last hours of the doomed pair had certain alleviations unforeseen by Law and which, had Miriam got wind of them, might have shortened beyond official edict the lives of the prisoners.

The fact is that Reeda and Smoota, being kind-hearted as well as curious and adventurous girls, took pity on the men they formerly had spurned, effected an entrance to their respective death cells, and there, forgetful of the awful dawn approaching, learned many things their youthful minds had been yearning to know. They later decided to complete their education at Radcliffe, because of its proximity to the Charlestown Navy Yard. There, as the saying goes, let us leave them.

As a reward for their tractable behavior while awaiting their executions, the two sinners were permitted to share the same lethal chamber. One must give the devil his due. They made a game attempt to drag in the chaplain with them when the latter suggested that, after a rollicking career of crime, they turn to religion at the finish, thereby setting the most lamentable example of spiritual duplicity to their fellow men.

Once the double arrest had been made, of course, the question of "*who*" no longer existed in connection with the Momblo murder. The question of "*why*" still was paramount and was only dispelled by Homer's masterful elucidation.

Our company was gathered in the Pratt back room, and included Lancaster Primway, his head still bandaged but decidedly unbowed. Before enumerating for the reader the other guests, the author takes pleasure in telling of results from the chance course of the assassin's bullet through the Primway's strict conscience, or the seat of it, as one might say. The lucky angle and level of that spot accomplished what is known to modern science as a frontal lobotomy, and left Primway a new man. The first indication of this personality change was that, when he first opened his eyes and saw, leaning over him, the moled and moustached Mrs. Nephi Allbrown, the convalescent Bostonian, chucking to the winds long generations of scruples and hesitations, made a feeble, though unmistakable, pass at her. The doctors, Hyacinthe Toudoux and Trout-tail III, however, assured Mrs. Allbrown and the delighted Ferdinanda that this reaction was normal, in lobotomy recoveries, and might recur, without causing undue alarm, throughout ensuing years and even decades, either steadily or periodically. For the first time in her long ordeal, Ferdinanda wept for joy. What happened as soon as she was left alone with the patient is none of our affair. Suffice to say that a few weeks later, after Primway had shocked all Boston by distributing keys to Louisburg Square's exclusive private park to all bums on the Common, smuggling Sinatra into a local meeting of the Junior League, and selling out the venerable firm of Primway and Leeks to an obscene tattoo concern, the long-enamored couple were made one, officially, and stayed that way virtually forever afterwards.

Primway had thrown all care and worry to the winds. He ate heartily, loved lustily, drank frequently, and swore that he would never do a tap of work again.

Needless to say, Ferdinanda, from whom bliss had so long been withheld, proved a lusty partner in a life of ease and frolic, which, all reformers to the contrary, is man's loftiest ideal.

We have strayed far from Blanc Mange, Wyoming, where our company had assembled to hear Homer's summing up. Among those present were: Miriam Leonard, who wore a fetching ensemble of chartreuse and French blue; Mr. and Mrs. Heber T. Allbrown; Mr. and Mrs. and the Misses Nephi X. Allbrown; François de la Cirage Dantan, or Frank Dante, as handsome and menacing as ever; Conductor Thomas Q. Rider; Chief Rain-No-More of the Blackfeet; Trout-tail III, chief medicine man of the same worthy tribe; Dr. Hyacinthe Toudoux, whose name is known and revered in halls of science the world over, and justly; Mrs. François de la Cirage Dantan, who was Ferdinanda Cushing and soon was to be Mrs. Lancaster Primway (although, in a manner of speaking, not quite soon enough, perhaps, from certain strict points of view).

Also there were in attendance Moses Lemmings; Orson, or Highpockets, Allbrown; Tarley G. Pratt, proprietor of the drug store, who was doing a land-office business in refreshments; and the remains, well-iced, of both victims, Isaac Momblo and the freckled Wen Shan.

"I wish to make a rather complete record of this investigation," Homer began, "because for so long the case resisted all my efforts toward solution. It is the first instance, I think, in the annals of criminology when the corpse itself has proved to be what is technically known as the "red herring.""

"I strove and delved for the motive which prompted the criminal, or criminals, to murder as inoffensive and humble a man as Mr. Momblo. And all the time, ladies and gentlemen, the reason was as plain as day. Mr. Momblo was killed because the law provides that, when a death occurs aboard an interstate train, said train shall be brought to a stop and the nearest coroner shall be summoned forthwith. Our adversary, therefore, wanted, first of all, to delay the Streamliner. Why?"

Homer looked around the circle, inviting an answer. Since none was forthcoming, he continued:

"Someone on the train must have been carrying information dangerous to the life or the schemes of the man who planned and perpetrated this dastardly crime.

"I had observed that Lancaster Primway, who occupied Bedroom A in the Car Masomenus in which we all were riding, was gravely worried and unnaturally anxious to reach his destination. So eager, in fact, that he appropriated a horse which still is at large, rode over to the Santa Fe, and made all haste to get to Boston.

"That, friends, was a slender clue, but led unerringly to my logical conclusions. I next was informed that Mr. Primway's former fiancée, Miss Cushing, was to be married to Monsieur de la Cirage Dantan and that many millions of dollars were involved. Wherever there are millions at stake, men will take long chances. Dantan or Dante, whose real name, by the way, is Frank the Fumbler, a member of the formerly notorious Spellman gang, met Miss Cushing in Hollywood at a time when she was pardonably annoyed with Primway. The latter, before his accident, had scruples against marrying a rich girl, however attractive, unless he could support her."

Primway blushed beneath his bandages and smiled. "Did I talk such rot as that?"

When Homer nodded good-naturedly and Ferdinanda forgivingly squeezed his hand, Primway shook his renovated head ruefully.

Homer then turned to François. "Had this man been content to stalk a fortune in a fair and open way, he might have got, at least, a handsome settlement. I was troubled that a girl as superb as Miss Cushing would wed such a heel, until I learned from her own lips that the marriage was a simple expedient on her part to gain access to Mr. Primway. As an actor's wife, she would be admitted to the M-G-M lot where Primway, according to his code, had taken refuge from temptation."

"I must have been an ass," Primway said, and sighed incredulously.

"For me to ascertain," Homer said, "that Mr. Dante was not of the French nobility, in fact, not French at all, but born in America, was child's play."

"But, Homer," Miriam said, "he was in Boston all the time we were on the train."

"Of course. He had a confederate, a member of the same old mob. I didn't worry about the confederate's identity, since it was evident that I could pick him up at will as soon as the motive came to light. There is only one man who could have killed Momblo and also shot at Primway with intent to kill."

"You're too smart for your breeches," the conductor said. "I wish I'd killed you instead of that sawed-off little drip—whatever his name was."

"I shall watch through the window when you're gassed," said Miriam, her eyes flashing angrily again.

"Help yourself," the conductor said, and spat into the coalhod— very nearly.

"May I watch, too?" Moses Lemmings asked. "He tried to pin the guilt on me."

"And very crudely," Evans said.

Heber T. Allbrown shifted uneasily in his chair and leaned forward. "He never played with Easter eggs when he was a kid," the coroner said. "If he had, he'd a known that the movin' egg, or object, always dents the one that's standin' still. The mark on that upper berth was hardly visible at all, while this poor little maverick's coco was busted clear through to his brain. I seen right away that the deceased must a been held under the berth while the murderer slammed it down and killed him."

"I told the sap to kill Primway himself," said Dante or Dantan. "If he'd followed instructions . . ."

"I used my head," said the conductor, defensively. "I said to myself, 'If I kill a man who's in the Blue Book, there'll be hell to pay. Whereas, on the other hand, if I kill some inconsequential little buzzard' . . . Ouch! Aaie!"

The outraged yelps of Rider had coincided with the sharp report of Miriam's automatic. She had neatly barked both his shins.

Homer looked at Miriam and smiled. "Please relax, my dear," he said. She sighed and promised.

"My slant was this," said the conductor, once the pain had sub-sided enough to permit him to continue. "So this Primway gets to Boston two days late. Frank can collect, just the same, and split with me. I was trying to save us both a lot of trouble."

"You didn't count on having Homer Evans as a passenger," said Miriam.

"That was where the breaks went against us," the conductor said.

"I spotted you the first day," Homer said. "You stuck out as the culprit from the start, and all along the way. Who else knew about the law concerning deaths on trains? Who, having vacationed out-side of Blanc Mange, knew the lay of the land, and how difficult it would be to get a coroner to the tracks? Who overheard Primway ask Moses to show him the way to the telegraph office, and there-fore was sure that Momblo, who had rung for the porter, was in his bedroom alone and unsuspecting and helpless and frail? Who knew how to unscrew the ratchet chains of the upper berth and screw them on again?"

"Well, who's goin' to get gassed?" the conductor retorted.

"I am," said Frank Dante, or Dantan.

"That fink always did think first about himself," the conductor said. "Too much ego. . . . Ah, well."

Homer reached for his drink and was about to sit down, when Miriam restrained him.

"You haven't said a word about Wen Shan," she said. "After all, poor Wen's as dead as these thugs are goin' to be next Thursday."

Homer's hearty laugh rang out. He took from the near-by table a porter's leather pouch, containing the application slips for res-ervations signed by the various passengers.

"It was from this list that the passenger list was typed," Homer said. "If you care to examine this signature through a reading glass, you will see that the signer, who was drunk when he took his pen in hand, wrote not Wen Shan, but Wm. Shand. The Wm. can easily be mistaken for Wen, and the Oriental flavor of the syllable 'Wen' would cause almost any typist to overlook the final 'd' which is scant and quite illegible in 'Shand.' As I told you, I could find no

Oriental tongue or dialect in which a name like Wen Shan occurred. When Moses brought me these signatures today, from the Los Angeles station master, I quickly saw what had happened. The late Mr. Shand, very drunk, arrived on the train too late for his baggage to be hoisted aboard, stayed in the Nugget until it closed, slept in the toilet, which is practically never used in a compartment car, and started drinking again the moment he awoke outside Salt Lake or Ogden. When a drunken man sees a horse, he thinks it would be fun to ride. That's all . . ."

"I'd like to ask," said Ferdinanda, "what it was that prompted this Lochinvar" (she squeezed Primway's hand again) "to send me a telegram reading 'May your voyage be packed with thrills'?"

Primway just then, enjoying his new-found freedom, was giving the Mormon girls an appreciative once-over; so Homer answered for him.

"Mr. Primway had always made it a practice not to overtax his brain. He wanted to let you know he was en route and ready to lay down his principles to save you from Dante, but instead of composing the telegram himself he selected from the Western Union handbook Message No. 292. This reads: 'Wait. Must see you before the operation.' Unluckily he shifted the numbers in his mind, an accident that happened to him frequently on the football field when signals were called, and wrote on the blank No. 929. No. 929 is in the Bon Voyage section near the end of the book and reads: 'May your voyage be packed with thrills.' Is that clear?"

"I'll do the thinking for us both, my dear," she said to Primway, who readily agreed.

"What about my towel?" he asked, feeling it incumbent on him to take some active interest in the proceedings.

"That is one little clue that gave the conductor away," Homer said. "In killing Momblo he got a small stain of blood on his hands. To wipe this off, he used one of the company towels from Momblo's compartment. This he threw away. Then, in order not to call attention to his act by leaving the fatal bedroom one towel shy, a towel which would not be found when the room was cased, he substituted for the missing towel one from Primway's bedroom next door."

Heber T. Allbrown scratched his head. "Why in tarnation," he asked, "didn't this Boston gent tell Miss Ferdinanda he was ready to do the wrong thing by her, when he finally got back to Massachusetts?"

"Mr. Primway did not believe in divorce," Homer said.

Primway blinked merrily. "Don't rub it in," he said. "I believe in practically everything, now the old onion's repaired. Let's let bygones be bygones."

Homer, Ferdinanda and Miriam nodded assurance and smiled, and the company dispersed.

MURDER ON THE LEFT BANK

Extra-Sensory Phenomena

"MY FATHER EATS FAST and heartily, my mother stays a long while at table. I take after both of them."

It was Megan Mallory speaking. The senior steward who waited on the Mallory table in the dining salon of the *Ile de France* understood almost nothing Megan said. But it was better, she had found, for her to use her kind of American when talking with a Frenchman, and let him have his native tongue. On the few occasions when she had tried her finishing-school French and one of the obliging attendants on the liner had countered with what he imagined to be English, the difficulties of communication had been compounded. Megan knew that her waiter was anxious to please her because she was young and beautiful, and her father was rich, from the French point of view. Also because her mother got her own way, anywhere, and in any language. Mrs. Mallory's school French was no better and no worse than Megan's, but Mrs. Mallory put behind it the force of her will and personality and the recipient had to understand, or else.

That same evening, when Mrs. Mallory had insisted that the red wine (a Chateau Lafitte, '28) be served ice cold in a champagne bucket, Megan had noticed that a lovely and distinguished-looking Frenchwoman about her mother's age had, very politely and surreptitiously switched off the hearing apparatus she wore in her ear.

Luke Mallory, Megan's father, who had a thriving wholesale beef and lamb business in Faneuil Hall, Boston, would not drink red wine, or still wine of any kind, no matter what anybody ordered or said, in any language. He either drank beer or champagne.

When Megan looked at her father, whom she admired wholeheartedly, she could not find a single point of resemblance that would stamp her as his daughter. And if she regarded her mother, so firmly established in the ways of Cape Ann's first families, she felt that had they not lived together practically all of her life, they would have had almost nothing in common. Megan had no illusions about being tough or forceful. She had no business head, no instinct for propriety; in fact, she was unformed.

Primarily, that evening aboard ship, she was excited and sad. She did not show too much of her excitement, for fear of seeming younger than she was, at seventeen. Because of the grief that was smoldering in the warm heart of her father, she had to repress her own sorrow. Her mother, unlike either of them, had to meet tragedy as the stern and rockbound coast, or the reef of Norman's Woe, stands up against a Nor'east blizzard.

Early that winter—it was now spring, 1949—Lieut. Fred Mallory, Megan's only brother, had died, from a ruptured heart which had resulted from his efforts to enter, while the war was still in progress, a branch of the service, the Commandos, for which his physique was not adequate. Having been rejected for the work he had wanted to do, it took all his persuasiveness to keep him in the Army at all. His tasks had been important and exacting, and not a little mysterious to his parents, friends and associates, but they involved no physical risk or danger, as far as anyone knew. At the time of his death, he had been attached to the European Recovery Commission, in some capacity that was military, in that he was still under the direction of the War Department, and seemed civilian in other respects. His father, long ago out of patience with post-war dilly-dallying, had wanted Fred to resign his commission and come home. His mother had assumed, in her positive way, that her son knew what he was about. Fred had written his mother every week, his father once a month, and Megan when he had the impulse. He was eleven years older than Megan, but one of the lovable things about him, from her point of view, was that he had never treated her as anything but an equal, in matters of years of experience. It was an attitude that had obtained between them ever since Megan could remember.

Fred Mallory's death had blighted the family plans as a stroke of lightning lops off the top of a tree, leaving a trunk without branches or leaves. His father had wanted him to go with him into the meat business and make some real money while individual enterprise still was valid in connection with the necessities of life. His mother had expected him to marry a Rockport girl, one of three or four who were eminently suitable. Megan, having seen little of him since Pearl Harbor, had wanted to get acquainted with him again. She had the strongest kind of feeling that they would get on, and help each other. They had money and, she thought, a relish for life. She had even believed Fred had health enough for his moderate purposes and only his sudden death had revealed his heart condition to her.

Even taking into account the relationship that had existed between her brother and herself, Megan was astounded when she had received in March a letter from Lieut. Robert Kitchel, "Bob," her brother's closest army friend. It came out of a dull leaden sky. There was nothing in the text to indicate that Bob Kitchel realized that Megan was a "kid" of seventeen. Fred must have carried his habit of referring to Megan as a contemporary into his away-from-home existence. And the writer assumed, erroneously, as far as Megan knew then, that she was going to Paris. The letter read:

> Dear Miss Mallory,
> You will pardon my writing, but Fred and I were pretty close, all through our part of the war and after, up until the end. His death hit me as hard as anyone, making allowances for what members of a family feel, if they are fond of someone who dies.
>
> Now a man, from hearing his best friend talk about folks he never has seen, gets an idea of people like you and your father and mother. I don't mean that Fred loved one of you more or less than another,

but it seems to me, in a case like this, he would have preferred me to write you, and not take the chance of agitating either one of his parents, until I had a clearer understanding of things. There may be nothing to my feelings that anything is wrong.

I can't get leave to visit the States. So I was glad when I heard you were coming. In fact, I was on the point of writing and asking you to come, only I could not take that chance, as your trip might have been for nothing.

If I were you, I would not say anything about this letter to anybody, before you get here and we've had a talk. I never know what I can do, in this man's army, but unless something comes up, I'll meet your boat at Le Havre. If not, I'll get in touch with you at your hotel as soon as possible after you get to Paris.

Your brother's friend,

(signed) Bob.

Sitting at the dinner table, in the first-class salon of the *Ile de France*, twelve hours out of Le Havre, having had about six *hors d'oeuvre*, soup, fish, duck, a salad, cheese and fruit, Megan, as she started on her dessert, reviewed in her mind her sensations of amazement on getting Kitchel's letter.

At first she had believed it was some kind of a test, a most severe one, intended for a mature woman, a confidante of her dead brother, a person of discretion and character. Her mother had been in the room when the letter had been brought to her, and had been politely aware that she had received mail and was reading it. The expected procedure would have been to make some comment, then describe the letter or show it to her mother. She had not been able to think of a plausible word to say, and certainly she could not show any part of it, or tell from whom it came. Lieut. Robert Kitchel had some time before written letters, almost alike, to her father and mother, which might have been copied or paraphrased from a book containing model letters to use on various occasions. Her mother

had remarked, not unkindly, that Fred had taken up with a lieutenant who must be very nice, but was not over-articulate. Perhaps, her mother had said, Lieutenant Kitchel expressed himself
more fluently in French, and therefore had been detailed, with
Fred, a fair linguist, as Harvard men went, for liaison service with
the Marshall Plan officials.

Megan relived in her thoughts, as she ate the magnificent ice,
the consternation she had felt while reading that letter. The experience had seemed to her then, and still did, as the only extraordinary thing that had occurred in her life, up to that time. Since then,
almost nothing had progressed according to Hoyle.

For no one had told her, or even hinted, up to the day she had
received Lieut. Kitchel's letter, that she was going abroad two
months later, for the first time in her life, to see scenes and places
Fred had described, her traveled classmates had talked about, and
re-establish ties with the Old World that was in such a mess and
whose history, traditions, manners, customs, art, music and literature had contributed such a large share to what was loosely
called her "education."

Lieut. Kitchel, in being matter-of-fact, had frightened her more
than he would have if the letter had conveyed a menace or a strain.
What had he meant? How had he got an idea that she was going to
Paris? He had specifically suggested that she say nothing to anyone, meaning her parents, about his letter. He had stated that
"there might be nothing to his feeling that anything was wrong."

The whole thing was a mistake. Lieut. Kitchel, perhaps, had
been injured in the head, or shocked so badly by battle conditions
that he stayed drunk most of the time. Fred, perhaps, had be-
friended him to help him. Fred was not as forceful as their mother,
but he had a similar kind of calm, which might have been restful
to a case of battle fatigue.

Megan tried to let the excitement produced by the letter sub-
side. She had answered it, after weighing the pros and cons. She
had been noncommittal, but truthful. In case she was in Paris
any time soon, she had written, she would get in touch with the
lieutenant. That was all she had written. She had concealed her

surprise and committed herself to nothing. She had tried to treat the matter as lightly as possible. Until, six weeks later, her father with a twinkle in his Irish eyes said he had a surprise for her, that he had booked passage for France.

Then she had nearly fallen out of her chair.

"This is all your father's idea," her mother had said. There could be no question of a joke, when Mrs. Mallory joined in.

Megan's first words astonished her parents a little, but they noticed nothing very strange.

"Where shall we land? At which port, I mean? Le Havre?" she had asked.

"Why, yes," her father had said.

"And who have you written to expect us . . . over there?" she went on. Her father turned away. Her mother looked at her severely.

"There's no one over there to write," Mrs. Mallory had said. "We wouldn't want to trouble the copy-book Lieut. Kitchel, and Captain Havemeyer, who was Fred's commanding officer, is out of the Army long ago, I understand."

"Then nobody knows we're coming?" Megan had asked, with a tremor inside.

"Not a soul," her father said. "Just the bloke at the French Line office on Boylston Street. I only got the tickets yesterday. Some other folks, who had reserved a suite, gave up the reservation."

From that moment, Megan had not thought of Lieut. Kitchel as a battle-fatigue casualty, but a man who might have been so close to death that he had developed psychic powers. Fred, she knew, had been interested in the study of psychic phenomena, as well as abnormal psychology, in his last years at Harvard. Miss Vincent, head mistress of the finishing school, had advised Megan and all the girls to steer clear of both of those subjects, if they wished to be acceptable in the best society. "My girls are seldom brilliant, but they do well, and wear well," Miss Vincent had said.

The nearer the *Ile de France* got to Le Havre, the more difficulty Megan had in hiding and controlling her emotions. No effort she could make would establish the conviction that she should not see Lieut. Kitchel. He might be the dumbest or the sharpest man in the world. He might be sage and cautious to the nth degree, or completely irresponsible. There was such a man. Fred had written of him, or rather, of his existence, and that he was a pal. And when had Fred had bores or fools as intimates?

Luke Mallory was smoking a vintage Havana perfecto, and sipping champagne, Cru Brut, '45. Edith Tarr Mallory was wondering whether she should stop Megan from eating so much. It seemed to do the girl no harm, but logic made it clear that so many thousands of calories must at least build up a tendency to corpulence, such as Mallory exhibited and even found a source of satisfaction. Megan was sure she would not sleep that night and wondered how long the dancing would continue, and if any young people would keep the vigil, to get the first glance of the shore lights of France.

The purser's assistant who, of all the crew of the liner, was slowest on the uptake, approached the Mallory table respectfully. Passing up Mr. Mallory and Mrs. Edith Tarr Mallory, who had straightened herself in a dignified way to receive the communication, the young man bowed to Megan and said:

"*Pardon, Mademoiselle* Mallory. *Quelqu'un veut vous parley au telephone.*"

"What's the son of a sea-cook sayin'?" demanded Mallory.

The assistant purser turned to Mallory and bowed. "Some gentleman will speak with Mademoiselle by telephone, monsieur," he said.

Mallory relaxed, and Mrs. Mallory sighed. "Probably some young man wants her to dance till all hours," she said.

Megan, after excusing herself, followed the purser's assistant. When, nearing the purser's office, she started for the "house" telephone connected with the liner's intercommunication system, her guide shook his head.

"It is from shore, your call, Mees Mallory," he said.

Her teeth began to chatter. "Which shore?"

"From Paris, mademoiselle," the young man said.

She followed, keeping her feet moving one ahead of the other, entered a booth, took down a receiver, and asked the operator:

"Is there a call for Miss Mallory?"

"One moment."

There was a succession of scraping, rasping noises, a few eerie dots and dashes in code, a whine of static, and then a voice, metallic, masculine.

"Miss Mallory? This is Lootenant Kitchel. Sorry I can't meet you tomorrow when the boat comes in. Things here are fouled up. Hear me?"

"Yes," she said.

"I can't hear you."

"Yes. Oh, yes," she said, as loudly as she could, which was barely audible.

"I'll ring you up and fix a rendezvoo, directly you get to the Prince de Galles."

"De Gaulle?" she repeated, stupefied. The hero of French resistance, she thought, was a general, not a prince, and she did not expect to "get to" him.

"So long. Nice to hear you."

Megan made a desperate little sound or two, unable to find words, most eager to preserve the connection.

The voice came over, worried in tone. "Are you oke? You don't sound so good. *Mal de mer?*"

"I'm all right," she said.

He understood, apparently, and hung up, with a "See you tomorrow night."

She could not tell her father, her mother, or a living soul. Or should she? She would not. Not yet, at any rate. There was no way understandable to her by means of which the psychic lieutenant could have known she was aboard the *Ile de France.* She would not sleep that night, or even sit down, or go where it was dark, the way she felt just then.

2

An Apparition, with Whiskers

ALL ALIGHT, THE *ILE DE FRANCE* moved steadily through darkness, presumably toward France, salons gay and animate, lower portholes awash, corridors and companionways dim. The last dinner of the voyage had been served and eaten; the final night was not to be like other nights at sea. Cherbourg would be sighted; then, at some eerie hour, the liner would nose behind the breakwater and inch up to the dock at Le Havre. Megan's dancing partner of that moment was a selectman of the town of Rockport, Mass., who had known her since she was a tot on the Cape Ann beaches. Selectman Parker had not crossed the Atlantic before.

Trunks and packing cases had been brought from the hold to the passageways and decks; cabin luggage was in heaps, in and outside of staterooms.

The young men were importunate enough that evening, but Megan danced a number of times with middle-aged men, because of what was stirring vaguely in her mind. Lieutenant Kitchel, who talked like a truck driver but who seemed to know everything two months before it was scheduled to happen, was expecting to meet a mature woman. The boys her own age—there were about twenty of them aboard, eight French, three assorted, and the rest Americans—seemed young and jejune. None of them, as far as she knew, had received prophetic mysterious letters, about which they could tell no one, or trans-oceanic telephone calls suggesting that they were to "get to" General or Prince de Gaulle.

"Where are you stopping, in Paree?" asked the Rockport selectman, Mr. Parker. "Your old man and I have promised ourselves
to see the meat markets together."

"Meat markets!" Megan repeated. "Mother has mentioned only
cathedrals, churches, museums, fairs, concerts, exhibitions and
historical monuments."

"Meat markets, Harry's Bar, and the Folies Bergère," Selectman Parker insisted drily. "And some of those secret gambling dens
around the Etoile."

"I want to meet Schiaparelli and Molyneux . . ." Megan began.

"That Molyneux murdered somebody years ago, didn't he? I'd
forgot he got away," the selectman said.

It is better not to try to indicate how Megan and Mr. Parker
pronounced the French words, but the distinguished Frenchwoman, catching a few syllables as they danced past her table
started switching off her ear phone, then changed her mind and
daintily removed it from her ear and dropped it into her handbag.

"I wonder if we sound to a Frenchman the way Charles Boyer
does to us?" Mr. Parker inquired.

"I think not," Megan said. "More like Victor McLaglen."

"You didn't mention where you're stopping in Paree," the
Selectman prompted.

Megan looked blank. "I don't know," she said. "Father doesn't
know, either. He fixed it up with the American Express in Boston so
that the American Express in Paris would make reservations, and let
us know on the boat train. Where are *you* stopping, Mr. Parker?"

"At the Prince of Wales . . . The frogs call it Ler Prance de
Gaulle," he said. "It was Thomas Cook who fixed it up for me,
around about Washington's birthday. Rooms are hard to get in
France, they tell me."

"You say the Prince de Gaulle is a hotel? And you're going to
stay there?" asked Megan.

"That's what I said," agreed Mr. Parker. "What's wrong with that?"

"Nothing," stammered Megan. Lieut. Kitchel, when he had
talked with her, must have been referring to the hotel, Prince de
Galles.

A bellboy in a red and gold-braid monkey suit approached her, obsequiously, with a tray on which was a form, and a French-style fountain pen.

"The purser says you forgot to fill in your Paris address on this declaration of entry," the bellboy said.

Flustered, Megan took the stylo, spread the form on the table and wrote, on the line the boy indicated: "Hotel Prance de Gaulle."

Some time later, Megan saw her mother coming, heading for her table.

"Whatever has got into you, darling?" her mother asked. "The purser just now handed back my declaration of entry, and your father's, and said there were discrepancies. You, it seems, gave as your Paris address an hotel—instead of the American Express. We don't know where we are stopping."

"I had a presentiment," Megan told her. "The American Express man on the train will tell us to go to the Prance de Gaulle."

A young man from Dartmouth came over and asked Megan to dance. She rose. Mr. Parker went into the bar. Megan's mother went into the Conversation Salon, where Mr. Mallory was waiting to take her where he could smoke another cigar. They decided the smoking salon, where the dancing was in progress, would be too noisy, and, if not drafty, would smell peculiar, what with French perfume, cognac, champagne, cigarette smoke, and the ship's orchestra trying to play "le Hot."

"Get everything fixed up all right, dear, about those papers?" asked Luke Mallory.

"Yes. But you'll visit no meat markets," Mrs. Mallory said.

"And you'll make no monkey business about that oral will of Fred's. What difference does it make? Let it alone. Let be. We'll take a look at where the lad was buried . . ."

Luke Mallory rose, averting his face.

"Let's go outside, where I can smoke," he said, and led the way to the promenade deck, where he leaned against the rail on the lee side. The night was cool; the sea was calm and phosphorescent.

"Luke," Mrs. Mallory said, "we've got to face this thing. Fred lived to be twenty-eight, and didn't have a bad time. He died—fairly quickly. The captain wrote he didn't suffer much. But I'm still alive, and I'm not a flighty or hysterical woman. . . ."

She controlled her voice with an effort. "Luke. Bawl if you like. I nursed that baby, and showed him how to walk, and one way to talk—the way folks do in Rockport. As a child he was careful. He didn't cut himself, or fall downstairs. Before he took a step, he thought about it, some. He did well in school, but not too well. I wouldn't have liked having a prodigy, and neither would you."

"He was sick before he died, wasn't he? Does a lad's mind work the same, sick or well?" Luke countered. "And what difference does it make, about the cottage?"

"Even if a man is delirious, he says and does things natural to him," Mrs. Mallory said. "Now you knew Fred while he was at Harvard. He had a good memory. He never did things twice if once was enough."

"He was a middleweight, and thought he should be a Commando," said Mr. Mallory, challengingly. "That was fine and logical, now wasn't it?"

"A few more cool heads in the Commandos wouldn't have done any harm," said Mrs. Mallory, tartly.

"The training he took strained his heart, as it was . . . Before they turned him down," Mallory said.

"His head wasn't strained. I've told you a hundred times, and, if necessary, I'll tell you a hundred more times. That deathbed will can't be explained. Fred had framed a will carefully, not a word too many or too few. Lawyer Gott had gone over it, and checked it. Fred was going to war. He hoped it wouldn't be a desk war."

Mr. Mallory broke in. "I'd sure like to know what in hell he was doing. Not so much while the war was on. That was four years ago, and more. But since then. Months with the Graves Registration Command. Now what sort of a job is that? And then the Marshall Plan?"

"Every time I talk about this, you try to change the subject," said Mrs. Mallory. "The will. Fred's will. That's what we're discussing. He had it typed, with copies, certified, and filed in your deposit box. Everything he had was to go to you, to be distributed as you saw fit. If you died, I was to be the executor."

"Who said you'd outlive me?" demanded Mallory. Then he softened. "Jesus knows I hope you do."

"It was always understood between all of us that whatever happened, Susie Lowe was to occupy the cottage at Loblolly Cove as long as she lived. But even that was written in Fred's will—the one he made when he had plenty of time. Then, on his deathbed, he dictated a will, in the presence of Captain Havemeyer, Lieutenant Kitchel, and other witnesses, including an army nurse. It was the same as the other word for word, until the last paragraph . . ."

"The lad was dyin'. He didn't even live to sign it," Mallory protested. He was heartily tired of the argument, if it was an argument. "I repeat. What difference does it make? He ended up the oral will sayin' 'To Susie Lowe, of Rockport, Mass., I give the small cottage.' You know damn well, and Fred knew, that Susie has no relatives or kin."

"That's the point," said Mrs. Mallory. "The way Fred and the lawyer fixed it, the first time, Susie would live in the cottage, as she is doing, until she died. Then it would still be Fred's, or belong to his heirs. What becomes of the cottage now, if Susie dies and nobody inherits it?"

"I don't know, and I don't care," said Luke. "Whoever it goes to, I'll buy it back—the town, the county, or the commonwealth, I mean."

"I intend to talk with someone who was there—when Fred made that last will, and died without signing it," Mrs. Mallory said.

"And while you're wasting your time like that, I'll be with Selectman Parker, in meat markets, or any place it suits me. And Megan is over here for a good time. Don't let me hear of you dragging her around anywhere, to reconstruct her brother's death scene. You run things in this family most of the time, Edith, and you do it well. But on that point, I'd like to have my way. Not a word to Megan about Fred, his death, or his will," said Mallory.

"That suits me," Mrs. Mallory said. "I'll make my own arrangements. She's old enough to find her way around, and she ought to improve her French. As for you, you can carouse with Selectman Parker. A fling will do you good, I suppose, after years and years with me."

Mallory looked at his wife closely. He had long ago ceased to be surprised by her flashes of intelligence, breeding and liberal-mindedness. But he was not deceived. She was intending to find out everything she could about Fred's deathbed oral will, in order to prove her point, or set her mind at rest about the matter. The small white cottage, a gem of the informal designs of early ship carpenters, which had stood two hundred and fifty years on the shore of Cape Ann, was worth in cash about two thousand dollars, land and all. The land was a rock ledge, with wild rose bushes, bay-berries, huckleberries, moss in the crevices, and small crabs, shrimps and tiny fishes in the tide pools, redolent of seaweed. Its sentimental value was incalculable to a daughter of the Tarrs.

One thing was clear. Edith intended that the Mallorys, for a while at least in Paris, should go their separate ways, each follow-ing his or her own bent. That would be swell for Megan, Mallory thought, and even better for himself. Would it be so jolly for Edith? She did not want to inspect meat shops, or get Schiaparelli's auto-graph on a girdle. What did Edith want? To prove that her feeling about Fred and the wills had not been silly or far-fetched. Edith could stand making errors of judgment, when decisions were close. It was logic itself she defended, she and her ancestors—and so had Fred. Logic could not fail, or their structures of beliefs and values tumbled down.

Mallory wondered if he should protest, or try to dissuade Edith. No. Let her have her head, and find in France what she most needed, he decided.

Soon after midnight, the ship's orchestra knocked off, to give the crew a chance to soap the decks and ladders, so that roust-abouts lugging baggage helter-skelter would have the maximum chance of breaking the trunks and their own necks. The hazards also were multiplied for the restless passengers. Already one woman had fractured an arm and a tall plump handsome Argentine gentleman had suffered a fit of hysterics, so that the ship's doctor, about five feet tall, had had to stand up on a chair to administer a calming hypodermic.

There followed hours of rushing darkness, without moon, and with a stiff breeze. The first lighthouses flashed dots and dashes, revolving. The horizon thickened. Megan had plenty of company for the vigil. About twenty young men, several older ones, and almost as many young women, and older ones. Some were speaking American, some French. Megan heard little that was said. Tomorrow the test would come. If the American Express man on the boat train sent them to the Hotel Continental, the Grand Hotel, the Ritz—and not to the Prance de Gaulle, she would lose her awe of Lieutenant Kitchel, or "Bob."

The first glimpse of the breakwater thrilled Megan, so did the lights of the port, the dawn, and the sight of Le Havre. She bore good-naturedly the incredible crowding, bustle and confusion incident to disembarking. She located the family seats in the first-class boat train. Their hand baggage was stowed on the racks. The train began moving, and Megan found herself growing lighter, her breath shorter, her cheeks rosy, her limbs trembling deliciously. She was in France, on her way to Paris. Her understanding parents had let her know that they trusted her, had confidence in her good sense, and were not going to keep watch over her in the Queen of Cities. They had put her on her honor, which neither she nor anyone had questioned, and her mettle, which was a different matter. If only she could speak French!

The doorway of their compartment opened, as they were speeding through the Norman countryside—none more compact, lush or beautiful in spring. The conductor took a slanting look at their tickets. Megan breathed again.

The second visit was from the passport inspector, who stamped their passports without looking at anything except the page number, which he misread.

Megan let herself go, and wished fervently that the American Express man would come, and have it over. But the third time the compartment door opened, as they were pulling into Rouen, a polite chap from the Customs chalked all of their bags without searching them for cigarettes, hidden money, or live birds or animals.

"You're sure about the hotel arrangements—that there are some?" Mrs. Mallory asked her husband.

"What the hell!" said Mallory. "The weather's fine. We'll camp out."

The compartment door opened. A sad-eyed stoop-shouldered man, one of the second-generation messengers of the American Express in Paris, entered and, without as much as looking at Mr. Mallory, handed Mrs. Mallory a slip of paper.

"Your reservations, madame," he said.

Coolly but firmly Mrs. Mallory handed the slip to Mr. Mallory, as if rebuking the messenger for having ignored the head of the house.

Megan was holding her breath.

"Mmmm," said Mr. Mallory.

Impatiently Mrs. Mallory retrieved the slip of paper, read it at a glance, drew herself up in astonishment, and looked wide-eyed at Megan.

"Le Prance de Galles," she said.

"I knew it," said Megan, weakly. "I heard voices."

"Anything wrong?" asked the messenger, uneasily.

Mrs. Mallory looked at Megan again, doubtfully, quite visibly perturbed.

"That remains to be seen," she said, curtly. There had been a great aunt in the Tarr family, the seventh daughter of a seventh daughter, who had had fits when certain ships were going down at sea, a thousand miles away, before the days of radio. A sensible woman like Edith Tarr Mallory was not amused by the prospect of a daughter developing extra-sensory perceptions.

There was still an hour before the train was due to reach Paris, in time for lunch. Mr. Mallory, now that all the formalities he had dreaded had been passed through safely without any of his money being confiscated, and hotel rooms were assured, felt like having a bottle of champagne. He asked his women folk to join him in the buffet car. Mrs. Mallory accepted with alacrity. She wanted a drink. Megan asked leave to stay in the compartment. She said she wanted to see the landscape. Actually she was glad of a chance to think things over.

The hotel was likely to be reached in sixty minutes or so. Lieutenant Kitchel, if he was as good as his word, which had proven to date so extraordinarily good, would "ring her up and fix a rendezvous."

She thanked her lucky stars that her parents had decided that she should be more or less independent. There would be a phone in her room, and her mother would not ask too many questions about where she went, or with whom.

She turned, looked through the compartment doorway into the corridor, and jumped two inches off her seat. She could not say, afterward, whether she felt outraged, startled, frightened or indignant. What she saw was a pale young man of less than medium stature who looked superficially like Ulysses S. Grant. His clothes were old-fashioned and wrinkled, he had the Grant hair, whiskers, stance and badly chewed cigar.

The apparition was not rude, exactly. He looked at her with no more expression on his chalky face than that of an ape. She saw that he was only half the age of Grant when Richmond had been taken. He looked like a student and a recluse. On the other hand, he was making himself at home on the first-class boat train.

Megan knew that he saw her, but could not be sure to what extent her image was registering. The whiskered young *farceur* turned his head, glanced down the corridor, and waited for someone to approach. The American Express man appeared. The whiskered young man stopped him and addressed him in French. Megan could not understand a word, but she knew the French was smooth and effortless. The American Express man, of the second generation, replied quite as fluently, took a list from his pocket, and found on it a name, which he checked with a pencil before handing the list to Whiskers.

As if Megan had been a sack of turnips or an ivory object of art, the whiskered young man, beady eyes hard, looked at her.

The American Express man asked him a question, and seemed a little disgusted when Whiskers shook his head in the negative. The American Express man shrugged and went on, out of Megan's sight.

The whiskered young man was about to follow, but he halted and stared at Megan again, this time directly. She flushed with anger.

"Well?" she snapped.

"Think nothing of it, Miss Mallory," the whiskered youth said, in faultless American.

Before she could pull herself together, the spook General Grant ambled away, with the slouch and limp of a veteran cavalryman.

3
The Handwriting on the Wall

MRS. MALLORY FOUND the Hotel Prince de Galles to her liking, much more modern and comfortable than she had expected, in fact. Thirty years before, her classmates at Miss Vincent's school had spoken about "roughing it" in Paris *pensions*, where toilets were merely holes in the floor and water had to be fetched from a lower courtyard. The Prince de Galles, clean, dignified-looking and spacious, in the broad leafy avenue Georges V, gave her a feeling of security and remoteness. She realized how tired she was, induced Mr. Mallory to have his noon meal with Selectman Parker, and invited Megan to lunch with her in the *salon* of their suite. Mrs. Mallory was not offended when Megan hesitated awkwardly before accepting.

"You mustn't keep me company, out of courtesy or consideration for me," Mrs. Mallory said, to give her daughter an "out." "I have seldom felt more self-sufficient."

She was speaking the exact truth. Not only that. She expressed it rather accurately—a rare pair of gifts. Megan longed to be equally candid, but she could not. From the moment she had entered on the train the suburb of Paris (Clichy) the girl had been tingling with impatience to see more, to roam in Paris, to force her obstinate brain to yield its store of French her teachers had so conscientiously deposited there, to become one of those to whom Paris is a second home, to be a cosmopolitan while she was young enough to enjoy that distinction. Lieutenant Kitchel, or Bob, had said, "See you tomorrow night," but he had also written that he could never tell what he could do in "this man's army." If, for instance, Megan should go out, find a quaint little restaurant with wonderful food and perfect service, at amazingly low prices, and then stroll past the book booths along the Seine, she might miss a telephone call from the lieutenant. Worse than that, her mother might receive it. Already both of them had been called a few times by mistake. There were then at the Prince de Galles two Mahoneys, a Mallois, and an M. Llory. Among the "M's" almost anything might happen on the hotel telephone.

It was painfully apparent to Megan that she was hesitating too long before agreeing to lunch with her mother, and that her mother was disappointed. Mrs. Mallory would not be disappointed if her daughter did not care to lunch with her, but Megan was showing herself unequal to a social situation. Megan should have carried it off better, if she could not at once make up her mind.

In the end, Megan lunched with her mother, having a generous plate of the chef's *hors d'oeuvre*, guinea hen *consommé*, a *sole Normande*, a lamb chop (rare), tomatoes with mayonnaise, and a mirabelle tart. When she ordered coffee served with the tart the waiter raised his eyebrows, and later, the head waiter telephoned up from the dining room to confirm the eccentric request. She did not get the coffee with the tart. When she did get the coffee she was glad she had not spoiled the tart with it. It tasted like something out of Macbeth, Act I, Scene One, the first few sips; then she began to get used to it.

"That's the way with things over here, I suppose," her mother said. "The best France has to offer gives a disappointing impression at first glance, then grows on one."

Surprised that her mother had been observing her reactions so astutely, Megan nodded in assent.

"You'll be going out this afternoon, I suppose. As for me, I shall take a nap, have tea, and go see a movie. I noticed as we came along in the taxi that *The Snake Pit* is playing, somewhere back there near the Madeleine. I like Merle Oberon," Mrs. Mallory said.

Had not Megan listened carefully to her school mistress, she would have reminded her mother that Olivia de Havilland and not

Merle Oberon was the star of *The Snake Pit*. But Miss Vincent had said:

"Girls. Remember above all things that you are not put on earth to set other folks right. Never correct them, if they say that Lincoln crossed the Delaware, or Elijah escaped bloodhounds by crossing the ice. If the person in error knows better, his slip of the tongue is not important. If he does not, it is rude to call attention to his lack of factual information. Cold facts are seldom significant. They clutter the feminine personality. I, for instance, am ordinarily well informed, but I could not give you off-hand the square root of almost any number, or even hazard a guess as to what hour the local dial indicated when Our Saviour walked out of the tomb. A European author, just recently, in addressing a class of English schoolgirls, cautioned them not to disclose erudition even if they had it. If someone asks you what city is the capital of Rumania, and you reply 'Bucharest,' do not under any circumstances observe also that the capital of Bulgaria is Sofia. Men do not seek out lovely young women when they need encyclopedias."

So, instead of correcting her mother, who was not a man but was ideal to practice on, Megan said, pleasantly, "Ah, yes!"

Mrs. Mallory looked sharply at Megan.

"I'm tired, I guess," said Megan. "Instead of going out today, I think I'll sleep and read. I have *Les Miserables* in French, and also in English."

"I've never read it," Mrs. Mallory said. But her love of order, in the realm of mind and of matter, was ruffled. Megan did not seem tired, but on the alert. No weary girl could have put away the lunch Megan had just eaten, and still keep her eyes open unless an inner dynamo was functioning. Megan had been jumpy on shipboard, toward the last. She had been psychic on the train. Now, in full enjoyment of youth, independence and vigor, she was going to fritter away a Paris afternoon in a hotel room and read *Les Miserables* in two languages.

Mrs. Mallory sighed. At least she could predict what Mallory would do, and, in a sense, understand it. Luke and Selectman Parker would eat like a couple of pelicans and then get fried. Luke knew there was a bar at the Ritz, could say something that might sound like "Ritz" to a taxi man, and probably that was where her husband and his friend would land. She expected that, about nine P.M., he would telephone contritely and say that he was tied up and could not get back for dinner. About two in the morning, either Luke would bring Selectman Parker home safely, or Selectman Parker would bring Luke. She wished she could relax as simply and wholesomely as the men did, but, alas for her, her mind would not stop working. Alcohol was undoubtedly a poison, and gallons of it must eventually have an effect on a person's constitution. Thus far, if his beer and champagne in quantities had done Luke any harm, she had not noticed it.

Three days passed, and nothing went according to plan except the wonderful good time enjoyed by Luke Mallory and the Rockport selectman. Mrs. Mallory tried to go out, once or twice, and found she still was too tired. She dug out the stilted letter of condolence from Lieutenant Kitchel, sent a polite note to the address indicated on the envelope, hid the Kitchel letter again beneath the sachet bag in her second dresser drawer from the top, and settled back to resting again. She was grateful because it made sense for her to wait at the hotel until Kitchel replied. Unfortunately, a long-established force of mechanical habit persisted, and she had placed in a corner of the envelope an American five-cent stamp. On the afternoon of the third day, it came back unopened. Ashamed of her blunder, Mrs. Mallory said nothing to the others about it. She simply asked a maid who spoke a few words resembling faintly London English to buy her some French postage stamps, inquired how many were needed for a letter going to an address in Paris, and placed the requisite number of French stamps over the American one. Then the letter was re- mailed. Mrs. Mallory, being of the old school, thought it would be brusque and indelicate to resort to the telephone, against which a party of the second part has inadequate defense.

But while the first three days in Paris were bearable, even restful, to Mrs. Mallory, and to Luke as if he had suddenly found himself in heaven, ascending higher and higher, Megan lost patience and weight. During the first night she did not close her eyes, and on the two occasions when her telephone bell clicked, then failed to deliver, her heart had raced. The feeling of awe she formerly had felt toward Lieutenant Kitchel had changed to smoldering resentment. But was this another test? Like the original letter? Or had he spied on her, somehow, and found she was in her 'teens, not old enough to know whatever he had to disclose? From both her father and her mother she had inherited persistence, patient on the one side, passionate and obstinate on the other. She would fight it out if it took all summer, she resolved, eyes dry and stinging with mortification. Then she realized that she was paraphrasing Ulysses S. Grant.

"Think nothing of it, Miss Mallory," she could hear that pale baboon-faced type with whiskers say. Could that be a cryptic message? From Kitchel? And if so, did it mean that she should not expect anything to happen, or that she was not to be discouraged by an unavoidable delay? Lieutenant Kitchel's voice, as she had heard it over the trans-Atlantic phone, had sounded as if he meant what he said, and his letter had had a ring of authenticity and good intentions about it.

She had reread his letter many times in those three days, and knew his address by heart. The floor maid had coached her to pronounce it, "Hotel Paris Dinard, 29 rue Cassette, Paris 6me." To say that in a manner comprehensible to a Frenchman required a succession of sounds and syllables something like this: "Oh tell Par-*ree* Dee-*narr* Van nerf roo Caas-*set* Par-*ree sieze*-ee-em."

She dare not leave the hotel to call at that address for fear the lieutenant would telephone from elsewhere while she was out. By that time, everybody with an Irish name beginning with an "M" was getting Mallory calls, and the Mallorys got three or four false alarms per day. It had been those false alarms which had kept Megan in a kind of sickly trance. Just as she was ready to abandon the whole affair and see the city, a teaser of some sort would prick the bubble of her resignation. And after her misgivings had been aroused, and her curiosity inflamed to such an extent, she could not accept a mere tourist's experience, and like it.

On the second night, she had reasoned thus. The lieutenant was not alarmed, according to his letter. He had only a faint suspicion that "something might be wrong." No doubt he had tried to get in touch with her and been shunted over to a Maloney or M. Aloi or Marconi or Dudley Field Malone, in the spirit world. Or Kitchel might have written a note that had gone astray. More notes went astray than were properly delivered in French hotels, it seemed. But such a man would not be likely to telephone, especially two or three days late, after two o'clock in the morning. Megan felt fairly sure of that.

So that second night, Megan got on her coat at a few minutes after two A.M., rode down in the elevator, and was crossing the lobby on her way to the door, with the eyes of every night employee fixed on her with quizzical astonishment. She heard familiar voices at the doorway, and then they called her name. Her father and Selectman Parker, leaning against each other like a couple of wooden soldiers, were entering.

"You're getting in late, daughter," her father had said sternly.

She could not insist at that hour, and with no explanation ready, that she was going out, and that *he* was the one getting in. She smiled, hiding her disappointment, helped her father get Selectman Parker aloft, and when the latter was safely in his room, she called the elevator man to help her with her father. There was nothing disorderly or sloppy. Everyone was cheery and good-natured, and enjoyed helping one another.

But Megan, the moment when she was saying "good night" to her father, for the fourth and last time, heard the telephone ringing in her room. How she made her getaway and flew to the next room, by means of the corridor of the suite, she could not remember, except that she had been swift. At the door of her room she had had to pause to insert her key and unlock the door. She had to close it after her, and her heart felt leaden because the telephone bell had stopped ringing. She had heard it at least four times. One-two-three-four. But when she got the receiver to her ear, the line was dead.

Choking back tears of mortification, she reproached herself bitterly. That was her punishment for acting like a quitter. She should have remained at her post. She pulled herself together, and signaled the operator on the hotel switchboard. She tried American, and her finishing-school French. Whatever the night switchboard man at the Prince de Galles spoke was neither one nor the other. He was a Hungarian refugee, who had written several creditable plays in his own language and in German. His French, among Hungarians, was adequate.

Megan could make nothing of what he said except that he was eager, pathetically eager to assuage her, and avoid any possible complaint about his accent. She decided to go downstairs to talk with him. Face to face, communication was easier.

There had been a call for Miss Mallory, in Suite 16, Extension 16-B. The voice had belonged to a man who spoke French with an English or American accent. The intelligent Hungarian playwright could not say whether it sounded like that of a truck-driver lieutenant or a baboon-whiskered Zazou.

"Did whoever called ask if I were awake—or apologize for phoning late? Did he seem calm or upset?" Megan asked.

The Hungarian shrugged, most deeply regretful that he could be of such little use.

Megan asked him if he always listened in, when outsiders were calling.

"Naturally," he said, and smiled. "One must learn what one can."

At least she had been warned to be careful what she said, if she ever got a chance to say anything.

Before two o'clock the next morning, the third after her arrival, Megan had laid out a plan of action to relieve her monotonous confinement to her room without risking the loss of another telephone call. She had read in the "About People" feature of the Paris edition of the *New York Herald Tribune* that the cream of the Existentialists gathered in the Café de Flore, between midnight and breakfast time and visiting celebrities like Orson Welles, John Steinbeck, Thalia Soteras, Billy Wilder, Larry Adler, John Hyde and Chowderhead Margolis were frequently among those present. Megan was not a celebrity hound, but at least she could sit quietly and listen to them speaking American. She had no idea what an Existentialist was, but if the members of the cult sat up all night they must have instincts that would prove interesting to an American traveler who could not leave her room in the daytime.

She had a conference with the Hungarian night telephone operator and he promised to relay promptly to the Café de Flore any calls for Mallory, Malloy, Moloney or any such name. The Hungarian selected a taxi-driver he knew, a White Russian, to drive Megan to the Café de Flore.

The night was balmy. As the taxi proceeded down the avenue Georges V, half-circled around the statue in the *place* de l'Alma, turned into the Cours Albert Ier, skirted the great *place* de la Concorde, crossed the bridge to the austere Chamber of Deputies, and started northward along the Boulevard St. Germain, Megan felt the thrill of adventure. She was hungry and thirsty, and anxious to sit quietly at a sidewalk table among Existentialists and visiting notables, breathing the night air and enjoying the great outdoors of Paris. The Hungarian would do as he had agreed, she felt sure. He and the White Russian had spoken well and affectionately of each other, as gentlemen who had known better days.

When she got out of the taxi, handed the Russian a crisp new 1000-franc note, the smallest denomination she had, accepted a sheaf of change and urged him, in pantomime, to take the customary tip, the chauffeur, a former colonel in the army of the late Tsar, had bowed and brushed her hand with his lips. She was touched and knew better than to insist on the tip. When, a moment later, she took a look at the *terrasse* she was confronted by a spectacle for which she had been in no way prepared. Practically every young man was wearing a beard of some sort. There were several like General Grant, others like Sherman, Sheridan, Early, James F. Garfield, John Alexander Dowie, the late Congressman George Holden Tinkham, Chief Justice Hughes, James Russell Lowell, Hailie Selassie, George V, and all the twelve Apostles. If any style of face decoration prevailed, it was the orang-utan fringe without mustaches, leaving the pale face bare, the kind Pat and Mike used to wear on the vaudeville stage. She had not seen so many whiskers since her mother had dragged her to the Twentieth Century-Fox production called *Brigham Young*.

There were no vacant tables on the *terrasse* and no one out there was eating. Megan decided to go inside, have a light supper if she could manage to order one, and venture back into the forest of spinach when the sidewalk crowd had thinned a little.

She had been aware that many females had been interspersed among the bushwhackers out front, and that they were dressed in all styles, from the formal to the drab, some feminine, some haughty, some mannish, others like gun molls, a few like girls on parole from a House of the Good Shepherd. Inside the café she glanced around, without seeing Orson Welles, Steinbeck, Sylvia Beach or even Chowderhead Margolis. But a table was vacant between two others at each of which only one man was sitting. The nearest one had a beard, but it was well trimmed and suited him. He must have worn it long enough to get the knack of it. He had an intelligent forehead, strong sensitive hands, and eyes that looked at her kindly, with just the right degree of appreciation and no fatuity whatever. He was eating what appeared to be a slice of toast on which was a thin layer of ham and toasted cheese, and on the table before him stood a tall slim bottle of some kind of white wine that was chilled but not iced.

Megan had been out of patience with herself because she felt so *gauche* and self-conscious. If the man sensed her embarrassment or hesitation, he gave no sign. He eased out the center table so she could seat herself without worming her way in, and replaced it after she had sat down.

There was a mild stir outside on the *terrasse*, and the man on Megan's left, whom she had not looked at carefully, got up, turned his back quickly to the door, and shuffled toward the kitchen. She was so startled that she dropped her handbag, which opened, spilling most of the contents on the floor. The man who had made his exit so promptly was the apparition, with Whiskers, who had looked her over on the train between Rouen and Paris—the one who had called her by name and advised her to "think nothing of it."

"Oh, thank you," Megan said, to the other man whom she had trusted on sight. He had retrieved all her little belongings but one, and returned them to her handbag.

"There's a letter under the bench," he said. "If you'll permit me . . ."

She moved aside so that he could push out the table. He stooped with graceful ease, and returned to her the letter, from Lieutenant Kitchel, in such a way that it was certain he had not read the address on the envelope.

"You're very kind, sir," she said. No effort she could make, however, concealed her perturbation.

The understanding man smiled, and Megan thought she never had seen eyes so tolerant and at the same time profound. She had read of countenances like that, but had assumed that a man must have been dismissed from the faculties of three or four American universities, or spent decades on a mountain top with some Hindu *guru* to project such a reassuring aura.

"Don't be startled. That chap wasn't really General Grant. Ghosts may inhabit this fantastic region, but they never walk, and if they inspire talk, they must have progressed little since passing to the other side," the man said. Then he introduced himself, not because, Megan knew, he needed company. Nobody could be more self-sufficient, not even her mother on a banner day. But the man beside her achieved his poise without rigidity.

"My name is Evans. Homer Evans," he said.

Her eyes sprung open wide. "That's like the name of the detective . . ." She had tried to stop herself. She knew before she uttered the words that she was in the presence of Homer Evans, the detective.

"The former amateur," he corrected her. "My days of detecting are over." He looked at her and she seemed to hear him add, although he had not said an audible word. "The war gave me enough of that."

"The war?" she repeated.

It was his turn to be impressed. "You *are* sensitive, Miss . . ."

"Megan Mallory," she said.

Through the doorway stepped two, then four, then six police officers, followed by a middle-aged man in plain French clothes, that is, a black derby, black jacket, striped gray trousers, patent-leather shoes and black gloves. The latter saluted Evans casually.

"Ah! Fremont," Homer said, pleasantly.

Fremont, with a relieved gesture, indicated to the six police-men who had entered so precipitously that they could go quietly, and find something else to do off the premises. As Fremont advanced to Homer's table, Evans rose and, turning to Megan, said:

"This is Miss Mallory . . . Chief of Detectives Fremont."

"Oh, God," gasped Megan, but both men pretended not to notice. She had read about Fremont, of course. Homer Evans, in order to have the fame he enjoyed, must perforce, exist. Someone was sure to meet them, somewhere. She had hit the jackpot. That was all. And wasn't it about time, after three days cooped up in a room?

"Since you're here, my friend," Fremont said to Evans, "my problem is simpler. Who was that type? . . . The one that went out into the alley by way of the kitchen just a minute ago . . ."

"Ulysses Grant Havemeyer is his name," Evans replied.

"What about him? Routine facts, I mean," continued Fremont. Then he asked permission to sit down, across the table from Megan. Homer had signaled, and a waiter was at Fremont's shoulder.

"You were about to order, Miss Mallory," Homer suggested. If Megan had been as old as Mother Machree, he could not have shown more deference. The nicest men must be like that, with girls who are quite young, Megan thought. To the waiter she said, for-getting all about languages:

"I want three of those, and a bottle of that," she said, indicat-ing Homer's "Croque Monsieur" and Reisling wine.

Homer interpreted, and looked at Fremont.

"*Un calvados . . . degustation!*" Fremont said to the waiter, who started away to fill the orders.

"Your errand can't be grave, or you wouldn't be drinking double applejacks," Evans remarked.

"A disappearance. That's all. Nothing too alarming, or definite. . . . One of the things your countrymen are always doing," Fremont said. "But what about the student with the beard, Ulysses . . ."

"Ulysses Grant Havemeyer. Nothing much. He's a regular in this quarter. Doing post-graduate work and research at the Sorbonne. Amazingly sharp mind!"

"He has!" interrupted Megan, astonished.

Evans and Fremont turned to her, and could not repress their smiles. Had they said that Hitler had been a jolly good fellow, the girl could not have been more flabbergasted.

"You thought he was a chump," Evans suggested. "Well. We're both right. In many ways the chap's deficient."

"You know something about him, mademoiselle?" asked Fremont. He understood well enough that such a flare of amazement does not result from nothing.

"He was on the boat train, from Le Havre—the *Ile de France* boat train, I mean to say—three days ago." The rest was not so easy. "He—he gaped or stared at me, when I was alone in our compartment—my family's compartment, I mean . . . And when I began to resent his impertinence, he said: 'Think nothing of it, Miss Mallory.' Then he went away."

"How did he know your name, mademoiselle?" asked Fremont.

Megan flushed. "I'm no good at reporting," she said, ruefully. And then she told about Whiskers having intercepted the American Express messenger to look at the passenger list.

Homer looked at Fremont and raised his eyebrows quizzically.

Fremont bristled. "Don't grimace at me as if this routine checkup is one of those ghastly affairs you used to mix yourself into."

Homer smiled again, and sighed. "You'll admit the behavior is unorthodox."

"Go on. What about Havemeyer?" Fremont said, sulkily.

"He's an Existentialist. Sometimes he writes for their magazine, *La Barbe*. He has a brother who was a captain in the American Army."

"Not Captain Leo Havemeyer?" burst in Megan, again startled out of her control.

"You know also the brother?" Fremont asked, puzzled.

"I don't know him. I know about him. He served in my brother's unit, during the war. He commanded it, in fact. He was with my brother when he died." Megan turned to Homer.

"Do you know where Capt. Havemeyer is now?" she asked.

"He's practicing medicine. He was a doctor, you know, in the Army," Homer said. "He now has an office in Rouen."

Fremont frowned. "An American, practicing medicine in Rouen? That doesn't make sense," he said.

"Americans are likely to do anything," Evans said.

"Whatever they do, or don't do, I must be getting along. Thanks for the information, both of you," Fremont said.

He turned to Evans. "You don't know monkey-face's address, by any chance?"

Evans shook his head in the negative. "Sorry," he said.

While they had been talking, the waiter had brought Megan three "Croque Monsieurs," and a bottle of Reisling. Megan had finished the three slices of toast, with cheese and ham, and one glass of Alsatian wine. Evans emptied his bottle, and she asked him to share the rest of hers.

"I don't drink much," she said.

Even with that opening, he did not remark about her youth. He did feel, however, that she was anxious about something, and tried to find out what it was, only in order to put her at her ease. When she admitted that she would like to telephone the Hotel Prince de Galles, to ask a question of the night telephone operator, he went with her to the booth, intending to put the call through for her. The booth was a new one, built of matched boards which had not been varnished or stained.

Homer stepped in, got the Hungarian at the Prince de Galles, stepped out to make way for Megan to enter, and was intending to go back to the table, to wait for her, when he heard her gasp. She had dropped the receiver which dangled on the cord, and was staring at nothing that Evans from the outside could see. He reopened the door of the booth hastily, touched her shoulder, and she clung to him with her left hand while with her right hand, making a determined effort, she pointed to a sketch someone had penciled on the wall of the booth, about at the level of her eye and just to the right of the instrument. Homer stepped closer, and relaxed. It was a drawing, quite a good one, of a sharp-faced, still rather benevolent old woman, just the head and shoulders. She was wearing a black shawl, the knitted texture of which the artist had conveyed with a few naive strokes of the pencil.

"Nothing to be afraid of, Miss Mallory," he said.

"It's Susie Lowe! My brother's and my nurse in Rockport. It's . . . Susie!" Megan said, more dumbfounded.

4

A Gleam in a Private Eye

AFTER DINNER, ON THE EVENING Megan started late for the Café de
Flore, Luke Mallory, his elbows on the Ritz bar, found that champagne was losing its mellowing influence. And as the magic of the
grape subsided, the voice of his conscience began to chant a mono-
tone. Ever since he had hit Paris he had been having a fine time.
He had done nothing constructive, had learned or unlearned nothing of consequence. He had slept like a top, dressed carefully,
enjoyed his daily session at the barber shop, relished his meals,
and looked forward to his hours of drinking with Selectman Parker.

It was not that Luke had been having too much fun. He was
troubled because Edith was not having any. Three days she had
been "resting." He had tried to lull himself into believing that she was
all right. Inwardly, now that the champagne had let down, he knew
better. She was being thwarted, somehow or other. She had failed,
he supposed, to get in touch with the people she had been determined to see—the ones who had been present when Fred had died.

Selectman Parker had been consulting a copy of *The Old
Farmer's Almanac* and jotting down a few figures on a sheet of
paper the bar man had given him.

"The way I figure," the selectman said, "when it's ten P.M. over
here, it's seven o'clock in Rockport." He then explained that, it
being Thursday evening, the Board of Selectmen were holding a
special meeting, and he had promised to call up Jason Wetherby,
the chairman, to confirm a proxy. So Selectman Parker excused

himself from the bar, and went out into the lobby to the telephone desk. Luke waited glumly. He was not in the mood to be left alone.

Six feet or so to Luke's left, at the bar, was a rugged square-shouldered man in his thirties whom Luke had seen at the Ritz off and on in the course of the preceding days. The man, who obviously was American, of Irish descent, wore the same suit every day, and the same hat and shoes, but the pants were pressed, the fedora brushed, and the shoes neatly shined. Because the man spoke French, and had the air of one who could handle himself, Luke assumed that he had been in the Army and for some reason had stayed too long in France after being mustered out. The young man invariably drank a small French beer, and paid for it with beat-up French bills of small denomination, or even metal coins. It looked as if he were short of money.

"Nice evenin'," ventured Luke, inching a little nearer the Irish-American.

"So, so," the latter said, without enthusiasm. But he turned toward Luke and smiled. He had steel-blue eyes, short stubby lashes, a scar on his forehead that was rather becoming, huge competent hands, and wavy rust-colored hair.

"Care for a drink?" Luke asked.

"No, thanks," the man said. "This hog-wash'll do. But much obliged."

Luke, three inches taller and sixty pounds heavier, looked down into the obstinate blue eyes.

"Come on," he said.

The other relaxed, as if resigned. "I can't buy back, not Heidsieck."

"All right. I'll switch to beer," said Luke.

The bar man, who had been listening because he could not help it, stepped opposite them.

"Mr. Mallory. Meet Monsieur Maguire," the bar man said.

"Monsieur, my necktie," Luke said, and Maguire grinned.

"My first name's Finke, with 'e.' That was pinned on me before the Wagner Act," the other man said.

"Mr. Feenk Maguire," the bar man repeated.

The two Americans shook hands.

"Two bottles of Burton," Mallory said to the bar man.

"We haven't any Burton, sir," the bar man said.

Mallory shrugged, and turned to Maguire. "What do you say we split a bottle of Old Crow?" he said.

Maguire acquiesced.

The bar man, astonished at nothing, uncorked a bottle of Old Crow and brought two old-fashioned glasses. Luke poured, and after he and Maguire had tossed off about three fingers of whiskey, Luke said:

"I don't touch this stuff as a general rule."

"Neither do I, at a hundred and fifty francs a shot," Maguire said.

They drank and chatted a while, long enough to be sure they were going to like each other.

"Where's your sidekick. Did he quit you tonight?" Maguire asked Luke.

"He's gone to the lobby, to phone," Mallory said. "Something about politics, back home."

"That's a good place for politics . . . about three thousand miles away," Maguire said.

"Yes," agreed Luke. Then he hesitated, but not long. "Do you mind tellin' me what you do over here? I deal in beef and lamb, in Boston, myself," ventured Luke.

At the mention of beef and lamb, Maguire's face, which was expressive when he was not watching himself, looked wistful.

"I'm a private eye," said Maguire. "I may as well come out with it."

"A private eye?" Mallory repeated.

"A detective," said Maguire.

Mallory looked at him with a new interest. When some new factor presented itself in a troublesome set-up, he tried to fit it in.

"Busy, just now?" asked Mallory.

"Are you kidding?" asked Maguire.

"Anything in prospect?" Mallory persisted.

"Thank you, sir," retorted Maguire. "My only big prospects are the office rent. Any day the building may fall down."

"Then you won't have to pay, I suppose," Mallory said. "Shall we move over to a table? I want to ask you something, in a business way."

It was at the table in the bar room that Selectman Parker saw them, a half hour later. They seemed to be talking so earnestly that Parker tactfully delayed his entrance. Luke had unburdened his mind to the young Irishman and felt a thousand per cent better. Maguire had in his pocket a retainer, in the form of American Express checks, properly countersigned. There were five of them, and each was good for 31,000 francs. What Finke had to do was to dig up all there was about the men, and the woman, who had been on the scene when Lieutenant Fred Mallory had died. He felt confident that he could do what had been asked, and had frankly told Mallory that the job was not worth $500, that $100 would be ample for expenses, and $100 more for a fee.

"If you can cheer up my wife, I'll give you $500 more, when I can hand her all the dope, and see her like herself again," said Mallory, with feeling.

"I'm damned if I see any reason why you shouldn't find out what you want," Maguire said. "First of all, there's Lieutenant Kitchel."

"You know him?" asked Mallory, pleased.

"Sure. I know Bob," Maguire said, laconically. "Here comes your friend. I'll be off and see Bob. Call you up tomorrow."

"Don't you do it," said Mallory. "Meet me here, about eleven."

"In the morning?" asked Maguire.

"For Christ's sake. Do you think I'm decadent, or something? I've only been over here three days. Sure I mean morning," Luke said.

"O.K., so long," Finke said. He was going through the doorway when he caught a side glance at Selectman Parker's dismal face as the latter entered.

"Now what's eating him?" Finke asked himself.

Prompted by a hunch, he lingered in the lobby, behind a potted rubber tree between the leaves of which he could see Selectman Parker approach Mallory. The selectman sat down; Mallory, then in high spirits, slapped him on the knee. Then the selectman said something, tersely. Mallory stiffened, and came up as if goosed with an awl from behind. All the relief had gone from his face.

Maguire was on the point of returning, to ask what was wrong. What the hell, he thought, it's none of my business. I've got a job that's a lead-pipe cinch, and 155,000 francs in my pocket. Supposing this info the selectman just spilled puts a crimp in it?

Instead of returning to the bar room—and not being inclined to leave the premises without some kind of a slant on what had developed—Maguire sought out the long-distance telephone girl. She was an alluring French brunette, svelte, full of languor and suppressed inner fire, with dark fathomless eyes, chestnut hair as groovie as a Chinese movie, and the shapeliest hands, feet, knees, throat and bosom Maguire had seen since late afternoon. Maguire knew then that he had done right in sticking around for a while.

"I was going to ask you somethin'," Finke began, smiling into her eyes the smile he kept for beauties who worked for a living. "One close look at you made me forget what it was."

She smiled the smile she reserved for nice men who were fresh just a little too soon.

"Then it couldn't have been anything personal," she suggested.

"That call you just put through to the U.S.A. for the Down-East Yankee," Finke said.

"Oh, you mean Mr. Parker."

"What did Parker hear that sunk him?" asked Maguire.

"That someone had died," the telephonist said. "I think a mademoiselle named Susie."

"Susie Lowe?" asked Maguire, startled.

"You know her?"

Maguire felt in his pocket for the American Express checks, and started away double-quick.

He was a detective who had no use for highfalutin theories, until he had a few facts to go on. He got right down to business. The one thing he disliked most was making a simple case complicated. He had known Bob Kitchel since 1944, and all that time the lieutenant had lived at the Paris Dinard, in the rue Cassette, over on the Left Bank. The Paris Dinard, during the occupation, had been the headquarters of the Nazi S.S. troopers, and as soon as they had cleared out, and the Americans had come into Paris, the rooms in that hotel which had been commandeered by the Boche had been taken over by the U.S. Army, G-6, a branch of the "intelligence."

The taxi fare from the Ritz to the Paris Dinard took Maguire's last two hundred francs. He felt lucky, so he waved aside the eighty francs change. He saw that a couple of French policemen, and a plain-clothes sergeant were in the lobby, so he showed the sergeant his special permit and went over to the desk.

"Lieutenant Kitchel," he said to the night clerk. "I want to see him."

"Who doesn't?" asked the clerk.

"Is he in?" Maguire asked, not in the mood for repartee.

"No," the clerk said.

"Where is he?"

"I've no idea," said the clerk.

Finke had a hunch that the French sergeant was listening. The latter was an honest-looking Alsatian type, a family man, no doubt, who kept his ears open by habit.

"Know when he'll be back?"

"I'm sorry," the clerk said. He meant it, in his mild way.

"When did he go out?" Finke asked.

"A few days ago. On Monday, I think," said the clerk.

"Today being Thursday," Finke said, drily.

The clerk glanced at the clock, which said twelve-thirty. "Friday, to be exact," the clerk said.

"Have it your way," Finke said agreeably. He took out one of his cards. "In case Lieutenant Kitchel comes back, give him this, if you please, and ask him if he'd mind giving me a ring at the office—my office."

"*Parfaitement, monsieur*," the clerk said.

"You said 'In case he comes back,'" remarked the French plain-clothes sergeant, sharply.

"Think nothing of it," Finke said, and, with a nod, left the hotel.

Finke remembered with dismay that he had no more francs, only the American Express checks which he would find it difficult to cash short of the night exchange window at the Gare des Invalides. That was a mile away, and he had no notion of walking that far. He covered the few short blocks between the rue Cassette and the Cafe de Flore, in the boulevard St. Germain des Prés, in a

few minutes, sat down on the *terrasse*, his smooth-shaven cheeks
and strong chin conspicuous among the rows and tiers of face decorations. Finke ordered a double Old Crow with cold milk on the
side, and when the milk was brought, took from it a cube of ice
and whittled out a disk with his jackknife. Leaving his drink untouched, he went straight in to the telephone booth, dropped in
the ice, which had melted down just thin enough to work the pay
apparatus, dialed a number and, when a sleepy voice responded,
said:

"Beaver?"

On the other end of the line was Beaver Chambers, the receptionist in the lobby of the U.S. Embassy, who was not on duty but
at home, in the rue Cadet.

"Finke? Well, how have you been?" Beaver answered.

"So so," said Finke. "Listen, Beaver. I want some dope and I
need it quick. Find out who's in command of the outfit Lieutenant
Robert Kitchel is in. It's attached to the E.R.P. headquarters. Ring
up the C.O., sounding official, if you can, and ask him where Kitchel
is just now. Then call me at the Flore."

"Tonight?" asked Beaver, doubtfully.

"Sure. Tonight. I'm not working for the State Department, or
the Encyclopaedia Britannica. I'll wait for your call. Now don't fall
down. Tomorrow you'll get an envelope, special delivery, with
10,000 francs inside."

Maguire hung up. Beaver, he knew, could always use 10,000
francs, or even ten hundred francs, or one hundred, for that matter.

Having talked with Beaver, Finke drew a deep breath and went
back to his place on the *terrasse*. More whiskers had moved in.
Extra tables had been jammed between others. The trees along the
boulevard showed emerald leaves in the glow of street lamps. Taxis
came and went. Finke listened now and then to conversations
around him, found them far over his head, and tuned off again.

It already has been related how, at 2 A.M., Megan Mallory arrived, and went directly inside the café. Finke was so deep in
thought when her taxi pulled up that he did not notice it, or her. It
was unusual for him to miss seeing such a striking young girl, or

old girl, either. Finke was figuring things out, not about Lieutenant Kitchel, Susie Lowe, or anything to do with Luke Mallory. He
was deciding that, since he could not drink up one hundred dollars' worth of Old Crow and present an express check for payment,
he had better brace the head waiter, or the manager, and see what
could be done about paying his check, when it came. That would
not be for quite a while and he was feeling so comfortable. Therefore, he decided to stop thinking and rest his cerebrum, cerebellum and medulla oblongata. He wondered if those three units in
his dome worked in relays or simultaneously, or if they were working at all. It had been so long since he had exercised them. Lucky
his present job was simple.

A waiter called his name and he went in to answer the telephone. Good old Beaver, he said to himself. Good old hell, he said,
soon afterward.

"Why didn't you put me wise that this Kitchel bird is hot?" asked
Beaver in an injured tone.

"Go on," Finke said, laconically.

"I routed that C.O. you specified out of bed. Lieutenant Colonel
'Wasp' Billings, it happens to be. I pulled the old line about special info for the Ambassador. The brass eagle asks to speak to the
Ambassador himself. Will I be in Dutch tomorrow morning, when
one of these birds has checked up with the other?" Beaver said.

"What's all the shooting about? I only wanted to know where
Lieutenant Kitchel is at present," Finke said, disgusted.

"And so does his whole department. For at least forty-eight
hours. They'll want me to tell who was asking. What in God's name
can I say?" Beaver asked.

"Take it easy. Take it easy. Just say that Mr. Luke Mallory was
inquiring. He's at the Prince de Galles," said Finke.

"On the level? I wouldn't want to get fired," said Beaver.

"Mr. Luke Mallory happens to be the father of an army lieutenant who died while Lieutenant Kitchel was with him. He's got a
right to ask, at any time of night, to see this pal of his son who
gave his all for democracy. If you get canned, come around and
see me. I'll let you cry on my shoulder."

Finke hung up. He went back to the *terrasse* just in time to see
Fremont and his cops cross to the Flore, and start to go inside.
Then he saw the uniformed cops go away. A little while afterward
Finke saw Fremont go, too. What the hell? And then it came over
Finke that Lieutenant Kitchel, who seemed to be A.W.O.L.—and
who could blame him?—hung out quite often at the Flore. Finke
dismissed the possible connection from his mind. What did French
cops care how many American lieutenants were taking a vacation
for themselves?

A little while later the crowd on the *terrasse* thinned out a little.
Some of the sidewalk drinkers liked to break the monotony by visiting a few of the cellar joints in the neighborhood, and after a few
drinks underground, up they came and sat on the sidewalk
terrasses again.

Homer Evans and Megan, at Homer's suggestion, had quit the
inside café in order to sit on the sidewalk, so that Megan could tell
him about Susie Lowe. They were far enough from where Finke
was sitting so that he did not hear. He only saw that a guy with a
better-looking spinach than the Existentialists wore had an un-
commonly good-looking girl with him, and that they found plenty
to talk about. All right. Let them talk.

After a whiskey or two, Finke got up, and walked over to the
head waiter, who was talking with the manager not far from where
Homer and Megan were sitting. Finke asked if the Flore could cash
an American Express check for $100. Both the waiter and man-
ager were explaining almost tearfully how much red tape was
involved, if they accepted any kind of traveler's checks payable in
dollars, when Finke heard a voice speak up behind him. He turned,
and saw it was the guy with the legitimate spinach who had with
him the young stunning girl.

"I couldn't help overhearing," Evans said. "Since I happened
to pass my bank late today, I've a supply of francs on me. Might I
cash your check?"

"Damned white of you," Finke answered, and tried not to look
bug-eyed when the man the manager had called Mr. Evans took
out a roll that would choke a mule, peeled off three packages of

thousand-franc notes, ten in a bunch, pinned together, flipped an extra thousand on top of them, and handed them over.

Finke, in his turn, took out one of the $100 American Express checks, and handed it to Evans, who, without seeming to glance at it, tucked it into his pocket.

"It don't need my signature," Finke said, a little weakly.

"I noticed," Evans said, but his amazing control did not reveal that he had read on the check the signature and counter-signature of Luke Mallory, the father of the girl at his side.

"I owe you about 8 francs change," Finke said.

With an easy gesture, Evans waved away the change. "There's a tenable theory that each of us has a limited store of energy. If we use it counting out and passing back and forth eight francs, at the present rate of exchange, we shall have less left for higher purposes."

"I always felt that way, so help me, but I never knew why," Finke said, and went back to his table. He paid the check, after drinking another whiskey, and walked across the boulevard, past the Brasserie Lipp, and across the rue de Rennes into the rue Madame.

"Who was that you gave all that money?" asked Megan.

Homer smiled. "An American," he said.

"He certainly didn't look like a Chinese," said Megan.

"A private eye," Homer said.

Megan was thrilled again. "A detective?"

"I wonder what Finke is up to," Homer said, half to himself.

"Oh, God," said Megan. "Must I go back to the hotel? I'll never have a night like this again."

"Would you do one thing for me?" Homer asked. "I'd rather you didn't mention the sketch of Susie Lowe to your parents. Not to anyone, for a while."

"I'll keep mum," Megan said.

"And could you also refrain from talking about Ulysses G. Havemeyer, and your encounter on the train?" he asked.

"I'll do anything you ask. But Capt. Leo Havemeyer . . . ? My mother's so anxious to find him," said Megan. "Is he on the hush list, too?"

"No. Tell your mother the doctor's in Rouen. She can find his address in the Rouen telephone book. There'll be one at the Ritz, if not at the Prince de Galles . . . Now may I take you home?"

Megan sighed, then braced herself. "Of course," she said. "It's got to end."

"Could we have lunch tomorrow?" Homer asked.

"Oh, God," was all she could say. "What time?"

A few blocks eastward, Finke Maguire was sizing up the lay of the land around the rear of the Hotel Paris Dinard. It was a cinch, he thought. He scaled a ten-foot wall, dropped into a courtyard, tried a door in another wall, found it locked. But the key was in the lock. He turned it, and before him was the kitchen entrance of the hotel. The doors and all the windows were locked securely. Finke found an old newspaper in an ashcan, took from his pocket a tube of mucilage, smeared it over the surface of the paper, pressed the paper against a pane of glass, pushed gently and when the glass cracked, drew the glued paper carefully toward him and without having made a sound took out the fragments of glass. He turned up his collar, and stepped in. The kitchen was deserted. He found the stairway, mounted to the third floor. He had noticed when he had asked the hotel clerk about Lieutenant Kitchel that from force of habit the clerk had glanced at a vacant space on the board, between keys No. 36 and 38. Kitchel's number must be 37. Finke, on the third floor, moved cautiously down the hallway, found the door marked 37, tried the knob, turned it, opened the door just wide enough and stuck in his head.

Instantly he was aware that someone had stolen up behind him, silently. A hand reached over, and closed the door sharply on his neck, so his head was inside. Finke kicked backward, viciously, with his right heel.

Something crashed down on Finke's skull, just a split fraction of a second after he heard an agonized yelp from behind. Finke became aware of a vast droning; he felt that he was wheeling and spinning, downward, and all the darkness inside his head was shimmering with violet stars. They all flickered out as he slumped.

5
Death Again

AT NINE O'CLOCK FRIDAY MORNING, Mrs. Mallory was up and dressed, having a light breakfast in her bedroom of croissants and shirred eggs, with post-war French jam and coffee. The jam was mostly blackberry seeds with a touch of saccharine, and had a bitter almond odor. But it was not actively toxic and the rest of the meal was tasty.

The telephone rang peremptorily.

"Ah," said Mrs. Mallory with a sigh of relief. That must be Lieutenant Kitchel at last, she thought.

She took off the receiver and placed it to her ear. A male voice, distinctly military, asked:

"Who's this? Mrs. Mallory?"

"Good morning, Lieutenant Kitchel," she answered, brightly.

"I beg your pardon," said the voice, irately. Even Mrs. Mallory, with her limited experience in military circles, realized that it could not belong to a mere lieutenant. The person with whom she was talking must be either a colonel or a sergeant.

"This is Lieutenant Colonel Billings," the voice said.

"Very well, Colonel Billings," she said, in her coolest New England manner. "I was expecting another call."

"Madam," the colonel's voice continued, still unwilling to be sidetracked, "did you, or did you not, telephone a receptionist of the Embassy just after midnight this morning, to ask about your son?"

"Lieutenant Colonel Billings," she said, nettled and disappointed, "I have no son. He died in a service you seem thus far to have survived. Furthermore, I did not call the Embassy, or any of its functionaries, either this morning, or at any other time. Good day."

The sharp edge on her voice had roused Luke in the next room. When he opened the door, he saw his wife trying grimly to hold back tears. There was nothing ridiculous in the way he hurried to her side and put his arms around her, or in the manner in which she let herself be comforted. When she told Luke what had happened, about her letter, improperly stamped, then the telephone call, he started boiling.

The phone rang again. Luke grabbed the receiver. "Mrs. Mallory, please, for Colonel Billings," a voice said, and then another took up the theme.

"Hello. Mrs. Mallory," said the rasping voice of the lieutenant colonel.

Luke all but growled and chewed the instrument. "And who the hell do you think you are, you fat-head?" roared Luke.

"This is Lieutenant Colonel Billings. Mrs. Mallory, if you please," said the colonel's voice, vibrant and spoiling for trouble.

"This is Mr. Mallory, and for two cents I'd go out there, wherever you are, and knock your block off. You talk to a woman who's lost her boy, ten to one on account of a blunder by some goldbrick like you . . ."

"Mallory, I'm sorry as hell," the colonel said. "Here's what happened. Beaver Chambers, messenger at the Embassy, called me out of bed last night, to say that the Ambassador—the Ambassador, mind you—wanted to know what had become of one of my lieutenants. A Lieutenant Kitchel. I thought it sounded fishy, so I got in touch with the Ambassador. He'd never heard of Lieutenant Kitchel."

"But I have," interrupted Luke.

"So have I," said Colonel Billings. "He's is my present outfit, and up to Monday was a most reliable man. He called me up, from the Café de Flore, Monday afternoon and said he might be out of touch the next day. That was O.K. That's quite in accord with what Kitchel might have picked up, or might be doing. But twenty-four hours went by, then forty-eight, and now it's about eighty-six hours, and no word from Kitchel. And nobody's seen him. And nobody can find him. Not the American Army, or the French police. Something's damned wrong. But for God's sake keep this quiet. Don't even tell Mrs. Mallory. I'm leveling with you, Mallory. I called back because it seemed to me, when I first phoned, that she answered as if I were Kitchel. Can you make sense out of that?"

"I sure can, but not now," said Mallory.

"She's listening, I suppose," the colonel said. "Why don't we have lunch, about one, at Fouquet's and talk this over?"

"If I can find the bloody place," said Mallory. "You couldn't tell me, off hand, who did stir up that call you pinned on Mrs. Mallory?"

"I've got a strong hunch. A guy at the Embassy who makes inquiries, now and then, for a few stray clicks around town."

Mallory got mad all over again, but not at Colonel Billings. Finke, he assumed, had got careless.

"And what was that all about?" Mrs. Mallory asked, after Luke had hung up. She was calmer, then, but still disappointed. "Did that Colonel tell you anything about Lieutenant Kitchel?" she asked.

Luke had to lie, fast. That was the way he liked to do it, if he had to lie at all. "Ah, darling," he said, "no wonder you haven't heard from the lieutenant. The colonel tells me that Kitchel's out of touch, on a special job, one that's a bit hush-hush. You'll get word from him in good time."

"Thanks, dear," Mrs. Mallory said. She was glad he was going to lunch with someone besides Selectman Parker. She was fond of the selectman, and was afraid that if he tried to string along with Luke on a long Paris bat he might die.

"And now," said Luke. "I'll be going."

He strode into the next room, dressed without his usual care, and instead of spending an hour in the barbershop, he hailed a taxi at the hotel door. Mrs. Mallory saw him hand a card to the chauffeur, to direct him, then enter the car.

Almost immediately there was a tap on an inner door and Megan stepped into her mother's room, looking radiant and brimful of life.

"I've got news for you, Mother," Megan said.

"Lieutenant Kitchel?" the words popped out of Mrs. Mallory's mouth. Megan was so startled she almost swallowed her tongue. Mother and daughter took a moment off in order to compose themselves, as daughters of New England should. They started over again.

"You have news, you say?" Mrs. Mallory asked.

"I know where you can find Captain Havemeyer," Megan said.

Mrs. Mallory was truly relieved, pleased and astonished.

"But how? You haven't been out of your room."

Megan smiled a little provocatively. "I dropped into the Flore about two this morning," she said. "That's the time people go there. . . . Orson Welles, Jean Paul Sartre, Tamara, Chowderhead Margolis."

Her mother raised her eyebrows. "You went out in the middle of the night, in Paris, alone?"

"Mr. Evans brought me home, and Lazio got his friend, Lvov, to drive me over," Megan said. She was trying not to play up her new connections ostentatiously, but the temptation was great.

"I'm amazed," Mrs. Mallory said, determined that she was not going to be the only stay-at-hotel among the clan. "Where shall I find Captain Havemeyer?"

"In Rouen," Megan said. "You can get his address and phone number from the telephone book . . . the Rouen telephone book. If there's not one at this hotel, there'll be one at the Ritz."

"I'll be going to Rouen this afternoon," her mother said.

"I'm lunching at the Voltaire, with a friend," said Megan, airily.

Her mother bit her lip, "Indeed," she said.

About ten o'clock, Homer Evans stepped from the downstairs doorway of his apartment building in the rue Campagne Première. He had bought the whole building, in 1944, because he liked the landlord and could not bear to see him suffer so cruelly from the postwartime restrictions, ceilings, taxes and complaints. His own apartment, on the fourth floor, was just as it always had been.

Homer stepped into his roadster as the garage attendant got out at the curb. He was on his way to the Prefecture to see

Fremont. The Chief of Detectives had phoned that he would like to see him, and Evans had offered to come around.

At the Prefecture, he was ushered into Fremont's office and found the Chief of Detectives in a mildly agitated frame of mind.

"This is a trifle, I suppose," Fremont began. "But long ago, I learned to step easily, whenever one or more of you Americans are concerned."

Without further explanation, Fremont led Homer to an alcove, through the Judas window of which could be seen the barred but otherwise open front of a cell known as "The Goldfish Bowl." That was for prisoners who required watching.

"Finke Maguire," exclaimed Homer, softly. "Was he drunk?"

Fremont looked at Homer reproachfully. "Had he been drunk, Schlumberger would merely have taken him home." Then the Chief added, somewhat reproachfully: "You know him, then?"

"Of him," Homer said. "Not much, but a little. I've been in Paris, off and on, for twenty-five years."

"Monsieur would then have been a boy of ten, when you arrived," the Chief said, wearily.

"He dates from 1944, as a Parisian," said Homer.

"I've been in Paris all my life, and I didn't know of him," Fremont said.

"Had he been French, and had you been twenty-five years in New York, you'd have known of him if he had been there since 1944," Homer said, comfortingly.

"Had the monkey not backed up against the lawn mower, he might have retained all his parts," Fremont retorted.

"What is Finke in for? And why am I consulted?" Evans asked.

Fremont sat down behind his desk, and waved Homer to a plain wooden chair. The Chief recounted how, on Wednesday, two days before, he had had a visit from Lieutenant Colonel Billings. The colonel had told him that a trustworthy young officer, a certain Lieutenant Robert Kitchel, of G-6, attached to the E.R.P. headquarters for special duty, had "lost contact" with his superiors, and in fact, with all the rest of the human race, as far as the colonel could ascertain. The colonel had asked Fremont to alert the Paris police to look for a trace of Lieutenant Kitchel. On Thursday, Lieutenant Colonel Billings had telephoned Fremont and suggested that extra measure be taken to locate Lieutenant Kitchel, who last had been seen at the Café de Flore.

"The Café de Flore, it had to be," groaned Fremont. "If there were crime committed there, it should be done by a barber who is being deprived of his means of livelihood."

"Bob Kitchel was clean shaven. Barbers are out," Evans said. "And what makes you think a crime has been committed?"

"The American lieutenant colonel was deeply worried. He is not the type to ask the French police for aid, unless a case is desperate," Fremont said. "But let me continue about the specimen in the Goldfish Bowl."

"A private detective," Homer said.

"Private detectives *and* Existentialists *and* Americans! I shall lose my mind," said Fremont. "And all I got for my pains last night, with my false raid at the Café de Flore, was a student with an 'amazingly sharp mind' who impersonates one of your dead generals."

"You haven't arrested young Havemeyer?" Evans asked.

"Naturally not. But we're watching him. He was the only one at the Café de Flore who took the slightest notice of a squad of French police in uniform, heading his way. Let's keep to the detective MacFeenk. Sergeant Schlumberger and a few men had been sent to keep an eye on the Hotel Paris Dinard, where Lieutenant Kitchel has roomed the last five years. About midnight, a little later, MacFeenk appeared there, made inquiries about Lieutenant Kitchel, and left his card, asking that Kitchel be requested to telephone MacFeenk at his office 'in case he returned.' *In case.* Lieutenant Kitchel had been returning there, quite steadily, for five years. But your American detective said distinctly, '*In case.*'"

"So you cracked him on the head and threw him in the Goldfish Bowl. A bit impulsive. No?" Evans said.

"You do me an injustice, and Schlumberger, too. The sergeant let him go his way," said Fremont.

"You had him tailed?" Evans asked, smiling.

"We did not. But after three o'clock in the morning, your MacFeenk climbed a high wall, dropped into a courtyard, unlocked a door into the back yard of the Hotel Paris Dinard, made an illegal entry in a manner most ingenious, stole up the backstairs, unobserved, so he thought, went straight to the room occupied when he is there by Lieutenant Kitchel, partly opened the door, stuck in his head and then kicked back at Sergeant Schlumberger who was directly behind him, gashing a hole two centimeters deep in Schlumberger's shin. It seems that Schlumberger is so sensitive in his shin that, without realizing what he was doing, he struck MacFeenk with a blunt instrument, to be exact, a chamois leather sack loaded with B.B. shot, and rendered MacFeenk unconscious. While MacFeenk was still insensible he was transported here, and placed where you see him. When a half hour after his arrival he opened his eyes and got to his feet, he began to complain. He has been ill-natured ever since, and before going further with him, I wished to have your advice."

The Chief drew a long breath as he finished his story.

"Call him in, but his name is not MacFeenk. It is Maguire. Mister Finke Maguire," said Evans.

"What's the difference?" asked Fremont. "There can't be another like him, who can raise such a fuss thirty minutes after having been black-johned by Schlumberger."

A moment later, Finke Maguire was ushered into Fremont's office. When Finke caught sight of Evans, he said:

"You here?"

Homer nodded. "I suppose you want to get out," he said.

"I've got a date at eleven. There's just time to make it," Finke said.

"You were crowned," Evans remarked.

"In spades," said Finke. "But I suppose, from the Frog point of view I had it coming. Any news of Kitchel?"

Homer shook his head. "Nothing that I know of," he replied. Fremont had been listening, trying not to be annoyed that a couple of Americans, under the circumstances, chatted as if they had met in a bar, and not in the Prefecture of Paris. To him, Evans said:

"Let Mr. Maguire go. He's O.K."

"If you say so," sighed Fremont, "but may I venture to hope that your friend will do no more breaking and entering on suspicious premises?"

"Think nothing of it," Evans said.

"That's what MacFeenk said to Schlumberger," grunted Fremont. "Also Monkey-face Grant to Miss Muldoon."

"Mallory," corrected Evans.

Finke was caught off base. "Mallory?"

"The lady you seen me with last night," Evans said. "I have no wife."

"Congratulations," said Finke. He handed Evans his card. "You're two up on me, already," he said, grinning. "But give me a chance to get square some time."

"With pleasure," Homer said.

Finke turned to Fremont. "Do I get back my 29,600 francs and four American Express checks for $100 each? I take it the guy who hit me didn't have robbery as a motive," Finke said.

Fremont pushed a button, gave an order, and an envelope was brought to Finke, who stuffed it in his pocket without looking inside. The Chief, observing, turned slightly mauve, and then glowed. Was Monsieur MacFeenk's gesture indicative of the American folly about the value of money, as if it had no importance? Or a touching and tactful tribute to the honesty of the department?

The Chief said "Au revoir" to Evans and "Adieu" to Maguire.

"May I drop you off somewhere?" Homer asked. "My roadster's here."

"Thanks. At the Ritz," Finke said. He was going to add, "And step on it" but he remembered his manners in time. Before they had driven off the Ile de la Cité, Maguire realized that asking Homer to hurry was like asking Barney Oldfield, at the finish of a record-breaking race, what had kept him. Without effort, Evans outdistanced the wildest taxi drivers, and pulled up at the Ritz at 10:58.

"Just in time for your date," Homer said.

Finke looked at him, at first without expression, but the grin broke through.

"I hope to God," Finke said, "that if ever the day comes when you and I have a long heart-to-heart talk, you'll do all the talking. I'm nowhere."

With that he turned and went into the Ritz.

Finke saw that Mallory, his client, was at the bar, and seemed to be as restless as a bear. He wondered if Mallory was still his client. Having nothing constructive to report, he had to take the initiative.

"Why didn't you put me wise that this Lieutenant Kitchel was hot?" Maguire began.

Mallory, who had been on the point of swinging on the detective, recoiled and bristled. "Did I tell you to phone the Ambassador? And half the Army? Or did I say I'd like to surprise my wife?" Luke countered. "And who told you Kitchel is hot?"

"A gumshoe with a sack of bird shot," Finke said, touching the back of his head. "I spent the night in jail. How'd you get on?"

"An army officer, pretty high up, I don't mind saying, called my wife this morning, and sounded off till she was half-cryin'," Luke said. "Said you'd egged on some guy named Beaver to wake him up in the middle of the night, with a cock-and-bull story about the Ambassador. And me, not having the nerve to tell her a lifelong friend of hers had died."

"That would be Susie Lowe, of Rockport, Mass., I suppose," Finke said.

Luke's eyes opened wide with astonishment. "You know her?" he asked.

"Never met her, but you yourself told me about Miss Lowe and the cottage by the sea. What did she die of?" Finke asked.

"How do I know?" demanded Luke.

"Don't get sore. You soft-soaped me into this easy little sinecure, just to set your wife's mind at rest. Already a U.S. lieutenant's vanished; the beneficiary of the will's kicked off, leaving no heirs; the cottage goes to hell knows who or whom, and I get my block socked so hard I don't even remember riding to the Prefecture and being tossed into the cell they call 'The Goldfish Bowl.' I'm sorry your wife was disturbed. But I went into this as innocent as a penguin. Naturally, after calling at Kitchel's and finding that he'd been A.W.O.L. four days, I phoned Beaver to get me the info about Kitchel."

"So what do we do now?" Luke asked, cooled off considerably.

Finke thought hard and fast. "The next best bet's Doc Havemeyer. I haven't seen him or heard from him for two or three years. Maybe he's in France, maybe not. I've got to find out," Finke said. "Havemeyer was a medical captain, on special duty. You say he was present when the will was made. As long as Kitchel's unavailable, Havemeyer's our bird. He's got a young brother who's half orang-utan and thinks he's General Grant. Maybe the young one knows where Doc is. I'll nose around the Café de Flore, and see you later, if there's anything to report."

"I've got a lunch appointment," Mallory said. "After it's over, around three or four o'clock, I'll be right here."

"Don't hurry with your lunch," Finke said, drily. He started away. He waited behind the rubber tree in the lobby until he saw Mallory go out and flag a taxi. Then he walked over to the long-distance telephone desk. At that hour of the day there was a blonde on duty. She was very chic and pretty, petite, full of animation and inner coolness, with ultra-marine eyes that sparkled, flaxen hair as fluffy as the conscience of a cuckoo, and the most enticing wrists, ankles, hips, nape and shoulders Maguire had set eyes on that day.

"I was going to ask you something," Finke began.

"Why not?" replied the girl. "If you don't spill it soon you may forget it."

"Just how am I to take that?" he inquired, feeling the back of his head again.

"Got a headache back there?" the blonde asked, then she added, "I've never had a headache in my life, but I thought they came in front."

She touched her fair forehead.

"I'll give you one some day," Maguire promised.

"Someone has to be the first," she said. "Now can you recall what brought you over here?"

"I want to call a guy in Rockport, Mass.," Finke said. He showed her his card.

"Ooooo," she said, with mock awe. "A detective."

"A private pair of mittens," corrected Finke. "But I know you can keep a secret. Don't tell anybody I made this call, if a long drink of water who lives in Rockport has the same idea."

"Who is this party you wish to communicate with?" she asked.

"He's chairman of the Board of Selectmen," said Finke. Within ten minutes the connection was established. Just in time Finke remembered that in Rockport it was only 9:30 A.M.

"I'm calling for Selectman Parker . . . That you, Mr. Chairman," Finke began.

"Yep," the chairman's voice said.

"Understand poor Susie died," Finke said. The clipped way of speaking the chairman had prompted Maguire to keep his words down to the minimum.

"Yep," said the chairman.

"What from?" asked Finke.

"Dunno," said the chairman.

Finke: "Anybody know?"

Chairman: "Nope."

Finke: "Where'd she die?"

Chairman: "In bed."

Finke: "Down t'the cottage?"

Chairman: "Yep. Funeral's Sunday."

Finke: "Much obliged."

Finke hung up. He asked for the charges, paid the blonde, handed her his card, to keep, this time.

"Whenever you want that headache . . ." he said, smiling.

She could not resist that smile. She wished he did not have it, or that someone she knew better did have it.

"You must buy your aspirin wholesale," she said.

"I'll bring an extra long tube," he said.

With that, he turned and left the lobby. He wondered how he could arrange to see the blonde and the brunette together, so he could date them in order without risking an anti-climax, or no climax at all. Paris was a great town in which to find women, he reflected. Better still, it was an easy place in which to lose them.

Homer Evans had driven his roadster to the Hotel Prince de Galles, permitted the doorman's assistant to park it, entered the lobby and sought out the telephone desk. The day operator was a redhead, with skin as clear and white as Cointreau standing in front of an ermine drape. Her cheeks were flushed with Tonkin Ruby (Lelong) and her lipstick was mixed especially for her by someone who was intimate with Raoul Dufy. The color of her hair was exquisite, but indefinable. Had it a background of lemon leaves it would have stopped a May Day parade through Red Square. She had a superb neck, shoulders, breasts, limbs, and curves, all of which beggared description. She was five feet seven inches tall, and sat on a swivel chair as gracefully as Dorothy Lamour perches on a giant clam shell.

"Good morning," Evans said, as if the redhead had been just a plain wholesome-looking girl like an English princess. "I want to call the postmaster at Rockport, Mass," Evans said.

"That's droll," said the redhead. "I've had two calls already for that town."

"You've had two calls?" repeated Evans.

"From two members of the same family, separately. Mr. Mallory and Miss Mallory. The girl you were out with last night," said the redhead.

"In that case, I won't need to call Rockport," Evans said. "Will you ring Miss Mallory's room and ask if it's convenient for her to speak with me?"

"It will be," said the redhead. "I'll just tell her you're here."

If only he would not smile like that, the redhead thought. American girls had all the luck. Aperitifs. Lunches. Money. Shows promise of being good-looking. Parents who do not care what becomes of her, and let her run wild alone on summer nights. And on top of it all . . . Mr. Evans—the perfect gentleman . . . Come to think of it, that tears it. If he was too respectful to me, I'd blow my top, or make a dive at him while he was driving.

Evans took up the house phone.

"Oh!" said Megan. "I can't tell you how glad I am that you've come early. I've tried not to be hysterical . . ."

"Come down. I'm in the lobby. My roadster's outside. Keep calm if you can," he said, and hung up.

He knew from her tone that she was deeply disturbed, in fact, grieved. Immediately Evans sensed that Susie Lowe was dead. He saw before his eyes that sketch of the woman wearing a dark knitted shawl, the placid brow, the sharp generous features, the effect of pallor and benevolence. In about a minute, Megan stepped from the elevator, Homer advanced to meet her and she took his arm.

"I understand," he said, "Susie Lowe died. She must have had a good life, and believed in the hereafter. It's only because you were startled, and cried out when you came upon that sketch in the telephone booth that you're unstrung." Homer felt sure that it had been the suggestion of telepathy, with her on the receiving end, that had shocked Megan. He was so right that Megan did not even notice that he knew about Susie's death without a word from her.

"You phoned Rockport this morning?" Homer said.

They were walking toward the doorway, with the eyes of the redhead and of all others upon them. They made a striking couple.

"Susie died quietly, and alone, almost surely in her sleep," Megan said.

"I could wish nothing better for myself, when the times comes, or for you," Homer said.

How tactful and delicate, thought Megan. He does not flaunt my lack of years in my face, even by failing to recognize that I must die some day. In her ears sounded a song she had heard Joe Turner sing. It was at the Righteous Athenaeum Arms.

"You're solid—about jazz?" she faltered.

He smiled. "My boots are laced way up," he admitted.

She squeezed his arm in a comradely spontaneous way.

"Well, all right then," she said. Her flurry of nerves had subsided.

They chose, or rather, Homer suggested for their appetizer the Cafe de la Régence, in the rue St. Honoré, from the *terrasse* of which there is a lively view of the foot of the avenue de l'Opéra, the Comédie Française, and the *place* du Palais Royal. As they sipped their drinks, vermouth cassis, since the day was warm and sunny, Homer did not tell Megan that Napoleon had played chess in the café before which they were sitting. He did remark, however, that the author of "Home, Sweet Home" had lived in the Palais Royal and disliked his native America which he had not seen for twenty-five years when he wrote the touching ballad for a London music-hall show.

Homer was not completely at ease. The vague connections between Megan, Luke Mallory her father, Finke Maguire, and the missing Lieutenant Robert Kitchel were not clear in his mind. He left Megan a few moments to go inside and telephone Fremont.

"Chief," Homer said, "I'm getting jittery in my middle age. I'm lunching with Miss Mallory at the Voltaire, *place* de l'Odéon. If by any chance you get word from or about Lieutenant Kitchel, would you mind giving me a ring?"

"Why, certainly," Fremont said, dolefully. "But don't delay your lunch waiting for the message—unless you have one of those abominable presentiments of yours."

"I'm as innocent of hunches as you are of clues," Homer said.

It was a more disgusted Fremont, but a man thoroughly aroused whose voice found Evans' ear, in a booth at the Restaurant Voltaire at 2:10 that afternoon.

"What's up, Chief?" Evans asked, taken aback by Fremont's intonation.

"The American lieutenant, Robert Kitchel, is dead. Can you, for old friendship's sake, come over right away?" Fremont said, and asked.

"To the Prefecture?" asked Evans, nonplussed.

"No. To No. 21 rue Cassette. It's only four or five blocks from where you are now," said Fremont, groaning.

6
Impossible Times and Places

WHEN HOMER RETURNED to the corner table Megan was aware that something had happened. Her first fear was that he had been called away. The night on the *terrasse* of the Flore, the drink at the Régence, the lunch at the Voltaire had been waking dreams for her, not in gushing romantic way. Those hours had fulfilled the vague hopes she had had, that every girl she knew had had, about the magic of Paris, that there was something for men and women in the City of Light that transcended experience elsewhere.

"Any notion where your father is?" Homer asked, without preliminary.

"Father?"

Homer smiled, to reassure her, but it was not a high-powered smile. "I'd like to locate your father, if I can. It's important," Homer said.

"He's in a Chinese restaurant," Megan said. Her mother had said that her father was "having some chop suey with a terrible-tempered Colonel Bang."

"Sounds like Wasp Billings," Evans said. He reflected. "There are quite a few Chinese restaurants, some in the Champs Elysées district for the Americans, others in the Latin Quarter for Oriental students and servants."

Megan tried hard, and up came the two syllables. "I've got it. Foo Kay's," she said. "That's what he told Mother."

In spite of the gravity of the situation Evans laughed heartily. "That's quite a Chinese restaurant, Foo Kay's."

"I'm sure that's what Mother said," Megan persisted.

"If anyone brought a mess of chop suey into Fouquet's, F-o-u-q-u-e-t-'s, the management would call out the riot squad. That's one of the traditional French cafés of world renown," said Evans.

He went back to the telephone booth, dialed Fouquet's, and asked to speak with Mr. Luke Mallory. At Fouquet's a bus boy went from table to table saying, not loud enough to annoy other clients: "*Monsieur Mallorée, s'il vous plaît. On vous demande au téléphone. On demande au téléphone Monsieur Mallorée.*"

Wasp Billings, tearing into a double portion of wild strawberry tart, took time off to say to Mallory:

"Expectin' any calls?"

"Not so's you'd notice it," replied Luke Mallory, who was eating crêpes Suzette arranged in stacks of four.

The boy kept on and on. "Better take a shot at it. Nobody else wants that call," the colonel advised Luke.

"No telling what 'twill lead to," agreed Luke. "I promised myself to take no chances with these foreign phones, but here goes."

When Luke heard Evans' voice, he pulled himself together quickly enough.

"I'm lunching with your daughter," the voice said. Luke had never heard it, but there was nothing against it, except that it sounded too mature for anyone Megan might have picked up.

"Eat hearty," Luke said.

"I've got to talk fast," said the voice. "A man in whom you're interested is dead. His body's just been found."

"Not that fine lad, Finke Maguire?" said Mallory, in horror.

"Not Finke. The man you sent him out to locate, Lieutenant Kitchel," the voice said.

"I don't know what to say. Poor lad. How did he die?" asked Mallory.

"I don't know yet. . . . Are you lunching with Wasp Billings, by any chance?"

"I am," Luke said. "Now why did such a thing have to happen?"

"Call Colonel Billings to the phone, if you don't mind. Say it's Homer Evans speaking."

"I'm sure sorry for the poor lieutenant. It's harder for the boys to die in peacetime, seems to me."

"We'll have a talk, later today," Evans said. "Now the colonel, if you please."

Mallory went back to the table and told Colonel Billings that Homer Evans wanted a word with him.

"Now how do you know Evans?" Billings snapped, irritated by the intrusion of something that might turn out to be work.

"He's lunching with my daughter," Mallory said. "And he's got bad news for you. Damn bad, Colonel. Your missin' lieutenant's dead."

That brought Wasp Billings out of his chair like a Jack-in-a-Box, an expression of fury on his face. Without a word he strode to the phone booth.

"What's this I hear about Kitchel?" he snapped.

"Dead," Evans said. "That's all I know. His body was found at 21 rue Cassette, not many minutes ago. Fremont's there already. Can you join us, right away?"

"I'll have the heart out of somebody for this," Lieutenant Colonel Billings said, and, slamming the instrument back on the cradle, he rushed out to where Luke was sitting, staring at nothing. "Sorry. Got to go," Billings said, and before Luke could object, the colonel left the restaurant on the double quick, hopped into his olive-drab Dodge and started like a shot off a shovel, leaving his chauffeur flat.

Luke Mallory had not had so many mixed emotions seething in his breast for years, shock because Kitchel was dead, bewilderment at who Homer Evans might be, resentment because Billings had abandoned him in a strange country where he couldn't say a word a soul could understand. Luke did not know where Evans and Megan were lunching, or where the body had been found. If he could find Finke Maguire, perhaps Finke could guide him to the rest of the bunch. So Luke paid the check, not knowing whether it was cheap or steep, tipped the waiter till he saw that the man was almost on the point of protesting, told the boy to get him a taxi, and was about to show the taximan Finke's card, with the office address of Maguire, Private Detective, when it occurred to Luke that he ought to break the news first to Edith. That would be tough, all right.

"The Prance dee Gal," Luke said, and in spite of his agitated state got a minor kick when the taxi driver seemed to understand. "By cripes. I'm learnin' to speak French," he said to himself.

Furthermore, the taxi took him quite directly to the Prince de Galles. Luke told him to wait, and, while the chauffeur and the doorman were gesticulating and uttering what passed in that country for human speech, Mallory crossed the lobby and took the elevator upstairs. He let himself into Suite Sixteen, and listened for his wife. No sound. Luke knocked, then opened the door of her room. Nobody there. He started pushing buttons. A maid, the elevator man and a garçon appeared in the order named. None of them could speak English, or grasp a word of it. They understood, however, that he wanted to use that illogical language with someone, and pointed to the phone. Luke caught on, and made a grab for the instrument.

"*Un moment, monsieur,*" said a voice.

"Speak English?" brayed Luke.

"One little minute, mister," the voice said.

Luke tossed the instrument in the general direction of the cradle and it was retrieved and set in place by one of the attendants. Luke was on his way downstairs. He brought up at the telephone desk. The redhead was at the switchboard, now free and unencumbered. She smiled at him, sweetly.

"Mister Mallory. So sorry to keep you waiting."

"That's all right. Where's my wife?" Luke asked, abruptly.

"In Rouen," replied the redhead.

"Ruin? Now see here, miss," spluttered Luke.

"It's a city." The redhead touched her fiery hair. "You know, sir, about Jeanne d'Arc. The English cooked her there."

Mallory tumbled. Edith had gone to a place named Ruin where Jeanne d'Arc was burned.

"How far is that?"

"Maybe two hundred kilometers," the redhead said.

"How'd she go?"

"On a train, I think. Adolphe" (she gestured toward the bell captain at his desk) "got the ticket."

Adolphe, who had seen how worked up Mallory was, had approached.

"It's all right, monsieur. It was a two-way ticket. She's coming back."

"I hope to Jehoshaphat she is," roared Luke. "Well, this beats me." Edith had come to Paris to talk with some folks about Fred, and see the churches, museums, art and stuff. Her first venture from the hotel had been to a city a couple of hundred miles away, more or less. Luke could not remember how long a kilometer was, but he thought Finke Maguire would know. So he hustled out, and found his taxi. He pulled out Finke's card, showed it to the taxi-man, who nodded and started away.

Finke was not at his shabby office or the shabbier back room in which he sometimes slept. Neither was he at the Ritz, but the bar man told Mallory that Finke had gone to Rouen, to see a Dr. Havemeyer.

With relief, Mallory saw Selectman Parker edging into the bar room through the doorway, as if he were playing a trout on a line.

"Well, thanks be to all that's holy. There's somebody left in Paris," Luke said.

Meanwhile, Homer had said to Megan: "A body has been found, over on the rue Cassette, a few blocks away. Why don't you let me leave you in the Luxembourg Gardens? That's between here and there. After I've talked with Fremont, I'll come back for you."

Megan's heart was beating fast. "A body?"

He nodded.

"The American Mr. Fremont said was missing?"

He nodded again.

"Not Lieutenant Kitchel," she said, barely able to utter the words.

Homer was surprised but he showed no sign. "Yes. It's Lieutenant Kitchel. Do you know him, too?"

"He was a friend of Fred's," said Megan. "Couldn't you take me with you?"

He hesitated. "You won't like it," he said.

"Please," she said. "I have a reason."

"All right. If you find the spectacle too tough, you can go over to the Gardens and wait," he said, doubtfully.

She was thankful, and also so frightened that she clung to his arm as they walked over to the rue Cassette.

No. 21 was a building divided into two sections. The corner wing, bordering on the short cross street, the rue Chevalier, was vacant and in ruins. A fire had gutted it, a few years before, and it had been unoccupied although the outside walls and a few partitions and floors remained. The occupied half was used by a small religious publishing house and a few apartment dwellers upstairs. There were three and one-half stories. A truck partly filled with crumbled stone, cement and rubbish stood in the cross street near by. Fremont, Sergeant Schlumberger, two officers in uniform, a truck driver and a laborer were standing just inside the lower ground-floor corner. Evidently the floor above with part of the outside wall and an inside wall of two had fallen to the street level, leaving a large pile of debris. The laborer and truck driver had been occupied in removing it. Just to one side, a body was covered with a blanket. Megan, in spite of herself, was trembling and her teeth were chattering. Her expressive eyes were wide open, and dry. A curious crowd outside was held back by two policemen.

"No question about identification?" Homer asked of Fremont.

"None," the Chief said. "It's Lieutenant Kitchel, all right."

"Who found him?" asked Evans.

Fremont indicated the laborer and truck driver. "They did, just after they resumed work at 2 o'clock," said Fremont.

"Where?" Evans asked.

"Under the pile of debris, over against the outside wall near the corner. These men had been digging here all morning and carting stuff away. When they got back after lunch, this man" (thumbing toward the laborer) "started shoveling and uncovered a foot.

He called the truck driver, they shoveled and tugged, and brought out the body."

"The devil," grunted Evans. "Then nobody knows just how it was lying."

"It was stiffer than a board," the truck driver said.

"He was the one who phoned the police," said Fremont.

"I didn't realize it was stiff before I tried to move it out," said the truck driver.

"The lieutenant had papers on him?" asked Evans.

"Everything," said Fremont. "U.S. Army credentials, and French identity card."

"How long ago did the floor above cave in?" Evans asked.

"Monday night. At six o'clock," Fremont said. "He must have been buried there, since then."

"But that's impossible," burst from Megan. All the men spun around to look at her. She was shaken but grim and determined.

"Why is it impossible, mademoiselle?" Fremont asked, kindly. He was astonished and perturbed.

"I talked with him last Monday evening, between 8:30 and 9," she said, a tremor in her voice.

At that point Wasp Billings, who had driven up, and overheard the last sentence, yelled from the driver's seat:

"And he reported to me Monday afternoon at 5 o'clock, five minutes of 5, to be exact."

Colonel Billings hopped out of his Dodge and strode over, taking in the situation with suppressed rage.

"The floor above this corner collapsed and fell down at 6 o'clock," repeated Fremont.

"Who said so?" demanded Colonel Billings.

"The concierge of the building was positive about the hour," Fremont said. "And so were five or six others who were near by."

Evans stepped forward and told Colonel Billings briefly all that had been disclosed to him. The others listened, and had no corrections to make.

"Who's this young lady?" snapped Billings, nodding toward Megan.

"Miss Megan Mallory," Evans volunteered.

"Miss Mallory said, if I heard her correctly as I drove up, that she talked with Kitchel at 8:30 or 9 o'clock Monday evening. That's two and a half or three hours after the cave-in," said Billings.

"There's some mistake," Fremont said. "The body could not have been placed under the debris after it had fallen. It was too far back, almost in the corner, and there was no sign that the pile had been disturbed."

"Where were you, miss, when you talked with the lieutenant?" the colonel asked.

"On board the *Ile de France*," Megan said. "He called me from Paris, while I was still at dinner—but toward the end of the meal."

Fremont said, aside, to Sergeant Schlumberger:

"We'll have to check up on all these hours and places." The sergeant nodded, then asked a question: "Could the deceased have been on the second floor, and fallen with the debris?"

"In that case he would have landed near the top of the pile," Evans said.

"What would he be doing on the ruined second floor of a vacant building, less than a block from his hotel?" demanded Billings.

"My head is whirling," Fremont said.

"When it comes to rest, get a full report of the lieutenant's movements last Monday," growled Billings.

"Monday was two full days before you requested my department to interest itself in the deceased," Fremont reminded him, somewhat tartly.

"When this old heap fell in, he hadn't been missing an hour," Billings reminded the Chief.

"What did he say to you, at 5:00 P.M.?" Fremont asked.

"That he might be 'out of contact' Tuesday," Billings said. He faced right suddenly and glared at Megan. "And what did he say to you, miss?"

Megan colored, from surprise, and hesitated, because she was blushing and his brusque attack had unnerved her.

"That he couldn't meet me at Le Havre the next day when the boat got in," she said.

"What else?" Billings acted as if the girl were a recalcitrant WAC.

Evans, the calmest one of the lot, interposed.

"She's perfectly justified in telling you to take your questions to blazes," Homer said.

Colonel Billings whirled on him like a badger prodded with a ramrod.

"You keep out of this," he barked.

Homer said, evenly, turning to Megan: "Let's you and I take a walk in the Gardens, as we'd planned. These gentlemen *and* soldiers should be able to clear up this matter."

Fremont made no effort to hide his consternation.

"My friend. Americans! Existentialists! Impossible times and places! You couldn't desert me . . . Leave me with this impulsive brass hat who barks and bites!" Fremont pleaded.

If Megan thought she detected the subtlest wink ever flashed from an eyelid, she was right. Fremont continued to groan and wring his hands, but said no more.

"Are you referring to me, you rattle-headed false alarm?" the colonel snapped at Fremont.

"This is an example of international amity, spread by the military," Evans said, casually to Megan. "Each American abroad is an ambassador of good will and loving kindness. And how the French reciprocate, with their famous politeness! It's more than I can bear."

"You'll both be held as material witnesses," Billings said, but he was losing his bluster.

"Held? By whom?" asked Evans, raising his eyebrows.

Billings looked hard at Fremont, who failed to respond. The Chief of Detectives shuddered as Homer and Megan walked down the narrow cross street, toward the matchless gardens of the Luxembourg, in full bud and blossom of a sunny spring.

"I wasn't being gallant," Evans explained. "I wasn't defending your finer feelings, but if I'm to represent you in this matter, I'd like to hear your story first, from beginning. The end, Miss Mallory, is not in sight."

Megan was so deeply horrified by the death of the man she had been waiting to hear from and to see that it seemed as if half of her were numb, feeling nothing at all. The other half was hearing Evans' words as if they were distant band music, on a street a few blocks away. He had spoken of "representing" her and that "the end" was not in sight. They would be allied, and together, then. The bottom of Paris would not drop out.

He led her to a couple of metal chairs near the statue of an odd-looking soulful man with a bevy of women's heads and shoulders draped below him, like ectoplasmic fragments upsurging from stone limbo.

"Chopin," he sighed.

"I wish I knew about art," she said, wistfully.

"It's supposed to hold up a mirror to life. So you have to decide also whether the mirror is true or false, and the life is thrilling or commonplace."

"Just now life's far from commonplace," she said.

"The crime, you mean?"

"You said 'crime'? Couldn't it have been an accident?"

"I'm afraid not," Evans said. "We'll keep our minds open, however."

Megan took from her handbag the letter from the late Lieutenant Kitchel and handed it over.

"Before I read it, tell me what led up to it, if you can," Evans said.

She told him about the references to Bob Kitchel in her brother's letters, indicating that they were much together and were friends. She told him about Fred's written will, and the oral will that superseded it.

"That's a very quaint and obscure point of law, about oral wills of certain citizens of Massachusetts," Evans said. "Was it ever discussed in your home?"

"Why, no. Both Mother and Father were surprised when Lawyer Gott, after consulting some other lawyers in Boston, told them the oral will was valid," Megan said.

"What exactly is your father's interest in Lieutenant Kitchel? Has he talked about that?" Evans asked.

"Hardly at all. It was Mother, I'm sure, who intended to see the lieutenant, to ask about Fred's death, the circumstances and all. Mother couldn't feel easy in her mind about the oral will, because there seemed no sense in it. And Fred, like Mother, was sensible," said Megan.

"Who was with your brother when he died?" Evans asked.

The list was not long. "Captain Havemeyer. Then there was Lieutenant Kitchel, an army nurse, a sergeant and a private. Mother has the names of all of them. They all made affidavits, certifying the will."

"The affidavits were forwarded through Army channels to your parents, I suppose?" Evans asked.

"I suppose so," Megan agreed.

"Who took the initiative in having the affidavits sent?"

"I haven't the slightest idea," Megan said.

"Who wrote letters of condolence?"

"All of them except the sergeant. He died in a jeep accident, before he got around to writing," said Megan.

"Do I understand that the nurse in question and the private have dropped out of sight?"

"I don't know where they are. I don't think Mother knows. That may be why she counted so heavily on seeing Bob Kitchel. And why, today, she started right off for Rouen when I told her, as you said I might, that Dr. Havemeyer is there."

Evans slipped Kitchel's letter to Megan from the envelope and read it, slowly.

"Thanks," Evans said, and asked if he might keep it.

She nodded.

"So you wrote him that you were coming on the *Ile de France*, and when. And he planned to meet you at the port, Le Havre? Was there no further correspondence? Just this letter? And your reply?" Evans asked, frankly puzzled.

"That's all," Megan said. "I couldn't understand why he assumed I was going to France, or that I would land at Le Havre. It was long after I got the letter when Father got the tickets and let me know about the trip."

"Your first trip?"

Megan nodded.

"How about your father and mother?"

"Neither of them has ever been here before."

"What was the text of your reply to the letter I have?" Evans asked.

"That 'in case I was in Paris any time soon, I'd get in touch with him.' That, because of the feelings of my parents, about Fred, it might be better if he did not write again until after we had met and talked," Megan said.

"In other words, you didn't want to stir up your parents' sorrow—involving your mother's fixed idea about the oral will. You wished to let the whole matter drop, for the sake of your father and mother. Whether Susie Lowe owned the cottage outright or merely had the use of it didn't seem important to you," Evans said.

"Exactly," said Megan.

"Why did you change your mind?" he asked.

"I didn't," said Megan.

"Didn't I understand you to say that Lieutenant Kitchel telephoned you on the *Ile de France*, from Paris, Monday evening at 8:30 or 9:00 o'clock?" prompted Evans. "He must have known where you were."

"I couldn't believe my ears. I didn't know what to think, what to say, what to do," Megan said, giving in her recital such dramatic proof of her agitation and perplexity on receiving the call that anyone would have been convinced.

Evans did not try to conceal that he was astonished. "Can you repeat the conversation?" he asked.

She gave him both sides of it, word for word, a bit apologetic about her own end.

"And then, when I got to the Prince de Galles, I waited for a word from him. Tuesday afternoon and night, Wednesday all day, except long enough to go down to the lobby at two o'clock in the morning. When I got upstairs again, my phone bell was ringing, and I couldn't get to the instrument in time. When I tried to answer, the line was dead." Megan told that part without waiting for questioning.

"Why 2 A.M.?" Homer asked.

She told him how she had arrived at 2 A.M. as the safest hour to leave her phone unguarded.

"Then, at 2 A.M., twenty-four hours later, you decided to risk it again, after your fiasco of the night before?" Evans' tone again was puzzled, but not skeptical.

"I arranged with Lazio—he's the night telephone operator at the Prince de Galles—to switch any calls for me to the Café de Flore," said Megan.

"Why the Café de Flore?"

"I read about that café in the Paris edition of the *New York Herald Tribune*, that celebrities like Orson Welles and Chowderhead Margolis dropped in there about 2 A.M."

"For an intellectual debauch?" suggested Evans.

"I'd been hearing French that I couldn't understand so long by that time that I wanted to hear some English," she said.

"Even if you couldn't understand the English of the Existentialists and migratory celebrities?"

"I wanted to get out in the air, and learn about Paris, feel it, breathe it, absorb at least something besides hotel walls. My nerves were getting jumpy, listening for phone bells that didn't ring, and others that brought voices for which I was just a wrong number," Megan said.

"And then?"

"Then I found *you*," exclaimed Megan. "Nothing has been the same, after that first breathless moment, when you pulled out the table so I could sit down."

7

Millions of Men, Millions of Records

GLAD TO BE ON THE MOVE, and toward a destination that made sense according to her plan to find out about her son's death, Edith Mallory sat by the window in a first-class compartment of a train from Paris nearing Rouen. She expected that Dr. Havemeyer, whose address, listed in the Rouen telephone directory she had consulted at the American Express office, was 3 bis rue de Caen, would tell her what he remembered. It was unfortunate, she thought, that the only witness immediately available was a physician. Doctors attended so many deathbed scenes that particular ones, she supposed, did not stick in their minds.

Still, Fred had been Dr. Havemeyer's friend, and Fred had died while dictating a will, before he had completed it, and signed it. A doctor on war service probably sees quite a few friends and comrades die, but none other than Fred had made an oral will. There were millions of men in the United States Armed Forces, and of those 350,000 were residents of the Commonwealth of Massachusetts. Only Lieutenant Fred Mallory had left an oral will. No other oral will had been offered for probate in Massachusetts since 1863. She hoped that Dr. Havemeyer had had some appreciation of the unique character of the occasion at the time he was listening to Fred's last testament. Most likely the doctor had not. A few learned lawyers in Boston had been mildly gratified because a rare point of Bay State law had popped up.

Not even Luke, Mrs. Mallory reflected, ruefully, and certainly not Megan, had brooded over the matter. And Susie—whom Mrs.

Mallory supposed was still alive—had not seemed to care, one way or the other. The small cottage on the shore of Loblolly Cove had been in the Tarr family for generations, and the Lowes had always been welcome there, what few there had been of them. Mrs. Mallory remembered only Susie and Susie's mother. Susie's father, Captain Jesse Lowe, had been lost at sea, like so many of his generation who lived on Cape Ann. Captain Jesse Lowe had had a nephew, Alrick Lowe, who had gone down on the same three-master. The name of Alrick Lowe was dim, indeed, but it had not faded from Mrs. Mallory's memory.

Soon after Mrs. Mallory had taken her seat in the only first-class compartment that had been vacant, a young man with rugged square shoulders, looking like a Boston Irishman of about thirty-four, opened the door of the compartment, glanced at the five empty seats and had sat down in the aisle seat facing the same way as she did.

She had remembered that the landscape between Paris and Asnieres had not been particularly thrilling, so she had read a while from a *Reader's Digest* she had bought in the railroad station. As she had glanced up from the *Digest* piece—"Is Supervised Necking Essential?"—she noticed that the young Irish-American type, with the large hands and rusty hair with natural wave, was drinking from a bottle of Old Crow, which he kept on the seat beside him.

Before the train got across the broad plain and back to the bank of the Seine, the young Irish-American tucked his bottle into the side pocket of his jacket and after muttering, perfunctorily, "*Au revoir, madame,*" left the compartment, turning aft. In that case, if need be, probably I should go for'ard, Mrs. Mallory said to herself. She wished she had lunched before taking the train.

When she got into a taxi at the Rouen depot and said "Trwa biss roo dee can," the chauffeur failed to understand her. He took her to the Hotel d'Angleterre, which he considered the best place for any woman who made noises like that. At the Angleterre there was a Swiss who, when she wrote for him "3 bis rue de Caen" pointed to the entrance of a street about a block away, farther back from the water front, and said: "Three *bis*, madame, signifies three and then some, but less than four, or, since the odds are all on one side, and three follows one and precedes five, three *bis* signifies, more properly speaking, beyond three and not up to five."

Mrs. Mallory gave him fifty francs in hope that he would stop before her ears began chirping like crickets. It worked. He bowed so low that she was able to get out on the veranda steps before he straightened up again, and knew she was gone.

It was no trick for her to find the rue de Caen. The odd numbers were on the left-hand side, more or less in order. They did not correspond very closely to the even numbers on the right-hand side. Also where Number 1 had been some years before, stood only a few fragments of broken walls, no roof, no windows, no doors, rubble heaped inside, and no roof overhead. No. 3 was normal—a concrete and plaster house three stories high, not more than one hundred years old, and in fair condition. Three *bis*, her goal, had a sixty-foot frontage, a common side wall with No. 3, and on the frame of the entrance was a brass plaque which read:

LEO HAVEMEYER
Médecin et Chirurgien

Mrs. Mallory pressed the bell, and a few moments later the door was opened by an apple-cheeked Norman woman of middle age, in drab peasant dress with a white apron and cap. The Norman woman asked in French if Mrs. Mallory wished to see *le docteur*. Mrs. Mallory answered "*Oui, madame.*"

The woman admitted her and ushered her into a spacious waiting room to the right of the entrance hallway. A broad staircase led upstairs from the hall. Everything was very solid and respectable, in the French bourgeois tradition. The furniture was correct, mostly period. The hearth was ornate and impractical. A few academic and quite worthless oil paintings with farm subjects and country landscapes hung in heavy gilded frames. The carpet was good Brussels. There was a bronze statuette of Beaulieu on a marble base. On the table was an assortment of out-of-date French magazines and newspaper supplements, illustrated weeklies, trade journals, and the like. Also current copies of the Rouen newspapers, and *Le Monde* from Paris.

The high ample French windows were curtained and draped, but the drapes had been drawn partly aside. Since the hallway was much lighter than the waiting room, Mrs. Mallory did not see for a few moments that across the room from the corner she had chosen sat the sturdy rust-headed Irish-American who for a short time earlier in the afternoon had been her train companion.

"Oh," she said.

Finke Maguire made no comment. Then it came over him that the woman before him was most likely Luke Mallory's wife, who had somehow got wind of Doc Havemeyer's whereabouts and had ridden down to Rouen to question Doc about her dead son. Finke tried to decide how to proceed. He had been hired by Luke to get what he could from Doc, in order that Luke might pass the info on to Mrs. Mallory, if Luke thought best. What was Finke's play now? he asked himself.

Dr. Havemeyer had a patient, with him. Finke had not been announced. So Finke at first was inclined to believe that he should beat it, take a walk along the waterfront, and think a while. Or did he owe it to Luke, his client, to get to Doc first, put Doc wise to the situation, and ask him to soft pedal gruesome details, if any. Finke made up his mind to see the doctor first. Either way it was awkward. He did not know Doc Havemeyer well. A reticent fish, Finke thought he was—a guy who had not fitted exactly in the Army, or a cerebral outfit like G-6 was supposed to be, and who had chosen to stay in France and practice in a God-forsaken burg like Rouen, where vice had been suppressed, women who were married wanted to stay that way, and the others wanted to get that way.

Rouen was bounded on all sides by junk, and abandoned railroad cars. Tourists were herded in rubberneck buses to see where Jeanne was burned, the place on the bank of the Seine where her ashes were dumped into the water, and then enjoy a meal in one of the three famous restaurants. It rained in Rouen oftener than in Paris, and harder. The fog was stickier. The history was gloomier. The art was heavier. The tourists took a gander around the Cathedral, and got into arguments as to which of the towers was the Tower of Butter. The guides gypped them.

When his turn came, the red-faced Norman woman showed him up the stairs and into Doc's office, which was above the reception room. Finke had a feeling that Doc was surprised to see him, but not as glad as he might have been. And what kind of a system was it for a doctor to have his office, with expensive equipment, up on the second floor, and no elevator in the joint? That flight of stairs was all right for a man in trim like Finke, but it was plenty long and steep. Pretty tough for sick or injured patients, Finke thought.

Another detail bothered Finke. He could understand a three-section window seat down in the reception room, making use of the bay window. What good was the same arrangement just above it, in a doctor's medical office?

The words that passed between Finke and Doc were conventional and plausible enough.

"Hello, Doc. Remember me? Finke Maguire?"

"Well, well," Doc said. "What brought you down here? There can't be anything wrong with you, and if there were, there's the American Hospital in Neuilly."

"You have a swell approach for drumming up trade," Finke said.

"I was only kidding," the doctor said.

The telephone rang. Doc answered it in his easygoing way. He showed mild surprise and faint regret.

"It's for you," the doctor said. "Sounds like somebody who's had maybe one too many." He sighed, and handed over the phone. Finke took the receiver.

"I'll leave you, so's you can talk," Doc said, and ambled from the office. One hell of a specimen for G-6, and no mistake, Finke thought. Or had Doc been good at the Simple Willie Stevens dodge?

"That you, Maguire?" asked Luke Mallory's voice.

"Yes," Finke said. He waited.

"My missus down there?" Luke asked, gruffly.

"Yes," Finke said.

"Well, what's going on? Damn it! Is somebody listening, so you can't talk?" asked Mallory.

"Let me call you back. You're at the Ritz, I suppose. Mrs. Mallory hasn't seen me, and if she did she wouldn't know me. She hasn't seen Doc Havemeyer yet. I'll call you a little later," said Finke.

"I got to tell you something," said Luke. He did not seem so drunk, to Finke. "Kitchel's been killed."

"Murdered?" asked Finke, incredulously.

Just as he said "Murdered?" Doc came back to the office, but he did not act as if he had heard.

"Stick around the Ritz," Finke said into the phone, and hung up.

"Somebody been murdered?" Doc asked Finke, with that sing-song way he had of asking questions, without any ginger in his voice. "In your line, that's not uncommon, I suppose."

Finke had to make a getaway. It did not prove to be hard.

"Just thought I'd say hello," he said, and extended his hand. "Take care of yourself."

"Too bad I can't join you, later on, but I got a case out in the country," Doc said. He didn't seem to care much, one way or the other. He shook Finke's hand, limply, then followed him part way to the door. Finke hustled downstairs as quietly as he could, let himself out the front door, and walked away. As soon as he was safely out of sight he made a beeline for the Hotel d'Angleterre.

At No. 3 bis Mrs. Mallory was ushered upstairs, and into Doc. Havemeyer's office. When she told him her name, he seemed to remember it, without undue surprise. He was polite and consider-ate enough, but apathetic. She braced herself and got right down to brass tacks.

"I'm Fred Mallory's mother," she said.

He nodded. "Fine boy. We were friends," Doc said.

His eyes are tired, she thought. So is his voice, and all the rest of him. He works too hard. Still there was not an air of activity around the place, neither downstairs nor upstairs. She could not explain to herself afterward why she got such a strong impression that he was homesick, that he could not face the prospect of stay-ing in France. She decided that, most probably, he was planning to leave Rouen, and Europe, and re-establish himself in America. Where in the United States? She could not place him by the way be acted and talked. What Mrs. Mallory had to say proved harder than she had expected.

"I don't want you to misunderstand what I'm about to ask," she began.

"I'll try not to, ma'am," he said. He was patient, not receptive, not wary or hostile.

"I seem to be the only one who thinks it's strange, Fred's making that last will. Naturally, none of us, neither his father, his mother, or Susie—she's the woman who got the cottage—would want to question anything Fred wanted to do, when he was—dying. I want to ask you, as a doctor, whether there is any chance that he was feverish, or delirious, or affected in any way—his memory, for instance. Are you sure he was acting consciously and deliberately?"

The doctor looked regretful, a little sad. "I wish I could be positive. There's a small chance he didn't remember too clearly having made the other will. It was my judgment at that time that he knew what he was doing. I didn't realize, of course, that there was very much difference between one will and the other."

"There wasn't really. I've magnified the difference, no doubt. I'm more sentimental about objects or belongings than I like to admit. It didn't seem natural to me that Fred would want the Tarr cottage to pass out of our hands, forever. Susie Lowe's alone in the world, as far as relatives are concerned. Was Fred aware, do you think, that if Susie should die intestate the property might go to the town, the county or the commonwealth? Did it seem to you that Fred acted as if he were doing anything—important? Did he know the end was so near?"

"We never tell a patient that he's dying, unless we have to," the doctor said. "Still, Fred must have known pretty well. Quite a few had gathered around. There were Lieutenant Kitchel, Sergeant Baring, Lieutenant . . . I can't recollect just now the name of that nurse. And there was a private. His first name was Judd."

"Judd Coulson," Mrs. Mallory said.

"Too bad how we lose track of people. Or maybe it's just as well," the doctor said.

"Doesn't the Army keep some sort of record of the veterans? Their current addresses?" she asked. She felt that she was getting nowhere, most likely because there was nowhere to arrive. Still, she was even surer than before that she could not stop until she had talked with Lieutenant Kitchel, the nurse, Judd Coulson, the private, and exhausted all sources of information.

"There were millions of men, and there are tens of millions of records. How well they match up, and who can find either of them's another matter," said the doctor, helplessly.

"If you were me, you'd let the matter rest, in other words," suggested Mrs. Mallory, without resentment.

"Folks can't ever figure right for one another," said the doctor. "I can't help you much, that's all."

They talked half an hour. In his uncertain way, never too sure of his own memory or judgment, the doctor told her all he could about Fred's work, his brief illness, his passing. She felt sure that everything had been done that could have been done, that Fred had not suffered much. At the end she had to admit that, as a result of her own efforts, against which she had been gently counseled, her misgivings and doubts were more inflamed than before she had talked with the doctor.

8
Was Humpty Dumpty Pushed?

AFTER MEGAN HAD TOLD HOMER what she could, in the Luxembourg Gardens, he said that he would telephone Colonel Lvov Kvek, the White Russian taxi driver who had brought her from the Prince de Galles to the Café Flore so early that morning, and had taken them back at dawn.

"Colonel Kvek usually calls at the Flore, and waits in line along the boulevard St. Germain about that hour, in case someone he knows wants to be driven home," Homer said. "He knows a lot of people who might want a service like that. He's very strong, and if need be, he carries them upstairs," Homer explained.

"Your own car is parked just outside the restaurant, where we lunched," said Megan, feeling suddenly empty and strange at the thought that she might be losing Homer.

"I'll have to use it, myself, for a while. I was going to suggest that Colonel Kvek escort you to the races at Longchamps. You'll be in time for the last three. It's a picturesque track, and some fine horses are running today. The colonel will tell you about everything," Homer said.

"And then?" she could not help asking.

"I'll need you, about that time," Evans said. "I'd like to meet your father—in a natural way that wouldn't necessarily suggest that I was involved in this case."

"Oh!" she said, brightening. "I'll do anything I can. I want to help you."

"While you're at Longchamps, I'll check up on a few details," said Homer.

So it was arranged. Colonel Kvek appeared promptly, was delighted with the assignment. Homer drove his roadster back to No. 21 rue Cassette. The body had been removed. Work had been stopped, of course, and the truck driver and laborer had been sent back to their department. Sergeant Schlumberger and a policeman in uniform were on guard. The Alsatian was glum.

"This is the kind of case designed to drive detectives mad," Schlumberger said. "Part of an old building chances to tumble on an American lieutenant. So our overworked staff searches haystacks for pins, while American lieutenant colonels go off like bunches of firecrackers."

"It's a pity the deceased lieutenant had to talk on the trans-Atlantic radiophone a couple of hours after having been buried beneath all this debris," said Evans. "That's the sort of thing that complicates a routine investigation."

Schlumberger looked at Homer reproachfully. "You've talked on trans-oceanic radiophones no doubt," he suggested.

"Several times," Evans agreed.

"You could swear, each time, that you could positively identify the voice?" Schlumberger asked.

"If I knew the voice well enough," said Homer. "There are distortions, due to transmission, reception and static interference. But certain tricks of enunciation, emphasis, pronunciation, the choice of words, the time, the place, the occasion, the subject talked about or discussed, would not depend upon timbre or tone quality. I might be able to raise my right hand and swear that So-and-So spoke with me, or I might not."

"I could swear that if anybody brought one girl out of several millions who had a monkey wrench like that to throw into our machinery, you, Monsieur Homer Evans, would be the man to produce her," Schlumberger said. "And no one but you could then take her from under the noses of chiefs and colonels before she had a chance to tell her full story."

"The influences were not propitious around here," Evans said. "I wanted her to tell the tale calmly."

"And be the first and only one to hear it," Schlumberger added. "Fremont trusts you, alas."

Evans put on an expression of hurt astonishment. *"You* don't?"

Schlumberger squirmed, remembering a few cases which, but for Evans, would still be open. He fussed and growled a little. "I trust Fremont. That's as far as I can go," he said. "Perhaps you'll tell him what the girl said, and maybe he'll tell me. In a muddle of this kind, we must all be as roundabout as possible."

Evans smiled. "I'll tell the proper parties at the right time," he said. "Just now, I need to have a look at this building. Is there a ladder handy?"

Schlumberger showed alarm. "I beg of you, Monsieur Evans, do not go climbing and scampering around those dangerous walls," he begged, indicating the ruins with a gesture.

Evans walked over and tried one of the walls, by leaning and pushing against it, at a point level with his shoulders.

"You're right, sergeant. They're not safe. Doesn't anyone interest himself, officially, in Paris, when death traps like this exist and the public is left at their mercy?"

Schlumberger narrowed his eyes. "France is not the United States, where there are dollars galore," he said. "The department that attends to demolition of death traps has had this building on its list since 1937. While the Boches were at the Paris Dinard, and so many of them walked back and forth I suppose this menace was allowed to remain, on the long chance that if walls fell, there might be Germans under them. In the week of Liberation, August, 1944, the order to proceed with wrecking this corner was transferred from the wire basket marked 'Current' to the basket labeled 'Urgent.' So the turn of this minor threat to public safety came only yesterday. Unluckily, as you know, part of the building took the liberty of collapsing of its own accord three days before the workmen got here."

While the sergeant had been talking, Evans had listened and assimilated all that was said, but also he had examined the standing walls as best he could.

"Let's hope no heavy trucks drive past," he said. "You might station a few men around, to detour large vehicles, until we can examine the premises with the aid of competent engineers."

"No one else will be imprudent enough to stand under there, where he may be killed," Schlumberger said.

"Ah," asked Evans. "You can swear that the late lieutenant was standing when the load fell on him?"

"Would he have gone in there to sit or lie down?" asked Schlumberger.

"I haven't yet counted the possibilities, but here are a few of them," said Homer. "Lieutenant Kitchel might have been placed there, dead or unconscious. He could have gone there conscious and alive. The wall may have fallen by accident at 6 Monday evening. Some outside agency might have brought about the collapse. The death might have resulted by accident, or, if there was a trap, it might have been intended for someone else. Who goes gunning for lieutenants in peace time?"

"The American might have wandered in there, to look around, and got killed when the wall collapsed. In fact, you'll admit that the chances are a million to one that the accident happened like that," Schlumberger insisted.

"We've got to find out when he died, and from what cause. Do you happen to know whether Fremont has called in the medical examiner?" asked Homer.

"Dr. Toudoux had leave to take his wife driving in the country today. In his place a young doctor or intern came, and said the deceased died because several tons of stone, plaster and dirt fell on him from a height of twelve to sixty feet," Schlumberger said. "My little son, aged ten, could have handled the job, and reached the same conclusions."

"Would you mind phoning Fremont to see that the body is not disturbed, or even undressed?" Evans said, very anxiously.

"A lucky thing, monsieur," muttered the sergeant, "that there were no amateurs of criminology in the days of Humpty Dumpty. Had there been a gentleman like you, helping the King's men, the cause of death would still be in question, and generations of children would have been deprived of the rhyme."

"It has never been proved that Humpty Dumpty sat on the wall of his own accord, or that he fell on account of his own contributory negligence. We don't even know whether he fell backwards or forwards," said Homer.

"I'll speak to Fremont about the body," Schlumberger said.

"There's no certainty that Lieutenant Kitchel died at 6 P.M. last Monday. All we can say with certainty is that he died before 6:01 P.M. last Monday," said Homer.

"The saints preserve the few straggling wits that wander like orphans through the desolation of my once flourishing intelligence," groaned the sergeant.

"Furthermore, I seem to recall dimly that the corpse was in a sitting position," Evans said.

"What's mysterious about that?" protested the Alsatian detective.

"All the King's horses and all the King's men could not have bent a corpse into a jackknife position, after it had been stiff so many days," said Evans, evenly. "You don't seriously suggest, on the other hand, that the lieutenant wandered into that ruined corner, beneath tottering walls, in broad daylight at six of a Spring evening, and sat down on the dirty floor, in a nice clean uniform. And remember! One hour before 6 P.M. last Monday, our lieutenant talked sensibly to the Terrible-Tempered Colonel Bang."

"If only I could go crazy," Sergeant Schlumberger said.

"And now, please, I want to look at Lieutenant Kitchel's room. Is it just as he left it?" Evans asked.

"It is just as we found it," said Schlumberger.

"Haven't your merry men tramped around, more or less?"

"They haven't emptied the mattresses and examined each thread of stuffing under a microscope or with chemicals, if that's what you mean," Schlumberger said. "No doubt you'll find something on the premises to make extra difficulties in the case."

"We set them up, then knock them over," Evans said.

Schlumberger gave instructions to the patrolman, and walked with Evans to the near-by hotel Paris Dinard. Evans smiled to himself. The sergeant's curiosity had been aroused to such a point that he could not let Homer examine the room alone. As they passed into the lobby, Homer said to the hotel clerk:

"Any idea what time the races will be over this afternoon?"

"I'll look at the paper," the clerk said, and having scanned the racing sheet continued: "Some pretty good horses are running in the 6th. Epinard III, Sanctuary, Prater Violet, and Nicholas II. About 5:30, I should say."

Homer asked for the key of Room 37, and the clerk handed it over.

Rooms have a way of absorbing and reflecting the personalities of occupants who live in them five years. The late lieutenant's indicated that Kitchel had been easygoing, unimaginative and impractical. It was about five meters by four, with a ceiling four meters high. There were two windows overlooking the back courtyard, a door into the hall, a washstand, a bidet, a large wardrobe with two drawers underneath, a wall closet with an opening four feet from the floor, and a sealed door that formerly had connected with No. 36. Kitchel had had some book shelves built. Ignoring the doors and windows, on the assumption that the routine work had been done well by Schlumberger, Homer went straight to the bookcase. He sighed and showed relief.

"We're in luck. I hate to run up against a blank wall, and have to reconstruct everything by means of cerebral strain," Homer said. "I love objects, material objects which can be labeled 'Exhibits A, or B.'"

"That is the most understandable thing I ever heard you say," said Schlumberger. "May I be permitted to look at the exhibits?"

Homer handed him five books bound in black cardboard with gilt lettering. They were uniform in style and makeup, and Schlumberger read the titles and dates, then groaned. They were all entitled *An Annual History of the Town of Rockport*. The dates were 1863, 1887, 1902, 1903 and 1933.

"Did Lieutenant Kitchel live in a town called Rockport?" the sergeant inquired.

Evans shook his head in the negative. "It's not as simple as that," he said.

"Why, may I ask, should he keep on his shelves five volumes of a town history about a place in which he did not reside?"

"If I could answer that," said Evans, "we might be nearer our solution."

"It would be a record, would it not, if we reached our solution without having decided on our problem?" asked the sergeant.

"As a matter of fact, the solution, if hit upon promptly, often reveals the essential problem," replied Homer.

Schlumberger touched fondly one temple, then the other.

"Ah, Humpty Dumpty," he mused.

"May I keep these books a while?" Evans asked.

The Alsatian grunted and nodded.

Before Homer went to the Ritz to meet Megan, he had another errand on his conscience. He ought to tip off Finke Maguire that Kitchel was dead and that Mallory knew it. Homer had a strong hunch that there was plenty of work for all concerned and that he might need Finke's help very soon. There were times when apostles of direct action filled the bill, and none others could qualify.

With his usual dispatch in city driving, Homer went to Finke's office and residence, 13 rue Pelican. He could not help remarking the condition of the old building, which never had been pretentious in its best days. It probably had been built about the time the town of Rockport had been founded, by Richard Tarr, in 1629.

Finke was not there. The concierge told Evans that as if she relished saying it. She looked like Kate Smith would if she had just received an insulting cablegram from Gerhardt Eisler. Homer knew without trying that there was no use asking when Finke might be back. So he drove to the Ritz. The blonde was just being relieved by the brunette at the switchboard. Neither of them knew a thing about Finke's whereabouts. Homer saw that the man talking with the bartender from across the bar looked as if he might be Luke Mallory, and was anxious that Mallory should not get a look at him until Megan introduced them as a matter of course. So he went over to an easy chair near the potted rubber tree Finke, unknown to Evans, had used as a screen more than once, and sat down to think. He had left the five annual histories of Rockport in his car, locked securely in the baggage compartment. An hour passed, and neither Megan nor Lvov Kvek put in an appearance. Why were they late? Others who had attended the races had come in, at least thirty minutes before. Then Homer's mind clicked back to the Paris Dinard and the names of the horses mentioned by the hotel clerk.

Homer rose to his feet, and went back to the telephone desk.

"Who won the sixth race, mademoiselle?" he asked the brunette.

"Nicholas II, Mr. Evans," she answered.

By the looks of Homer's face, she assumed that he had backed some other horse.

"Did you lose much, sir?" she asked.

"I seem to have lost, temporarily, a couple of friends," Homer said.

"You make friends so easily, Mr. Evans," the brunette said. "Don't you?"

"More easily than I find them," said Homer.

The switchboard began flashing owl eyes and buzzing at disconcerting intervals. The brunette's lovely tapering fingers and wrists began to flit, draw, insert and release while her mobile voice responded, assuaged and chided. With an understanding shrug Homer went back to the easy chair behind the rubber tree to resume thinking about the riddle in which Megan had involved him. There must be a reason why Lieutenant Kitchel had been reading about Rockport, Mass., and it would have a connection with the fact that his deceased friend, Fred Mallory, had owned a small cottage there, on the shore near Thatcher's Island, at a place called Loblolly Cove. But why the years 1863, 1887, 1902, 1903 and 1933? A reading of those year books would disclose a common factor, Homer hoped.

He wished Megan would show up.

Then he saw her, such a picture of radiance and youth that he forgave her in advance for keeping him waiting. At her elbow was Colonel Lvov Kvek, but not in his taxi driver's rig. He was wearing a stovepipe hat, evening clothes, with a white satin lined cloak, and a muffler of jade gray silk. His hands were gloved. On one arm was a hooked stick.

Homer watched the pair advance. Kvek halted before another easy chair in which an elderly woman with a fine head of silver hair and a high forehead was sitting motionless, as if she had been there for years. Homer saw Kvek's handsome face light up, as he greeted the woman, bowing over her hand which she extended list-lessly.

"Your Highness, little dove," Kvek exclaimed.

"Ah, Prince Kvek. What is it the English poet says? 'Time, like a wounded serpent.' Surprising, for an Englishman. Such penetration. That's just how I feel . . . the dying snake, biting and rebiting myself as much to inflict pain as to hasten release into oblivion. You know, Lvovshki, that I have clung to hope for our cause, that I've never surrendered. But between you and me, this spring, when the buds emerged and the sun shone strong, I was depressed. I fear we will not go back to Russia. The cursed Bolsheviki are there to stay."

Kvek threw his arms around the lovely old lady and lifted her two hundred and fifty pounds from the chair in an impulsive embrace.

"You haven't heard, Anastasiuschka, darling? Today we were given a sign. We have courage again. Also, in my case, funds."

"Don't raise my hopes," the Countess Pluishkin begged.

"No one told you who won today at Longchamps?"

"The horses I once knew are all dead," said the Countess.

"Nicholas II!" shouted Kvek.

The sophisticated and callous bystanders in the front lobby of the Ritz were touched by the spontaneous demonstration of joy which ensued. After it had passed its height, Homer rose and Megan, who had been so amazed on learning that her escort was a Prince, caught sight of Evans and fairly ran to him.

"I'm late. It's terrible. I couldn't help it. . . . But, oh, it's been such fun. The colonel. . . . That's what I call him. I can't pronounce any of his names, won lots of money, and so did I. I haven't counted it. Neither has he. A horse won, named for somebody the colonel had served. The colonel emptied his pockets, urged me to bet every cent I had. Then he sold the taxi, and bet the proceeds, just before the race got started. We won. Almost nobody else did. It took quite a while to collect, and he was so anxious to stop and change into evening clothes. Did I do wrong? I couldn't spoil his pleasure. I felt, somehow, as if he hadn't felt as good as that for a long, long time. . . . I felt, to tell the truth, that you would have wanted me to humor him."

"You did exactly right. What were the odds?"

"I think the horse paid 17 to 1. We bet on his nose, and that's how he won, by sticking it out farther than the other two horses who were running beside him," she said.

Homer grinned. "Then Lvov has the price of seventeen taxis. Before you start out with him, tonight, be sure that he buys himself another cab, before he spends his winnings," Evans said.

Her face had fallen. "You mean, you won't be with us?"

"I've got to do some reading, in connection with the case," he said.

"Oh," she said, disconsolately, "couldn't I read aloud to you?"

"I'd rather you witnessed the White Russian celebration. I never shared their politics, but their enthusiasm is an example to the world, when they let themselves go."

He saw that she still felt bad, and added:

"We'll have breakfast at the Closerie des Lilas. I'll tell you then about my findings."

"Yes. Yes," she said, eagerly. "I'll celebrate. I'll be ready. I'll be there."

"I'll call for you," he said. "Now I want to meet your father, just to pay my respects."

9
To the Junk Yard—Sooner or Later

FROM THE HOTEL D'ANGLETERRE, as soon as he had got out of Dr. Havemeyer's office, Finke called the Ritz in Paris. The blonde was on the switchboard and Finke assumed she would listen in, but what could he do, and what did he care? Lieutenant Kitchel, whom he had described as "hot" was now "cold." Luke Mallory finally responded on the other end of the line.

"Tell me everything you know," Finke said. "I couldn't talk in Doc's office."

"I told you everything. Lieutenant Kitchel's been murdered," Mallory answered, huffily. "And since when have I got to tell *you* things? I thought 'twould be the other way around."

"Can a guy be in two places at once?" countered Finke. "How was Kitchel murdered?"

"I haven't the foggiest idea," snapped Mallory.

"Then how do you know he was murdered?"

"Come to think of it, I don't," admitted Mallory, as if that idea had just struck him. "A guy called me up, somebody I don't know, and said a man he thought I was interested in was dead, that his body'd just been found."

"Found where?"

"I don't know. He didn't say."

"Who found the body?"

"He didn't say that either."

"Didn't you ask him anything, for God's sake?"

"I didn't have a chance," Mallory said.

231

"But you call me up all the way from Paris to Rouen to say Kitchel was murdered?"

"I shoulda said his body'd been found. But don't start tellin' me what to say and what not to say."

Finke broke in. "At least you probably know who it was that tipped you off."

"His name was Homer Evans, and he was lunching with my daughter. That's all I know about anything," Mallory roared.

"Homer Evans!" repeated Finke. "Oh, no! Don't tell me he's Johnny-on-the-Spot again. And how is it your daughter, who don't look a day over sixteen, is out all night with this guy, Evans, who you don't know?"

"You know this Evans, then," grunted Mallory.

"We've met," Finke said. "He cashed a $100 check for me, one o' yours, got me out of jail this morning and drove me to the Ritz to see you. How did he happen to phone you about Kitchel?"

"I was lunching with Wasp Billings, at Foo Kay's. Megan must have told this Evans where I was, and he phoned me to find out if Colonel Billings was there. Billings talked with him after I did, and beat it, leavin' me flat, and also his own driver, who'd been look-ing in a shop window, not three doors from Foo Kay's. The colonel drove himself, he was in that much of a hurry."

"How nice! Then you know that a guy named Evans called you and told you a body's been found and that it was Kitchel's. Try not to get any more information till I get back there. Some things, so they say, are so terrible that it's better not to know about them. You're as careless a client as you are a father, I would say."

Finke hung up. What should he do next, he asked himself. Maybe Kitchel had been murdered, maybe not. Finke was inclined to think he had been. And Evans? At least the *garçons* at the Flore called Evans by name. So one of them might know where Evans lived; how he came by so much jack; how come he was so thick with Mallory's daughter, three or four days after the kid hit Paris; how Evans knew Finke himself was in the hoosegow and wanted to get out; how Evans knew Wasp Billings.

There were plenty of questions, and damn few answers. Finke
decided to take the next train back to Paris. He had an hour and
more to wait, so he thought he'd take a walk. He did not care a rap
about Joan of Arc or cathedrals, or Beaulieu, and although he
hadn't eaten since the night before he had no appetite. He went
into the Angleterre bar, drank a double bourbon with a bottle of
Bass for a chaser, and started out with no destination in his mind.
Soon he found himself on the edge of a dump where some old
barbed wire, G.I. cans, elephant iron, twisted rails and girders, iron
wheels and maybe a hundred abandoned railroad cars were standing on a rusted side track that ran from the riverside to the dump.
It was a dead scene on what looked like a dead land. A clumsy der-
rick was working a quarter of a mile away, at the corner of the field,
loading scrap iron into a camion. The methods were all wrong, but
Finke was used to that.

As he started along a kind of path by the old spur track, glancing idly at the railroad cars, he noticed that some of them, about a
dozen or so, were of the old type, Class III, with dinky compartments having doors on both sides, and no connection one with
another. Of course, there was no glass in any of the windows and
most of the wood had been salvaged for firewood or kindling by
the people in Rouen. The French Government, Finke thought, could
finance itself, without aid, if it went into the junk business.

Finke looked at a compartment window, a few yards from where
he had come to a halt to try to figure out whether any of the junk
had commercial value. He touched the back of his head, still good
and sore, and blinked. He looked again, harder. What seemed to
be a woman, wearing the cap and tunic of an American Army nurse,
was sitting in one of the old third-class cars. If she was thinking,
Finke remarked to himself, the subject must be a deep one. She
had not seen or heard his approach. Finke started walking again
until he was beneath her paneless window.

"*Bon soir,*" Finke said.

The woman turned her head, and looked at him, saying nothing,
not in the least startled or surprised. She had straight straw-colored

hair, fairly tidy. Her army cap was at the exact angle to give her an appearance of rakishness her lethargy belied. Her eyes were brown and wary, like those of a pig, without the swellings around the edges.

"Enjoying the scenery?" Finke asked.

The woman acted as if his original "*Bon soir*" had just reached her brain, by a process of delayed action.

"*Bon soir, musseer?*" she said in a low flat voice, and a Middle-Western American accent. "*Come on tally voo?*"

"Forgotten your American?" Finke asked. His face was just below the level of her elbow which was resting on the window sill.

"I was looking for the first-aid station," she said, in American. "It used to be around here somewhere."

"There's nothing around here now but junk," Finke said.

"Sooner or later, everything gets to be junk," she said, and rose. With a little difficulty she pushed open the door, and stepped from the compartment to the running board along the side of the car. The step was quite a distance from the floor of the car. She had on a short skirt, and showed quite a bit of her leg.

Finke whistled softly. The leg caught him off base. It was a strong shapely leg, from the knee down, at least. American rather than European. Country, not city. He was about to ask her where she was from when the rotted running board gave way and she pitched forward into his arms. Instinctively he had braced himself to catch and steady her.

"One advantage junk has," Finke remarked. "It don't have to be dependable."

A faint smile changed ever so slightly the lower part of the woman's face and seemed to increase the wariness of her eyes. They were between hazel and brown.

"You liked my leg," she said, as if she were saying that he liked tapioca pudding. It was a kind of general observation, no displeasure, no satisfaction, either.

"Sure I did. The other one's about the same, I suppose," said Finke. He did not know just where this was leading but since he had started out without any objective, he thought he might as well proceed.

The woman raised her skirt and showed both of her legs, to just above the knee. She did it in a matter-of-fact way, and looked down at them, dubiously.

"They're not too thick—on the heavy side?" she asked, as if she wanted his opinion, but was prepared for an unflattering one.

"You probably ride bicycles or something," he said. "The calves are developed . . . But not too much. I'd say your legs are O.K."

He had noticed that her skirt was navy blue, that her shoes were American and comfortable but not flat, and that her stockings were sheer nylon. With her uniform tunic, army flannel shirt, and cap, all olive drab, the effect was unusual, quite definitely strange. He made no comment on that.

"Did you find the first-aid station?" she asked.

"Not yet," he said.

"I was almost sure it was around here, somewhere. Probably the captain will know," she said.

He was about to say "You must have been in the service," but then he decided to let her talk without prompting.

"The captain?" he repeated.

"He lives in this town. I was going to see him and ask him. I found his house, all right. Then I didn't go in. I'd made up my mind, then I changed it. I like changing my mind, when I feel like it," she said.

Silently Finke said, "You like wearing a regulation cap and blouse, with a WAVE's skirt, and civilian shoes and nylons," and it occurred to Finke that her liking to change her mind might be hooked up somehow with her wearing an assortment of clothes that were not banal. Could it be that she had not liked taking orders in the Army, and maybe before or after the Army, she had not liked taking orders in civilian hospitals, where some doctors like running nurses ragged as long as they can get away with it? Also he figured that Dr. Havemeyer was probably the only American captain in Rouen who might know where a certain field hospital had stood, while the shooting war was in progress. He decided to take a flyer.

"Doc Havemeyer's sure to know—about the first-aid station," he suggested.

"I'll go back and ask him," said the woman. "This time I'll go in."

"Mind if I walk with you? I'm headed that way, toward the railroad station," Finke said. "I'm Finke Maguire," he added. "I was an M.P."

"The M.P.'s won the war," she said.

Finke looked at her closely, but she gave no sign that she was kidding or making a dirty crack.

"Did you know Lieutenant Kitchel—Bob Kitchel, by any chance?" asked Finke.

"I saw him Monday. I had a drink with him in some Paris cafe. I'd made up my mind to look him up, then I thought, what's the use, but I ran into him anyway, so I said, what's the difference."

"Sure. Bob was a good guy," Finke said.

"I haven't told you my name," she said. "I thought of telling you, when you told me yours, then I couldn't remember yours and forgot about telling you mine."

"Finke Maguire," he said.

"Agnes Welsh," said the woman.

"You were a lieutenant?" he asked.

"I had the rank of lieutenant," she said. "I was a nurse. I wanted to be a model, and got turned down."

"I didn't know they had models in the Army, but I wouldn't be surprised. I wouldn't be surprised at anything they had or didn't have in the Army," said Finke. "By the way, did you know Lieutenant Mallory—Fred Mallory?"

That had a startling effect on her. She winced, her eyes opened wide, and she pulled herself back together with an effort.

"Fred was a good guy," she said, flatly. "He found my legs O.K. Not too thick, I mean."

"Seen him lately?" asked Finke.

"Not since he died," she said. "Only a couple of times in a dream. It's funny, isn't it, how you see people in dreams after they've died? I knew a woman once whose sister had a parrot, and after the sister died the parrot kept on using the dead woman's voice. I used to go over to their house, just to hear the parrot. I can't explain it, but I got a kick out of it, somehow, hearing a live voice of a woman who was dead. I dream about the parrot, too, once in a while."

"The parrot dead?" asked Finke.

They started walking toward the doctor's office, and talked as they went along.

"Parrots live a long time. That's funny, too, that parrots live longer than people. Some say they live a couple of hundred years," said Agnes Welsh. "And I should have told you they don't have models in the Army. It was before I went into training I was turned down for modeling."

"I see," Finke said.

"What difference does it make?" asked Agnes Welsh.

"Your legs are absolutely O.K. Thin legs are strictly for atrocity propaganda, and Hollywood," said Finke. "You mustn't be morose about those gams of yours . . . Fred liked 'em, you say."

"He talked just like you, when I told him about getting turned down for modeling. He said there wasn't a better pair at the Embassy or the Marshall Plan headquarters. He told me to ask Dr. Havemeyer—the doctor was a captain then—to prove that what he said was sincere."

"You asked the captain-doctor?"

"I thought I wouldn't. I thought I was bothering too much about my legs, and ought to think of something else. But I changed my mind, and asked him."

"That was before Fred died?"

"Not long before. A month after Fred was dead, I got my discharge from the Army. Doc thought I ought to rest. I didn't care much, one way or the other, so I resigned and went back home. When I found how different things were back there, I came over here again. But at first I didn't look up anybody I knew. Not until I ran into Lieutenant Kitchel. He said I ought to see Doc Havemeyer. Everybody seems to get the notion, every now and then, that I ought to see a doctor. So I hired a bicycle and came down here today."

"Kitchel said that Monday?"

"While we were having a drink," she said.

"Bob was there, when Fred died?" Finke asked.

"Sure. He was Fred's best friend. Quite a few times the three of us went out together. Fred didn't mind if Bob was with us."

"Fred's mother's in town. Had you heard?"

Agnes Welsh blushed and looked troubled. "She hadn't heard about Fred and me, I hope. He and I both understood that what we did didn't mean anything permanent. We both were leveling. So many of the men and girls got intimate, and liked each other's company—you know what I mean."

"Sure I do," Finke said. "Had you talked much with Fred—about modeling and that sort of thing—before you got together? You know . . ."

"No. Not before. When I told Fred about modeling—he was the first person I'd told, since it happened. My talking about failure got Fred worried, and he advised me to tell Captain Havemeyer. Things didn't go so well between us, after that. I didn't see much of Fred until a few days before he died, when the captain called me in to take care of him." She stopped talking and walking suddenly, and looked at Finke apologetically. "I've talked too much, again. You'll give me the brush off," she said.

"Not so's you'd notice it," Finke said, and he meant it. He risked one more question.

"Ever meet a guy named Homer Evans?" he asked, brusquely.

She thought back and shook her head. "No. No one by that name," she said.

"Well, thank God for that," said Finke. And silently he gave thanks, also, that at last he had something to report to Luke Mallory, an item for men only, if Mallory wanted it that way. And something told Finke that Mallory would want it that way.

Finke made up his mind to take no chances. He would watch Agnes go in to see Doc Havemeyer, and would do his damnedest to fix it so she wouldn't mention having talked with him, or seen him. That might work and it might not. Agnes was a walking nervous breakdown. No telling what she'd forget, remember, say or do. Anyway, Finke would hang around, join her when she came out of Doc's house, and go back to Paris with her. He was not going to lose her, if he could help it. "Jeepers!" he groaned. "Two hundred kilometers on a bicycle." He wished Mallory had paid him five grand.

He escorted Agnes Welsh as far as the corner of the rue de Caen, saw her mount the steps, push the bell, and enter when the Norman woman admitted her. Then he beat it as fast as he could to the Hotel d'Angleterre, phoned the Ritz, told the brunette, who by that time was on duty, to tell Mallory that for a reason he said Mallory would later understand, he had decided to return to Paris "over the road."

Then he hustled back to the rue de Caen, posted himself in a convenient ruined doorway, and glued his eyes on Doc Havemeyer's house. The lights came on in the streets, and about the same time in the downstairs hallway and reception room, and the upstairs office.

Finke strained his eyes, but he could see nothing or no one moving inside.

"What the hell?"

At 8 o'clock, the light in the second-story office went out. Two minutes afterward the ground floor lights in the reception room went dark. The dim light in the hallway, dispersed through a glass chandelier continued shedding its baleful glow, a color between Grand Rapids oak and kumquat.

"I've got to take a quick gander at the back of the house." There were only front and back, as far as windows were concerned. Havemeyer's house had had a common wall with No. 3 and although there was a passage two feet wide between No. 3 bis and No. 5, both walls were as blank as Finke's reports to Mallory had been.

Feeling nervous about leaving the front door unguarded, Finke ran, under cover of darkness, through the passageway and before he could stop himself in the walled backyard felt a blinding stinging blow on the forehead, just above his eyes. He was thrown backward so violently that in falling his head hit a terra-cotta open drain three meters away. Finke went into what is known in the trade as a "long tunnel." He did not know how long he was out but, on regaining consciousness, he took no chances. He lay still, looking up at the stars which were almost obscured by the damp atmosphere. Then silently he crawled back through the passageway, and stood up just before he got to the sidewalk, keeping close to the wall of No. 3 bis so as not to offer a target against the dimly lighted street.

Nothing happened. If anyone had seen him, no one cared, it seemed. Finke fished in his pockets, and found everything there, including his francs and American Express checks.

"Whoever it was didn't roll me," he muttered.

He ducked across the street and looked at the face of No. 3 bis. The hallway light was still burning. A clock struck nine. He had been out nearly an hour. Of course, Agnes would be gone, but he had to try. He mounted the front steps, pushed the doctor's night doorbell and the regular one, too. Both sounded somewhere inside, one loud and harsh, the other medium. One was tuned to "A," and the other clanged "G-flat." A dismal minor third.

After quite a wait, he heard shuffling footsteps, then the door opened a few inches.

"The doctor's not here," said the Norman woman, much disgruntled. She started to shut the door.

"No, you don't," Finke said, and inserted his foot. The Norman stamped on it. He shoved his way inside and when she started to yell, cut off the demonstration by means of a stiff right uppercut under her chin. He hadn't meant to do it. The action was instinctive. Anyway, Miss or Mrs. Normandy went out cold. Finke banged on the reception-room door, then went up the stairs two or three at a time, and looked back. No response. He tried the door of the office. It was locked tight, a heavy lock and also a Yale lock. No chance of going in there, short of breaking down the heavy oak door.

Finke found another door, back of the staircase, and it was unlocked. He switched on his flashlight. The room was empty. Evidently it was the doctor's bedroom, which connected with another behind the office. Finke took a quick look at both rooms. They were tidy and quite as they should be. The bed had not been slept in, but the cover was turned down. Finke tried the door from the back room to the office. That had two locks, like the other office door. He could not get into the office. Why in hell should he?

He hustled downstairs again and hopped nimbly over the Norman woman who was lying on the hall carpet. The reception-room door was unlocked. He went in, turned on the lights and looked around. All was in order. He went back into the dining room behind the reception room, then into the kitchen. On the table was a small lamp, lighted, and near it were a pair of store spectacles and a Buffalo Bill wild Western in French. The Norman woman had been reading, so it seemed.

Before he could get farther, the Norman woman regained consciousness and got moaning to her feet, holding her jaw. She spat out a tooth, and, seeing Finke, started to yell again. He had her in a strong half nelson, in an instant, his left hand over her mouth.

"Listen. This is no hold-up. I'm a friend of Doc's and I want to see him."

She tried to struggle, gave up the idea, and indicated that the doctor was not at home.

"When did he leave?"

"About seven," she told him, shivering with fright, or something else. He did not have time to find out about that.

"A woman came to see him. Where is she?" Finke demanded.

"Several women came this afternoon," she said.

"The last one, with an army cap and blouse and a short navy skirt," he said.

"That one asked for the doctor. I said he wasn't home. She went away," the Norman said.

"How soon after you let her in?"

"Just a minute or two, maybe four or five," the woman said.

That checked with the time Finke had gone over to the Hotel d'Angleterre.

"When'll the doctor be back?"

She shrugged her shoulders. "Who knows?" she said. "Where is he now?"

"I don't know. In some other town."

"Don't he leave word where he can be reached?"

"Not always. Not tonight," she said.

Finke swore disgustedly under his breath and pulled out his American Express checks. He showed one to the Norman woman.

"Know what these are?" he asked.

She nodded.

"The one I'm giving you, to keep your trap shut, and get another tooth, is good for 31,000 francs," he said.

She reached for it.

"Just a minute. How'll I know you'll keep mum about this visit of mine?" he asked.

She pulled a rosary out from under her blouse and touched it. "I swear," she said.

He gave her the check, went out and closed the front door behind him. He heard her slip the chain, so he could not get in again.

Finke beat it to the railroad station and went to the baggage room. He slipped the baggage man 1,000 francs, and looked over the bicycles. All were for men. He described Agnes as best he could, and the man assured him he had seen no such woman.

Five bicycles were parked in a rack in the parking space between the station and the city. One was a woman's, but while Finke was watching, a woman, not at all like Agnes, came to recover the wheel and, mounting it, rode away.

Near by was a bicycle repair shop, still open. Finke made inquiries there. The patron remembered having seen a woman like Agnes, as Finke described her, ride along the main street toward the waterfront early that afternoon. Her bicycle was in good order, it seemed to the repair-shop patron.

"This is getting me nowhere," Finke grunted to himself. Then he had an impulse he tried to dismiss and could not. He walked down the street, turned right and went back to the junk yard. With the aid of his flashlight he found the abandoned Class III coach in which Agnes had been sitting when he spotted her. He walked around the coach, flashing his torch. On the side away from where he had stood talking, and caught Agnes when she had fallen, was a woman's bicycle, with a plate attached to one of the handlebars indicating that it was the property of Machin, Frères, of 68 rue Cardinal Lemoine, Paris 5me.

He rode the bicycle back to the railroad station, feeling like a fool, but nobody noticed it was for women and priests. Finke found the *chef de gare*, or station master, and asked him if he had seen any American women boarding a train for Paris that evening. The station master, an observant obliging man, described Mrs. Mallory, and then Agnes Welsh. They had got on the 8 o'clock train separately. Either or both might have been bound for Paris. Finke went to the ticket window. The man there remembered having sold a one-way ticket to a woman answering Agnes' description. She had been in a terrible hurry, and there had barely been time to make out the ticket and hand it to her before the train had pulled out of the station.

Finke was so disgusted with himself that he had a good mind to ride that woman's bike all the way back to Paris, himself. But instead he waited for the 10:15 train, the next one running, checked the bicycle in the baggage room, and sat grimly, smoking and thinking all the way back.

Some of his thoughts were dark and heavy. Some were not so heavy. Some were not so dark. He had something, and again he had nothing. He had not the nerve to tell Mallory whom he had found, and how he had let her get away. He would first have to catch up with Agnes Welsh again. When he got through with her, she wouldn't give a damn whether she had legs both alike, or none at all, he promised himself.

He was so hungry that every time he saw a lighted *bistro* or hash house along the way, he felt faint and started swearing.

10

Post-Mortem

HAVING MET MEGAN'S FATHER and Selectman Parker, Evans suggested that they go with Megan and Colonel Kvek to the Coque d'Or, in the rue Mouffetard, behind the Pantheon, for a Russian dinner and the celebration Kvek was planning. Countess Pluishkin joined them at the bar.

Luke Mallory contrived to get Homer aside, and Evans told him that Lieutenant Kitchel's body had been found under a pile of debris in the corner of a ruined building less than a block from the hotel in which the dead lieutenant had lived since late 1944.

"The police believe Kitchel's death was accidental," Homer said.

"And what do you believe?" asked Mallory.

"Wasp Billings is investigating, on behalf of the American forces," Homer told him. "Fremont, chief of the Paris detectives, is a capable man. They'll leave no stone unturned."

"You didn't answer my question," Luke said. "Do you think the lad's death was accidental?" he repeated. Luke had not made up his mind about Evans, who looked as if he might know a lot, and said so little.

"I think it would be better if anyone who might be responsible for Kitchel's death believed that everyone else had swallowed the accident theory," Evans replied.

"I get you," Luke said. Then he remembered something and looked crestfallen. "I've talked too much already," he admitted.

"To whom?"

"A guy named Finke Maguire. He says he's met you," Luke answered.

Evans smiled and relaxed. "Finke's all right. He's not the garrulous type. Anyone else?"

Luke thought hard, and shook his head. "Nary a soul," he said.

"Did you tell Finke over the telephone?" Evans asked.

"Yes. I did," said Luke, feeling guilty again.

"From here?" Evans asked.

"From a booth by the switchboard," Luke said.

"Who was on the switchboard? The blonde?"

"I think so," said Luke. "You don't mean, she listens in?"

"It's possible. I'll find out what, if anything, she knows," Evans said.

Luke looked at Evans sharply, still undecided about him.

"Might I ask what's your interest in the case?" he demanded, bluntly.

Evans smiled. "I'm an old friend of Fremont's. I've lived in Paris, off and on, a number of years. The Chief has formed a conviction, I'm sure I don't know why, that all incidents, accidents or problems involving Americans have peculiar aspects of their own, not necessarily comprehensible to Europeans. So, before he gets in too deep, when Americans seem to be in difficulties, he asks my advice."

"I see," said Luke. That was what he said, but he still was puzzled. "You're ducking this Cossack jubilee where you're sending the lot of us," Luke said. "You'll be dishing out advice somewhere else?"

"I've got a few errands, and some reading to do," Evans said. "And I'd like very much, when Mrs. Mallory gets back from Rouen, to have a talk with her."

"She never killed anybody, as far as I know," Luke said. "But if she wants to talk with you, I've no objection. I only hope you'll bear in mind that she lost a son, herself."

Evans could not find a word to say. Megan stepped over softly.

"I know we shouldn't keep you," she said to Homer. And glancing at her father, she added: "We'll be all right."

Recovering, Evans smiled, made an easy gesture of good-bye to Mallory, and walked away.

It took Homer less than five minutes to drive from the Ritz to the E.R.P. headquarters. The guards at the entrance stepped forward as if to halt him, saw who he was, then nodded recognition. In the lobby of the fine old building Homer went straight to the receptionist's desk, where the night man was sitting.

"Tell Colonel Billings I'm on my way up," Evans said.

"Yes, Mr. Evans," the clerk said, and reached for the phone. Homer crossed the lobby, entered a long marble corridor and walked toward the rear. As he reached the fourth door, it opened, and he stepped inside. Anyone who had witnessed the scene and heard the exchanges between them at 21 rue Cassette would have been astonished to see how glad Wasp Billings was to see Homer and with what respect Evans extended his hand.

"At last," Evans said. "Sorry to keep you waiting."

"Got anything?" Billings asked.

"A lot of questions," Homer said.

"Shoot," said Billings.

"Was Kitchel neat and careful of his appearance?"

"Just soldierly. He didn't primp," Wasp said.

"Tell me about his drinking," Evans asked.

"He drank damned well," Wasp said. "That's why he was picked for several jobs. He could take it, all right. Ordinarily he didn't have to stall, or waste good liquor. He seemed to know when he had all he could stand, and seldom took the extra one."

"That was when he was working, I suppose," Evans said. "Was it the same when he was off duty?"

"When he was drinking for pleasure, he didn't take nearly as much," said Wasp.

"How about Havemeyer?"

"Nothing but a beer, now and then. He used to drink more, when he first came over. He was quite a gay one, so they say. Used to be the life of a party. The war, or something, toned him down. He worked hard. He didn't go to pieces, exactly. But he stayed more by himself, and was quiet. Toward the last, before he resigned and went into private practice, it looked almost as if he didn't know what to do with himself. He couldn't make decisions, I mean."

"Where's his home?"

"A little place called Mount Washington—not the one in New Hampshire. It's a small town tucked into the corner of Massachusetts, with New York State and Connecticut both a few yards away. There's one rock, he told me, where the view takes in miles of three states. The town government's Massachusetts, the nearest post office is in New York."

"He talked a lot about it, if you know all that," remarked Evans.

"He seemed to long for it, all right. Only it was no place for a doctor. . . . No practice, there."

"So he stayed in France, quit Paris, and went to Rouen," Homer said.

The colonel nodded.

"What about his nurse—the one he liked to have on special cases?" Evans asked.

"I've forgotten her name. I'll find out. Won't take a minute." Colonel Billings already had started dialing. He said a few crisp words into the phone, and replaced the instrument.

"Anything strange about the death of Sergeant Baring?" Evans continued. "He was another witness at young Mallory's deathbed."

Billings reached for the phone again, and again spoke a few words. He replaced it. The phone bell rang. He picked up the instrument, crooked the headpiece so his hands were free, and made a few notes on a pad.

"Thanks," he said, and hung up. He turned to Evans. "The nurse was Lieutenant Agnes Welsh. She was one of the best. Went through hell. This year, long after the worst had let up, she got nervous and tired. Doc Havemeyer advised her to rest. She was discharged and went back to the States. Columbus, Ohio."

"Fine," said Evans. "Get a full report on her actions, whatever she's been doing, important or trivial. I'll want it tonight, and then, as soon as possible—a matter of minutes—I want to talk with her by phone."

Billings looked as if he were about to show the side of his character he kept in front, nearly all of the time, but he bit his lip.

"Now what in hell has a girl in Columbus, Ohio, got to do with a lieutenant dead in France?"

"Not much, if Nurse Welsh is actually in Columbus, Ohio," Evans said.

The phone rang. Billings took no notes this time.

"Sergeant Baring died in a jeep accident that could not have been foreseen or avoided by him," the colonel said. "It was in the *place* Notre Dame, just off the Pont au Double, where the old car tracks curved around."

Evans nodded. "I know the layout there," he said.

"A big *camion* with a big trailer was turning left, following the car tracks. Baring in his jeep was approaching, headed north toward the island. Baring timed it so he'd miss the trailer, but when it pulled out of the way, a truck was beyond it, headed south. The truck and jeep collided. There were two Frenchmen on the *camion* pulling the trailer, two more on the truck that hit the jeep and killed Baring. We looked up the records and questioned all four of the French, so did the Sûreté Générale, and there was nothing suspicious about any of them or their connections."

Before he left Wasp Billings, Evans said he was going to have a talk with Dr. Hyacinthe Toudoux, the French medical examiner and world-renowned toxicologist. After that he had five large books to read, which he planned to do in his apartment in the rue Campagne Première. He would be either with Dr. Toudoux at the Prefecture, or at home. Billings promised to phone him the moment the report on Agnes Welsh was received over the trans-Atlantic phone and decoded.

"Let me decode it myself," Evans suggested. "The boys over there can make as much sound and fury as they like, to get quick results. On this side, the fewer who are in on this, the better."

Evans rose. "I am not in as much of a hurry for a report on Private Judd Coulson. Tomorrow afternoon will do. I want his I.Q. and present whereabouts, most of all," Homer said.

Billings nodded. "His I.Q. won't be hard, but I can't say as much about Judd's whereabouts. He was a rolling stone."

"With so many of our countrymen obscured in moss, a smooth stone ought to be easy to spot," Evans said.

They shook hands, and Evans departed. He drove straight to the Prefecture, and went to Fremont's office. The Chief of Detectives looked as though he had been grilled by himself.

"What news of Dr. Toudoux?" Evans asked.

Fremont groaned. "He's coming. I didn't dare tell the details. Only that you were promising him an experience he would not like to miss. He's due any minute."

"If you don't care to face him, I've a good suggestion. Pick up the Existentialist named Ulysses Grant Havemeyer. Let him think he's suspected of having beaten up an American from Mississippi, on Monday afternoon. If he offers an alibi, hint that the assault may have occurred on Tuesday, or even later. Check on everything he says, then let him go, and tail him," Homer said.

"He's been tailed since Friday morning just after two A.M.," Fremont said.

"How lucky!" said Evans.

Fremont, hearing footsteps in the corridor, made a quick and inglorious exit through a side door. The Chief got out just in time so that when Dr. Hyacinthe Toudoux burst into the office, Evans was there alone to receive him. Evans hurried toward the irate medical examiner and clasped his hand.

"We have a case that will eclipse your fame," Homer said.

"If not as a toxicologist, as a swordsman," Toudoux said, unbending. "For should the case not come up to your promises and expectations, sufficiently to atone for my dear wife's disappointment at having our holiday cut short, I shall send you my seconds and on the field of honor churn your tripes."

"I'll give another promise," Evans said, smiling. "If I am the challenged party, I'll choose sabres for weapons."

"Where is this body?" demanded Dr. Toudoux.

Without further ado, Homer led the doctor to the room in which the body of Lieutenant Kitchel, still bent L-shaped and fully clothed in uniform which was covered with dust and loose plaster lay on an extra-wide slab. Dr. Toudoux looked at it coldly and then at Evans.

"Proceed," he said.

"The body was found under tons of debris on the ground floor of an old building which had collapsed, and had been there since Monday last, at 6 P.M.," said Homer.

"Am I to understand that you know the hour and cause of death? What was it you expected from me?" cried the medical examiner, almost choking with rage.

"A false certificate," Evans said, calmly. "With your reputation behind it, no one will raise a question. The young novice who was sent in your place was willing to say that this man, an American lieutenant, died last Monday at 6 in the afternoon, when part of an old building fell on him. He meant well, poor chap. Youth is hasty."

"My seconds!" roared Toudoux.

"Before you sabre me to bits," Evans said, "will you tell me how a young man in the best of health, sitting on a concrete floor, can be struck from above with at least 2,000 kilos of rock and concrete fragments, also loose dirt and plaster, without having his skull crushed, bones broken, or showing signs of struggle or suffocation?"

Dr. Toudoux took a quick angry look at the body again, felt the head, neck and shoulders, glared at the face, and turned to Evans, a picture of embarrassed contrition.

"Love is all that matters, but it plays havoc with the scientific mind. To the artistic, perhaps, it corresponds in rhythm. A scientist, perhaps, when love flies in, should retire from active service, and let Cupid feed upon his laurels. You will not, I beg of you, disclose to others how obtuse I have been," Toudoux implored.

"The others have been obtuser," Evans assured him. "Even such a sterling character as Fremont. I shall spare him and withhold from you the bloomers he has made concerning this unfortunate victim. Had not the assassin been clever, I should have let wild horses drag me in separate directions before sending all the way to Fountainebleau for you, and causing a pang of disappointment to enter your wife's bosom."

"I recall who brought us together, in that fantastic mummy affair,"* said Dr. Toudoux.

* *Hugger Mugger in the Louvre.*

"Then you'll issue the false certificate?" Evans asked.

Toudoux turned green and purple again. "That is a joke not funny," he said, trying to control himself.

"I'm serious. It will serve a temporary purpose, and in the meantime you can carry on the post mortem of your illustrious lifetime. In the end, when you have triumphed over a most cunning descendant of Cain, the full truth will come to light," Evans said.

"But a false certificate, undersigned by Toudoux! My fingers would refuse to hold the pen, even should I dominate my conscience."

"As a Frenchman, and one of our Allies, do you wish to ascertain when and how an American soldier died, and then let the criminal go free?" Evans said.

"My friend. You can do anything with words. Furnish me with an honorable pretext for a dishonorable betrayal of my professional integrity, if you can."

"Nothing easier," Evans said. "You issue the misleading certificate as a decoy, to entrap the culprit. You place justice on the pedestal with honor, that is, the universal with the personal. Only large souls are capable of that unselfish outlook."

"Enough! No doubt you had the certificate typed in advance. I only need to sign," the doctor said, resignedly.

Evans nodded. "And now to work," he said. "First of all I must ask you a question. You are familiar with the action and symptoms of all kinds of poisoning that have yet been used for criminal purposes."

"Or for any purposes whatsoever, criminal or beneficent," said Hyacinthe Toudoux.

"What is the longest period of time which may elapse between the administration of a poison and its fatal effect?" Homer said. "In other words, how long after a murder is committed by a poison with delayed action before a victim dies?"

"There are cumulative poisons. Small doses are given, day after day, for weeks, sometimes months," Toudoux replied.

"I know. But a single dose?" Evans asked.

"First let us find the poison. I can then tell you all about the time element," the medical examiner said.

"There's a request I'd like to make, without too much explanation. I want to undress the corpse, with your aid, and take charge
of the garments. Then, before you touch the body, I want to go
over every millimeter of the skin with a powerful magnifying glass."

Dr. Toudoux looked at Evans searchingly. "You suspect, in advance, how the poison, if there is a poison, was administered?" he
asked.

"Just a shot at the moon," Evans said.

"Had this young man done anything drastic, that would furnish a motive for a crime as spectacular as this?" asked Dr.
Toudoux.

"Only as you and I," said Evans, sighing.

"Master criminals do not shoot mosquitoes with V-2's, or bom-
bard whales with neutrons," Toudoux observed.

"Amateur criminals, especially if mentally deranged, do not
follow patterns already catalogued and cross-indexed in the books,"
Evans said. He was at the same time peering at the dead lieutenant's hair, "Ah, capital!" he said. "Look here. I want you to make
a mental note of this, so you can substantiate it later."

Toudoux looked through the strong glass. "I see only human
hair and very ancient lime mixed with dust and dirt, finely granu-
lated."

"Exactly," Evans said. "If a cushion of this soft dirt fell first on
the lieutenant's head, it would serve as a buffer between the cra-
nium and falling chunks of rock and concrete."

"It would also start a young man struggling and endeavoring
to save himself, first of all by raising his hands and arms to protect his head," Toudoux remarked.

"A young man who, under such circumstances, should sit down,
back to the wall, legs outstretched, arms at his side, to await further disaster, would run the danger of being considered eccentric,"
Evans said.

"Americans are nothing if not eccentric," said Toudoux. "That's
what we logical French love most about them."

The two men worked in silence for a while; then Evans uttered
another muffled exclamation. He pointed to a scratch on the back

of the dead lieutenant's right hand, about an inch beyond the lower joints of the middle and third finger, almost perpendicular to the fingers.

"Looks like a scratch he might have suffered accidentally against a rough spot under a table top or a shelf," said Dr. Toudoux. "No one could die from that."

"Now have a look through the glass," Evans urged him.

"A perpendicular puncture!" exclaimed Toudoux.

"A clever bit of camouflage," Evans said.

"A skilled hand. Indicates a surgeon . . ."

"Or a nurse?" Evans suggested.

"The victim's hand remained stationary. The cutting object moved. How fortunate you thought of the magnifying glass," the medical examiner said.

"Don't overlook the fact that the vertical incision was made first," Evans said.

Dr. Toudoux groaned and turned back to his gruesome work again.

"I've got to go," Evans said. "Would you mind having that scratch photographed and some enlarged prints made? You'll leave the tendons, arteries, veins and skin intact, quite naturally."

The doctor nodded, but deterred Evans gravely. "Before you go, I wish to say that if there is a poison of any kind or description in these soldierly remains, I'm prepared to eat this huge marble slab."

The telephone rang. Evans answered.

"I've got the report on Nurse Welsh," Colonel Bit lings said.

"I'll be with you in ten minutes," said Evans, and ten minutes later he entered Billings' office. He glanced at the cablegram, and drew in his breath sharply.

"Don't tell me you can decode it at sight," Billings said, ruffled.

"A few words, toward the end," Homer said. He sat down, took up paper and pencil, and in a few minutes the message was clear.

"Our nervous nurse is back in France, most likely. At least she embarked at New York eighteen days ago, and got off at Le Havre nine days later," said Evans.

"Then she could have been in Paris last Monday," Colonel Billings said.

"Undoubtedly," agreed Evans.

He was dialing Fremont's number. Schlumberger answered.

"I want to locate an American woman named Agnes Welsh. Check the small hotels. Don't let her know she's being traced. Phone me at home if you have any luck. I'll take over from there," Evans said. He added a description of Agnes and other details from the cabled report.

"Thousands of hotels," Schlumberger grunted.

Evans chuckled as he replaced the instrument on its cradle. Before he said good night to Colonel Billings, Homer asked him casually:

"Did any of your gang in G-6 have a talent for drawing?"

Billings nodded quickly. "Kitchel did," he said. "Bob had a knack for sketching people that most professional artists lack. We used his ability in more ways than one. Sometimes he drew portrait sketches from verbal descriptions of suspects, again he took an individual from a group photograph or one with too complicated a background, and made a line drawing we could photostat and distribute."

"Thanks," Evans said, with satisfaction, and drove to his comfortable apartment in the rue Campagne Première. Soon he was deep in the history of Rockport, year 1863.

11

The Annals of Rockport, Mass.

SEATED IN HIS FAVORITE READING CHAIR, at his sturdy library table, with the green-shaded light adjusted perfectly, Homer Evans read rapidly, a line at a time, of people and events in Rockport during 1863. The local historian of that period was Amos Parker. Most likely an ancestor of Selectman Parker he had met that evening at the Ritz, Homer thought. In 1863 the Civil War had been raging and feeling ran high among the Cape Ann folks, among whom, if there had been any Southern sympathizers they were not mentioned in the book. Toward the middle of the volume, Homer found what he wanted, an item occupying about a page and a half in which it was set forth that a citizen of Rockport, Massachusetts, one Erothius Crandall, had by means of an oral will, witnessed on the battlefield, left a schooner, the *Mazie B.*, and whatever else he had, to his partner, Jonathan Lake. There had been three witnesses, all of whom had filed affidavits with their company commander. When the War Department had passed on the matter to the Attorney General of Massachusetts, the latter had pronounced the will legal, according to a very early Massachusetts law which had not been amended or repealed.

"That's that," commented Homer with a sigh, as he closed the volume and took up the one covering the year 1887. He had to read almost to the end of that year before he saw anything that seemed to be relevant. There was an announcement, quoted from the Rockport *Review*, of the birth of a son, Alrick, to Amos Lowe and Jane Alrick Lowe, both of Rockport. Most likely, Homer thought,

the Lowes named in that item would prove to be related to the late
Susie Lowe. Probably he could find out more about that from Mrs.
Mallory or Selectman Parker. He was about to set aside the book
when a series of illustrations grouped at the end arrested his attention. One of them so intrigued him that he stood up, the open
book in his hands before him, and walked the floor a while in contemplation of it. It was a reproduction of a pen-and-ink sketch,
not badly done, of Land's End, a part of Rockport two to three miles
distant from the center of the town and used principally by
lobstermen who had shacks along the shore for storing pots and
tackle, and boathouses for their Cape Ann dories and oars.

There were separate sketches, inserted and on a larger scale,
of Thatcher's Island with its famous twin lights and the light
keeper's cottage, about a mile off shore; and Loblolly Cove with
the Tarr cottage and the Norcross shack.

Homer put the book down, and paced the floor, not uneasily,
but as if he were enjoying a walk along the shore of a far-distant
land which suddenly had come close to him. Land's End he could
see, in his mind's eye, with a few low windswept trees, blueberry
plains, sweet fern, wild roses and the enigmatic granite boulders,
rocks and ledges. That must have been, in its day, one of the most
entrancing lonely spots on the New England shore, and yet so easily accessible to those who could walk a couple of miles. Long Beach
with its stretch of fine white sand, and Gloucester, then one of the
world's most important seaports connected with the fishing indus-
try, were just to the south. Pigeon Cove, with its renowned quar-
ries was just north. The coming of the automobile had changed all
that, in so far as natural isolation was concerned. Land's End had
become a populous summer colony, and the whole area now was
webbed with well-paved narrow side roads, curving and twisting
like the footpaths of old. In winter, with the summer folks away
and the lobstermen's trade spasmodic and hazardous, there must
be something approaching the old-time desolation, known to the
red men, and the European fishermen who wintered on the New
England shore from the Newfoundland Banks. Many of those had
liked it so well that they had stayed and had become early Americans. Those families, the Tarrs, the Lowes, the Parkers, and the

Gotts, among others, were Eastern pioneers, not much concerned with politics or religion. The men worked and went down to the sea in ships. The women waited, and sometimes wept, ashore.

It was characteristic of Homer that when he read, he gave himself over to the author and the author's creation, whether the text was reportorial, fictional or critical. He could reject nothing until after he had given himself a chance to feel and understand it. As he walked back and forth in his elegant apartment he felt like a Tarr or a Parker, a fisherman from the Banks trying out a new wilderness, a ship's carpenter building a cottage and painting it white, a lighthouse keeper in the middle of a nor'east blizzard, a member of the crew of the Straightsmouth life-saving station pulling his oar in one of those indestructible Cape Ann dories toward a rocket in the darkness ahead.

He was glad that the case had to do, in some way, with the town of Rockport, which he had never seen.

As he was about to take up the next volume, for 1902, he felt a tug at his consciousness. Perhaps there was more in 1887. He read further and was well rewarded. Another birth announcement. This time Homer's pulse quickened and he tapped his knee with the book. A girl, Lois Havemeyer, was born to Lou Havemeyer and Amanda Havemeyer, who was Amanda Cheever.

"Lou was right on hand, along Perkin's wharf, with the cigars, ten-cent Blackstones," the historian wrote.

Again Homer was about to push aside the 1887 volume when an item toward the end brought him up short.

"I'm rushing this wonderful development," he said. "What's the matter with me? I'm crowding the tempo. After all, I haven't got to catch a train."

He read, mused and pondered, poured himself a drink of bourbon, Rolling Fork, and chose Evian as a chaser, which he liked to drink first, to clear the way for the ripe corn flavor. Rum when it rained, brandy in the autumn, bourbon in the spring. He sipped the drink. Then he read, half aloud, from the text of Amos Parker:

"Mandy Cheever, who left Lou Havemeyer's bed and board without notice, while her baby girl was four weeks of age, sent a card from over in New York State that she was sorry but would not be back. Lou was released on the 16th instant from the town lockup where he had been held for recuperation. He shipped this morning (the 18th instant) on the *Bessie Alrick*, Capt. Jess Lowe, with a cargo of cedar posts and masts for Nagasaki. Their daughter, Lois, is being cared for by Mrs. Amos (Alrick) Lowe."

Homer took another sip of bourbon to clear his head. Surely Mrs. Mallory or the selectman could straighten out those Lowes, Havemeyers and Alricks. Now for 1902. He read almost to the end of 1902, having noticed that as town historian Gunnard Carlson had succeeded Amos Parker. Gunnard Carlson had a style more terse and precise than that of his predecessor.

"The *Bessie Alrick*, Capt. Jess Lowe, set sail on Labor Day, Sept. 4, for the South Seas, object, whales. Among the crew was the skipper's nephew, Alrick Lowe, and some Scandinavians and a Portuguese who signed at the last minute because several of the able seamen who had signed to go with Capt. Lowe were laid up with mumps. Mumps is no complaint to have aboard ship or any other place if the sufferer is an adult."

Two pages farther along, Homer chuckled again. "Like mother, like daughter," he said. The item read:

"Lois Havemeyer, daughter of Lou Havemeyer and Amanda Cheever, who left these parts a little over sixteen years ago, departed for a destination she did not announce, by means of the Boston train on the 12th of September, P.M. She left a note thanking the Lowes (Amos and Jane) for all they had done for her, and saying she did not want to be a burden any longer. That puzzled Mrs. Lowe, because Lou Havemeyer, Lois' father, has paid board and lodging for the girl regularly, when able to work. Lou was arrested in Gloucester for attempting to wreck a waterfront saloon but was released when sober, twelve hours later. He has taken a job at the quarry in Pigeon Cove for a while."

Homer rose and paced a while again, and the expression on his face had an element of tenderness.

"I'm beginning to love Lou Havemeyer with all my heart," he said. "But I'm wondering why it is, with Havemeyers all over Rockport, that neither Dr. Havemeyer nor Ulysses Grant

Havemeyer is known to such a sterling Rockport Citizen as Edith Tarr Mallory, for instance. There is much to be clarified in this fascinating tangle."

The telephone rang. Homer took up the instrument, and without waiting to hear who was on the line said, with mock peevishness:

"Must you interrupt my reading?"

"Not necessarily," said the voice of Fremont. "My own evening and this much of the night have not been spent in sedentary pursuits, and the same could be said for Sergeant Schlumberger."

"Why don't you both come here? I'll have a *casse-croute* sent over from the Coque d'Or," Evans said.

"If you produce any more dead bodies this night, for any reason whatsoever, our friendship will fade," Fremont said.

"No bodies," said Evans.

"We come, then," Fremont said.

Homer stacked the five annual histories of Rockport and telephoned an order to the Coque d'Or. When he had made himself as clear as he could to the head waiter, who had served as a Major in Colonel Kvek's former regiment, he asked to speak with Megan Mallory. The uproar was wholesome and epic, but after an interval Megan's voice came to his ear.

"I thought I'd check up, to be sure you're not bored," he said.

"But this is wonderful," she said. "I've laughed, cried, danced, and sung in strange languages. And even if I had been miserable, the sight of father, doing a *kazotsky* and playing a tambourine, locking elbows with noblemen and officers, would have given me a bang. He hasn't let himself go like this since before Fred died. I think he never enjoyed himself so much. And Mother. The Russians adore her!"

"Your *mother* is there?"

"Selectman Parker went to the Prince de Galles to pick her up as soon as she got back from Rouen. About ten-thirty or eleven," Megan said.

"Phone me"—he hastily gave her the number—"when the party breaks up, if it does. And, by the way. That taxicab. Has Lvov got one, for the morrow?"

"Forgive me, Mr. Evans. I haven't had the heart to mention any practical subject. These men and women, living in a dream . . . Who could be cruel enough to wake them or arouse them? Bring them back to reality, I mean. They actually think the Bolsheviks are ephemeral. I'm beginning to think so myself," said Megan, breathlessly.

"It may be better that our breakfast meeting take place before you go to bed. And I'd like your mother to be present, and not your father. The selectman I can take or leave."

"The way Father and Selectman Parker are drinking vodka, I think what you wish will work out of its own accord. I'll phone you, then. And thanks for calling. It meant a lot to me, just knowing you were bridging the chasm with a thought," she said.

"My thoughts tonight are swarming like bees in black hair, as the Afghanistanian poet so aptly expresses it," Homer said. "*Au revoir*."

She wondered how she would look with her hair dyed. Black.

The *casse-croute*, or snack, served the police officials by Evans, included fourteen dishes, six cold and eight hot. The Russian major also sent vodka, kvass and a phonograph record of a band in exile playing the former Russian anthem. Homer put it on the machine and when Fremont and Schlumberger, eating voraciously and drinking cautiously, shook their heads at Evans' vagaries, he exclaimed, "Was ever such noble music put to such questionable words?"

"Or valuable time to such outrageous purposes?" Fremont groaned. "Have you lost interest in that orang-utan student who impersonates General Stonewall Grant?"

"I've been on the verge of undue haste this night," said Homer. "I nearly missed learning that a fine upstanding American, in turn favored and buffeted by fate, passed out ten-cent Blackstone cigars on November 26, 1887."

"I have learned more vital facts than that while involuntarily overhearing citizens talking to themselves in a public *pissoir*," Schlumberger said. "But I have no doubt you'll fit your trivial findings into this case."

Evans smiled. "Let's have Fremont's report first. I'm more interested in the Existentialist suspect than ever."

"Did you say 'suspect'?" asked Fremont, looking stern, through a mouthful of gray caviar. "Well, disabuse yourself. In my long service to France I have come across quite a few alibis. Those offered by your monkey-faced false general, who slinks through kitchens at the sight of a squad of police, have the *Premier Prix*, the all-time record. Furthermore, they have all been verified and substantiated. Listen: On Monday last, at 2 P.M., your decadent young American had his breakfast of one croissant and black coffee at the Café de Flore. He saw there the late Lieutenant Kitchel, and an American woman who looked like an army nurse. Monkey-face had an argument with the waiter about the croissant, and discarded five he claimed were stale before one was produced which he accepted as freshly baked and then consumed. He made a few trips to the telephone booth, to inquire about trains to Le Havre, getting two wrong numbers and finally Information at the Gare St. Lazare. Over the phone he had a dispute with the telephonist at the railroad station and used language no one would be likely to forget."

"Right," interrupted Evans. "French slang expressions, I suppose."

"Very easy to remember," Fremont said.

"Almost too easy," Evans remarked.

Fremont went on. "Monkey-face took a train at 3:24, arriving in Le Havre at 7:45. Having misplaced his ticket, he was stopped at the gate, had an altercation with the agent, who took the number of his passport and his Paris address. That evening later, in a café of none too good repute known as 'Le Ménage Foutu' (The Broken Home) Monkey-face ordered a pair of Frankfort sausages, specifying that the mustard must be of Dijon. The waiter brought the two sausages, with a jar of mustard stolen from American Army stores and bearing the label of a concern in Lompoc, California."

"The only American mustard equal to that of Dijon," Evans said.

"Monkey-face did not think so, evidently. He swung ineffectually on the waiter, who had been a sparring partner of Jean Stock,

ELLIOT PAUL

our French middleweight. Monkey-face was ejected forcibly, called the police, got into a row with them, and was escorted to his hotel, where, before going to sleep, he insisted that his mattress be changed for a harder one. Mind you, those incidents have all been checked."

"And the next day, returning to Paris on the boat train, Ulysses Grant Havemeyer made himself obnoxious to Miss Megan Mallory, apparently without flirtatious intent," Fremont said.

Homer sighed. "Then he could not have been in Paris at 6 P.M. on Monday when the building fell in the rue Cassette, or between the hours of 5 P.M. and 6 P.M., a sixty-minute interval in the course of which Lieutenant Kitchel died. Alas."

Ready to explode, Fremont blurted out: "And still you ask me to trail him. On the off-chance that he may commit some murder still unperpetrated? I am short of help. Like every department in France, we are short of money."

Apparently sympathetic, Evans nodded. "I'll relieve you of the task as soon as I can," he said. Then he turned to Schlumberger, who, superbly fed and warmed with vodka, beamed and smiled.

"Mine was a lucky assignment. In one of the first hotels I tried, *place* de la Contrescarpe, an American woman had registered about eleven o'clock. She had filled out her registration slip in her own handwriting, and it disclosed the number of her passport, which she had left with the proprietor, according to custom, and I have in my pocket. Her name is Agnes Welsh. At present she is asleep or lying quietly, unclothed except for a string around her neck which supports an army tag. Her clothes, a brown shirt, tunic and blouse, O.D. shorts and brassiere, a navy-blue skirt, nylon stockings, and shoes of an American make, are over, on and around a bedroom chair. In front of her door is stationed Officer Weber and on a neighboring roof, from which he can see Miss Welsh sleeping bare on the bed, and her effects on the chair, is Officer Champs."

"Please do not discipline Officer Weber if you find him with his companion on the roof," Evans said. "Plain-clothes men are only human."

"Sub-human," grunted Fremont.

The phone rang and the moment Evans dislodged the instrument such sounds issued forth that Homer turned to Fremont and Schlumberger before risking his ear at the receiver and whispered: "Toudoux."

"*Ici Evans, l'amateur,*" said Homer into the phone.

"There is not a trace of poison of any kind, form or description anywhere in this body, except a faint trace of chloral hydrate, $CCl_3CH(OH)_2$. My wife's gentle cat has a small two-weeks' old kitten who could lap up such a temporary hypnotic and an hour later play with its fond mother's tail," roared Toudoux. "I should challenge you to a duel, after all."

It was seldom Homer Evans showed such gleeful satisfaction. "That's capital," Homer said.

"The woods of Boulogne. Sabres! Daybreak!" bellowed Dr. Hyacinthe Toudoux, and slammed back his instrument with such force that an electric spark, false blue, skipped all the way along the wire to Homer's hand.

Fremont and Schlumberger rose to go.

"You must continue your reading," Fremont said, sarcastically. "No doubt you'll find more testimonials to the famous American generosity."

Schlumberger merely sighed.

After cautioning them both to keep close watch over Ulysses Grant Havemeyer and Agnes Welsh, Homer bade them good night, and went back to Rockport, 1903. The item that interested him was on the 232nd page, dated Christmas day. Homer, so susceptible and sensitive, felt the cold chill of tragedy and relentless fate as he read:

"It is with sorrow we report that the schooner *Bessie Alrick* went down off one of the Micronesian Islands, Long. 70° E., Lat. 30° S., on Dec. 25, with Capt. Jesse Lowe; his nephew, Alrick Lowe, aged 17; and several Scandinavians, also one Portuguese, whose names are known on High but are not inscribed in our local records. Capt. Lowe leaves a widow, Bessie Alrick that was, and a daughter, Susie Lowe; a brother Amos and Amos' wife, Jane Alrick. The two last-named are father and mother, respectively, of the boy who found untimely a watery grave. The late Captain had a host of friends in Rockport and all over Cape Ann. A fuller report will be made upon the return, if God wills it, of the three-master, *W. P. Rogers*, of Gloucester, whose crew picked up floating relics of the *Bessie Alrick*."

With a pang of real regret Evans read, a few pages later, that the *W. P. Rogers* of Gloucester went down with Capt. Sims, First Mate Hornblower, and a list of Cape Ann seamen off Cape Hatteras and with it all supplementary information about the fate of the *Bessie Alrick*.

He took up the fifth volume dated 1933. "Came approximately 11,000 dawns, and now let us see," Homer murmured. He opened the book, not at random, exactly, but to a place where it had been spread and kept open many times before.

"What luck," he said, for on a right-hand page was a group photograph of Rockport women over sixty years of age, and among them, with her shawl, sparse parted hair brushed flat, and her smooth quite noble forehead, was Susie Lowe. Moreover, it was the photo from which the sketch in the phone booth of the Café de Flore had been drawn. Homer turned to the back end pages and there was a pencil sketch almost identical with the one he had seen at the Flore, the same size, the same characteristics of good line drawing by an untrained hand.

Still Homer was not satisfied to renounce the history of Rockport. He read and read, and on page 136 he found an obituary of the man of whom he had become fond, Lou Havemeyer. The town roisterer and reprobate, hardest worker on a hardworking cape, devil-may-care, more sinned against than sinning, gave up the ghost, as the 1933 historian, Fennel Parker, expressed it "at the venerable old age of about 80-odd winters, and hard ones." He left debts amounting to $2.60, and personal property valued at $3.00 even, "and a host of friends who may have deserved worse and got better than Lou did in certain respects." His lawful wife, who was Amanda Cheever had not been heard from since the post card from New York State in 1887. His daughter, Lois, had been last seen on a Boston P.M. train in 1903 immediately after which Lou "had taken a job in the Pigeon Cove quarry for a while."

All the Lowes, including Susie, had gone the way of all flesh.

The Tarr cottage, neat and ancient, now belonged to the town, the county or the commonwealth, but nothing had been done about that.

Homer, as he relinquished the Rockport history, so eloquent and fragmentary, was reminded of the Persian bard who ages ago had written:

> "Myself when young did eagerly frequent
> Doctor and sage, and heard great argument,
> But always I came out
> By the same door that in I went."

He hoped Mrs. Mallory could cast a beam of light into the dim corners of the annals he had read of Rockport, Massachusetts.

Then he thought of Finke Maguire. He ought to call up Finke and brief him a bit, as one detective to another.

Finke's voice came to him huskily, and with undertones betraying that the world, his oyster, had been drilled by a submarine enemy and spoiled.

"So it's you," he said.

"The very same," Evans said. "I'm about to start a mission of reconnaissance and thought you might like to join me."

"Whatever you say," Finke said.

"I'll drive to your place. Can you be down in ten minutes?" asked Evans.

"Such as I am," Finke said, and hung up. "Now what the hell?" he grunted to himself.

When Evans drove up to 13 rue Pelican, Finke was standing at the curb. His concierge was glaring at his back through a slit in a shutter. Finke turned and thumbed his nose in tandem style, with both hands, then got in the car beside Evans.

They started away.

"One can get a nasty wallop from one of those taut-wire clothes-lines," Homer remarked sympathetically. He had seen the welt across Finke's stern forehead.

Finke was dumbfounded for a moment; then it dawned on him that his backyard assailant in Rouen had been an inanimate object. He started to swear softly, then let himself go.

They drove in silence, to the Ile de la Cité, across to the Left Bank, toward the Pantheon and beyond, and Homer parked the roadster on the edge of the *place* de la Contrescarpe.

"Wait here a minute," Homer said.

Finke grunted.

Evans turned a corner, and beckoned to two officers, Weber and Champs, who were standing on a roof. They climbed down.

"You can go now," Homer said, and rather sheepishly they thanked him and walked down the hill side by side. Homer went back to the roadster.

"I want to show you something for your report to Mallory," he said to Finke.

Homer touched his lips with his fingers. He climbed nimbly to the low roof. Finke followed. Homer located the hotel window. It was still open, and on the bed the sleeping woman was lying, in a pose that would have thrilled Rembrandt. He stood aside, indicated the direction to Finke, and whispered:

"The deathbed nurse, Miss Welsh."

Finke's reaction was so sudden, violent and unexpected that Evans had barely time to duck by the smallest fraction of an inch the wild left jab and wilder right cross that started his way. In missing Evans, Finke, blinded with exploding temper, lost his balance, his footing, started falling from roof to sidewalk and clutched Homer's coat. Homer lost his equilibrium, too, and both crashed from low roof to hard sidewalk, head first, so that both were aware of an impact, a galaxy of indigo and magenta stars. Then all was plush and black.

12

Logic, Farewell

IN THE SMALL HOTEL ROOM near the *place* de la Contrescarpe, Agnes
Welsh awoke. She had slept deeply many hours. Consequently the
transition to consciousness was not instantaneous. As she opened
her eyes she was aware that two men on a near-by roof across the
street were staring at her. At the same moment she remembered
that she was naked and that one of the peeping gentlemen was
Finke Maguire, whom she had last seen in the rue de Caen, Rouen.
Before she had a chance to size up the other man with the well-
trimmed Van Dyke and blue cheviot suit, she saw Finke lead with
his left, bring his right across, and, in an effort to avoid falling off
the roof, clutch the other chap's clothes and cause both of them to
tumble head downward to the sidewalk below, in the midst of a
small curious crowd of early risers.

Like a startled wood creature, Agnes sprang from bed to rug,
covered her nudity with the first garment handy, dressed in less
time than it takes to tell of it, ran down the single flight of hotel
stairs and, ignoring the proprietress who was watching her suspiciously from the desk, darted out on the sidewalk. She had to halt
in her tracks, again like a pursued wild animal, to case the terrain
and decide which way to flee. The street leading down the hill to
the Pantheon was fairly wide. On one side was a high blank stone
wall. Shops and dwellings lined the other. None of the shops was
open. There was no cover in that direction. The only alternative
was for her to control her impulse to run, walk along the edge of
the quaint *place* and into the rue Mouffetard, which even at that

hour of the morning was alive with pushcarts, local market people and exigent customers.

From the doorway of what appeared to be the entrance of a bazaar, Agnes paused to look back. She saw Finke and with him the man in blue cheviot and the beard. They seemed to have recovered from their fall and to have effected a reconciliation. Together, they were headed for the front door of her hotel. They entered, side by side. With a sinking feeling Agnes then remembered that she had left her passport with the proprietress, for the police to peruse and O.K. She had had no baggage with her when she registered, and had told the proprietress that her "things" would be delivered this morning. Nevertheless, the woman had asked and she had paid a week's rent in advance, amounting to 1750 francs, plus 20 per cent tax, 350 francs, and another 12 per cent tax, 210 francs, a total of 2,310 francs. In terms of U.S. money that meant about six dollars. "Let it go," she thought. But she would somehow have to get her passport back.

Stepping back into the bazaar, Agnes saw at a far corner of the courtyard, beyond the booths and counters some of which had been uncovered and were ready for business, what appeared to be a narrow passageway. It might lead into another street and thus make her getaway easier, she thought. So she walked in that direction. As she drew nearer she saw that the opening was not a narrow alley, as she had at first supposed, but a tunnel, the walls, floor and ceiling of which were finished in bright-colored mosaic, with Kremlin blue, pale vermilion, white and gold.

She entered the tunnel and proceeded a few yards beyond a closed door. She heard voices and wild music. A short distance ahead she saw daylight and realized that the egress did, as she had hoped, lead into a sloping street parallel with the rue Mouffetard. Before she reached a point where there was another side door, it opened and a lean solemn man, somewhat disheveled but stiffly correct, stood directly in her way.

Coincidentally, the door she had already passed opened, a tall man in evening clothes, and wearing a monocle, stepped out behind her. He had a champagne bucket of melted ice in one hand, and poured the contents over his head, leaning forward and gasping.

The man in front of Agnes stared; then his face was transformed with a beatific smile.

"Mornin', Lieutenant," he said.

She had never seen him before. "Gggood morning," Agnes replied, feeling trapped.

"Better late than never," said the tall spare man, and, taking her elbow hospitably, ushered her inside. Agnes thought she must be dreaming. She seemed to be in Old Russia. The walls were like stage sets of the Chauve Souris. Russian counts, princes and officers were talking, crying, dancing and drinking with countesses, princesses and ladies, some with white hair, some with gray, others with hair dyed yellow or black.

She could not get away, because the stranger was holding her elbow. He was an American, a New England Yankee, no doubt of that. Without ceremony he steered her toward a tall heavy man and a distinguished middle-aged woman. The woman was relatively sober, as sobriety went in that fantastic place.

"Edith, meet a friend o'mine," said Selectman Parker, thickly.

Mrs. Mallory was most gracious. "How are you, Lieutenant?" she said, and looked out across the banquet room and alcoves with a tolerant smile and a sweep of her hand. "Can you believe this is real—and earnest?"

"I just came in," Agnes stammered.

"Better late than never," Selectman Parker said. "Luke. Want yuh t'meet a friend o'mine."

"I didn't get the name," Luke said, as he reached toward Agnes' timidly outstretched hand and instead grabbed a near-by cake that was covered with whipped-cream frosting.

Agnes' professional habits asserted themselves. She took up a napkin and wiped Mallory's hand clean, dipped a corner in an ice bucket, washed his fingers, dried them on a dry corner, and tossed the napkin on a service table near by.

"Thank you. Thank you very much, Lieutenant," Mallory said, with Irish courtesy reinforced with Russian vodka.

Selectman Parker wandered a few yards away, where he was taken in charge by the Countess Anastasia. Megan, sitting at a table for two, in a comparatively safe corner, with Colonel Kvek, noticed that her father was being gallantly attentive to a young woman, attractive enough in face and build, but rather surprisingly dressed—an army jacket, shirt and cap, a navy skirt, and civilian shoes and stockings.

"Who's the woman talking with Father?" she asked Kvek.

Kvek turned his head discreetly, leaned forward, and whispered in Megan's ear:

"Secret Service."

Megan, amazed, looked again. "In that outfit?"

Kvek nodded. "She used to be seen often at the Café de Fiore, and I picked her up—as a client, of course—several times in a fish restaurant, *place* de l'Odéon."

A flash of recollection—a phrase from one of Fred's letters, came to Megan.

"The Méditerranée. Sea food specialties? Fish stew fine, but not like a Cape Ann chowder?"

"Exactly. The Méditerranée. She used to be in company with an American lieutenant—charming fellow—I never knew his last name. She used to call him 'Fred,'" Kvek said.

Megan, pale, sober now and resolute, got herself together. She described her brother as best she could, without disclosing the relationship. Kvek, afraid he had been indiscreet, sensing that Megan had been fond of the Lieutenant Fred, was about to hedge. Megan already knew. The strange woman who had frequented the Café de Fiore, was reputedly in the Secret Service, wore an assortment of clothes that required some kind of explanation, had dined often with her late brother, at the Méditerranée. . . . Why had Fred never mentioned the woman in his letters? He had written lots about Lieutenant Kitchel, who had been found dead the day before—the day that had not ended but stretched: the appetizer at the Régence, lunch at the Voltaire, the spot marked "X" where the body was found, Longchamps, the races, and a White Russian evening and night. Fred had written plenty about Judd Coulson, the private who had acted as orderly for Bob Kitchel and himself, but nothing about dining with a Secret Service woman at the fish place.

"Could I meet the woman—not while she's with Father?" Megan asked.

Kvek sighed. "You Americans are intuitive. No use to withhold anything from you. Yes. She is the one who dined with . . ."

"My brother," Megan said.

The former colonel in the not too recent army of the late Tsar got that tip just in time. He might have let it drop that he had driven Miss Mallory's brother and the mystery woman to a certain small hotel where neither of them lived as a rule.

"I am honored to have driven for him," Kvek said.

Agnes Welsh was becoming desperate. She had to get away, and whenever she tried, some gentleman, overwhelmingly drunk and polite, took her in charge. She could not help being thrilled, almost drunk, with the wild Cossack songs, of love, passion and nostalgic longing, outpourings of the vast restlessness of the White Russian soul. It seemed incredible that she had got into such a party—a dream in which she walked and made no progress. She had a feeling of menace around her. She knew Finke Maguire, whom she had believed had left her flat in Rouen, had only pretended to ditch her, in Doc Havemeyer's house. Finke must have followed her. He had seen her, plain, from the rooftop. He could not have known where she was going to sleep that night, because she herself had not known. She had planned to stay in Rouen, then changed her mind. She would have to go back, some day soon, to get that rented bicycle. And now there was the problem of her passport.

As suddenly as everything seemed to happen to her lately, Agnes saw her chance. The Countess Anastasia, who had been whirling round and round showing Selectman Parker how to do the European fast waltz, got dizzy. Agnes, who could assert her authority as a nurse, took the aged countess by the arm and led her into the passageway. Exhausted, the countess sat down on the step and fell fast asleep. The tiled tunnel was empty, both ways. Agnes ran softly toward the rue Tournefort.

Homer Evans, who had quickly understood and forgiven Finke's outburst of chagrin, had accompanied Maguire to the hotel in the *place* de la Contrescarpe, hoping for a talk with Agnes Welsh. When it became all too clear that the nurse had taken alarm and flown, Finke started one way, Evans the other, to pick up her trail. Neither was anxious to tell Fremont and Schlumberger that they had been within sight of the nurse, then lost her.

It was not Finke's day. Given his choice, he elected to go toward the Pantheon. Evans chose the rue Mouffetard, and took time out for a long telephone conversation with Wasp Billings, in the course of which Homer asked for data as follows:

Everything on record concerning Dr. (former Captain) *Leo Havemeyer, and Ulysses Grant Havemeyer.*

All information on record about their parents, and their lives from the beginning to the present.

All gossip or information that could be gathered in the region of the town of Mount Washington, Massachusetts, and the adjoining corners of New York State and Connecticut.

"Did you find out about Judd Coulson's I.Q.?" Homer asked.

"It was 132 when he was a kid," Billings said, reluctantly.

"Quite an army," remarked Evans. "Privates with intelligence quotients twice as high as the members of the United States Senate."

"Hell. Judd was only an orderly in my outfit," Billings said, with an air.

"Quite," observed Evans, drily. "In a wonderful position to keep tabs on lieutenants in positions of trust. Who did the dog-robbing for Captain Havemeyer?"

"A lad named Devs Smith. He's now in Indo-China. He was the only American we could find to lend the State Department who wanted one to go to Saigon and pal around with their straw emperor, Bao Dai. Smith parleyed Indo-Chink," Billings said proudly.

"Another private, I suppose," commented Evans. "Did Buck Private Smith know the Indo-Chinese language before he joined the Army?"

"No. He heard there was an opening out there in Saigon, and took lessons on his time off," Billings said. "Shall I contact Devs Smith?"

"No," Evans said. "Doc Havemeyer's near by, and still alive."

"I don't like the way you say 'Still alive,'" Wasp Billings said.

Evans was not anxious to find Nurse Welsh, himself. He hoped that Finke would catch up with her. He might have need of Finke, and did not want him to develop an inferiority complex, or express his resentment of Homer's astuteness by means of fisticuffs.

As Homer crossed over to the rue Tournefort in order to enter the Coque d'Or by the street door, he rounded the corner just in time to see Agnes Welsh. She was dressed in the clothes Schlumberger had described, and was turning into the small rue Amyot. Homer followed reluctantly. He wanted to get to the White Russian party while Megan and her mother were still there. So he kept Agnes in sight, without arousing her suspicion, until two bicycle policemen wheeled along. Evans showed them his credentials, indicated his quarry, and asked one of the officers to tail Agnes. The other he requested to telephone Fremont, so that the task of following Agnes might be turned over to some experienced plain-clothes men.

Then Homer hurried back to the Coque d'Or. He found Megan still happy and excited, but somewhat disturbed. Quickly she told him about the woman who had appeared at the party, and related what Kvek had said about her connection with Fred.

"I've asked Fremont to keep the woman in sight," Homer reassured her. "I just saw her in the rue Amyot, headed toward the boulevard St. Michel. The detectives won't lose her."

Megan was torn between admiration and awe. "You know everything in advance," she said. "I suppose you even know her name."

"Agnes Welsh, Lieutenant Agnes Welsh," said Homer. He did not tell Megan all that Finke had told him, particularly of Agnes' dismay when the possibility arose that she might meet Mrs. Mallory face to face.

Then it struck Homer all of a sudden that it was mighty odd that Agnes Welsh had dropped into a White Russian carouse. From what Finke had said, Evans had assumed the girl was not the gate-crashing type, but manifestly shy, timid and ill-at-ease.

"Who brought Agnes in here?" he asked.

"Selectman Parker," said Megan.

"Ah, well," sighed Homer. "The unexpected. The aromatics in the cuisine called life."

"Don't tell me you also can cook," Megan said, on the verge of asperity.

"When I taste my own cooking, I'm not vain. It's only when I sample that of others that frequently I think highly of my own address," he answered.

"Oh, God," Megan breathed. "The daily bread."

White Russians of both sexes were sleeping in chairs, on the floors and on tables. Others were carrying on merrily. Luke Mallory and Selectman Parker had taken a good look, one at the other, and decided that they each must take the other home. Luke had a dim qualm about his womenfolk but before he blinked around to locate them he felt sure that the chap, Evans, would be on hand to do the needful. When Luke and Selectman Parker got out in the morning air, they decided there was no time of day like morning, and that they would walk back to the Prince de Galles. So, helping each other and getting in each other's way, they meandered down the hill toward the ugly Greekified roundhouse with pillars, in which France keeps in crypts a few samples of her honored dead.

When they reached the rue des Ecoles, a modest funeral procession was marching raggedly, two and two, behind some carriages and a hearse. Absentmindedly Luke and Selectman Parker fell in to bring up the rear, and, talking of this and that, moved slowly, in evening clothes, at the tail of a column of mourners in mufti. No one seemed to mind, until a young Irish-American, who had been searching futilely along the broad Boul' Mich' for Agnes Welsh, caught sight of his client and the client's friend from the old home town. He wished he had knocked himself out instead of letting Evans know what a sorehead he was. American drunks in soup and fish, tagging along behind solemn funerals, are practically sure to run into trouble. What the hell? Was a private mitt his client's keeper? Finke decided yes, and trailed along the sidewalk.

Mrs. Mallory was trying to learn, without asking, how it happened that Megan had met with such a charming cosmopolitan American and why Mr. Evans was so anxious to ask her "a few questions." It was too early for the Closerie des Lilas and too late for the Café de Flore.

"Let's go to the Brasserie Royale. No one I know ever goes there, so we're not likely to be disturbed," said Evans.

"But—Mr. Evans," objected Megan. "Isn't that the big place almost across the street from the Café de Flore?"

"Exactly," Evans said. "No one is safer from interruption in Paris than he who is in an unfamiliar café of a familiar quarter."

When they were seated on the rue de Rennes side of the *terrasse* of the Royale, Evans turned to Mrs. Mallory.

"I had hoped you could tell me about a man of Rockport, who died in 1933," Homer began. "He was more than 80 years old, expansive in his habits, and loved more for his breaches than his observances. He made good use of public facilities, such as lock-ups. He had many jobs in his day, but held none of them long. His wife flew the coop soon after his daughter was born, and the daughter quit him sixteen years later."

"That would be Lou Havemeyer," Mrs. Mallory said.

Megan was trying not to bubble with amazement at Homer's knowledge of her summer town.

"Mmmm. Havemeyer," repeated Evans, and waited. "A good tough family," he added, musingly.

"Lou's name wasn't really Havemeyer. That is, he wasn't called that in Spain. I never knew what his family was, in the old country. Lou didn't learn to read or write until he went to evening school in Rockport, I've been told. Lou, himself, said that when he got to America, and some official in Boston, at the pier, asked him something, most likely his name, Lou was so excited and grateful for having reached the Promised Land by steerage that he murmured "Ave Maria" or "Hail, Mary," in his native tongue. Naturally, he did not know what the inspector was asking him. The official, in a hurry and not too fussy about foreign names, inscribed him as Lou

Havemeyer, Lou for Luis, and Havemeyer was as close as the immigration man could come to Ave Maria."

"His daughter was known as Lois Havemeyer," Evans suggested. Then he sighed disappointedly. "That won't fit, will it? If Lois had married and had children the offspring would not be Havemeyers."

"If you were trying to link him up with Captain Havemeyer, there's no connection," Mrs. Mallory said. "And Lois was not the marrying kind."

"Lois' careful bringing up by Jane Alrick Lowe, then, didn't take?" asked Evans.

"Lois was wild as a hawk, and a girl never came by it more honestly," Mrs. Mallory said. "Lou was as reckless and improvident as they make them, and Amanda Cheever didn't bother about a ceremony until Lois was in prospect, and only then, I believe, because Lou had a job painting the Congregational minister's launch and Mandy was afraid he'd lose it if he became an unmarried father."

"There are not many Spanish Protestants," Homer remarked. "I can't recall ever meeting one."

Mrs. Mallory smiled. "Lou and Amanda were married by the priest at Annisquam," she said.

"How did Lois get on with Alrick Lowe? They were raised together, more or less, and about the same age?" Homer asked.

"I was only nine years old when the *Bessie Alrick* went down, with Alrick and all hands," said Mrs. Mallory, "but I heard a lot of talk, and listened. Alrick Lowe, as I heard it, was a boy who never got caught if he did wrong."

"You mean, Lois got the blame?"

"She was always getting into something, and wouldn't take the trouble to deny it. Amos—he was Jane's husband—corrected her, in the old-fashioned way, until she got too big."

"I understand," said Homer, grinning. "They had to think of other ways . . . Loss of privileges, extra turns at drying dishes, short rations of frosted cake—that sort of thing, you mean?"

"I suppose that was the long and short of it," said Mrs. Mallory.

"And meanwhile Alrick kept out of trouble, and ducked most of the chores?" asked Homer.

"It must have worked out like that," said Mrs. Mallory.

"An ideal setup for a spirited young daughter of the irrepressible Lou and the wayward Mandy, who must have inherited a sense of humor from both sides of the tree," said Homer. "The note Lois left seemed to indicate that Lois had a touch of Spanish pride, about money, I mean. She 'didn't want to be a burden any longer.' Those were her words, I believe."

Mrs. Mallory looked at Evans in astonishment. "You know more about—Rockport—in a way, than I do," she remarked.

"Oh, no," said Homer. "But that girl, Lois. She'd be sixty-two this year. I'd like awfully to meet her."

Mrs. Mallory nodded and shrugged. It was evident that she did not know whether Lois Havemeyer was alive or dead, and if she did not, it was unlikely, Evans thought, that anyone else of Rockport would know. He dropped the subject of Lois. He looked at Mrs. Mallory and smiled.

Megan closed her eyes. She knew the effect of that smile. "Here goes," she said, and gripped the table.

"The Mallorys are working at cross purposes, with a common objective in mind," Evans said. "You, Mrs. Mallory, are troubled on account of the oral will your son made, and want to find out all you can about the circumstances."

"Yes," she said, returning his gaze unwaveringly, but with pain in her eyes.

"Your husband, in order to help you, has employed a fine young private detective, Mr. Finke Maguire, his idea being that Finke would dig up facts which your husband could present to you, to save you frustration and suspense.

"I met Megan under rather piquant circumstances, involving the younger of the Havemeyer boys—not of the Cape Ann Havemeyers, it seems. I offered to represent her," Evans continued.

"Mr. Evans is a famous detective," said Megan.

"Then tell me, Mr. Evans," said Mrs. Mallory, summoning all the force of her stalwart personality, "do you—I have no idea how

much or how little you know about Fred—but do *you* think I'm
making a mountain of a molehill? About that will, I mean."

"I do not, Mrs. Mallory. But please let me tell you finally and
frankly that your son was not murdered!"

It was a stiff jolt, but she took it, and looked up at Evans again.

"Are you sure?" she asked, steadily.

"Quite sure," Evans said. "But where you see a mountain, I am
convinced there is not a mere molehill, but a range of mountains
stretching far behind the front one. I will say, as positively as I
told you your son's death was not contrived, that . . ." he hesitated.

"Whose was contrived?" Mrs. Mallory gasped.

"Lieutenant Kitchel's. And there is a link between that cowardly deed and the Tarr cottage in which Susie Lowe lies dead today. Fantastic! Unbelievable! Incomprehensible as it seems! We
must work together, and ferret out this crime, and the criminal, or
criminals," Evans said.

Megan touched her mother's hand, which was trembling.

"What shall I do?" asked Mrs. Mallory. "I'm anxious to help."

"I'll have to ask a few more questions," Evans said. "First of
all. Your son's effects. Were they sent to you, according to the usual
procedure?"

"Yes," she said.

"Were there among them any books?"

"A few. Mostly about psychology, and political economy. Some
treatises on philology and comparative languages," she said.

"Any history?"

"None."

"No local history . . . No yearbooks about Rockport?"

"None," she said.

"Have you read the yearly histories of Rockport?"

"Not very far back," she said. "I—I am Rockport. What could I
read about it?" she asked.

"Did Fred read the year books?"

"He began when he was in high school, but he didn't go far back.
What he wanted to find out, he asked me, or someone older," she
said.

Evans sighed. "I feared as much," he said. "That makes things harder—the solution, I mean . . . Still, in a way, it helps. Someone else may have told Fred about oral wills."

"Or he might not have known what he was doing," Mrs. Mallory said, doggedly.

"There's that," admitted Evans. "But somebody knew."

"I'll find out," she said, grimly. Then she modified her statement. "We'll find out," she said, and looked straight at Evans.

He braced himself. "Now comes the most difficult question of all. Do you believe in the double standard, Mrs. Mallory?"

Mrs. Mallory did not flutter an eyelash.

"I do," she said, calmly. "I have a daughter and I had a son. What would have been best for him would not necessarily be recommendable to Megan. That may not be logical, superficially, or fair to members of my sex, but that is the way I feel about it."

"That would be the consensus in Rockport?" Homer continued.

"Yes," said Mrs. Mallory. "A town as old as Rockport does not have to try modern experiments that were A.B.C. to the Armenians, the Portuguese and the ancient Greeks."

"If it should transpire that Fred and an army nurse had found in each other's company, in war and its aftermath, what would not be recommendable to Megan, you would not be impelled to bellow or climb shade trees, or think hard thoughts about the young woman?" Homer asked.

Megan was gasping and spluttering. "Am I not to be consulted about what's good for me?" she demanded, with asperity.

"No," said Mrs. Mallory. "No, my dear. You are not."

Megan drummed with her fingers. "God damn it," she said.

Mrs. Mallory got back to brass tacks. "Mr. Evans. If I should meet any young woman who had made hours pleasant for Fred, I should thank her. And if she intimated that my son had—made hours pleasant for her I should feel even more satisfaction and gratitude. However, if the question arises when Mr. Mallory is present . . . How shall I make myself clear? If Mr. Mallory should assume that I would be shocked, I shouldn't attempt to set him right. Luke doesn't care as much about what people do as what they condone."

"There are two schools," Evans said, but he was much relieved.

"You had something definite in mind?" Mrs. Mallory suggested. "Someone, I should say."

"There is a young woman whose service in the Army brought her within the range of your son's unusual understanding and sympathy. Her nerves became unstrung. He gave her what he thought was good advice. In short, her name is Agnes Welsh, she was the nurse Dr. Leo Havemeyer preferred to help him handle difficult cases, and she was, as you know, one of the witnesses at your son's deathbed," Homer said. "Furthermore, she is now in Paris. You met her tonight," Evans said.

"God bless her," said Edith Tarr Mallory.

"Logic, farewell!" Megan muttered.

13
Death Is a Frequent Caller

FINKE MAGUIRE WAS WALKING along the sidewalk of the Boulevard St. Michel toward Montparnasse and was just about to brace Luke Mallory and Selectman Parker, with a view to escorting them back to the Prince de Galles. Two bicycle policemen, wheeling side by side, diverted his attention. They came to a halt at the corner of the rue Abbé de l'Epée, and, obviously by prearrangement, were met by two men whom Finke sensed at once were either thugs or plain-clothes detectives. The funeral procession was moving at a slow pace, so Finke took a chance, stood in a convenient doorway, and watched.

One of the bicycle cops indicated covertly something or some-one just out of sight in the rue de l'Epée. Both plain-clothes men nodded assent. The bicycle policemen wheeled back toward the river, in the opposite direction from which they had come. The two plainclothes men, after a brief consultation, separated and started shadowing someone. Finke sauntered out of his doorway and when he got as far as the corner saw, about half a block down the rue de l'Epée, Agnes Welsh, still in her conspicuous outfit, walking nervously away. The movements of the plain-clothes men made it obvious that Agnes was their bird. He did not have to make up his mind to let his client and the selectman shift for themselves. The decision was automatic. Luck was with him, once again.

Agnes, unaware that three men were on her trail, turned left, toward the river, on the rue Guy Lussac, took the rue St. Jacques as far as the boulevard St. Germain, which she crossed, then turned left again to the rue Boutebrie and entered a hotel. It was a snug disreputable little place called Hotel de la Reine Blanche. Finke had little trouble keeping Agnes in sight, up to the moment she went inside. His problem was to keep out of the way of the two dicks who also were following the girl. He saw one of them enter a courtyard on the opposite side of the rue Boutebrie, from which he could watch the front of the hotel, and the other go scouting to find the back door.

"What the hell?" thought Finke. "Those dicks don't know me." So he took a chance, hustled over to the Boulevard St. Germain, bought a cheap suitcase, several heavy cans of fruit to give it weight, and a large batch of newspapers from the corner newsstand, so the cans would not roll around. He made sure there was a back entrance to the Hotel de la Reine Blanche, into an alley opening into a courtyard from which the boulevard could easily be attained. The official dick was across from the mouth of the alley. He could not lose the girl if she tried to get out through the rear.

Finke walked around to the front door of the hotel, went in, and reached for the registry pads. The proprietress was a motherly woman getting on in years. She asked Finke how long he was going to stay. He said until the next morning. She looked at him as if she were about to ask another question. To forestall it, Finke said:

"I'm expecting someone!"

The woman nodded and pressed a button for the maid, who proved to be a rather good-looking robust girl of thirty or so with short hair and a husky voice, at the same time somewhat naive and very sophisticated. Finke looked down at the maid's ankles. She had on nylon stockings. He had her tabbed all right. She was one of the girls who had been officially reformed in 1945 and still found the old ways best. A man could talk sense with a veteran like the maid, if he used the right approach and had not left his wallet back home on the piano.

While the proprietress and the maid were deciding which of the rooms would do for Finke, and whoever Finke was expecting, he saw coming down the narrow stairs a Zazou who looked like General Grant, and whom he recognized as Ulysses Grant

Havemeyer. The pale young Zazou with the spinach tossed his key on the desk and glanced at his mail box. The proprietress took from the box (No. 11 Finke noted) a printed circular and handed it to the Zazou. The latter crumpled it, tossed it on the floor. That irritated Finke.

"Don't you smarty-pants learn manners at the Sorbonne?"

The veteran maid was about to pick up the crumpled paper.

"Wait, mademoiselle. You have enough stooping to do," Finke said.

Ulysses Grant Havemeyer's face lit up with sarcastic amusement which riled Finke still more.

"Pick it up, General," Finke said, tersely.

"Pick it up yourself, flatfoot," was the reply.

The maid, whose long familiarity with the ways of men prompted her to avoid trouble, tried to stoop again.

"Please, mademoiselle. Don't strain your back," said Finke.

Young Havemeyer laughed derisively.

"I got a good mind to land one on that silly fringe of yours," Finke said. "Now pick up that paper. Americans around here have got to set a good example."

"If you put it that way," the pale young man with whiskers said. His change of manner was baffling and caught Finke off guard. The Zazou stooped, reached for the crumpled pamphlet, then, like a spring trap, came up all the way from the floor with his fist, which landed on the point of Finke's jaw. It was a sterling wallop but not quite good enough. Finke blinked, saw stars, heard owls and crickets, but his reflexes did wonders. One hand caught the General's beard, the other, the left, jabbed into young Havemeyer's breadbasket almost to the spine. Then, kicking the incautious young man smartly in the shins, Finke grabbed his head with both hands and pressed on his nose.

The crumpled piece of paper was still on the floor.

"Pick it up," Finke said. "I must say, I think more of you for that haymaker, but you know what Dempsey said of Carpentier. 'You're a good little man.'"

"I'm going to be actively sick, I'm afraid," said young Havemeyer, who had lost his bravado.

"O.K. Beat it back upstairs and be sick in your room. I'll pick up the paper myself," Finke agreed, good-naturedly, but as he stooped, so did the maid. Their foreheads bumped, both saw stars, and reeled against the wall. As Finke recovered, and just as he was seized from behind, he caught a flash of Agnes Welsh's face above the stair rail in the dimness of the second floor. She had seen and heard him all right.

Finke tried to twist out of the arms of the man who had pinned him from the rear, and another man stepped in front of him. The one in front made an almost ludicrous grimace of recognition. Having been on duty at the Prefecture, he had seen Finke in the Goldfish Bowl not forty-eight hours before. While the proprietress and maid looked on regretfully, unable to help Finke, the front plain-clothes man showed Finke his credentials.

"Come along with us, monsieur. We want to talk with you," he said.

Finke looked at him, then at the other. Both were plain-clothes officers, but not the ones who had tailed Agnes.

"I never saw a quaint little corner of Paree so thick with dicks," Finke said to himself. But he saw no reason why he should not talk with someone, almost anyone.

"*Bien, messieurs*. Let's all go to the Prefecture," Finke said. He waved to the maid, Amelie, who had that hard look all girls of her profession, reformed or unreformed, assume when cops of any kind or description put in an appearance.

"See you later, Amy," Finke said, and the girl smiled. She hoped he meant it. So did the motherly proprietress. Finke had shown the women that the days of chivalry are not dead, even if chivalry is.

As soon as Finke and one of the plain-clothes men started toward the sidewalk, the other said he would stick around. Finke caught on that they had been assigned to shadow young Havemeyer. Finke made sure the dick in the courtyard across the way, one of those responsible for Agnes, was on the job. Monkey-face was upstairs, casting his cookies. Agnes was upstairs, guarded front and back by good men and true.

"Look! Let's make this a threesome. I got to talk to Fremont," said Finke.

"Fremont?"

"The Chief. He and I are just like that," Finke said, crossing his fingers.

"That is the double cross," the plain-clothes man said. "You will not attempt it, please. Will you tell me why we should bother Monsieur Fremont? You caused him some inconvenience on Friday morning, early."

"That was Schlumberger who crowned me," Finke said.

"If this proves to be a hunt of wild geese, Lieutenant Schlumberger will doubtless crown you again, more emphatically," said the dick. But already they were headed for the Prefecture, which was not far away, just across the Seine, on the Ile de la Cité.

Fremont was in his office. He glared at Finke.

"What now?" he grunted.

"Can we speak privately?" Finke asked.

Fremont motioned for the plain-clothes man to retire. "Why were you brought here?" Fremont asked.

"Disorderly conduct. I clipped a Zazou who wouldn't pick up a paper he threw on the floor, at the Hotel de la Reine Blanche," Finke said.

"Any particular Zazou?"

"One you were having tailed. I didn't know it at the time. Was that Evans' idea?"

"You mean Ulysses Grant?"

"The same."

"There is no penalty whatsoever for clipping Ulysses Grant, at any time or place. He has led us on a pointless excursion. I'm not surprised that he is at the Hotel de la Reine Blanche. He lives there. He had rented Room 11 at least two years."

"Never mind Grant," Finke said. Then clearly and succinctly he told of his meeting with Agnes Welsh, who had been seen with Lieutenant Kitchel on Monday afternoon, a few hours before Kitchel's death. "If I were you, I'd have her in for questioning. Tell her you want me and Homer Evans present, and delay the grilling a while, to let her get good and soft. She registered at the Hotel Llhomond in the *place* de la Contrescarpe last night some time."

"I know," said Fremont.

"She registered at the Reine Blanche less than an hour ago this morning," Finke said.

"Without a passport?" asked Fremont. He made a grab for the phone. He asked his operator to get the Reine Blanche and waited a moment, impatiently. Then he heard the voice of the proprietress.

"You have a tenant? An American called Agnes Welsh," Fremont said.

"*Oui, monsieur,*" the woman's voice said.

"She filled out her registration slip, according to law, of course," Fremont said, with a shade too much mildness.

"Monsieur, I can explain. She is known to me, over a period of years. When the American soldiers were here, and all of us were urged to make things easy and pleasant for them, she used to spend a night here now and then. . . . Mademoiselle is a nurse, an American Army nurse, or was."

"Go on," Fremont said. "Did she spend those nights with fellow Americans?"

"Not Americans, monsieur. She's a nice girl. Only one American, monsieur. Invariably the same one. Also a lieutenant," the woman said.

Fremont almost jumped into the phone.

"His name?"

"Lieutenant Mallory. I haven't seen him lately."

"Fred Mallory?"

"Ah, yes. Fred Mallory."

Fremont was no longer doubtful. The nurse who had tumbled into his lap had been the sweetheart of the deceased Fred Mallory, and had talked with the deceased Bob Kitchel on the afternoon of Kitchel's accident. Fremont still swore it was an accident, in spite of Evans' insistence on foul play and Dr. Toudoux's noncommittal fury.

The Chief pressed several buttons. Schlumberger was first to arrive. He and Finke greeted each other like game cocks in separate cages, about a foot apart. Fremont sighed, and turned to Schlumberger.

"Lieutenant, would you mind going with Monsieur MacFeenk to the Hotel de la Reine Blanche in the rue Boutebrie?" Fremont asked. "I want you to bring back an American female lieutenant he will indicate."

To the plain-clothes man, Fremont said:

"Go back to Monkey-face until further notice. There is a restaurant on the corner from which you can see the front door if you find it necessary to eat."

"I shall find it imperative," the detective said.

"What's the idea of tailing this Zazou?" Finke asked.

"The idea comes from Monsieur Evans," said Fremont. "He is not lacking in ideas, a fair percentage of which prove to be sound."

Finke and Schlumberger were driven in a police car to the Reine Blanche and, after a word with the anxious motherly *patronne*, were directed upstairs to No. 12 in which Agnes Welsh was resting. Schlumberger trudged up first, with Finke a couple of stairs behind him. When Finke got to the landing, he saw Amelie standing just inside the doorway of No. 13. The door was ajar, so Finke, beckoning to Schlumberger to hold his horses a minute, stepped into No. 13, closed the door, and, clasping the maid in his arms, drew her roughly to him. He kissed her on the mouth. She was rigid at first, then relaxed, then began to shiver, clung tighter, and relaxed again.

"That was in the cards. I felt it coming, when you started to stoop, downstairs," Finke said. "A guy needs a good matter-of-fact woman after getting the run around from one of them neurotic dames. I'm going to hang on to the room I asked for here until I feel now is the hour we must say good-bye. Does that louse up any of your commitments?"

"Quite a few," said Amelie, lips parted, eyes smiling.

He kissed her again, until she shivered and slumped. He straightened his clothes. She smoothed her hair. He beat it out again. Schlumberger was patiently waiting, in front of No. 12. Finke listened at No. 11. The voice of Ulysses Grant Havemeyer was singing, low and mean, *"Oh, listen to the tale of Willie the Weeper."*

"He seems to have recovered," Finke said to himself.

Schlumberger tapped softly on the door of No. 12. The song about Willie the Weeper in No. 11 stopped abruptly.

"Come in?" said young Havemeyer's voice, from No. 11.

Schlumberger, ignoring the response from the wrong room, tapped again, louder on No. 12. Havemeyer began singing again.

Finke shook his head. Schlumberger, undiverted by "le hot," rapped again, staccato and insistently.

"Who is it? *Qui est là?*" asked a girl's voice from inside.

"It's me, or I," Finke said. "Remember Finke? In the old junk-yard by the river?"

"What do you want?" asked the voice. It was Agnes all right.

There were sounds of footsteps ascending the stairs. Finke wheeled around. Homer Evans and a tall Russian in faultless morning dress, black jim-swinger, striped pants, Homburg, spats, gloves and stick.

Homer greeted Schlumberger with surprise and Finke with approval. He introduced Colonel Kvek, without explanation.

"What is it you want?" came the voice of Agnes Welsh from inside No. 12.

From No. 11, the voice of Ulysses Grant Havemeyer stopped, then resumed singing, but with less gusto.

Evans, having no way of knowing whose voice it was, paid only perfunctory attention.

"Go away!" cried Agnes' voice from inside No. 12. Evans guessed who she was.

"Miss Welsh. We're only anxious to talk with you," he said.

"Who are *you?*"

Homer turned the knob. The door was not locked or bolted. The others looked in from the hallway. Agnes was lying on the bed, in her O.D. blouse and cap and navy skirt. The khaki shorts were damp and hanging from a radiator pipe, drying, and the nylons were suspended from the towel rack, also drying.

"You've no right to come in here," Agnes said.

"Please don't be alarmed," said Homer.

"The Chief of Detectives merely wants to question you at the Prefecture," Schlumberger added.

"I'm an American," the girl said, sitting up on the bed. Her bare legs were outstretched, toes pointing upward.

"Evidently," said Schlumberger, glancing at the legs, then looking at them with frank approval.

"Nothing like American legs," said Finke from the doorway.

"You gave me the brush-off," Agnes said to Finke, resentfully.

"I can explain," Finke said.

Homer took charge. "It's clear that Miss Welsh needs dry hose. What size?" Then he glanced at the nylons. "Eight and a half. Lvov. Would you mind stepping across to the Bazaar St. Michel for a pair of American nylons, midnight mist, and panties with a 32 waist. They won't have them in olive drab, but robin's egg would go nicely with the brown, dark blue and pale Tyrian nylons. The shoes are black, of course."

By that time Agnes Welsh seemed resigned to the company. She got off the bed and sat in the only chair, at Homer's insistence. Lvov bowed and left. Finke stepped from the doorway into the room. Neither he nor anyone except Kvek, who paid no attention, noticed that Ulysses Grant Havemeyer opened his own door, softly, and tiptoed along the corridor toward the back stairs, which he descended. There was a connecting doorway, between the kitchen of the hotel and the kitchen of the corner restaurant, also called La Reine Blanche. It was only eleven o'clock, but the Spanish rice was ready. Havemeyer took a seat, apparently his accustomed seat, in a sheltered corner, ate his lunch with relish, and left by the main door of the restaurant. Unobserved by Fremont's dicks he joined the sidewalk crowd along the Boulevard St. Germain. Five minutes later he arrived at the Café de Flore, where he greeted a waiter, was greeted in turn, and ordered coffee and brandy.

He spilled the brandy clumsily, then blamed the waiter unjustly. The head waiter came over, and several tourists gawked as the mild altercation proceeded. The manager took a hand, and refused to serve another brandy gratis. So young Havemeyer denounced them all, ordered another brandy, and eventually paid. There were at least six other Zazous on the *terrasse* at that hour, nearly noon.

None of them paid the slightest attention to young Havemeyer, but the help eyed him balefully, as usual.

By that time, Kvek had returned to the Hotel de la Reine Blanche with eleven pairs of sheer nylons, the right size and shade, and six robin's egg panties, all hand embroidered and unique. The gentlemen were about to leave the room but without self-consciousness Agnes wriggled into the nearest pair of panties, and drew on a pair of the nylons. She looked almost happy because every man present indicated approval of her legs.

"They're not too heavy?" she asked, and looked from face to face, hopefully.

"Girls of your height, not too tall, should have sturdy legs. Otherwise they look diminutive," Homer assured her.

She slipped on her right shoe and said softly "Ouch," then looked down at her ankle, through the nylon.

"I must have scratched myself," she said. "I got so in the habit of scratching in my sleep, during the war, that I still do it, sometimes. I was dozing when you guys tapped on the door."

"Please don't imagine for an instant that you're suspected of anything," Evans said. "The Chief believes you can help him, if you will."

"Of course I will. But what about?" asked Agnes.

"Bob Kitchel. He was killed, you know, in an accident last Monday," Evans said.

"Oh, yes, I remember. Mr. Maguire told me that. So many die. You see them, talk with them. Then you don't. I got used to that," she said.

"Colonel Billings spoke most highly of your work," Evans said. He paused, then continued: "Madame downstairs was glad to see you back at this hotel."

Agnes lost all the poise she had gained. She flushed to the roots of her hair, and her eyes grew hard. "All right! I used to stay here all night! With a man! A lieutenant. He's the only one who ever touched me, or ever will."

The awkward Alsatian, Schlumberger, went over and put his arm across her shoulder. "Maybe you'll feel love again," he said, quite tenderly. "Some lucky fellow, some time. This is France. Nobody's going to pry into your affairs that are personal."

She relaxed again. She got her fur up like a cat, and relaxed just as easy and completely.

They took her, at Evans' suggestion, to the Reine Blanche restaurant for lunch, before going to the Prefecture. The two plain-clothes men, in the innocent belief that the pale young American Zazou was still in the hotel, waited, sighed and fidgeted.

Agnes ate, not heartily, but enough. Finke, between rice and the *calda*, excused himself, went back to the hotel and found Amelie on the third floor. He clasped her to him, and playfully she pushed him over on the bed. Ten minutes later, Finke joined his associates for dessert. He ate three orders.

Then they all strolled down the boulevard, in the May sunshine, over sidewalks dappled with the shadows of plane trees. They crossed the bridge of Saint Michael, and saw the fishermen along the quais. They stopped to watch a man in shirt sleeves pull in a minnow, with a shining tackle and spliced bamboo rod worth at least ten thousand minnows. They entered the Prefecture, which, under the circumstances did not seem as gloomy as usual, and Fremont, who had lunched Aux Armes de la Ville, near the city hall, had divested himself of much of the care which had beset him. A building had fallen. An unlucky young American had been killed by falling debris. No poison. No suspects. No motives. Nothing there. Nothing here. No foul play anywhere, unless Monsieur Evans had rabbits in his sleeves.

The party escorting Agnes Welsh entered his office. In order of entrance, they were:

Agnes Welsh; Finke Maguire, with a new look in his eye; Colonel Lvov Kvek, former officer in the none too recent army of the very late Tsar; Lieutenant Schlumberger, defender of the fifth freedom known in Europe as *amour*, *lieb*, *amor*, *love*, (by tenor singers) *loaf*, (by Central Europeans) *larv*, (by prelates) *sin*. Homer Evans was the last to enter and he beamed at Fremont.

"You look like the canary who has swallowed the milk punch," Fremont said, in an attempt to put the conference on an informal comfortable basis.

"Miss Welsh," Fremont said, after seeing that she was seated where the light was not in her eyes, and no one could look down at her, "let me simplify this formality by telling you what has been reported to me of your movements, which, to us, seem bizarre. If I say anything inaccurate, interrupt. If you do not protest, we shall consider that you confirm my statement. Yesterday, early in the morning, you left the Hotel de la Université, rue Saints Pères, where you have been properly registered since a week ago last Thursday. You rented a bicycle from Mechin Frères in the rue Cardinale. You were seen riding the said bicycle several hours later down the main street of Rouen, toward the waterfront. In a field of junk you were observed sitting alone in an abandoned third-class railroad car, French, by Mr. MacFeenk. You told him you had bicycled from Paris to Rouen to call on an old comrade-in-arms, one Dr. Leo Have-meyer, who lives in a house he owns at 3 bis rue de Caen. You changed your mind about the reunion and instead went to the junkyard to sit alone in an empty railroad car on a rusted side-track no longer in use. Having talked of this and that with Mr. MacFeenk, touching on your girlhood ambitions, your legs, and your friendship with the late Lieutenants Fred Mallory and Rob-ert Kitchel, you started on foot, leaving your bicycle leaning against one side of the railroad car, where Mr. MacFeenk had not noticed it, walked to the rue de Caen, entered No. 3 bis with the avowed purpose of calling on Dr. Leo Havemeyer.

"Although Mr. MacFeenk waited hours in front of and near the house, No. 3 bis rue de Caen, to accompany you back to Paris as you had agreed, he did not see you emerge, and by making inquir-ies learned locally that you had bought a railroad ticket, one-way, in haste for Paris and had departed on the 8 o'clock train."

At this point, Agnes interrupted. "Mr. Maguire stood me up. I rang Dr. Havemeyer's doorbell, asked to see the doctor, was ad-mitted, and was told by his housekeeper a few minutes later that the doctor was not in the house and might not be back until late that night. Then I left by the front door, looked around and called for Mr. Maguire." Her face puckered and tears came into her eyes. "He stood me up. I knew he would," she said, almost sobbing.

Evans spoke kindly to her. "There's a discrepancy, Miss Welsh. You said, if I understood you correctly, that you told the housekeeper when she answered the door that you wished to see the doctor. The woman admitted you, then a few minutes later informed you that the doctor was not in the house and might not be home until late that night. Was anyone in the house besides the housekeeper? Did she speak to anyone else to get her information? Is it likely that she did not know, before admitting you and keeping you waiting, that the doctor was away, if he was?"

Agnes opened her mouth to answer. No sound came. She was utterly motionless and expressionless, except that she seemed to have caught her breath. She did not start breathing again, and before anyone could reach her, she slid to the floor, falling sidewise, toward the left.

Evans was the first to try to lift her up. He carried her to Fremont's desk. There was no bench or couch in the office. He listened for her heartbeats. There were none.

Then he turned to the others with an agonized expression.

"I have let this girl die," he said, so grieved and chagrined that the others, shocked into silence and immobility, suffered with Evans, too.

Fremont already had pushed buttons. A physician was in the doorway. He gazed at the girl, stretched face upward on the desk, with Evans supporting her head. He tried the heart, respiration, all the tests.

"She is dead," he said.

"But the cause. Why did she die? In my own office, surrounded by friends?" demanded Fremont.

Evans had regained his composure, if not his self-esteem and confidence.

"Send for Dr. Hyacinthe Toudoux," said Evans. "Let no one else go near her."

Homer turned to Finke and Schlumberger.

"Go back to that hotel—the Reine Blanche. You, Finke, find out about what Monkey-face has been doing, what he did all morning, every minute of this day! Lieutenant Schlumberger, check up on every man, woman and child who has set foot on the second floor of the Reine Blanche today, when and why, and how long."

Evans turned to Fremont. "I've been a fool," he said. "We should have put everyone under guard, not merely have them followed and left unprotected. Old friend. I want you to search the Reine Blanche. Put on all your best men. I want fingerprints from Rooms 11 and 12. From all the door latches and knobs."

As Finke was about to start out on his mission, Evans said:

"Finke. Get the story from that maid. Most likely she'll come through—one way or another."

14
A Profound Sense of Fatality

As one by one the small company gathered in Fremont's office started away, the Chief, sitting in a chair reserved for visitors because the body of Agnes Welsh still lay upon his desk, sank deeper into gloom.

"An American lieutenant dies in a building collapse, but he is what you call 'hot' and I am made to look like a dunce. An American former lieutenant, female, has heart failure while being questioned in my office. Can you imagine what a hostile press can make of that?"

Evans, who had waited in order to see Dr. Hyacinthe Toudoux, looked down at the floor.

"I am the fool," he said.

"At least, if you should take to folly, you would do it in the grand manner. I am only one of the junior fools, like Rabelais' small devils who were able only to thunder and lightning a little around the head of a cabbage," said Fremont.

The door opened. Dr. Hyacinthe Toudoux came storming in, and pulled up just short of the desk. He stared down at the body of Agnes Welsh with protruding eyes. He turned to Evans.

"Another?"

Evans rose as if he had to force himself to take the slightest action. He went to the desk, removed the right shoe from Agnes' once sturdy foot, reached under the navy-blue skirt, rolled down the sheer nylon and exposed a scratch on Agnes' ankle.

He looked up at Dr. Toudoux. The doctor sustained his gaze an instant, then turned away.

"The same?" the doctor asked.

Evans nodded.

Fremont came up out of the chair. "Do you mean to say that this woman did not die of heart failure?"

For the brief fraction of a second Evans hesitated, and then said:

"Her heart failed. That's all we can say just now."

Dr. Toudoux nodded. The desk blotter with its imitation-leather backing had slipped to the floor. He reached down for it, and tore it all the way across, throwing the pieces violently to the floor again.

"Another certificate?" he asked Evans, as soon as he could control himself sufficiently.

"Coronary thrombosis," Evans said.

"Have the body removed to my laboratory," Dr. Toudoux gruffly said to Fremont. "If you please, my friend," he added, softly, ashamed of his own discourtesy.

Fremont pushed a cluster of buttons, and the attendants promptly appeared with a stretcher.

The telephone rang. It was Finke, for Evans.

"First of all, the Zazou's disappeared. What Schlumberger's saying to that pair of dicks who were watching in front and behind would make Wasp Billings sound like Henry Wadsworth Longfellow," Finke said, disgust and admiration contending for mastery in his voice.

"That's unfortunate," said Evans, more like his calm self again. "What else?"

"Amelie, the maid, came through, all right. She told me Doc Havemeyer was at the Reine Blanche this morning. They're old acquaintances, it seems. For five years, he's been seeing her once a week, on Saturday or on Monday, with a thousand-franc note in one hand. . . ."

"That's fortunate," Evans said. "I grasp what you mean."

"And Doc adores his kid brother. In fact, on the days he's been coming up from Rouen to spend an hour with Amelie, he also has dropped around to the Zazou's room and either handed the kid or left for him enough dough to keep him going."

Evans interrupted. "It couldn't be that Doc was in Paris last Monday afternoon?" he asked.

"He was. And don't say that's fortunate, or unfortunate. It's a fact," said Finke.

"Keep digging. And call me later at Billings' office," Evans said. "I'm going to break the news about Agnes to him."

"It's fortunate it's not me who has to do that," Finke said.

He heard Finke chuckle as the phone clicked at the other end. Evans replaced the instrument. He turned to Fremont.

"Chief. We seem to have lost Ulysses Grant, for the nonce," he began.

"I shall order those two turnips who were tailing him to grow whiskers and dress as American generals, until further notice," Fremont bellowed.

"He'll turn up, where the shot and shell are thickest, no doubt," Evans said, unworried.

"You remarked that something in MacFeenk's report was 'fortunate.' Could I be informed about that?" asked Fremont, as if he needed badly an item that could be so described.

"Dr. Havemeyer, the former captain attached to G-6, was in Paris, at the Reine Blanche this morning, and talked with the Zazou," Evans said.

"I shall have him brought in for questioning," said Fremont. "If his heart fails in the process, so will mine, I promise you."

"Let's let Dr. Havemeyer follow his own devices," Evans said. "Should we get trace of his whereabouts, have the same two men who lost his young brother keep him under observation, discreetly. Their Existentialist lilacs will not be noticeable the first couple of days. Do not insist on slouch hats and a cavalryman's stance. Having been guilty of such a bloomer will put them on their mettle, in the interest of their monthly pay."

"Shall I also detail the pair who were assigned to the unlucky Miss Welsh?" asked Fremont, dejectedly.

"Four tails might prove too many. They'd get in one another's way," Evans said.

"Did I understand you to say that you are going voluntarily into the presence of that American lieutenant colonel who barks and bites?" asked Fremont.

"First I'll have a chat with Dr. Toudoux," said Evans, and made off for the laboratory and dissecting room.

Dr. Toudoux stopped his gruesome work when Evans entered. No assistants were present.

"We are back in the Middle Ages," said Dr. Toudoux. "The days when cowardly killers had to be caught in the act, or all was guess-work. No proof. No antidotes."

"You know whom we have to thank for that," Evans said.

The medical examiner clenched his fists and the veins swelled on his forehead. "The ones we have to thank for all France's misery, for the world's disintegration, the future's threat."

"You were reluctant to discuss Lieutenant Kitchel—the method, I mean—even with me," Evans said, but not reproachfully.

"And you would not give me a lead. I don't blame you. I should never have disclosed this fiendish outrage until I was sure you grasped the nature of it. There will be no supplementary certificates, my friend. I, Hyacinthe Toudoux, who have loved and served science all my life, am proud to swear falsely."

"I was sure you'd feel that way," Evans said, and clasped the doctor's hand. "Thanks to the criminal folly of a few publicists, who think of nothing beyond sensations, too many know of this technique already. But the knowledge must not become general, or murder may as well be added to the curricula of our public schools, our grade schools, even. And the police will act merely as morticians."

"The atom bomb at least lacks the menace of selectivity," the doctor said.

"And nominal cost," said Evans.

"The simplest of equipment."

"Anonymity of whoever lets it drop."

"Dead silence."

"Disunity of time and place."

"I regret having had to bring this to your attention," Evans said, "but if humanity is safe from anyone, it is Dr. Hyacinthe Toudoux."

"And his friend, Homer Evans, whom he had unfairly abused ofttimes," said Dr. Toudoux.

Then the two men, each great in his way or ways, sighed deeply, and brought to their aid their profound sense of fatality, Olympian irony and determination to cling, for however short a time, to life, which they appreciated and relished so keenly.

"I will make you a wager," Homer said.

Dr. Toudoux looked at him questioningly.

"That before this year has expired, you will have found the counter measure," said Homer.

"I shall sleep very briefly and infrequently meanwhile," said Dr. Toudoux. "Eulalie! Bliss! Farewell!"

"We shall explain to her, and make her the proudest woman in this or any land," Evans said. "I leave you to continue, with the fate of thousands or millions in your hands. The same photos, corresponding enlargements. I go a-hunting V-2's with butterflies."

Evans walked from the room, through a corridor, out a door, across a courtyard, under an archway, across a sidewalk and strode square into the side of a moving bus. He was thrown back and sideways, and landed face up on the sidewalk.

"In effect," he said to himself, as he picked himself up and dusted off his clothes. "I had better cling to the surface of the earth before I find myself six feet under it."

He hailed a cab, and drove to the *place* de la Concorde.

15
A Small World

LESS THAN TEN MINUTES LATER, Evans was with Billings in the colonel's office.

"I've been in touch with Washington," Billings said. "I had to be sure. I've got permission to tell you about the work of my outfit, certain general aspects no outsider has been told."

Evans nodded. "Good. I've surmised quite a lot, but that's not enough. The time has come to get tough."

Billings, the fire-eater according to reputation he had nurtured so carefully, sighed. He was too angry to let himself go.

"That fine girl . . . After Bob Kitchel. How many times I've said to all my gang, individually and sometimes to a few of them together: 'The Commandment says, Thou Shalt Not Kill. Except, naturally, in self-defense. There wasn't room on those stone tablets for a lot of stuff that has to be implied. Go easy with the weapons,' I told 'em. 'Lots of the boys and girls have different assignments than ours. We're dealing with the stuff that Shakespeare called "dross." Just lousy money, that's all. And most of that is phony. G-6 has no room for trigger-happy people. Forget that bayonet training with the stuffed dummies. We're on the scene with the green.'"

"I thought as much," said Evans.

"You can imagine," Billings said, "when you think of how in peace time, in the States, jobs of counterfeiting can be slick, and passing 'the queer' is only a skilled trade, not even a profession, that when a powerful government, organized from top to bottom as few governments have been, goes in for making and spreading false money, the possibilities can hardly be exaggerated."

"Exactly," Evans said.

"Hitler's boys made quite a few billions of what look even to most experts like good U.S. bills—fives, tens, twenties, and fifties. Not so many fifties, but quite a number. Just the fifties would go into the millions. And if you knew in what far corners, and near metropolises they turn up. And what the temptation is, for men like mine, who have to get along on Army pay; how we had to check up on our personnel before we accepted them, how we had to watch them afterward, what they did, what they spent, who their friends were, you'd have a headache in December that you felt in May.

"It was bad enough during the war, but since, with Black Markets running wild in every country, and travel restrictions lifted, our job has been a rat race.

"No one could say how much of that Hitler-brand American money got over to the States. His gang, the big boys, I mean, didn't count on losing the war and being tried and hanged. And the ones who should have been hanged and were not, are still organized, some living the life of Riley.

"The top Nazis and their fixers in other countries, including our own, acquired plenty of U.S. money that was genuine. They collected it through the Bunds and Sängvereins, in a hundred ways, and cashed it where they could. When it got more and more dangerous to use the Hitler counterfeit stuff, which still can get by most banks, some Heinie hit on a scheme. Soon tourists from the States, who were Nazis under cover, began bringing bills with them. They listed them on those Treasury forms the French give out at the ports, and took back to the States an equivalent amount that was 100 per cent pure.

"So our outfit has to get the name and address of every man and woman who applies for a ticket on a liner or a plane from the U.S. to France, and any of them to which the slightest suspicion can be attached is investigated, as secretly as possible, by the Treasury boys and G-6, before they sail or take off," Billings said.

Evans nodded and smiled. "So anybody in G-6 over here would know, fairly soon, if a man like Luke Mallory went to a travel agency in Boston weeks ahead of sailing time and asked to be informed when passage would be available."

"Right," Billings said.

"However sterling a citizen Luke appeared to be, if he were closely connected with one of your men, alive or dead, his affairs and his record and his actions would be closely checked," said Evans.

"As a matter of course," Billings said.

"Any man who signified a preference for the French Line would land at Le Havre," Evans continued.

"Most likely," agreed Billings.

"Bob Kitchel quite often met boats, and rode on boat trains, I take it."

"Yes," Billings said.

"Now," said Evans, "I'd like to hear about Dr. Havemeyer. From the beginning. Whatever you've got."

"He was a damn good operator," said Billings.

"And you let him resign," Evans remarked, casually.

"Like almost everybody else, he got too damn tired, till he didn't seem to care whether school kept or not. That's our main occupational hazard, in this kind of work. Poor Agnes was the same, only worse. She had what amounted to a nervous crack-up, and Doc eased her out, with my full approval."

"Tell me more about Doc," urged Evans. "He had a change of personality, as I understand it. What was he like before he lost his pep?"

Billings reached into a drawer of his desk and pulled out Doc's folder. He referred to it, now and then, but spoke partly from memory.

"He was born . . ."

Evans leaned forward, all attention. "Might I hazard a guess? It'll help me, right or wrong."

"O.K.," agreed Billings. "Look into a crystal, if that gives you a kick."

"I'd say, about—around June, 1903," said Evans.

"June 12, 1903," Billings said. "Did somebody tell you?"

"No," Evans said. "Nobody told me."

"Shall I go on?" Billings asked.

"I'll try not to interrupt too often," Evans said.

"His name is Leo Havemeyer, that's all. No middle name. Not Leopold or Leonidas or Leon. Just Leo. He was born in Mount Washington, Mass. The certificate was signed by a country doctor from over in New York State. His father is listed as Sawyer Havemeyer, his mother as . . ."

"Not Lois?"

Billings looked slightly annoyed. "Lois. L-o-i-s. So what?"

"God be praised! I've not been chasing noon at four P.M., as the French say," Evans said.

"Look," said Billings. "You know me, and you know my setup. If I've had to hold out on you, that was orders. You're not under any official restraint, I presume."

"The last thing I'd do would be to confuse you with unconfirmed conjectures," said Evans.

"We're in this together," Billings said. "Now Doc was nuts about his mother, from his childhood till she died. And his old man was dotty about him, and used to jump up and down with chagrin because he couldn't seem to produce any more kids, till twenty years later, when this gander-gutter, bandy-legged false alarm who thinks he's General Grant came along. And damned if Sawyer Havemeyer didn't die six weeks or so before his second son was born. The old man knew Ulysses Grant Havemeyer was on the way, but he never saw him, or knew whether the child was a boy or a girl."

"Let's hope he watches from above. But not steadily. Just when conditions are propitious," Evans said.

"Nuts to metaphysics," Billings said. "Let's stick to the records, and the hot poop the boys in the States have gathered. Leo, that's Doc, went to grammar school from 1908 to 1914, and he was a whiz with the answers. Skipped two grades."

"One reason he was spotted for G-6, I suppose," Evans said.

Billings nodded. "Doc went through high school in three years, when it should have taken four. He was popular with his class, and somewhat of a headache to the teachers. Fair athlete, strong on the morale. He sang like a thrush, yodeled in the bargain, and played the zither his old man taught him. He could throw his voice, too, the way Edgar Bergen does.

"In 1919 he went to Harvard, and waited on table to help pay his way. Did odd jobs. Tutored. Kept up in his studies, and got his B.S. in 1923, *cum laude*. Harvard didn't do him any harm and he got a lot out of Harvard. The month before he graduated, his old man died, from falling out of one of those tall trees on Mount Washington, Mass., and landing head down on some granite. Just after the commencement was over, and Doc took a summer job as ventriloquist with a carnival that played New England resorts and fairs, his brother was born, July 3, 1923.

"Doc entered Harvard Medical, went through with not much money and plenty of fun, and got his M.D. in 1927. But his mother died a month later, on the fourth of July, 1927, and that hit Doc so hard that while he was interning at the Massachusetts General, he didn't mix much with his old college chums or any of the gang at the hospital for a few months. Then he loosened up again. In 1930, still without any dough to speak of, he joined the staff of the Boston Psychopathic Hospital, and was there until 1936. But he got a bug about the sea, and took a post as ship's doctor with the American Export Lines. He still had nothing much in the way of money, but he went all out for Republican Spain."

"Stout fellow," Evans said.

"On the *Exeter*, speaking good German, he got to know a Kraut stewardess, a female hairdresser, also *echt Deutsch*, and a couple of Heinie stewards. And what he gleaned from them about Hitler and the Reich brought him to Washington, in 1936, voluntarily. He was turned over to me. He'd gone to the Library of Congress, sized up some of the librarians, and asked one he believed he could trust who he should talk to about what he'd learned from the traveling Krauts. The librarian sent him to my outfit. I liked him right off the bat, and he was assigned to practice medicine in Yorktown, where he stayed three years, and did plenty for his country. In 1939 he was transferred to G-2, and became a specialist in that truth-syrup technique you hear so much about, but not all there is to hear. In 1942 he went to England, with G-6, then to France, then, in August, 1944, to Paris."

"Was it about that time he underwent that personality change?" Evans asked.

"That's when we noticed he was different. Later, in 1946 he quit the service and bought a house in Rouen. He came to see us now and then, but had little to say. Honest to God, when I think back, it's hard to realize he's the same Doc Havemeyer who held up his end so well through thick and thin, from 1936 till the war was in the bag," said Billings.

"A man, or a woman, for that matter, ought to be listed as a casualty the day he or she gets into a uniform," said Evans, with as near to bitterness as he ever permitted himself to go.

They sat silently a while, Evans thinking over what he had heard, and rounding out his conception of Dr. Leo Havemeyer. Homer roused himself, prepared to continue.

"Mind if I telephone Fremont?" he asked.

"Pray do," said Billings.

When the connection was established Evans asked: "What about Ulysses Grant Havemeyer?"

"Monkey-face was seen at the Café de Flore after having left the Reine Blanche by means which will cost two of my officers dearly. He left the Flore by other means as mysterious, after some talk with an Indo-Chinese. My entire force shall grow beards, wear slouch hats, and pretend they are generals, without pay, if both the young crazy Havemeyer and his older brother, of the regular habits, are not found in suitable condition for grilling before eight o'clock tonight," Fremont said. "We've lost the doctor, too. He's not back in Rouen."

Billings, at Evans' suggestion, had been listening in.

"Both of them gone. By God, if anything happens to Doc!" Billings muttered.

"I've developed a sudden deep interest in Devs Smith, the dog-robber prodigy who's in Saigon, let's assume," said Evans. "Could

I have a full report on him? Especially how, where and when he learned Indo-Chink?"

"Isn't that pretty far afield?" grunted Billings.

"Small world," Evans said.

16
No Standards Apply

WHEN EVANS STEPPED OUT of the E.R.P. headquarters in the former residence of the Dukes of Toussaint-Ferron, Lvov Kvek drove to the curb in Evans' roadster. This was by prearrangement. When Homer had noticed that his White Russian friend had brought to the unlucky Agnes Welsh eleven nylons, he understood that Kvek's winnings on Nicholas II had been spent. So he had asked Kvek to be his guest and helper until the case was solved, the criminal or criminals caught, and the time had come for more relaxation, after which a few elementary questions of a practical nature might be faced.

The first call was at the laboratory of Dr. Hyacinthe Toudoux, where Homer hastily examined the blown-up photographs of the scratches on the late Lieutenant Kitchel's right hand and the right ankle of the late Agnes Welsh. The medical examiner looked over his shoulder. Kvek, meanwhile, said a few sincere prayers, in Greek Orthodox fashion, for the repose of the two souls which formerly, according to his beliefs, had inhabited the bodies which rested on adjacent slabs.

"I expected this, but, nevertheless I am relieved," Evans said, touching one photograph, then the other.

"The same hand with the identical instrument made both scratches. The instrument was probably of nickel-plated steel, and had recently been sharpened on a small grinding wheel of stone, one of the old-fashioned kind installed in so many small restaurant kitchens. The nature of the scratches indicates that the instrument, no doubt improvised from some utilitarian object that would in itself attract no attention, had no handle. It must have been short. Not two inches long. The grip of the fingers that held it was tight but not too firm," said Evans.

"What could it be?" asked the doctor.

"Let me think," said Evans. "What is there, on my person, let us say, that could, by means of a small sharpening or grinding wheel, be adapted for the purpose? Not an empty fountain pen. That has two nibs. Ah." He touched his belt buckle, then unfastened it.

"The prong of the buckle of a belt," said Dr. Toudoux.

Evans nodded with inner satisfaction and went with Kvek to Fremont's office.

"May I telephone the Terrible-Tempered Colonel Bang?" he asked. Fremont nodded wearily. Homer dialed.

"Colonel Billings," he asked, "where did Judd Coulson live, when he was with your outfit?"

"At the Paris Dinard, naturally. And so did the Orientalist, Private Smith. And I may as well tell you that Coulson has been lost without trace. He was last seen in San Francisco, but that was three months ago," the colonel said.

"Thanks," said Evans. He asked Fremont if he would be in his office another half hour. Fremont nodded, dejectedly.

Evans asked Kvek to drive him to the Hotel de la Reine Blanche. The Russian had taken Homer there that morning because that was the hotel where Fred Mallory and Agnes Welsh had gone together, in the years when both had been alive. Evans went into a huddle with the maid, Amelie, Finke Maguire, and the motherly manager.

"The pox of race prejudice has never infected this place, madame?" he asked of the motherly woman.

"We've had a few black men, and women, some who spoke French, others who pretended not to understand it," the woman said.

"Any Orientals?"

"Not many. There's one young man, whose name is Po Dingh, according to himself and his papers. He has Room 14, has rented it several years. He's not here now because he works in a restaurant in the Latin Quarter somewhere."

"In the rue Cornu," said Amelie.

Evans thanked them, and smiled. "Finke," Evans said. "Will you come with Colonel Kvek and me? I shall need you tonight, in the interest of your client."

"I'm glad somebody does," Finke said, and Amelie playfully grinned and nudged him with her elbow.

Finke, Kvek and Evans went back to the Prefecture in the roadster. Fremont was pacing the floor.

"I want you to get in touch with your Black Chamber, which is supposed not to exist," Evans said to the Chief. "I've become interested in a certain Oriental with an Indo-Chinese name, Po Dingh or Po Dinghh, who has lodged at the Reine Blanche some years, who works in a restaurant in the rue Cornu, near the Ecole Polytechnique, and who wears suspenders."

The look Fremont gave Evans was piteous indeed. "Americans, Existentialists, and now, Orientals," he murmured. "On top of that, our Black Chamber, the mere address of which would not be disclosed even to the Commissioner, the Prefect, or the Minister of Justice, who wears suspenders *and* a belt."

"I'll talk with our Ambassador, with President Truman, if necessary, to grease the channels," said Homer. "What I want is simple. The *dossier*, or file, about Po Dingh. We are all aware that the situation in Indo-China between the Communists and the natives who have been induced to give lip service to Bao Dai is acute. The problem of colonies, and the encirclement of Red China and Red Russia, has prompted your Secret Service to keep close tabs on Orientals who live in Paris. I don't want to question Po Dingh until I know a few things, primarily, whether or not he amplifies his income as a restaurant worker by teaching Occidentals his language."

Evans snapped his fingers, suddenly, and without ado took up the phone and dialed.

"Colonel Billings," he said. "Try Saigon for a trace of Private Judd Coulson, with the high I.Q. This is just another shot at the moon, but it's worth a phone call. I'm at the Prefecture."

Evans turned to Fremont. "Before you start on Po Dingh, tell me about the steps you have taken to find Doc Havemeyer," he said.

"All restaurants and cafés are being checked systematically, also concierges, railroad stations, buses, moving-picture theaters and other places of amusement; drug stores, anywhere medical books or medical and surgical supplies are exchanged or sold; airports, public and private planes, all roads of egress from Paris, especially those leading toward Rouen. He is not in Rouen. On that I can stake my monthly pay," Fremont said.

"That leaves only one way out," Evans said. "That simplifies our search."

"One way?" Fremont stiffened. "Had this American doctor killed himself, we should have found the body."

"I was not thinking of that. The Seine, I mean," said Evans.

Fremont's jaw dropped and his eyes went blank, like those of a haddock. "There are no passenger boats plying between here and Rouen."

"Just an idea," mused Evans. "I have learned that in 1936, when Dr. Havemeyer had passed with credit through Harvard University, Harvard Medical, a stiff internship at the Massachusetts General, and four brilliant years at the Boston Psychopathic Hospital, he took a job as ship's doctor on a liner which is not top grade, and spent nearly three years aboard. His mother died, just before he went a-sailing. He had been touchingly fond of her and close to her, spiritually, all his life. He took aboard with him his young brother, Ulysses, twenty years his junior, who was then twelve years old. The lad, whom you know ever so slightly, had proved so smart in the lower grade schools that Ulysses was graduated at the age of ten. Dr. Havemeyer quite wisely wanted his young brother to wait a while and see something of the world before entering Prep school. A pupil a few years younger than others in his class is at a disadvantage. It does not take much of a stretch of the imagination to assume that, when Doc Havemeyer's mother died, Doc was at her deathbed and there was plenty of time for talk . . . Doc may have promised to take good care of Ulysses, who must have needed supervision."

"With that I agree," Fremont said, fervently.

"I have vague reasons for thinking that in his last talk, or previous talks with his mother, Doc Havemeyer's feeling for the sea might have been engendered. That's only guesswork now, but we have to go on something. Will you alert whoever you can, on both banks of the Seine between here and Rouen, to watch for Doc, and/or his whiskered brother? Kvek will drive me and Mr. Maguire along all roads bordering the right bank of the Seine, downstream from here. We may be able to spot Doc or Ulysses or both, somehow. And please get in touch with the police of Rouen and urge them to give me every facility, with no regard for red tape and ordinary formalities."

"I should have covered the river," Fremont said, sadly. "But not many criminals in the last century or two have stationed themselves on slow-moving river craft to be caught like frogs on lily pads, at anyone's leisure. I won't deny that such a ruse might occur to Americans, to whom no standards apply."

"Have you taken in a safe-blower's kit lately? Drills, soup, and so forth?" Evans asked.

"A few," said Fremont.

"Lend me one, in working order, if you please," Homer said.

Finke, who had stood around like a bump on a log, somewhat sulkily, brightened. "The old ways are often the best," he said, and grinned.

"I once heard of a Basque who could eat a motorcycle, handlebars and all," Kvek said. "My teeth are strong. Perhaps I could scuttle a ship without making a telltale explosion."

Finke clapped Kvek on the shoulder. "You an' me'll get along," he said.

"Let's go," said Evans.

First, at Evans' suggestion, they drove to the Prince de Galles. Homer had promised Megan and Mrs. Mallory to take them to dinner that evening, and he had to beg off. The redhead was at the switchboard.

"Miss Mallory's room," Evans said, with a smile, and added: "You're looking particularly well this afternoon."

"I fixed myself up, in case you came along," she said. "Miss Mallory's gone out, and I thought if you were disappointed, you might cry on my shoulder, and see how it is."

Homer was astonished. "Miss Mallory's gone out? Did she leave word for me?"

"No. A slim well-dressed monsieur came in, about five feet seven, I should say. Wore an Oxford gray suit, French shoes, and a nifty gray hat. He had nice eyebrows, kind of thin, not just alike. His voice was something like yours. He said you were tied up, had sent him over and wanted her to have tea with him, so you could join them later. Said you couldn't be reached just then . . . She'd understand."

"Go on," Evans said.

"She was disappointed at first, then braced up. She was ready and dressed in half an hour. The young guy sat down here, reading . . ."

"Reading what?" Evans asked. He had never been more shocked and startled, so completely nonplussed, but he controlled himself. If he got the redhead excited, her memory might play tricks.

"Oh, I forgot to tell you something else—about their talk, I mean." She looked at Evans wistfully. "If just once in my life I could find a man who'd worry about me, the way you do about . . ."

"Please. Not now," said Evans, earnestly.

"All right," she said. "The guy in gray mentioned that he'd met Miss Mallory at a party last night. And the magazine he was reading's over there in the chair right now, the chair next to where he was sitting."

Evans walked over, picked up the magazine and looked at it. It was in French and English and German, got out by anti-Soviet Russians in exile. There was a slip of paper torn off a sheet of paper and inserted as a bookmark in an article about the horse, Nicholas II. It was the May issue of the magazine and was dated some time before the triumph at Longchamps of the horse named for the late Tsar. Evans put the magazine, bookmark and all, into his pocket, and returned to the switchboard.

"Something else I haven't told you," said the redhead. "While he was waiting, maybe five minutes before Miss Mallory came down, the man in gray went into the bar and talked a minute with the chap you call Selectman Parker, who's in Room 24 when he's here. He's out now."

"The selectman seemed to know him?"

"As far as I could tell," the redhead said.

Evans stood a moment, making decisions. He telephoned upstairs to Mrs. Mallory, and asked to postpone their meeting until the next day for dinner. Nothing that Mrs. Mallory said indicated that she knew Megan had gone out. Homer thanked the redhead, and hurried out to the roadster.

"Finke! Lvov!" he said. "Something has developed. I can't go down river with you. I'll fly to Rouen and join you there. Drive along the river, as we'd planned. If you spot either one of the Havemeyers, don't warn them. But if there's time, drive as fast as you can to Rouen, and go through that house at No. 3 bis rue de Caen with a fine-tooth comb. Tie up the housekeeper and gag her, or do anything you have to, so she won't be in your way."

A taxi came along, Evans hailed it, jumped in, and rode back to the Ritz Hotel. Selectman Parker and Luke Mallory were at the bar.

"You talked with a young fellow in Oxford gray, at the Prince de Galles bar earlier this afternoon," Homer said.

"What time?" asked the selectman. Parker was submerging the father and mother of a hangover with the broth of a pelt from the dog that had bit him. He was drinking vodka, straight. Luke, in better shape, was sticking to Old Crow.

The chagrin that possessed Evans when it came over him that he had been too perturbed to get the approximate time from the redhead made him bite his lip.

"Did you talk with more than one man in gray?" asked Evans.

The selectman shook his head. "Just one. Some feller who said he met me at the party, wherever it was."

"Did you place him?"

"Didn't have to. He placed me," the selectman said.

"Was he Russian?" asked Evans.

"No. He couldn't stop for a drink," said the selectman.

It was no use. The selectman could be of no help. Evans looked at Luke, who asked him what he'd have.

"Another time. The American girl you met last night, Agnes Welsh, has died. I've got to go to the Prefecture," Homer said.

Mallory was sincerely sorry. He remembered having met some American woman in uniform. "That's terrible," he said. "What took her off?"

"Coronary thrombosis," Evans said, and hurried back to his cab.

"To the Prefecture," Homer said. Then he reconsidered. His brain was stuttering. He breathed deeply and tried to pull himself together. "No. Wait a moment more," he ordered the driver. Homer went back into the Ritz. The brunette was on duty at the telephone desk. Homer gave a number, without observing the usual amenities. Wasp Billings answered. "Meet me at Fremont's office as quickly as you can. Miss Mallory's been kidnapped. And forget about the Zazou. Have your people on the lookout for a trace of Miss Mallory, and a young man in Oxford gray, with a gray hat, French shoes, about five feet seven. Give the orders, then hurry to the Prefecture," Evans said.

He hung up before Billings could answer, regained his cab and in a few minutes was with Fremont. Schlumberger was there. Evans told them what had been told him. Billings came in, breathing hard. Evans repeated his story. They all were stunned into silence.

Homer was the first to speak. "Have you a list of shoe stores which make a specialty of odd lasts, specifically the kind by means of which heels can be heightened and soles thickened, for men who want to add as much as possible to their height?" he asked.

Schlumberger nodded and pressed a button.

"How about coiffeurs for men, who pluck eyebrows?" Evans continued.

Schlumberger nodded again and pressed another button. One clerk appeared, then another. Schlumberger told them what was wanted and they came back promptly with the lists. Homer scanned them rapidly.

"He wouldn't go where he was known, or where he'd be too conspicuous. Somewhere in the Latin Quarter. No. Most probably Montparnasse. There are plenty of whiskers down there, and gigolos. Ah. Here's a shoe store in the rue Delambre, and around the corner, in the boulevard Raspail, André and Simone, hair dress-ers. Will you come with me, Fremont? Schlumberger can send out the descriptions of Miss Mallory. She'll be wearing stylish clothes suitable for late afternoon and dinner. The man in Oxford gray should be stalked cautiously and asked for his papers. Have him searched, take everything, no matter what, from his pockets. And check the prong of his belt buckle. It may show signs of having been sharpened," said Evans. He was self-possessed again, tense and alert, but in control.

"What would anybody want with the Mallory girl?" demanded Billings.

"I'm hoping for the best. If the man who killed Kitchel and Miss Welsh suspects we're on his track, and God knows he should, he may be holding the girl as a hostage, to strike a bargain. He wants a chance to get away, and he knows what all of us would do to save an innocent lovely girl of seventeen. I can think of no way in which Miss Mallory could be of other use to him. She knows nothing that would constitute a menace to his plan," said Homer.

"Did poor Agnes know anything?"

"She might have, or he might have been afraid she did," Evans said.

"If they've got aboard one of those tugs or motor scows, they couldn't get her out to sea," Fremont said.

"Better look for her in Paris," said Homer. "Finke, Kvek and all the riverside police are checking every vessel."

Homer started out with Fremont, in the latter's sedan. They tried André and Simone without success, but in the rue Vavin they learned that a young man, freshly shaven, with a recent haircut and wearing Oxford gray had had his heavy eyebrows plucked, and had been fussy about the job, so that one would be more arched than the other, and the other a millimeter narrower on the out-side. He had brown eyes.

Fremont groaned. "Four-fifths of the men in Paris have brown eyes."

"What kind of shoes was he wearing?" Homer asked. No one in the shop could remember.

"Then he had the French shoes. He called first at the shoeshop," he said.

He and Fremont went to the shop in the rue Delambre, one hundred and fifty yards away. There the proprietor and his wife, agitated by a police visit, said they had sold a pair of shoes to a man in Oxford gray with heavy beetling eyebrows. The shoes had built-up heels and soles.

"What did he do with the ones he was wearing?" Evans asked.

"Left them with us, to give to someone who might need them," said the proprietor.

"Trot them out," Fremont ordered.

The proprietor's wife looked crestfallen, if not frightened. "Already I've given them away, to an old man who was so tired from tramping that he sat down on the curb outside," she said.

"Would you know him if you saw him?" Fremont asked.

"He was not one of those who beg around this quarter. He had a gray shock of hair, and hadn't shaved for a few days. His eyes were watery and the rims of the lids were red and inflamed. He touched his old hat and thanked me, and asked God to bless me," said the shoe man's wife.

"I join him in that request," said Evans. "You meant well, and God intends nothing easy for Monsieur Fremont and me, that is clear."

"You mean, of course, that our Zazou no longer looks like an American general," Fremont demanded.

"We cannot count absolutely on that. There may possibly be confederates and accomplices. Dr. Havemeyer is five feet nine, and my five-feet-seven estimate came from a telephone operator who had other things on her mind. We can absolve the Indo-Chinks on account of their eyebrows, which need no plucking, as a general rule. By the way, any reports on Po Dingh?"

They had got back into the sedan, leaving the shoe man and his wife uneasy but sustained with their innocent intent, if all they had said had been true.

"Po Dingh has taught a few pupils, among them two American privates, the rudiments of his language. He has avoided taking sides

between his countrymen who wish to remain under the protection
of the French, and the faction which wants independence, even if
it means a Communist regime under Ho Minh," Fremont said. "The
restaurant in the rue Cornu is frequented by Oriental students and
other Orientals of the Latin Quarter, some of whom have French
girl comrades. It is in Category III but does not charge the maximum prices permitted by the regulations. A meal can be had, soup,
some kind of Oriental concoction with bits of this and that, rice,
biscuits made on the premises, candied ginger, and tea for 150
francs."

"Do white people go there much?" Evans asked.

"Soldiers did, and now a few G.I. Bill of Rights veterans who
study mostly contraband tobacco and illicit gasoline, and who can
blame them," Fremont said.

"Let's go to the Reine Blanche. I want another look at the Rooms
No. 11 and 12, and a talk with Amelie, the maid of all work," said
Evans. "I have never been as worried in my life as at this moment."

"I have not your gifts or your intellect, monsieur," said Fremont humbly, "but if I had I should be as desperate as you."

At the Reine Blanche, Homer first checked with Billings by
phone.

"Judd Coulson's in Saigon, with Smith and Bao Dai. They all
are living like emperors, and our boys seem to be carrying it off
better than the native Pooh Bah," Billings said.

"More power to them, all except Bao Dai," Evans said, and hung
up. He mounted alone to Ulysses Havemeyer's room, and found a
roll of charts standing in a corner of the disordered clothes closet.
He unrolled them, and his eyes hardened. On each one was a lon-
gitudinal cross-section of a man or woman's body, showing on one
the glands, and on others the bones, tendons, arteries, organs,
veins, and muscles. The charts had been acquired in Cambridge,
Massachusetts, years before, and the cover bore the name of Leo
Havemeyer, in the doctor's handwriting as it had appeared in his
student days.

Evans took the charts along, rolled on their attached stick. He
braced Amelie in the hallway.

"Know any girls who live peaceably with Indo-Chinese?" he asked.

"A few. Why not? The Orientals are generous and kind," she said, a bit defensively.

"Pick out one of those girls with a good heart, a pal of yours you've known some time, and arrange for me to talk with her as soon as you can. I'll want more of your help, and there's no reason you shouldn't be paid," Evans said, reaching for his wallet.

"This may help to catch whoever killed that nurse, poor kid?" Amelie asked.

Evans looked at her closely. "Killed? Who told you she was killed?" he asked sharply.

"Nobody," said Amelie. "I'm as psychic as hell."

She returned Homer's look, and waved away any suggestion that he should open the wallet.

"Just give me credit for a little sense," she said. "If a woman drops dead naturally, half the flics in Paris don't start searching a joint like this."

17
Confound Confusion!

SINCE THE MOMENT HOMER HAD BEEN TOLD by the redhead at the Prince de Galles that Megan had been lured away, he had forced himself with all his will to attend to the various seemingly trivial details that might help him save her life. The whole pattern and importance of the case, which previously had offered him an intriguing puzzle on which to exercise his ingenuity, had faded into the background. Murder was dastardly, final, cowardly and against all man's honorable instincts. Murder, as applied to Megan Mallory, he found so hard to accept, as a threat or a fact, that his thinking had become blurred. And since his mind stood between her and destruction, he had to have solitude for self-discipline and concentration.

He already had set in motion whatever machinery there was to get trace of her. So he asked Fremont to show him to a private office at the Prefecture where he could not be disturbed, and to see that he was not interrupted unless there was news of Doctor Havemeyer, Ulysses Havemeyer the Zazou, or a young man answering the meager description he had got from the telephone operator at the Prince de Galles.

Homer first examined his decision not to let either Mrs. Mallory or Luke Mallory know about the terrible danger their daughter was facing. The suspense, cruel enough for him, would be unbearable for them. He must act. But first he must think. What did he know about the killer or killers? They had no regard for human life. They had a method against which most of the modern science of criminology, police investigations or precedents were all but useless.

Still, they were human—abnormal, depraved, cunning to the point of madness and bolder than insanity itself, nevertheless human. They felt safe and sure of themselves. . . . Suddenly he sat up straighter and grew tense. Did they feel safe? Had not the security they had enjoyed been somehow shattered, so that the abduction of Megan and the holding of the girl as a hostage had had to be improvised?

That, he felt, was the key to their new behavior. What had alarmed them?

He tried to shut all else but fundamentals from his mind. Doc Havemeyer, for instance? If, that morning, Doc had planned to disappear, he would not have visited Amelie at the Reine Blanche, or gone to the Reine Blanche at all. He would have sent the money to Ulysses, as he had done many times before, no doubt. He would not have gone directly to the one place in Paris where he was known, and surely not for the purpose of killing Agnes Welsh who herself did not know beforehand where she would be that day. He might have killed Agnes *because* she had seen him. Amelie might already be dead, or might die later. The Zazou might be dead. There was nothing positive, in the scientific sense of the word, identifying Ulysses with the new young man in gray, five feet seven inches tall, perhaps.

Furthermore, if Ulysses, the Zazou, had *planned* to change character and appearance and become the young man in gray, who spoke "something like" Homer Evans, himself, he would have bought his built-up shoes ahead of time. No shoes the Zazou was known to have possessed were missing from his room, except the pair he had been wearing when he had left it, which had been *after* Homer had heard him singing American jazz songs, and with a flair few Europeans could counterfeit.

The detailed material furnished by Wasp Billings had made it clear that both the Havemeyers were talented mimics and impersonators. The Harvard *Crimson* and *Lampoon* had been rich in reference to Doc's popular acts as a ventriloquist, on the occasions when Harvard men of his class had got together, and had quoted some of the witty dialogue between him and his dummy, Boola-Boola, at the expense of Yale and all it signified. Homer himself had seen the Zazou take off the late General Grant, and keep the act day after day. In the brief sketch of Ulysses Havemeyer he had received from Billings, Homer had learned that Ulysses had been born at a private hospital in Boston on July 3, 1923, about six weeks after his father had died. Between the time his mother, Lois Havemeyer, had died, and January, 1942, when at the age of 19 Ulysses had entered the Army, by virtue of the draft, Ulysses had been with his brother, Leo, who had cared for the boy with a touching tenderness. Leo's solicitude seemed to have been poorly rewarded. All reports agreed that Leo had been unable to see any of Ulysses's faults and that the boy had been scornful of his older brother, had shown him little courtesy, and always had maintained a superior attitude, mainly on the strength of Ulysses's more brilliant record in school and his identification with advance-guard movements in the fields of art and behavior that Leo did not pretend to understand.

From the age of 19 until after the war, Ulysses had no such sheltered existence. He was sent to a training camp in Texas where he antagonized all the Southerners he met, deliberately, and with a passion that got him more than once into an Army psychiatrist's office or a ward for observation of mental and nervous misfits. Ulysses got out of all those perilous spots by making monkeys of the psychiatrists on their own ground, to such an extent that two of them had to be discharged from active service and ended in institutions as patients themselves. In fact, Ulysses stirred up so much trouble in that Texas camp, and so cleverly within the letter of Army Regulations, that a brigadier general, in exasperation, had him transferred to the loneliest coldest spot in the Aleutian Islands, and there, at sub-zero temperature, in snow and ice, and with soldiers as unlucky as he was, but more deserving, he had shivered out the war.

Homer could imagine how fast Ulysses, once discharged, sped to Paris, and the unselfish protection, funds and blind devotion of brother Leo. Or could it be that Leo, with devotion that verged on the pathological was the victim of a guilt complex concerning Ulysses, and, as a border line case was a little off, and was using Ulysses's vicious qualities cunningly, not possessing enough ruthlessness himself to carry out his designs?

Or were the two in league, as they might have been year in, year out. It was aboard the *Exeter*, Homer recalled, that Leo had experimented with the tricky sodium pentathol, or truth serum, technique. Surely Ulysses must have picked up a great deal of knowledge about the use of hypodermics.

As hard as he tried to keep his mind at work, searching, associating, deducting, groping, Homer had to pause, frequently, to re-establish any kind of self-control. Megan Mallory was in the hands of the worst killer or killers that had come within the range of his experience. Megan's fine mother, the best product of Cape Ann, had she known what was hanging over her daughter, would have turned to him. Luke Mallory, good liver, square shooter, fine American, adoring father, would have put it squarely up to him. Fremont, Billings, and yes, Finke Maguire, were looking to whom for guidance? To *him*. And Megan—with her youth, her candor, her "breathless moments"—who did she expect would save her, if she were able to think at all?

"I've got to do it," Homer said, over and over again, to himself, and as often he admitted, with despair, that "he was nowhere." He knew how Lieutenant Kitchel and Agnes Welsh had been killed, and shared that awful knowledge only with Dr. Hyacinthe Toudoux and the killer or killers. Therefore he suffered a thousandfold. Every moment he waited, the situation grew worse. If Megan were being held as a hostage, her captors could not delay much longer in sending someone, Mr. or Mrs. Mallory or Homer, himself, their proposition for ransom. Homer knew well what it would be. Not money. He had reason to be sure that the criminals did not lack money, or need a cent more. Unless he was mistaken, they would be better off with less. A chance to get clear, to escape? And where? Nowhere in the United States, in France, or any country familiar to them. Could it be Indo-China?

What would Homer say, if faced with a choice like that? Would he let murderers get away, to live in ease in a dim dream world of the Orient? Would he let Lieutenant Kitchel and Agnes Welsh go unavenged? He had no difficulty answering that question. To save Megan, yes. But what about the dread secret of the method? It was not a secret, alas. It was common property, for all who wished to kill. Murder had been stripped of many of its principal risks. Another Nazi heritage to infest and destroy the world that force could not conquer.

Brrrrrannnnnng! The telephone bell. With enforced calm Homer took up the instrument, and said, "*Ici*, Evans."

"Fremont," said the voice. "The girl was seen leaving the Voltaire about five o'clock. Twenty minutes later she was alone, at the Flore. She had a drink, then left a message for you—to meet her at the Prince de Galles at 9 P.M."

"You're sure?"

"From my most reliable men," Fremont said.

Not five seconds later Evans was in Fremont's office, and Fremont had ordered his sedan. They were driven at breakneck speed to the *place* de l'Odéon, where Homer warned the chauffeur to slow down and approach the Restaurant Voltaire at a pace that was not conspicuous. On the off-chance that Fremont might be known and recognized, Homer asked the Chief to wait in the car. The Chief acquiesced, trying to subdue his nervousness, but when he saw Evans enter by the main door, hand his hat and topcoat in a casual manner to a waiter standing by, and seat himself at a table in the small room containing the bar and cashier's desk, as if he were a customer who had all the time in the world, Fremont's hair almost stood on end.

"He's a cool one, Monsieur Evans," the chauffeur remarked.

"Inversely according to the acidity of the pickle he is in," groaned Fremont.

Inside the small bar room of the Voltaire a more tranquil scene could hardly be imagined. Madame Lotte-Briquet was at the cash drawer behind her wicker barrier, perched on a stool and idly shuffling some government forms. Her daughter, Philomele, who

looked like her, on a different scale, was at the silver-plated coffee
machine, which was complicated enough to heat the Luxembourg
Palace not far away. Monsieur Lotte-Briquet was seated behind the
high polished mahogany bar eating a large portion of wild strawberry tart, with *crème d'Issigny*. Hippolyte, the head waiter came
in and stood by Evans' table.

"You're early, Monsieur Evans, or late. The sweetbreads Rossini
are no more, and the roast pheasant is not yet in the oven,"
Hippolyte said.

"I just came in for a cup of your inimitable coffee," Homer said,
with a smile at Philomele that caused both her and her mother to
drop whatever they had in their hands and smooth their dresses
behind.

"You're alone," remarked Madame.

Evans looked around him, as if the idea surprised him.

"So I am," he said.

"That healthy young American girl was here for tea," Madame
continued.

"With another," said Philomele, as if imparting the information gave her satisfaction.

"You'll never make a hostess," the proprietor said to his daughter. "Murders have been caused in this historic restaurant by re-
marks less indiscreet than that."

"Ah! My friend in Oxford gray," Evans said.

"They didn't seem to have much to say to each other," volunteered Hippolyte, the head waiter. "So I took the liberty of escorting them upstairs, to see our Gold Book—the famous signatures,
examples of wisdom and wit."

"No doubt they were impressed," Homer said.

"I think so. I was not present. Something told me that the young
man wished to be alone with mademoiselle, so I came downstairs,"
the head waiter said.

"God. I am in a nest of magpies," groaned the proprietor.

"Anyway," said his wife, enjoying his discomfiture. "They came
downstairs separately. Mademoiselle came through this room from
the staircase entrance. The young man had gone directly to the

street, through the family entrance, to call a taxi. The taxi arrived. Mademoiselle got in. The taxi drove away."

"And later, not half an hour ago," said Philomele, "another gentleman inquired if mademoiselle and her escort had been here. He was from the Russian Embassy, so he said."

"Not at all. From the White Russian club," corrected her mother.

"Mademoiselle told you, I take it, that my friend had preceded her to the street to find a taxi," Evans suggested.

"Exactly. She spoke to me, and told me how much she liked our place, and how thrilled she had been to see the autograph of Anatole France, in the Gold Book," said Madame Lotte-Briquet. "She asked me the time. I told her five-fifteen."

The coffee was finally ready, Evans drank it, paid, said "*Au revoir.*" He joined Fremont, who had become so impatient that he had bitten the inside of his cheek.

"She was alive and talking at five-fifteen," Evans said. "Let's try the Café de Flore."

At the Café de Flore, the head waiter greeted Evans pleasantly and told him that Miss Mallory had been there, arriving at 5:30. She had sat on the *terrasse* until 6 o'clock, drinking two vermouth cassis. "Just before she paid and left she asked me to tell you that she would be at the Prince de Galles at 9 o'clock," the head waiter said.

"She was alone?" asked Evans.

"Quite," said the head waiter.

"She left by taxi?" Homer asked. "Alone?"

"But, yes, monsieur," said the head waiter.

"You didn't happen to know the driver?" Homer asked.

"Why, yes. It was old Crapaud. He'd just started work for the day, or night, I'd better say."

"Did you notice what kind of a handbag she was carrying? The color of her dress, for instance? Anything about her clothes?" asked Evans.

"She looked wonderful, a little flustered and embarrassed, it seemed to me. But that was natural. Her handbag—let me think— it was a large one."

"Ah," said Evans.

"Her dress was of an indefinable color, some would call it mauve, some silver, others gray. It made an agreeable sound," the head waiter said.

"Perhaps taffeta?"

"I know little about fabrics. It was stiff but not forbidding," said the head waiter.

"You have a memory," said Evans, gratefully.

"That's why I'm on my way to the summit of my profession," the head waiter said.

Fremont, meanwhile, waiting in the sedan, had burned his mouth by inserting in it the live end of a cigarette. Evans asked the chauffeur to take them back to the Prefecture, and on the way repeated to Fremont what had been said. On their arrival, he sat with Fremont in his office, thinking, sometimes aloud. The dragnet, of course, had been set for the taxi driver, Crapaud.

Timidly, at last, Fremont ventured a remark.

"Homer," the Chief said, "the Mallorys, each one separately, have been playing detective, *n'est-ce pas?* Monsieur to get facts for Madame. Madame to get facts for herself. And now, is it not possible that Miss Megan is taking a hand? Let us formulate a hypothesis. Let us say that Miss Megan, who is surely very bright, either suspected at once or soon after seeing the man in Oxford gray that he was an impostor. Might she not have decided, recklessly, to go along with him and get some facts for you? If so, will she not impart what she has learned at 9 P.M. when she meets you at the Prince de Galles?"

"That is possible, and frightening," Evans said.

The telephone rang. Finke Maguire was on the line, and Evans took over the instrument.

"We spotted Doc aboard a barge near St. Germain," Finke said. "No one else, except the barge people were in sight. He was sitting on a keg, taking in the scenery, certainly taking no trouble to hide. He smoked his pipe and rode along, that's all. He didn't catch on, I think, that anyone had noticed him from shore. So I had Kvek drive me down here to Rouen, as fast as your roadster would go.

Quite a bit faster than it ever had gone before. I didn't consult the French police. I took care of the Norman dame with another American Express check, told her Doc wouldn't be home until late, and sent her out to visit her sister. If that dame's in cahoots with Doc, or ever has been, I'll change myself for a chamber pot."

"She left you in the house?" asked Evans.

"Sure."

"Found anything?"

"Not much. The only thing that looks fishy was just as fishy the other day, the office on the second floor, with a hard flight of stairs between it and patients down below. That bay-window seat in the office. But it's solid. Must have been built in solid, with the walls, like the one downstairs. And in one of the bookcases—Doc's got as many books as you have, almost—one hundred and forty-nine volumes of a *History of Rockport*, from 1800 to 1948, inclusive."

"They're all there?"

"I didn't count 'em," Finke said.

"That all?"

"Not sensational, is it?" said Finke. "Any suggestions?"

"Just one," Evans said. "Take out the volumes for the years 1863, 1887, 1902, 1903, and 1933, and bring 'em back to me. Fix it with the housekeeper so Doc won't know you've been there. I don't have to warn you to be careful about fingerprints and everything on those books. The chances are, if you close up the gaps, Doc won't notice the missing dates. And check with the local post office and letter carriers about mail for Doc from Indo-China or any cards or letters he may have sent there."

"Roger," said Finke.

"Then hurry back," Evans said. "I'll leave word at the Prefecture where you can find me, at no matter what hour."

"Roger," Finke said. "Roger O'Rooney."

Finke, after he replaced the receiver in Doc's office, hurried to the bookcase. He looked at Lvov Kvek with such a woebegone expression that the Russian was touched. All the volumes Evans had requested were missing. They left the house, checked with the post office with no results whatever, and were driving toward the Paris road when Kvek brought the roadster to a stop. He peered at a house by the roadside.

"What's loose?" demanded Finke.

"That house! It must have been built by the same architect who built the doctor's house. They're not exactly alike, but the bay windows and that awkward construction are similar," Kvek said. "I've been with Monsieur Evans on cases before, and he has said: 'When anything odd or coincidental comes to your attention, stop, look, listen and think.' I have stopped and looked, I am listening."

"And by cracky, I'm thinking," Finke said.

He hopped out of the roadster and, followed by Kvek, went to the front door, rang the bell, and when a genial ordinary Frenchman responded, Finke showed his credentials, and asked if he might take a look inside.

The Frenchman was agreeable, and if his wife, who appeared, was less so, the man was master of the house. Finke made straight for the bay window in the downstairs living room.

"Jumping Jehoshaphat!" he yelled, and was up the stairs two at a time. Kvek followed, four at a time. The French couple made exclamations including: "*Mais, alors!*" "*En effet.*" "But *messieurs.*" "What is it that passes itself?"

"Holy smoke," yelled Finke, and grabbing Kvek around the waist lifted him jubilantly into the air. They locked arms, did a few steps of the *kazotsky.*

"From now on till hell freezes over, we're blood brothers," Finke shouted. "You had a hunch. You handed me this tip on a platter."

"I am happier than when the horse Nicholas II stuck forward his muzzle as a Heaven-sent sign!" said Kvek.

"Don't be afraid, my dear," the Frenchman said to his cowering wife. "One is an American, and therefore crazy."

"But the other. The one who dances with his bum?"

"Russians are the only ones crazier than Yanks. That is why America distrusts them, and there must be war, they say," the man declared.

Lvov hugged and kissed the Frenchman. Finke tickled the wife's ribs and slapped her fanny. They ran back to the roadster, made a

U turn that could have been done on an inflated thousand-franc note, and headed back for Doc's house.

"We've got the drills," cried Finke.

"And the soup is mellow," boomed Kvek.

"Before we blast those solid window seats I'm going to phone Evans," said Finke. "If he says he knew this all the time, I'll beat his brains out, then mine."

18

After All, They Are Americans

AT NO TIME OR PLACE in his eventful life did Homer Evans spend an hour so hideous as the one that passed while he sat or paced the lobby of the Hotel Prince de Galles between 9 and 10 that evening.

He was there at 8:45. He talked a while with Lazlo, the night operator, and with Adolphe, the bell captain. He had a drink of whiskey with Luke Mallory, Selectman Parker, and the blonde from the Hotel Ritz who had promised to guide and protect them at the Moulin Rouge and the Bal Tabarin later on. Mrs. Mallory, he learned, and with immense relief, was attending a performance of *L'Avare* and *Les Précieuses Ridicules* at the Comédie Française, Salle Richelieu. Neither of her parents had asked where Megan was.

At 9 o'clock Homer started watching the door. After fifteen minutes, he glanced at his watch and could not believe that it was running, the time seemed so long. Megan, if she came at all, he thought, would be punctual. Nothing that had been told him about her movements, words or behavior that day had made sense, and now he was forced to acknowledge all that.

By prearrangement with Fremont, Wasp Billings and all concerned, it had been agreed that persons or messages for him would be sent immediately to the Prince de Galles. At 9:05 there was a phone call from Finke Maguire. In as few words as possible Finke told him how Kvek had spotted the similar house to that of Doc Havemeyer, and that the window seats in the bay windows, on the ground floor and second floor had been open, underneath, with good French sense of economy of storage space and amplitude of foot room.

"Finke," Homer said, trying not to betray his own terror. "You have found the key to an important factor in this case."

"We'll soon know what's hid in there. I've got the holes drilled, the soup tamped in, and the fuse all set. Want to hear the explosion over the phone?" Finke asked.

"In Heaven's name, no. Don't blow up the evidence. We can't let Doc know, yet, that we're on the track of it," said Homer. "Cover up any traces you've left, and drive back here to Paris, as fast as you can. No. Better park the roadster, and fly. Charter a plane, if one isn't scheduled. I need you on the spot and I need you badly," Evans said.

Finke, disappointed, said O.K. His not to reason why.

At 9:20, an Oriental, well-dressed and urbane, entered the lobby and approached Evans.

"Po Dingh," the Oriental said. "My girl and Amelie are outside, if you wish to speak with us all coincidentally."

"I want to ask you a few questions," Evans said. "And first of all, I wish to assure you that I am your friend, or, at least, not an enemy or spy."

Po Dingh looked at Evans inscrutably, and smiled.

"I am like the Irishman who sang and played bridge," Po Dingh said, somewhat ruefully. "The Irishman was known as a bridge player among musicians, and to bridge addicts he was always called a tenor singer."

Evans summoned a smile, not his best. "In other words, the French Government sleuths suspect you of Communist tendencies while the party members think of you as a tool of Bao Dai," Homer suggested.

"I try to keep a foothold on both rafts, knowing not which will sink first. My unhappy country," Po Dingh sighed.

"You gave lessons, did you not, to an American private soldier named Devs Smith, who wished to learn your language?"

The Oriental bowed assent. "I did, for three hundred francs an hour."

"Did you happen to find out in the course of your association with Smith whether he was friendly, and in the confidence of another private, Judd Coulson?"

"They were as thick as thieves—that is a bad comparison, perhaps. Like David and Jonathan, shall I say? Or has that a perverse implication which, in case of the two hearty young Americans, is inapplicable?"

"They were both very smart, I understand," Homer said.

"You'll pardon me," said Po Dingh. "Smith was apt as a linguist, superficially. Coulson was smart. He was smart Occidentally and Orientally, he had hindsight and foresight. He did not even talk loosely, of the high affairs in which he was involved, when drunk, which happened after dinnertime every night. Smith talked when drunk, which was every other night. He had half the stamina as well as half the intelligence of Tuan Coulson. I was fond of both of them, because they treated me as a friend and assaulted several persons who thoughtlessly were discourteous to me on account of my color. Actually, I am of a richer hue than Coulson, but not as dark as Smith."

"They're together now, with Bao Dai, in Saigon," Homer said.

"May they enjoy the good life while it lasts," said Po Dingh.

"Smith must be the more adventurous. He went East first, and joined the—should I say 'Emperor'?" Homer asked.

"Ah, no. Coulson maneuvered Smith's mind, so that Smith did the hard study to learn our language, went to Indo-China, found 'pickings fine and easy'; then Coulson joined him, at little risk," said Po Dingh.

"Did the two private soldiers, both orderlies, talk much about their respective officers?"

"They shared all of what they called 'the poop,' sparing no one," said Po Dingh.

Evans rose and extended his hand. "Po Dingh," he said. "If ever you need help or recommendation, please let me know."

"If I could be of further service, I should be honored. Bao Dai, who somehow has flimflammed your State Department, is a comical man, but tragic for his country—my country. Ho Minh, a better man, will be liquidated by the Russian Communists the moment Ho's patriotism ceases to be useful to Moscow and becomes, in fact, a hindrance."

"Oh, there's one question more," Evans said, casually.

Po Dingh smiled, "The sixty-four-dollar question, no doubt," he suggested.

"You are a sensitive, intelligent man," said Evans. "Yes. This is the sixty-four-dollar question. Were either or both of the privates I have mentioned thick with Ulysses Grant Havemeyer?"

"They were. They tried to be. They wanted to use him, and he them. They believed for a while that Ulysses Grant Havemeyer could help them, that is, put them in the way of what they called 'heavy dough.' What he wanted of them was less tangible. The 'poop' concerning his own brother," said Po Dingh. "Is that credible or sense making?"

"I shall be in your debt always," Evans said.

"I prefer it that way," Po Dingh said, and with a graceful bow, backed away a few steps, respectfully, then left the lobby.

The redhead came in from the back room where she had been dining. Evans rose and asked her to sit with him.

"Will you do me a favor?" he asked.

"You're in trouble," she said.

"Big trouble," Homer said. "Please call the Café de Flore, get Jean, the head waiter, and ask him if he's seen or heard from Miss Mallory."

She sighed. "All right, damn her," she said, and did as requested.

"No soap," she said, on her return.

Homer rose and walked back to the switchboard with her. "Try Madame Lotte-Briquet at the Voltaire. Use my exact words. Ask her 'if anybody saw the man who was with the girl, Mr. Evans' friend, leave the Voltaire by the family entrance, or saw him in the taxi in which she drove away'."

As she was repeating the message, to get the exact wording, the clock struck ten.

She dialed. Homer stood by.

"Madame Lotte-Briquet?" she asked. "Did anybody see the girl who was with the man, no, the man who was with Mr. Evans, no, the man with the girl who was Mr. Evans' friend. . . . Oh, par*don. Vous ne comprenez pas Anglais?*" the redhead started to repeat the question in French.

"She doesn't understand English!" Homer almost shouted.

The few people in the lobby looked around, and Luke Mallory, the selectman and the blonde waved from the bar.

They all saw Homer Evans sprint out of that lobby and through the swinging doors to the sidewalk at a rate that would have caused Jesse Owens or Paavo Nurmi to blink and consider retiring from competition.

Homer held up just long enough to tell the detective stationed outside to phone Fremont and have compiled a complete list of passengers for planes leaving Le Bourget, via the Gare des Invalides and bring it without an instant's delay to the Voltaire. Homer flung himself into a taxi and gave the Voltaire's address, in the *place* de l'Odéon.

"What a fool! What a damned unforgivable jackass I've been!" That was the theme he muttered, with variations, all the way. Before the taxi had fairly come to a stop in front of the restaurant, Homer jumped out, dashed into the family entrance, up two flights of stairs, and finding the door locked to the empty banquet room in which the Gold Book was kept, crashed into it and broke it open. He pressed the light switch. The chandeliers blazed. He saw a closet door, also locked, broke that, and there was Megan, stark naked, except for tape over her mouth, her hands tied behind her, and her ankles bound tightly together.

He clasped her in his arms, carried her from the closet and stretched her on a table. Taking a microscope from his pocket he went over her skin, millimeter by millimeter, while her blushes surged all over her lovely body. He found only a contusion on her jaw.

He was so weak when he had finished that he sank to the floor, recovered, tore the tape from her lips, kissed them, bruised and sticky as they were, drew back, looked supremely foolish, and said:

"It was stupid of me to take so much time finding you."

As weak and cramped as she was she forced a rueful smile.

"You're a thorough man, Homer Evans. A once-over from you is really something. Perhaps you can tell me what happened."

"You were tagged, stripped and abandoned," Homer said.

It was only then that Homer noticed that Schlumberger, his back to the *corpus vivendi*, was in the smashed doorway, holding back quite a clamorous throng.

"Patience! Philosophy! They are both Americans," the Alsatian lieutenant of detectives was muttering weakly to all concerned.

19
The Naked Eye Is Inadequate

WHEN THE REDHEAD at the Prince de Galles, who had been waiting around on the chance that Evans would reappear, in a mood that called for consolation, got his telephone call about 11 P.M. she was thrilled to hear his voice.

"Would you mind, without disclosing your errand to anyone in the hotel, going to Miss Mallory's room, choosing a suitable outfit for the evening, not formal but—well, you know. And omit nothing, no garments from the skin outward, I mean. I don't want it advertised that she has lost all her clothes—that is, she has none to wear. Bring the complete set of habiliments to the Restaurant Voltaire, if you will be so kind," Evans said.

"That place must have perked up since I was last there," the redhead observed.

"All will be explained," said Homer.

"Why bother? Girls will be girls," said the redhead with a sigh.

Before the redhead arrived at the Voltaire, Fremont came puffing in with the list of airplane passengers.

"This is incredible! According to the records Mrs. Mallory's flown the coop," the Chief exclaimed.

Homer took the list and scanned it. His eyes, bright and alert, traveled downward and rested on a name:

Mme. Edith Tam Mallong

That was as close as French clerks are likely to come to "Edith Tarr Mallory." Mrs. Mallong, it seemed, had bought a ticket for New York on the de luxe evening plane, a reservation having been canceled just in time, as happens nineteen times out of twenty. She had ridden in a bus operated by the French Airlines from the Gare des Invalides, leaving about 7 P.M. that day, had boarded the plane at Le Bourget at 8 P.M. and at 11 was three hours by air, headed for La Guardia field, New York, which she should reach at 8 A.M.

"The French eventually will have to recognize the integrity of names in print and, by reducing the amount of their paper work about one thousand per cent, will probably develop more accuracy with what remains. Mrs. Edith Tarr Mallory, described here as Mme. Edith Tam Mallong, is at present enjoying the last act of *L'Avare*, in the Salle Richelieu. Please have your men verify that, discreetly," Evans said.

Megan, who was wrapped in a huge linen table cloth, while a nurse-masseuse was relieving the bruises and strain of her wrists and ankles, laughed happily.

"Ah, youth!" Fremont said. "One moment at death's doorway, deprived of all artificial covering, the next amused by the perplexity of a veteran police officer who should, fifty years ago, have chosen a less exacting profession more suited to his mental endowments."

"You are in an enviable position," Homer said. Meanwhile, Schlumberger had closed what was left of the outer doors of the chastely ornate banquet room, blocked off the view from the hallway with a screen, and, with Fremont, was listening attentively.

"Our young man formerly in Oxford gray and built-up shoes— the shoes you will find inside that old-fashioned carpet sweeper, no doubt—knocked out Miss Megan with a blow of the fist on her mandibular plexus as soon as they were alone in this room. Then he took her clothes off . . ."

"Oh!" Megan cried in dismay.

"Just a hasty glance. He was in a deuced hurry," Evans assured her. "It takes a close and thorough inspection to do you justice. The naked eye is inadequate."

"I beg of you," Fremont interrupted.

"The man in Oxford gray took off his own clothes, hid some hastily and stuffed others into Megan's handbag, which is the size of a small suitcase. He went downstairs, deceived Mme. Lotte-Briquet without letting her get a good look at him, and got away. But, of course, there is no perfect getaway, any more than there is a perfect crime. Dressed as Megan, he spoke to Madame in French. When it was brought to my attention that Madame understood no English, many things became clear. First of all, that Miss Megan was still in this building. She knows the rest."

"*I* know nothing whatsoever," growled Fremont.

"The man in Oxford gray went to the Flore, wearing Megan's clothes. He was an excellent female impersonator—passed as a girl, had a drink, and left a message for me. He wanted me to fall for the hostage theory, as I did, until he was well on the way to America, still being mistaken for a girl.

"You know how incorrigible your countrymen are about names of foreigners, Fremont. At the Gare des Invalides, he submitted Megan's passport, perfectly in order. But the clerk jotted down not Megan's name, but her mother's, which also appears on the document. And he botched up Mrs. Mallory's name so badly that your officers, watching planes, muffed the gambit completely. In silver taffeta and high-heeled shoes, he rode on the bus to Le Bourget and now is over the ocean blue, not 'thinking about nothing' as Lindbergh did, but with many schemes in his head. He knew I was after him, and getting closer, not to his trail, which he blazed with ludicrous care, but his motives. This noon, or thereabouts, he had to give up one plan and think of another. So he decided to go to Indo-China and join the happy group of whoopee boys around Bao Dai. Two of his acquaintances were there, and had found 'pickings' amazingly good."

"What did he want of me?" asked Megan. "Just my clothes? Did he think I believed his tale about being sent by you?"

"He counted on your adventurous nature, your urge to play detective," Homer said.

"He's getting away," groaned Fremont.

"Have him taken into custody on the field in New York, and sent back by the next fast plane," Homer suggested.

"On what charges?"

"Conspiracy to defraud the French Government," Homer said.
"Not murder?"

"That can wait, if it need be used at all," Homer said.

Fremont was about to excuse himself, to give orders about the arrest and return of the *homme-femme* in silver taffeta.

"Just a moment," Homer said. "We've got to find his pants."

"Here they are," said Schlumberger, dragging out a pair of Oxford gray trousers from behind a cold radiator.

Evans beamed. "Ah, another slip-up," Homer said, drawing from the trouser belt straps a leather belt with nickel-plated buckle. He glanced at the buckle, and sighed with satisfaction.

"With this he has written his doom," said Homer, and showed it to Fremont, Schlumberger and Megan, who now was fully dressed. The redhead stood behind her. "You'll perceive that this prong has been sharpened with an emery wheel."

"May I sleep before you tell me why?" Fremont asked, pathetically.

"Pray do. But keep the belt as an exhibit. Let no one tamper with it. Also label the shoes. The plane will reach New York in the morning. We can have our young man back tomorrow morning, in custody of the officers who fly the plane. No need for an extra G-man. No publicity. I'll have Finke Maguire take charge of him at Le Bourget."

"As you say," agreed Fremont, dubiously.

"Meanwhile," Evans continued, "I'm leaving Paris for Rouen, on an errand of mercy."

"May I go with you?" asked Megan. "After your close check-up, you'll admit that I'm physically fit."

20
"The Night My Father Got Me"

HOMER, DRIVING THE ROADSTER WESTWARD, with Megan beside him, was unusually pensive. He did not appear bewildered. His mind was on the right track but he needed more confidence and intensity, more amperage and less voltage, perhaps.

"Don't tell me where we're going, or why," she said, dreamily. Homer was not quite at ease about Megan, either, but that was background uneasiness, and not on his account, but hers. He had led her into an experience which she had found fascinating. His artistic sense urged him to avoid an anti-climax. Six or eight other senses were equally insistent that he watch his step.

"Some of our most wonderful music ends pianissimo," he said. "A maestro once told me that records of those diminishing masterpieces never prove popular and never sell in large numbers. Recording companies dare not make them."

"You're afraid I'm going to be troublesome," she said. "I'm not. Thank God, I'm young, only seventeen. Not even at the age of consent . . . What an absurd legal phrase."

"An even more absurd poetic phrase," Homer said, and smiled.

"Don't you see, Homer," she said. "My being a minor, as they say, saves us—me, I mean. I can say—and it makes sense—that we— that I, that is, must wait for clocks to tick, and the world to whirl and move around the sun—quite a number of times. Otherwise, whatever might happen, if it happened, would be unfair to you. I must be strong, and think of consequences to others, which, if they occur too soon. . . ."

"It's all very simple," Evans said. "You have a sense of values, rare at any age. Have all the fun you can, and don't do anything that seems the least unnatural to you."

"Or premature?"

"Nothing is as unnatural as prematurity, unless it's procrastination," Evans said.

They drove across the *département* known as the Ile de France—the heavenly island. One vista was superseded by another more poignant. The road and river approached and parted, and Megan let herself lean closer as stream and highway touched, and was more circumspect, for the sake of balance, when the pavement and the Seine seemed mutually resigned to separative space or distance.

"I don't know which is more solid, to talk or not to talk," Megan said. "In either way lies madness."

"I'm trying to compose myself," Evans said.

"I know," Megan said, contritely. "For a supreme effort, having nothing whatsoever to do with me. I'll be impersonal, so help me Moses."

"For the sake of our case," Evans said.

"The guilty must be punished. . . . I feel right about that. They're cruel and mean, and spoil life for others," said Megan.

"I've spent much more time and effort trying to shield the guilty from punishment than ever I did endeavoring to convict them," admitted Homer.

"You shield killers?" asked Megan, incredulously.

Homer sighed and relaxed. "The murders in this mixup are incidental," he said. "Our problem has other aspects, of deeper consequence."

"I wish time could be cranked down to slow motion, like a movie camera," Megan said.

"I shall have to leave you to your own devices for an hour or two," Evans said, as they entered the outskirts of Rouen. "Drive along the waterfront, seek beauty in the miles of junk deposits, visit the Cathedral and let its merits atone for its clumsy imperfections, and see a few historic spots related to the martyrdom of

Joan of Arc. Meet me at the Angleterre, on the *terrasse*, for a late lunch. I want you to learn that wild duck may be eaten extra-rare."

"If you said it was all right, I'd eat a muskrat alive," Megan said, and swiftly brushed his cheek as she moved over into the driver's seat and he stepped out. Her manner lost its buoyancy an instant. "You don't fool me, always," she said. "You're going into something rugged, not dangerous, the kind of thing that can make you sick, if it goes wrong."

"Good girl," he said, and pressed her hand. "Good head."

"The brain is woman's secondary nerve center," Megan said.

"I shall miss these little talks," Evans mused, as he headed straight for No. 3 bis rue de Caen.

The stalwart Norman woman opened the door. "The doctor's back from Paris. I'd like to see him. Evans is the name," Homer began.

She ushered him into the downstairs waiting room in which there were no patients. He heard her walk upstairs, tap on a door; there were a few words of murmured exchange; she descended again.

"Go up," the woman said. Homer was inclined to agree with Finke Maguire that the Norman specimen, so buxom, healthy and matter of fact, was not in league with Dr. Havemeyer, or anyone. There had been a phase of the case during which Homer had suspected that Billings might have planted this typical Norman country female in the house. But Evans knew lots of Frenchwomen who were, on principle, "not curious," as they expressed it. They wanted to know only what was needful and good for their circumscribed lives. Doc's Norman was in that group, Evans thought. She had lost a tooth, got a smack on the jaw, and come into possession of 200 easy dollars, or 62,000 francs. Some of the doctor's patients were understandable, others whacks. What could be more natural? The doctor did not seem to care a fig whether he practiced successfully or not. She knew blacksmiths, longshoremen and café keepers like that. Normandy was full of indifferents, especially the men.

When Homer entered the doctor's upstairs office, so ill suited for the reception of emergency cases, he decided to waste no time on his approach. Dr. Havemeyer, looking tired but otherwise about the same as usual, regarded him questioningly.

"What seems to be your trouble?" Doc asked.

"I want to talk with you about your mother," Evans said.

The doctor was astonished, but too weary to react, so he could make no adequate response.

"Who are you?" he asked.

"Your friend—if you'll have it that way," Evans said. "You've been carrying a load on your mind, and if I know something of what it is, it won't hurt you to hear me talk about it, or say a word or two yourself."

"My own fault! I came up against a decision, and played it wrong. Why don't you arrest me, and have it over?" Doc asked.

"I'm not the police, or a Secret Service man—this year—or a treasury agent, or a strolling member of the F.B.I.," Evans said. "I'm a citizen, on the sidelines, and I want to see you get a fair deal. What you've been up against is fabulous, fundamental, unique."

"If you've got nothing on me, what's your angle?" the doctor asked, bluntly.

"I've been reading and learning about your mother, and that fine old grandfather of yours, Lou Havemeyer," said Evans, with such contagious enthusiasm that Havemeyer lost his ennui.

"You?" he asked.

"Yes," said Evans, beaming. "Also your father—and your foster father, who never chanced to meet. A fascinating group. A live, American group—with a dash of Spanish and German and plenty of that rockbound New England femininity, the salt of the sea and the shore. Let me tell you what I've surmised, and see what we can make of this rare pickle. Nothing's hopeless, you know."

"This has been hopeless from the start. I played it wrong. I shoulda done one thing; I did another, and couldn't stop. Why don't you turn me in?" asked Doc, again, as if he was reluctant to make an effort to save himself.

"May I start talking about your mother? You can stop me if I'm wrong," suggested Evans.

"Can't we leave her out of this? She's dead," Doc said.

"Such women never die. They live a good life, and the spice of it lasts," Evans said. "Let me talk a while. You modern doctors, with a flair of psychoanalysis and high psychiatry, make your patient do the talking . . . and it all comes out nonsense. Reverse the roles. I'm the doctor, with the gift of gab. You're the patient. I'm going to talk you deaf, dumb and blind, and most likely you'll listen, and some of it will make sense. This isn't any childhood problem. Nobody dropped you on your head, or made you so jealous you pulled off kittens' tails. You came up against something dramatic and wonderful, when you were approaching middle age. A plague on these experts who trace everything back to the nursery. If that school were sound, we could let kids vote if they were fairly normal at the age of four."

"Go on," said Doc. "This is just the kind of talk about his mother that stimulates a man." He actually grinned.

"'It is the perfume of her dress that makes me so digress,'" paraphrased Evans.

"Let's have a shot of Calvados," Doc said, and, reaching into a drawer of his desk, produced a jug and glasses.

"The layman's sodium pentathol," said Evans, grinning of his own accord and sipping the eighty-year-old, aged in oak, distilled apple brandy of the country.

"It liquefies the brain—in time," Doc said, and drained his glass. He gasped. "That's the first drink I've enjoyed in years."

"About four years and a half?" asked Evans.

Doc looked surprised. "You didn't read about that, anywhere, or did you?"

"Between the lines," said Evans. "But I won't be mysterious. I'll get down to brass tacks, but it takes a lot of those to lay a carpet."

Doc nodded.

"Until some time in late '44 or early '45, you were gay," Evans said. "You were a bad influence, but good company. You liked folks. They liked you twice as well. You were, in fact, old Lou Havemeyer—which last name, by the way, was derived from Ave Maria."

"Good Christ! Am I Spanish, on top of all the rest?" asked Doc.

"I envy you," said Evans, "but I'm partly Norman."

"I must have got a lot from the Cheever side, too," said Doc.

"A fine tough family," Evans agreed. "You'd have been the first, if you'd resisted temptation."

"A man get's tired; that's the worst of it," Doc said.

"He gets a second wind," Evans said, reassuringly. "And has more fun."

"I had fun, but never any cash to spend," said Doc.

Homer nodded. "We'll talk about us later," he said. "Just now—your mother. She was brought up, unless I am badly mistaken, by a couple of Rockport folks named Lowe—Amos and Jane Lowe."

"Go on," said Doc, somewhat cagily.

"She had a foster brother—no blood relation—named Alrick, who was everything she was not, played close to his vest, never was caught in the jam pot, and took advantage of your mother's good nature, and likable weaknesses."

"She got the best of him," Doc said. "In a way."

"May I speak plainly?"

"Sure."

"At the age of 16, when a girl like Lois Havemeyer is grown up, your spirited *mater* seduced the prudent Alrick, more or less for the hell of it," Evans said.

"'The night my father got me, his mind was not on me,'" quoted Doc, who knew his A. E. Housman. He poured another Calvados for Evans and himself.

"But how could you possibly know that?" Doc asked, as an afterthought.

"A man's intuition," Evans said, drily. "Let's continue. Alrick, not a sterling character, beat it off to sea with an uncle, Jess Lowe, leaving Lois to face the Moody and Sanky music. She didn't care too much about that. Nevertheless she thought it best to clear out of Rockport. She went to Boston and got herself a job under the name of Mrs. Lois Havemeyer, on account of the visible signs that were developing. Soon she took up with an otherwise nice young man whose name—such things do happen—was Sawyer Pratt."

"That's what it was," Doc murmured. "A young man with a moniker like that has two strikes against him and a cinder in his eye when the third starts coming over. No?"

Evans nodded, and took up the narrative.

"Your mother had had the name Havemeyer quite a while and liked it, on old Lou's account. Anyway, according to the Massachusetts records, Sawyer got permission to change his name from Pratt to Havemeyer. He got a job as a carpenter, fixing up a big lodge and some cabins on the pond at Mount Washington, Mass. There you were born. Your parents stayed on at the lodge, as caretakers, through summers when a few rich summer people were around and winters when they were lucky to see anybody once a week, on the main road where the post-office box stood."

"We had everything except money . . . a margin, I mean," the doctor said. "They meant to get married, but never got around to it."

"When did she tell you? About Alrick and the rest?" Homer asked.

"When I was at Harvard. She used to come up to Boston to see me and we'd get comfortably tight at Jake Wirth's. She and Dad— that's what I called Sawyer—were happy enough, but he knew I wasn't his child, and it burned him up because he couldn't produce one. God knows he tried and tried. That's where I stuck my oar in," Doc said. "The technique of artificial insemination was new then, more or less. I'd got wind of it, and on another beer evening with Ma I asked her why not give Dad a surprise and his heart's desire. So I sent her to a doctor I knew."

"Result? Ulysses Grant Havemeyer!" said Evans. "I can understand that seldom has one half-brother felt so much responsibility for another."

"The whole thing went wrong. Dad died. But happy, thinking he'd hit the combination at last. Ma died a few years later. She and I had some fine days together at the end. That's when she told me everything she'd overlooked before."

"And you, with a tough New England conscience, had a very young and trying kid brother on your hands," said Evans.

"I did the best I could," said Doc. "Let's hope he doesn't turn out badly."

That hit Evans hard. The job he had started was worse than he had bargained for. Still, he tried to keep control of his nerves.

"Tell me about Rockport . . . Your sudden interests there," he suggested.

"As best I can," Doc said, and put the Calvados away.

21

Fantasy? No, Reality

"My life had been rich and eventful enough, up to the time I went down to Rockport for my grandfather's funeral. Old Lou Havemeyer, town reprobate. But until I saw that town on Cape Ann, and the folks who lived there, the shore, the islands, the churches, the old-fashioned schools, I'd known nothing much about towns. Mount Washington, Mass., wasn't a town. It was a woodland estate, with a few unprosperous farms around it, and some perch and pickerel in a lazy high pond.

"In my high-school days, I'd worked in a grocery store, then a drug store. At Harvard I tutored and waited on table. I never missed a meal, or wore patched pants. But I'd never had a bank account, or money for a vacation, or any to spend on girls. I'd never enjoyed community life, except on the campus. Those few days in Rockport—I stayed on after Old Lou was buried—got me all stirred up. I had roots in that town, and some crazy feeling for the sea. My brother was ten, and already knew more than I did. But I wanted him to grow up some place—Rockport, in fact. I always felt as if he understood me too damned well, and I hadn't caught the hang of how his mind worked, at all. Does this sound mixed up?"

"Impressionistic," Evans said. "And I love the Impressionists. The truest artists ever."

"Good. It's nice, not talking to a dumbbell. That's another thing that's held me close to the kid brother. Whatever else you can say, he's one who doesn't have to have the 'i' dotted four or five times."

"He's quite an amateur showman, like you. I've read about your ventriloquist routine with your dummy, Boola-Boola," Evans said.

Doc looked at him, surprised and for a moment lost the thread of his talk. He waited a while, before he resumed. Evans showed no impatience.

"I couldn't quit the Boston Psychopathic without notice, when I got the impulse. A couple of years later I signed as ship's doctor on the *Exeter* of the American Export Lines, and what had been cooking all over the world began to boil. I learned plenty about Spain, and our own blunders there. I found the Nazis had honeycombed all our liners with agents. When I felt I had to go to Washington and spill what I had, I was put in touch with Wasp Billings. From then on, my private affairs had to wait," Doc said.

"I suppose your brother learned a lot about, for instance, your sodium pentathol technique," Evans suggested.

"The kid was smart about everything," Doc said. "He had a curious inquiring mind. He liked to use it, any way at all. Besides, he was skillful with his hands. My fingers are all thumbs."

"He had it tough in the Army," said Evans. "Texas, the Aleutians."

"I couldn't help him, then," Doc said.

"It's ironic, isn't it, that you, who'd had so little money, got into a department of the service where large amounts, both good and bad, were like Tennyson's cannon, to the right, the left, and in front of you, all the time."

"They thought I was indifferent to money. And I was. I tried to be—until . . ."

"Everybody, all Americans, I mean, dream about their first million. You found about a million, in perfectly good American bills—here in Rouen. Perhaps on the site of that huge junkyard. No one else was in on the secret. That was just a little more than you could stand. . . . Am I wrong?" Evans asked.

"It did something to me. I couldn't make decisions, after that, until I made a wrong one, and got off the track," Doc said.

Evans was never more sympathetic. "It seems to me a setup like that would have tempted any man," Evans said. He went over and touched the solid window seat, significantly. "The money's in here," he said.

"You know everything," Doc said. "And, believe it or not, I'm glad. I'm tired. I'm fed up. I'm finished."

"You walled it up here," Evans said, touching the window seat again. "That was why you bought this house, cheap, and kept up a pretense of practicing, just stalling for time—and clarity. Don't think I can't understand how maddening your situation was. This stuff had been collected from bad citizens for foolish, criminal purposes. If you turned it in, where would it go? How much would be wasted? Who would benefit? And on the other hand, what could you do with it? If you spent it, the men you'd been working with would know. They had to keep tabs on everybody. You couldn't sneak it through two sets of customs barriers. I've figured that a million in small bills would fill two army trunks. You tried and tried for a solution, and couldn't confide in anyone, or ask for help or advice. In the States, you could use the money, but you couldn't get it there. The top Nazis who had known about it were dead. Then a possible solution came to you by the merest chance. Fred Mallory got sick. You knew he was going to die. He showed you his will. That cottage in Rockport—on the shore of a cove that was deserted more than half of each year. You read, in your *History of Rockport*, about the Massachusetts law on oral wills. You knew that when Fred died, from the heart condition he had, he might appear for quite a while to be conscious after life had passed. You had manipulated dummies. You were a ventriloquist. You were surrounded by people in the death room who trusted you, and some of whom were too nervous to register details.—Miss Welsh, for instance. So you made it appear that Fred willed the cottage to Susie Lowe, your aunt."

"I didn't know how important the cottage was, to anyone but Fred," Doc said. "I didn't think anyone would care much who got it."

"Will you answer a few questions?" Evans asked.

"If I can," said Doc. "I wish you'd turn me in, and have done with it."

"Let's not be hasty," said Evans. "The million you found is intact. Wasp Billings is a friend of yours. . . . Oh, by the way. Tell me about Bob Kitchel. How did you and Kitchel get on?"

"All right, up to the time Fred got sick, and I let on to Bob that Fred's case was hopeless. Bob was a layman, smart, not flashy, loyal. But he thought a lot of Fred, and figured, probably, that I was giving Fred up too easily. Actually, there was nothing I could do but wait for the end. If I could have showed Kitchel Fred's heart, swollen up twice or three times its natural size, and ready to give out any minute . . . But men who don't know about hearts think that while there's life, there's hope. Fred knew better, but not Bob. Bob figured I'd gone to pieces, and wasn't much of a doctor any more. Who could blame him? But the best doctor in the world couldn't have helped Fred Mallory at that stage of the game. His number was up. . . . And I was confused enough to take advantage."

"Of course," agreed Evans. "That cottage. That cove. There were so few ways you could hope to get a million in cash into America. That one seemed made to order."

"It looked easy on that end," Doc said, sighing.

"Once you'd figured out how to land the money, you started planning how to get it out of France. You settled in Rouen, where you could load a yacht to suit yourself; take it across the ocean with only one man to help you; wall up your money in the ballast with concrete, put it off on Thatcher's Island, establish your relationship to Susie Lowe. You knew she wouldn't live forever. You were a blood relation, and could prove it. It looked to you as if luck had turned your way. You'd studied navigation. I suspect that somewhere along the line you broke down and told your young brother something—maybe not all—about unlimited funds for him and for you."

Evans said that very casually, but it was the crux of what he needed to know. Doc did not dissimulate.

"I got pneumonia, a bad virus pneumonia, and felt as if I was going to kick off, myself. So I told the kid," he said.

"He was pleased?"

"It solved the only problem he had. He and I could steer a motor boat from here to Loblolly Cove, put off the stuff, go on to Boston and check in properly. We couldn't let anyone else in on the deal. We knew it might go wrong. It was worth the chance, that's all. And the kid didn't think for a minute I'd die—too soon. The kid had never thought I was too bright, and he was pleased and surprised that I'd played the thing so carefully. So he waited."

"How did he feel about Kitchel?"

"He thought Bob was stupid. He underestimated nearly everybody. That was his way. No. He didn't worry about any of the deathbed witnesses," Doc said.

"You told him about the will—the way you faked it?" Evans asked.

"He guessed it, somehow. I'm not a good liar. Never was," said Doc.

"Ulysses wasn't impatient? He didn't fret about waiting?" Evans asked.

"No. 'We've got time and money, and I've got brains,' he said. He talked cocky, like that," Doc said. "But mostly to me, I hope." Doc looked appealingly at Evans. "You won't have to involve the kid. He's done nothing, really," Doc said.

Again Evans felt most uncomfortable.

"I, personally, won't charge him with anything," Evans said. "As far as you're concerned, it's up to Billings, I suppose, but the Wasp isn't as tough as he makes out. When he sees a million, in small bills, it won't look to him like a bale of hay. And he knows a man has got feelings about a million. What is there about that figure that sets Americans off? Say $900,000 and they don't blow their tops. And a billion's too much, too many naughts strung out together. I'm excited myself, when I think of that window seat. . . . By the way, don't use a hammer around there anywhere. The bench is drilled and primed with nitro-glycerine."

"Christ!" said Doc. "How come?"

"An associate of mine who's naturally impulsive," Evans said. "Think nothing of it."

"For God's sake, turn me in," said Doc, once again. "I can't hold out much longer."

"Think of Rockport, and the cottage. I think you'll be able to live there, and practice on the Cape. You'll even be able to start a bank account, probably in the Rockport Savings Bank," said Evans. "But tell me. What started Kitchel reading Rockport history? And how did he hit on the years 1863, 1887, 1902, 1903, and 1933?"

"He was down here quite a few times, and I had those volumes marked." Doc went over to the book shelf, and recoiled in surprise. "Those volumes are gone!"

"I've got them. Kitchel must have borrowed them, informally, to keep you off your guard," Evans said.

"He died, then, thinking I let Fred die, or killed him?" asked Doc, sadly. "I hate to think that. It's so damned wrong. I wouldn't do a thing like that, for any number of trunkfuls of greenbacks. I must have been half crazy, for the last four years or so, but not desperate enough to think about murder. I'd have waited till Susie Lowe was a hundred, if she'd lived that long. Are you on the level, when you say you're going to try to square this for me? So I can go back, without this nightmare on my mind?"

"I've done a favor or two for Wasp Billings," Evans said. "Quit worrying."

"That isn't easy," said Doc. "Why am I built like that? Probably that louse of a father I had. My heritage from Alrick Lowe. Mother never let anything get her down. Neither did Lou Havemeyer. They'd have tried to snag a million, at the drop of a hat. They'd have taken the long chance."

"We'll get this tangle straightened out," Evans said. But he knew of the blow that was yet to shake Doc Havemeyer. That made Homer feel guilty as he said, "*Au revoir.*"

22

Out of Multiplicity—Unity

ON THE *TERRASSE* OF THE CAFÉ DE FLORE, among the whiskers and the inexpensive talk, sat Megan Mallory, breathing the spring air, hearing without listening to the chatter, aware of the beards and pale faces without attempting to classify them. She was content. Homer Evans sat beside her, on her right, and on the next chair, beside Homer, sat Mrs. Mallory.

"You have set my mind at rest," Mrs. Mallory said.

"Body and soul," murmured Megan. "But, confound it, time and tide."

"You've made quite an impression on my daughter, Mr. Evans," said Mrs. Mallory, drily.

"That was a cinch," Megan said. "The question is, what have *I* got across?"

"I shall be counting the days until you reach the age of consent," Evans said, smiling.

"Your intentions are dishonorable, I take it," said Mrs. Mallory, grimly.

"Oh, quite," Evans said, and Megan, brightening, squeezed his hand.

"I sometimes think I was born either too soon or too late," said Mrs. Mallory. "In my day, we girls knew pretty well what we were about, but the men did not like to have us express ourselves too boldly, in words."

"In the beginning was the Word," remarked Evans.

"And the end is not yet," said Megan.

"In the middle is the father with the shotgun," Mrs. Mallory reminded them.

"We're drifting away from discussion of the case," suggested Homer, who was thoroughly enjoying himself.

"I want to thank you, Mr. Evans, from the bottom of my heart. I've been reassured that my son Fred was not capricious or illogical. He died in a rational way. As to Dr. Havemeyer, who was tempted so sorely, I forgive him freely, as Fred would have done. He shall live in the Tarr cottage, which is Luke's and mine, and he shall practice in Rockport and be accepted there. I respect Lieutenant Colonel Billings for his humane decision. The Army, our Army, is better led and organized than I had dared to hope."

Mrs. Mallory took a long sip of her green mint frappe.

"The other nations, unless possibly, some day, the French, will never understand that we have a civilian national defense, and that by virtue of its healthy amateur qualities it has beaten and will continue to get the better of all the old-fashioned military and political setups, or dictatorships," said Evans.

"I still don't understand about the sketch of Susie Lowe in the telephone booth," Megan said. "Nothing up to that point—when suddenly and unexpectedly I saw it—had given me a jolt like that."

"Kitchel liked to draw and did it well. He used that booth frequently, and had Susie on his mind to the point that she dominated his unconscious doodling," explained Evans.

"How did he know what Susie looked like?"

"There's a group picture of Rockport sexagenarians, in the 1933 year book. Kitchel spotted Susie there, and drew her on the back flyleaf. The department used Kitchel quite often to draw imaginary sketches of suspects, from written or oral descriptions. Also to make good line drawings from photographs. He had had no training, but he was born with a flair. Not much imagination, but sound representative instincts," said Homer. "The fact that he wasn't a known artist made him more useful to G-6, as Doc Havemeyer, being more or less obscure, was handy to use the truth serum, when truth seemed lacking and was *de rigeur*. Billings' men did lots of things illegally, in order to get legal results. Once truth is known,

it becomes easier to prove it. In other words, the solution leads
back to the problem."

Megan beamed. "That I shall cherish in my thoughts, yet unformed," she said. "When in doubt, solve, then explain."

"It's comforting to hear you speak of doubt," her mother said.
"I thought the younger generation was never in doubt."

"That's why we need art," Evans said. "To keep our doubts
alive."

Homer escorted the ladies to the Prince de Galles. "I shall be
busy in the morning, but later . . ." he said.

"I'll mark the calendar before going to bed," said Megan. "That
will be the start of counting the days."

"I shall talk with Luke, if he's in shape for it, until he agrees
with all we have said," Mrs. Mallory promised. "Good night."

At eight o'clock next morning, Homer was sitting with Fremont,
Schlumberger and Dr. Hyacinthe Toudoux in the dingy office of
the Prefecture. The plane from New York was not due for a while,
and Evans had much to say. Finke Maguire had been sworn, deputized and equipped with American and French credentials by means
of which he could take over the young man who had been apprehended in New York, and legally sent back to France to answer a
list of charges.

The complete saga of Dr. Havemeyer, his mother, Lois; his
grandfather, Lou, his father, Alrick Lowe, and the million sealed
in concrete, had been lucidly disclosed, and thoughtfully assimilated. No one present, not even Evans who had had his million from
birth, had failed to appreciate what the sight of that amount in
greenbacks signified, symbolically, practically and psychologically.

"Now let me tell you about Ulysses Grant Havemeyer, with
whom we still must deal, alas," Evans said. He sketched the circumstances which preceded Ulysses' unorthodox birth, his childhood, boyhood, school days, and the Army experience in Texas and
the Aleutians.

"That was the contrast which embittered and unhinged him,"
Evans explained, and they all nodded. It was as clear as the lure of
the million. His having turned against his brother, who had done

so much for him—as a matter, partly, of atonement—was harder to accept.

"The paranoid," Evans reminded them, "turns first on whoever is nearest and dearest."

Dr. Toudoux nodded; Fremont and Schlumberger scowled.

"It is ninety to one he would have killed his brother, to get all the money, once it was safely in the States," Fremont said. "For that, and two murders actually committed, he shall be guillotined."

"He won't like it," Evans said.

"How did he stick a syringe into Lieutenant Kitchel, and Miss Welsh? Either one could overpower him," Schlumberger asked.

"That was simple," Evans explained. "In each case he doped the victim mildly and temporarily with chloral hydrate. He had no difficulty in placing a few drops in Kitchel's beer; and Amelie has told us that Ulysses stopped her and exchanged a few words while she was on the way to Miss Welsh's room with a glass of cider. See how cleverly our young criminal reasoned, and took circumstances into account. Both Kitchel and Miss Welsh had for years been drawing on their reserves of nervous energy, in connection with their exacting work. Both had learned to stall off fatigue, and keep going beyond the point where a normal person would find it necessary to rest. So Kitchel, feeling the effects of the knockout drops, forced himself to the telephone and called Lieutenant Colonel Billings to sign off duty. There he got drowsy, Ulysses slipped into the booth, made the injection, then the scratch. Miss Welsh was already in bed, exhausted, when the $CCl_3CH(OH)_2$ sent her deep into the arms of Morpheus."

"What I can't get through my head," Fremont said, "is why he scratched them with a sharpened belt buckle prong after he had injected—whatever it was—with the hypodermic needle. Wouldn't that call attention to the puncture?"

"Again our criminal was extraordinarily clever. Both Kitchel and Miss Welsh, when the chloral hydrate wore off and they were themselves again, unknowingly doomed, would have felt sore spots where the needle had been inserted. As it was, they must have felt soreness. So they glanced at the area in question, and concluded they had accidentally scratched themselves. Had either of them suspected he or she had been stuck with a hypo needle, he or she would have raised an alarm.

"While I am on the subject, the fatal injection was made with an empty syringe. The new instrument of cowardly murder is the air we breathe, introduced in the veins instead of the lungs. Foolish publicists already have printed far too much about that technique, which was devised by the Nazis to slaughter Jews at a nominal cost, without bullets or expensive gas apparatus.

"Lieutenant Kitchel must have started for his hotel, after telephoning the Wasp. Probably he felt giddy when he was at No. 21 rue Cassette, so he entered the shelter of the ruined building, sat down to steady himself, and died before the corner walls collapsed and buried him. That accident delayed and confused our investigation from the start."

"It had me baffled," Fremont admitted, and sighed.

Evans continued. "Ulysses, always the exhibitionist, set up such a glaring string of alibis that I got suspicious right away. He expected momentarily that the body of Kitchel would be found, and it was not, until days later. That got on his nerves. He had seen Agnes Welsh talking earnestly with the lieutenant just before the murder was committed, and since Agnes was a witness at Mallory's deathbed, and had been in Rouen, presumably in touch with Ulysses's brother, Ulysses got panicky and put her out of the way. His method had worked before; it was easy. There was little risk. He was all-powerful. Then just afterward, he found out that I was on his trail. You know about his impromptu getaway, and his plan to wait a while in Indo-China, with his Army acquaintances and the fantoche, Bao Dai."

"What made him so afraid of Kitchel? That's what I'd like to know," asked Fremont. The others sat forward to listen more intently.

"Kitchel had been detailed, had always been the member of G-6 to keep tabs on Doc Havemeyer. Each one in that organization was under the special surveillance of another, for security's sake. First, Kitchel found out about Doc Havemeyer's odd interest in Rockport, and saw the marked volumes which told me most of the story about the Lowe relationship and the cottage. Kitchel knew that Doc had planned, as soon as he could get out of the service, to settle down and make some money. Then he observed that Doc, instead, was apparently wasting his time in France, not in Paris but a river port. His practice was hardly a practice at all. His house was unsuited for the work of a general practitioner. What could be the conclusion? Not that Doc had lost his interest in getting himself financially established, at last, but that the solution lay in Rouen, and not in the practice of medicine. Kitchel started drafting a report to Billings, suggesting an investigation. Ulysses, now as busy as an ant, and not at all patient, as he made his cautious brother believe, got wind of Kitchel's suspicions through the garrulous orderly, Smith, and Kitchel's own dogrobber, Judd Coulson. All three were pupils of Po Dingh, and were frequently together, and could try out their Indo-Chinese in cafés, after plenty of beer. They liked to show off.

"Ulysses immediately assumed that Kitchel was suspicious about that oral will, as he was, but that was a secondary consideration. He had to erase Kitchel, and he did, helped by the knowledge, also obtained through the orderlies, that Kitchel had written to Megan Mallory, and that the Mallorys were coming over."

"Who telephoned Miss Mallory after Kitchel was dead?" asked Fremont.

"Ulysses, of course. He wanted her to land in France without raising the question of where Kitchel might be, for a while, until the body was found. He was an excellent mimic, as you know. He even passed for Megan, at the Voltaire and the Flore, very cautiously but effectively. The *patronne* at the Voltaire did not get a good look at him, and the waiter at the Flore had seen Megan, at some distance, only twice. Of course, he had her hat, makeup and gloves. He touched his cheeks and lips with Caron's "Victoire" and made discreet use of her perfume, Caron's "En Avion." He had always liked dressing as a girl, in amateur shows and impromptu parties. That's another paranoid obsession."

"I shall attend the guillotining," Fremont said.

"Finke ought to be here with him, soon," Evans said.

At Le Bourget, Finke watched the big airliner descend, presented his papers, and put Ulysses, none too gently, into Evans' roadster.

"At least, the French Government could have sent someone besides a washed-up M.P. to meet me," sneered Ulysses. "Was this humiliating reception Mr. Evans' idea of a joke? I shall deal with Mr. Evans, once I'm free of these trumped-up charges."

"Listen, Ape-face. This is too early in the morning to rile me. For your own good, keep your trap shut, if you can. If not, I'll button it up, but good," was Finke's rejoinder.

"You can't intimidate me. Your brute force'll get you nowhere. If I were you, I'd watch my driving. Your reactions are sluggish this morning," Ulysses said.

As a matter of fact, Finke was so mad that he was driving atrociously. He slowed up, and made a turn without signaling. Two other drivers yelled at him.

"Perhaps I'd better take the wheel. You're rattled," said Ulysses. "Me, I'm calm."

Finke gritted his teeth, but when he got into Paris, as far as the rue du Four, and darted across that tricky crossing of the rue de Rennes, he veered a little and rubbed a front tire against the traffic island.

"I can't bear incompetence," sighed Ulysses, blowing smoke from his cigarette into Finke's eyes.

Finke kept one hand on the wheel, and with his right he smacked Ulysses hard across the bridge of his nose. Ulysses grunted, and from then on was silent. Finke kept his eye on the traffic and the busy tangled streets. He finally brought up at the Prefecture, got out on his side, walked around in front of the roadster, opened the right-hand door, and Ulysses, inert and limp, tumbled out into his arms. The bridge of the Zazou's nose was discolored ludicrously, both eyes had No 1 shiners.

"All right. All right, cream puff. I'll carry you in," Finke said, and suiting the action to the word, slung Ulysses over his shoulder, walked past the guards to Fremont's office, and, entering, dumped his burden into a chair.

"Good morning, gentlemen," he said, and thumbing toward Ulysses, growled: "Here's your bird."

Dr. Hyacinthe Toudoux was already on his feet. The medical examiner stooped to listen. Fremont came up like the spring of a trap. Evans sat still and smiled.

"*Nom de Dieu!* He's not breathing," the doctor said.

"Somebody hit him," said Fremont, looking hard at Finke.

"No heart action. No pulse. He's been dead at least five minutes," said Dr. Hyacinthe Toudoux.

Fremont pointed an accusing finger at Evans.

"You planned this assassination. You and your countryman, MacFeenck!"

"Oh, no, Chief," said Evans. "I might have anticipated this, but I didn't contrive it. But it's rather lucky, all around."

"So help me," said Finke. "I only poked him in the snoot. He— he got my goat, damn him. A little tap like that couldn't kill a man, not even an Existentialist."

Evans looked at Toudoux, who was swelling like a turkey.

"Another coronary thrombosis. The usual photographs, just for us," Evans said. "And if Fremont insists, you can chop off his head. His twisted brain, in fact, should go to the Ecole de Médecine, where it will serve a useful purpose."

"But the method! Three Americans dead. Two in my own office," groaned Fremont. "The press!"

"Two murders and a suicide, abetted by what you Americans call 'a poke in the snoot,'" protested Schlumberger.

Evans shrugged. "The alternative? A full disclosure?"

Fremont and Schlumberger hesitated, but Dr. Toudoux stepped in.

"Monsieur Evans is right, as usual," he said. "You don't want to advertise how easy murder has become, a drop of chloral hydrate, an air bubble in the veins, no unity of time or place, the alibi made easy. We are poor if not bankrupt, our department. We are understaffed. Do we want citizens dropping dead, like flies?"

"Science stinks," muttered Fremont. "Take this body away, and forever hold your peace."

Evans placed his hand on Finke's shoulder. "You don't know your own strength," he said, drily. "But think nothing of it."

COACHWHIP PUBLICATIONS

COACHWHIPBOOKS.COM

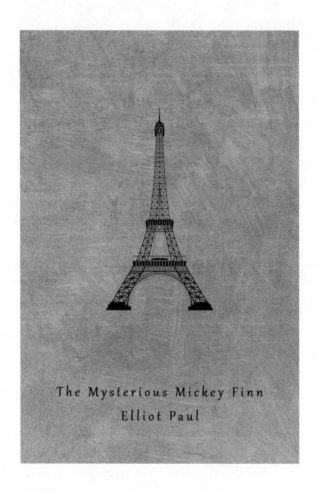

The Mysterious Mickey Finn

Elliot Paul

The Mysterious Mickey Finn
ISBN 1-61646-293-0

Coachwhip Publications

Also Available

Hugger Mugger in the Louvre

Elliot Paul

Hugger Mugger in the Louvre
ISBN 1-61646-294-9

COACHWHIP PUBLICATIONS

COACHWHIPBOOKS.COM

Mayhem in B-Flat

Elliot Paul

Mayhem in B-Flat
ISBN 1-61646-295-7

COACHWHIP PUBLICATIONS

ALSO AVAILABLE

Fracas in the Foothills

Elliot Paul

Fracas in the Foothills
ISBN 1-61646-296-5

COACHWHIP PUBLICATIONS

COACHWHIPBOOKS.COM

The Black Gardenia
Elliot Paul

The Black Gardenia
ISBN 1-61646-313-9

COACHWHIP PUBLICATIONS

ALSO AVAILABLE

Murder Ends the Song
ISBN 1-61646-298-1

COACHWHIP PUBLICATIONS

COACHWHIPBOOKS.COM

Murder on Tour
ISBN 1-61646-170-5

CPSIA information can be obtained
at www.ICGtesting.com
Printed in the USA
BVHW07s0127131018
530013BV00003B/630/P